'Bury my mare at Glenrowan'

Horse's soul

'My horse fights with me and fasts with me, because if he is to carry me in battle, he must know my heart and I must know his or we shall never become brothers. I have been told that the white man, who is almost a god, and yet is a great fool, does not believe that the horse has a spirit. This cannot be true. I have many times seen my horse's soul in his eyes.'
Chief Plenty Coups - '500 Nations' - Alvin M Josephy Jnr

The excitement of the chase and riding a fast horse

Indeed, that is what it was, a well-trained buffalo horse, but the owner had not thought to tell us so. It was even swifter than mine, and I felt no little anxiety as I saw it carry her into that sea of madly running, shaggy-backed, gleaming-eyed animals [buffalo stampede]. In vain I urged my horse; I could not overtake her, and my warning shouts were lost in the thunder and rattle of a thousand hoofs. I soon saw that she was not trying to hold in the animal, but was quirting it instead, and once she looked back at me and laughed, her eyes shining with excitement. On we went, up the slope for a mile or more, and then the scattering herd drew away from us and went flying down the other side of the ridge. "What made you do it?" I asked as we checked up our sweating, panting horses. "Why did you do it? I was so afraid you would get a fall, perhaps be hooked by some of the wounded." "Well," she replied, "at first I was scared, too, but it was such fun, riding after them. Just think of it, I struck four of them with my quirt! I just wanted to keep on, and on, and I never thought of badger holes, or falling, or anything else.'
My Life as an Indian: The Story of a Red Woman and a White Man in the Lodges of the Blackfeet by James Willard Schultz

Simultaneously Published in Australia, United States, the UK, India,
Germany, France, Italy, Canada, Japan, Spain and Brazil
This novel is a work of fiction despite the use in some cases of real names
which feature strictly as a dramatic device. all characters are the products of
the authors imagination and any resemblance to actual persons is entirely
coincidental

TABLE OF CONTENTS

Preface

There are many books about Ned Kelly. Some are brilliant in their fact gathering and research like Ian Jones, Ian Shaw, Peter Fitzsimons and Keith McMenomy. Others are divided between hero worship and villain-murderer. Justice Phillips analysed the evidence to answer the question whether Ned received a fair trial. His conclusion was that he did not receive a fair hearing because Judge Barry misdirected the Jury. Barry excluded from the Jury's consideration the issue whether the police had intentions of shooting Kelly rather than apprehending him. The Police had it appears boasted about what they would do with the Kelly Gang, took body bags and a lot of ammunition and went into the Ranges disguised as gold fossickers. Julian Burnside Q.C. makes a similar point about the issue of self defence not being allowed by Judge Barry. He also says the nature of the wounds on Lonigan show he had drawn his weapon when asked to bail up. He further says that his inexperienced Barrister asked too few questions of the only witness, McIntyre, who changed his story several times.

My lecturer in constitutional law at Adelaide University, Professor Castles, also wrote a book analysing the background with his customary tenacity but was only able to partially complete it before he unfortunately died. If only I could have learnt from him to be a resolute hunter of facts than just maybe I would have got better marks in my final year exams but I would drift off in his lectures, and am afraid to confess, wander in my imagination of other things which usually occupied a foot loose and free teenager. His daughter, who had assisted him with researching the background material, admirably completed the book for him. Professor Castle's father, who lived at Benalla near Glenrowan, saw Ned's mother and brother, Jim Kelly, shopping in the town accompanied by their grandchildren. His book is a detailed research about the last days of Ned Kelly. It tells us, through the bad publicity of the Press, Kelly was poorly thought of by the general Public, and one could assume from this his chances of getting a sympathetic jury would have been slim more so when the trial was transferred to Melbourne. His fate was of course not assisted by poor legal representation in a time where the defendant could not give evidence on his own behalf, and his Counsel advised him not to make a unsworn statement due fear of him appearing too flash before a Jury. To be fair to his lawyer, he was inexperienced and had only a short time to prepare the case due to Ned, at a late stage, not being able to raise the money for his barrister of choice. Ned along with McIntyre were the only two witnesses to the events of Stringybark. The book says that McIntyre visited him in Gaol, and Ned greeted him warmly. McIntyre appeared uncomfortable with the statements put to him by Prosecution, and was anxious to see that Kelly was not portrayed in too bad a light. In his later statements after the trial McIntyre does, as I am able to read it, say the other three shot had not surrendered but went for their weapons. He is of course guarded in his comments and anxious to re-establish his credit with Police after suffering what some others may have thought was the ignominy of hiding the night in a wombat hole, and to assist their aims to have Kelly convicted and hung. Kelly and his men could have shot the Police from their hidden positions near the creek if that were their intention but asked them to surrender. Their intention was to take their horses, guns and ammunition because they were poorly equipped, and to release the Police to walk out of the Ranges. The book further deals with uncovering the background dealings by the State to ensure Kelly would not escape the noose.

One matter I thought should have occurred at Trial was to object to Judge Barry hearing the case on the grounds of bias and prejudice. It may not have been a concept well known at the time although it is a common principle of justice. Barry had stated at the trial of Ned's mother [where she was convicted by a jury and imprisoned for three years for assisting attempted murder] that if Ned were present he would have given him twenty one years in gaol, and this said without having heard his evidence. Barry, despite his public good works, was known to have given severe penalties to the lower classes especially ex-convicts, and where the authority of the State was challenged in murder prosecutions, death penalties to defendants without a lot of discrimination as to their complicity in the offending. The end result may not have been any different if the case was supervised by another Judge but with Barry there was little opportunity for any evidence favourable to Ned to have been admitted.

The book 'the Kelly Gang Un-masked' by Ian MacFarlane attempts to redress the balance away from hero worship, and put their version with a careful and detailed examination of the evidence. It is not easy to come to any firm conclusion about these matters because the facts are not clear. It is clear that Kelly at times stole stock and sold them in N.S.W. over the river. He admitted this freely himself. There was an ongoing enmity between the Squatters, being the landed gentry, and the small Selectors. Often the animals of the small Selectors grazed the roads and were distrained by Police and sold on the urgings of the Squatters who wanted the Selectors gone. I think Kelly saw taking the stock and horses of the Squatters as fair game. The battles were not much unlike the struggles between the cattle barons in America with the sheep herders and fencing.

Although my book is pro Kelly, I do not want to be an apologist for unnecessary violence and criminal conduct. My gut feeling is and I argue the facts show Kelly wanted to avoid unnecessary death, and act with integrity and respect for human life unless it was unavoidable. Saying that, he was not a soft touch if others were intent upon doing him or the members of his Gang harm, killing them or unjustly treating his family or others facing the same fate at the hands of the Police, the Courts and those controlling the Government. At Stringybark, the Police when asked by Kelly to bail up, the evidence appears to be those shot went for their guns. Most persons, in those circumstances where your life is threatened, would defend themselves. Kennedy was said to be retreating when shot but that does not mean that he was not shooting as Ned said he was. He faced a difficult choice when he lay dying– either leave him to suffer a slow and painful death or to end it. I know the relatives of the Police who were shot at Stringybark have deep feelings of resentment at the hero worship of a bushranger whom they see as a murderer, and that is understandable if you accept Kelly had no right to approach them that day, or to shoot at them irrespective whether they were shooting or attempting to shoot at him or his men.

There are some incidents however which do give an insight into his character. Kelly says at Glenrowan he had, when in the bush at night, the opportunity to shoot police nearby and did not. Some writers have said that Ned did not have the temperament for a revolutionary, that is I expect someone who thinks little about the death of others in political struggles. I agree with them. The fact that he appears to have directed his support men waiting in the wings at Glenrowan to not get involved supports this. If they had intervened, the result may well have been different with Kelly succeeding but it would have been at the cost of many lives. The Kelly Gang shot no one at Glenrowan which seems remarkable over the period of the shooting. Two in the pub died from the hail of Police bullets, [it may be argued it would not have happened except for Kelly holding them at the pub] Joe was shot and the boys probably suicided but that was the extent of it. They wanted to release the hostages and a number of attempts were made but they were forced back by the Police and others shooting at them before eventually getting clear.

During his raid on the towns and banks, he did not shoot or physically harm third parties. He appeared to be at pains to explain the injustice he and others suffered at hands of the Police and Judiciary [Jerilderie letter]. He was polite and generous to woman seeing they were not harmed. There is much to like about him– the saving of a drowning boy when at school, standing up to a bully in the fist fight, and doing his best to support his mother and young siblings in difficult circumstances. He was I understand always seeking a resolution whereby his mother would be released. There is his courage in attempting, single handed and alone, to free up his two young boys, Dan and Steve, in the besieged pub, and to face the firepower of the Police and their supporters. He could have escaped on his mare who came to him at the critical moment of his capture. Ned was good to the local policeman, Bracken, when taken to the pub with the others, argued and joked, and did him no harm. At his trial, when given the opportunity to speak on his own behalf, he spoke eloquently choosing his words carefully. He answered Judge Barry in a logical and dignified manner refusing to be brow beaten or cowed and gave back as good as he got. I say there are good grounds to have sympathy for Kelly, and the verdict of the general Public, over a century of analysis and study, is almost unanimous in their assessment. To see the opening of the Australian Olympics with a grand display of horsemanship and Kelly impersonators is an acknowledgement of how the people now see him - as a national folk hero.

It can reasonably be said that Ned's troubles were caused by two persons – Fitzpatrick attended the Kelly hut seeking to arrest Dan for horse stealing. He had been at a pub for three hours before and did not have a warrant with him. There are differing versions of what occurred when he got there. It said that Dan was not there and he waited around. Later when Dan arrived and was arrested, it is alleged Fitzpatrick tried to molest Kate Kelly aged fifteen years. Dan, his mother and two of their friends grappled with him taking his revolver. He received small cut to his wrist which he said occurred when Ned arrived and fired at him. Ned denied being there. It is said the Police wanted to construct a case against Ned because they suspected him being the ring leader in the horse thefts but didn't have the evidence to charge him. In any event, Fitzpatrick received only a superficial wound, those present bandaged it for him, gave back his pistol and he left on the understanding nothing would be said. Within short time Ned and the others are charged with attempted murder which in the circumstances are highly inflated charges. At the trial before Barry there was the evidence of Fitzpatrick and doctor for the Prosecution . The doctor could not confirm his wrist wound was caused by a bullet. Further it appears unlikely that Ned, who could have handled Fitzpatrick with one hand tied behind his back, would come into the room firing his pistol. Again it is unlikely, if he did shoot as alleged, he would have missed his target being an excellent shot. The later events, Stringybark, the Banks and taking over the towns and Glenrowan, show he always deferred to giving others the opportunity to comply. The jury in the Fitzpatrick trial was made up of several ex police, a shanty keeper who did business with the police and others who were prejudiced against the Kelly's. Most people even those against the Kelly's thought the sentence of three years hard labour on Mrs Kelly was severe, and three months would have been sufficient. The other two said to be present received six years. As is evident from Barry's statement at the trial, Ned and Dan had little chance of a fair hearing, and to spend the best years of their lives in gaol was not an alternative they or anyone for that matter could willingly accept.

When hiding out in the Ranges with Joe and Steve they bailed up and sought to defend themselves from a heavily armed Police contingent of four, three of whom chose to draw their weapons [rather than surrender as McIntyre did]. There was no turning back when the three policemen lay dead. Is it right to defend yourself against a system that offered you no prospect of justice and years in prison, and in Barry's case, suggested you were guilty in open court without hearing your evidence? If Barry had said to the jury in the Fitzpatrick trial the prosecution evidence is weak, the injury superficial and applied only a short sentence, and indicated he would do same for Ned and Dan, they would probably have surrendered themselves. But he was not that sort of a Judge- more a hanging Judge. And before that, if sensible charges had been laid for the Fitzpatrick affair by the Police, such as assault rather than attempted murder, it may have all been avoided. But these are wise words after the event and life, as is painfully apparent, will often take a unexpected course for the worse. Fitzpatrick left the police force three years later and it was said by the Chief Commissioner of Victorian Police ' the ex constable's conduct during the time he was a member of the force was generally bad and discreditable to the force.' Kelly said to Judge Barry during his sentencing to hang 'I'll see you there where I go,' and 11 days after his execution Barry died.

Cookson's interview with Ellen Kelly 1912

"My God! My God! and I was innocent—innocent as this dear little baby here! And I was thrust into prison like a common thief! Justice! No: there's none on this earth! I swear it again that I never hurt the man. I never hit him. I remember it all as if it were yesterday. He tried to kiss my daughter. She was a fine, good-looking girl, Kate: and the boys tried to stop him. He was a fool. They were only trying to protect their sister. He was drunk and they were sober. But his story was believed. If he'd been badly hurt he would have richly deserved it. But I never hurt him - before God I didn't. They swore I hit him with a shovel. It was untrue.
Before that black day when Fitzpatrick came we were so happy. It was a lonely life, but we were all together, and we all loved each other so dearly. Dear little Kate! I can see her now, bustling about the place, keeping things tidy, helping outside whenever she got a chance; always bright and cheerful, just like a sunbeam about the house. And they dragged her poor mother away from her and lied, and sent her to prison for three whole years. After that, nothing but misery. And it has been nothing but misery ever since.

My main interest however in Kelly is to look at his life anew as it were as an exceptional horseman, and in an imaginary sense, try to describe the part his grey mare played in his life. There is understandably very little written about this. Only a few tantalizing lines can be gleaned from the vast amount of literature and historical record that exists. A further statement came recently in the release of correspondence by an eye witness, Sutherland, when writing to his Parents in Scotland about what he saw happen at Glenrowan siege. It makes interesting reading. Sutherland describes the scene and at the end says-

'the hair enclosed is from the tail of Ned Kelly's the famous murderer and bushranger's mare. His favourite mare who followed him all around the trees during the firing. He said he wouldn't care for himself if he thought his mare was safe.'

That statement is similar to two other statements at the time including what Kelly says. The mare came to him and offered him a chance to escape. She did this in the heat of battle, when the shooting was intense, and the Police had decided to shoot the outlaw's horses yarded behind the Hotel. That the mare was there offering him the opportunity to escape is remarkable and Kelly saw it as such when he spoke about it to third parties afterwards, and to his Mother when she visited him in jail.

The other interesting piece of evidence comes from the Jerilderie Letter. Ned says-

> 'out of the thirty head of the very best horses the land could produce, I could only find one when I got my liberty. Constable Flood stole and sold the most of them to the navies on the railway line...he, Flood, is the greatest horse stealer with the exception of myself and George King I know of.'

Ned clearly owned a number of horses before he was imprisoned for three years. I expect he would have learned much from his mother's parents, the Quinn's, who bred and supplied Harry Wright, the bushranger, with horses to evade the Police. Ned and his relatives knew the Police were always going to give them problems. The Traps were generally doing the work of the Squatters [large land owners] and harassing the small selectors including impounding their stock. That is not to say it was all one way and it is not disputed that Kelly and his mates were running stolen stock across the River Murray to be sold in N.S.W. If they were to evade the Police, it would only be by having the best horses and being expert bush horsemen. The horses they rode would need to be long winded, athletic and durable. They had to be able to cope with covering vast distances over steep hills and mountains, through boggy terrain and often in the dark with only moonlight to guide them if that. Most of the daring raids by Kelly Gang were carried out when there was a full moon, but as endurance riders will know the moon can be covered by clouds and then it is very dark. Riders today will have a torch but Kelly would have no artificial light to assist him and would have to rely upon his horse. On a few rides at night I have had my torch give out and faced the same worrying experience. The American Civil War is interesting to study being one of the last wars where horses were extensively used, and close relationships were formed between the rider and his mount. It was said about perhaps one of the best cavalry horsemen in the Civil War, General J.E.B. Stuart, who was only young when given his command for the Confederates –

> 'I believe Stuart's got eyes like a cat,' the officer said. 'Sometimes on a dark night he has come galloping up to a post where I was in command, when one could scarcely see one's hand before one. It never seems to make any difference to him; day or night he rides about at a gallop.' 'He trusts his horse,' Vincent said. 'That's the only way in the dark. They can see much better than we can, and if men would but let them go their own way instead of trying to guide them, they would seldom run against anything. The only thing is to lie well down on the horse's neck, otherwise one might get swept out of the saddle by a bough. It's a question of nerve. I think not many of us would do as Stuart does, and trust himself entirely to his horse's instinct.' With Lee in Virginia - a Story of the American Civil War - G. A. Henty

My interest in horses started when I was young. As a child all I wanted was a pony. My dad rode a big, white horse to do stock work. We were not horsey people as such and a horse was there to do a job. He was not keen for me to ride. For what reason, I do not know. Maybe it was because our workman Harry was dragged with his foot jammed in the stirrup. I can still see Harry's head wrapped in bloody bandages and sitting at the dining table looking a sorry mess. It was then my Dad probably heard for the first-time disturbing things like workers compensation insurance. His indifference made me even more determined.

When Dad's horse was tethered to post next to shed and he was taken up with the shearing, I went to his horse and tried to get into the saddle. I was only about seven years old. He was far too tall for me to climb up. I went and got a bin to stand on. I needed two. It was a shaky arrangement at best but I managed to pull myself inch by inch into that well used saddle. Why the horse didn't pull back or knock me off I don't know. He seemed to understand it was my first time, and stood still putting up patiently with my clumsy and childish attempts. My heart was thumping. I had climbed tall pine trees and a high windmill but what I felt from the saddle of that horse was nothing like I had ever experienced. We owned the world, and he would take me to every part of it in a few giant strides. I was hooked, and I would use every power I possessed as child to get a pony.

Unfortunately, I was a sick kid. I would in the cold night air of the South East have attacks of asthma and croup. In those days there was not any useful medication. All we had was a wood stove, kettle and steam. Some nights I choked up that bad, I thought I would not get another breath. If it wasn't for my mum, I think I would have turned blue and died. I spent several weeks in the Adelaide Children's Hospital being operated on. I would spend the day drawing horses and bullets coming out of rifles which were a series of dots in a line using my ruler. My Dad would visit and we would play draughts, a thousand-year-old game, on a board. He would, now and then, let me win. My Mum promised me a pony when we got back to the farm, and I lived for that day. When back home my parents went cold on the idea after the workman got hooked in a stirrup and dragged.

If I were to get a pony, I had to look for outside help. The local parish Priest, a big, rough Irishman called Father Dempsey who, apart from making us kids recite the catechism off by heart every Tuesday at school, led me to believe in the power of prayer. Ask and it shall be given to you the Bible said. With all the innocence of nine-year-old child, I prayed at the foot of my rickety, iron bed every night for a pony. I was persistent. Nothing happened. I was beginning to become a doubting Thomas. One ordinary Sunday, Frank Sanford, a friend of my parents, arrived from Naracoorte at our farm in the first Holden ever built. Frank was a car salesman. He said the teenage girl living next door to him in Naracoorte, Christine Edwards, was riding to our farm on pony. It was something he had arranged off his own bat. She arrived some time later, and was sore and rubbed from the long ride. She was riding him for a Parent and their child. He was a piebald pony- black and white - and his name was Boxy because of his head I later learned. I thought his head was beautiful. Christine, as luck would have it, was too sore to ride him back to Naracoorte, and so the pony stayed with us on the farm for a couple of weeks. At my insistence, my Parents phoned the owner and asked if I could ride him. With the characteristic generosity of country people, the owner said yes. The pony had girth sores and I could not use a saddle. In any case we didn't have one that fitted him. I rode him every day bare back, and came off many times. I was learning to ride just like the Indians did. The pony was kind to me in that he stopped every time I fell off, and waited for me to get back on. I was broken hearted when the time came for him to go back. I pestered my parents until they phoned the owner to see if he would sell him. He said his boy got asthma from horses and he would sell. It was the one-time asthma did me a good deal. From a doubting Thomas, the almost impossible coincidence of circumstances whereby that pony came to be delivered to me when all appeared lost, made me as a child, a firm convert and believer.

We did not have a float. The pony was ridden to Hynam and then my Dad rode him from there to our farm. I was waiting at the bottom of our long drive. I waited for hours and then saw a speck in the distance. They slowly came into view. He was a solid man about five foot eleven but the pony about 14.1 hands carried his weight easily as he trotted happily along on a loose rein. I could barely contain my joy and excitement as the two came into full view. How much better is it to see your Dad riding your pony to you than having him delivered in truck or float.

I got up in the dark that morning, and went my pony to make sure he was still in his paddock. It was pitch black and I called out for him. I was still in my pyjamas. I stroked his neck and felt his whiskery, rubber muzzle. I was immensely happy as we stood there in the darkness of an empty, frosty paddock. I finally had my pony. It was a dream come true. I remember a bit of moon peeped out from the ink black sky above us. Someone was sneaking a glance from the heavens. I swear I could hear the angels giggle with mischievous delight in the tentative union unfolding before them. The angels they say are the ordained message carriers of God, and although I am conflicted as to the Jesus thing, I believe something supernatural delivered that piebald pony to me as surely as I stand here today. I rode my pony everywhere...all over our property tending to the lambing, to the local villages and into the big town of Naracoorte where my Grand Father stabled him in the chicken shed. He and the chooks seemed to get on quite well. And then a long distance out to my Auntie's farm on the Bordertown road. The pony made me a healthy boy again.

After University, I played some polo and then endurance rode for many years including breeding horses. I used well-bred stock horse blood lines from N.S.W. over part Arab mares bred by the Wilsons of outback fame. When I was in my twenties, the Wilsons, who had outback properties, purchased an Arab stallion from England [Lady Wentworth] and let him run loose with the station mares in the wide expanses of the Australian outback. As some of you may know it is a pretty dry, harsh and unforgiving environment, but it produced the best, hardy horses you could find. It's a bit like wheat...the best milling wheat to make quality bread comes from the dry Mallee. Every year they, or a canny horse dealer, would transport hundreds of these horses to Adelaide. They were nearly all grey, and looked identical like peas in a pod. The stallion must have been pre-potent for he stamped them all much the same. They were nice types and could be bought for fifty dollars apiece unbroken. The grey mare on the front cover of the novel with Ned in his prison uniform is China Doll, a mare from my bloodlines, who went on to win the Quilty in Queensland. The Quilty is the pinnacle of Endurance events in Australia and probably in the World along with the Tevis Cup in America. China Doll represents in my opinion the ideal type of horse - an all-rounder, do anything, refined yet durable horse - by a well-recognised Australian Stock horse breeding infused with sensible thoroughbred blood for speed and length of stride and the hardiness and staying ability of colonial bred Arab mare. Often it is only in the high, mountainous country like Scone that you are able to get good horses with trusted blood lines established since early 1900's and before. The flatter areas of course went to motorbikes but motorbikes were not all that useful in high country and consequently horses were not replaced.

I sometimes watch the races on the television around Melbourne Cup time. One day before I depart, I might have enough money to go. The coverage previously with Simon O'Donnell and his offsiders was great. Francesca Cumani, the English trainer's daughter is a doll, and she rides track work as well. You would think a girl like that would be wrapped up in a mink coat, sporting high heels and drinking French champagne all day, but no... she is out there riding those hot headed, inbred thoroughbreds as game as any jockey worth his salt. Don't let me forget Johnny Letts joking in the saddle as the winning jockey and horse return to scales, Bruce with his encyclopaedic knowledge of form and breeding, and Clare. This is a second edition and I cannot leave the racing scene without saying Winx and McEvoy in my opinion are the best horse and jockey in the World. McEvoy's ride in 2018 Melbourne Cup was astonishing to watch coming from behind in a superb display of horsemanship. Racing in Australia must take a lot of credit for this and the Melbourne Spring Carnival in particular is organised with such efficiency, professionalism and flair accommodating overseas guests, trainers, horses, the public, high fashions not to forget the battler and mug punter. It is constant joy to me to hear the Irish lilting accents so often associated with fine horse flesh. The television coverage is fascinating and thrilling to watch... you see the owners and hangers on go ape shit with excitement when their horse brings home the bacon. Well - I probably would too as I need a buck as much as the next man - but I hope you will forgive me when I say their elation doesn't bear comparison to having riding relationship with your horse over many years. It is only through many hours in the saddle, riding day and night, out in the bush, beach and mountains in the rain, wind, storms and sunshine that you will experience a closeness, an understanding, an affection with your horse that is near spiritual and impossible to put into ordinary words.

Sometimes animals who have a close relationship with their owner or friend appear capable of receiving urgent thoughts, messages, and cries of distress from long distances away. A word used to describe this is telepathy - that is the transmission of information without using any of our known sensory channels. Aborigines would know it as spirits moving about in the night. I recently read that when they have a nightmare, they get up and grab a stick from the fire and wave it about their head to scare off the spirits. A simple example happened to me. One night after an argument with my parents I left home and ran to the back paddocks near a swamp. I was about nine years old and I did not want to go back home. It was dark, difficult to see your hand in front of your face, and cold and eerie for a child. I could hear the chorus of frogs in the swamp nearby and it was loud like a bar when they had 6 pm closing. Even so I could hear my Ole Man hollering from long distance away but he could hollow all night for all I cared. At about midnight I could hear a terrifying sound, a grunting and groaning, and it was getting louder and louder, and coming closer and closer. It was too dark to see what was causing the frightening sounds. I was terrified and thought monsters were coming from the swamp to devour me. If I ran, I could end up in barbed wire fence. Then all of a sudden out of the darkness right in front of me was the neighbour's big, old, black dog. He was grunting and groaning as he went because he was aged and arthritic. I was overjoyed to see him as he was me, and we warmed and embraced each other. We had often played together when my mum visited. They had a small garden pool in which we as kids romped and played. He was too old to work and would excitedly sit by pool wanting to be in the fun barking and carrying on like a young pup. You could see that he loved being in the company of kids. That dog had to negotiate in the middle of the night about three miles of sheep fences not easy to get under or through, a railway track and road, and several large paddocks to get to me, but he did. I have often wondered what made that dog come to me at that time. It was not on route to another farm house. Did something pass in the air that night that alerted this old dog to get up from his bed and go. Somehow, I think he sensed I was alone and troubled, and he came. Peter Fitzsimons in his recent book Ned Kelly gives a rollicking good yarn based on lot of detailed research. He says 'seemingly from out of nowhere, his mare Music trots up to him - all saddled up and ready to be ridden - only to be shot for her trouble by the police.' What made this mare, about which little is written and known, go to Kelly when he was in dire trouble? I can believe that where a very close relationship has built between horse and rider, the senses become highly developed between the two, and a communication about which we know little and cannot be scientifically explained, sometimes in situations of life and death passes from one to the other.

The artist Nolan in his iconic Kelly paintings has I reckon got it about right. You see Ned on a thoroughbred looking horse but Ned has no legs. That is because he is a centaur - half horse half man. Nolan also captured the spirit of the Kelly Gang; you see in one painting a policeman hightailing it away from Kelly because the public knew they were frightened of the Kelly Gang. You see in another painting Steve dressed as woman on his horse because he attended and competed in picnic races using this disguise. You see the Police and woman's faces peering from under a bed in the infamous Aaron Sherritt shooting about which I have chapter, 'are you old enough.' With their heads poking up, they look like startled meerkats spooked by a predator which is probably not too far removed from having Joe Byrne issuing threats after blasting the dissembling Sherritt in the corridor of his hut. There is a lot of drama, excitement, violence, colour and movement in the Kelly story which Nolan has captured in his what I think to be the naive/primitive Kelly series of paintings. If a kid produced a painting like that you might scold him and send him back to do a proper job, but having said that, I confess I like them very much; they are childlike, the landscapes show the essence of Australia, and the characters evoke deep feelings. Nolan had an anti- authoritarian streak and he admired the dreaming quality he saw in aboriginal paintings long before they became popular. He is reported as saying that the picture Glenrowan was like the final act of an opera with all the protagonists lined up on a fateful stage. Evidently when Nolan travelled to the Greta District with Max Harris to do his research and speak to the relatives of Ned, they would not speak to him as was their custom with nosey strangers from the big smoke. Nolan's grandfather was a Police officer stationed at Beechworth and had vivid memories of Kelly - maybe that had something to do with the silence.

In many of the Kelly books I have read, as good as they are in their research and facts, I have felt there is something absent, something missing. I am tempted to say soul. I say this not out of any disrespect for the other writers because they are much more learned than me about the historical facts and their books are all very interesting, painstakingly researched and beautifully written. I say it because I always think of Kelly and a horse as being inseparable; and sometimes when I have finished reading a book about him...well... to be honest I get the uneasy feeling he could have been peddling a push bike up in the Ranges or at Glenrowan to avoid police capture. Kelly's reliance on a good horse would have been vital to his liberty and very existence, and to my way of thinking his relationship with his horse is a indispensable part of the story. And sadly, it has been missing. If you don't have a close background and experience with a horse, it can be difficult if not impossible to find the right words to get this relationship across to the reader. Even if you have the experience, it is still difficult. I hope I may have been able to get somewhere near in my chapter 'Lucille, why doncha come back where you belong' where Kev, the Cobb and Co buyer and their lead driver, whilst accompanying Music in the railway stock crate of slow goods train to Melbourne, decides to hang himself because of a failed marriage. In *'like a virgin'* I try to get across the need for a good rider to progress slowly, and to understand that to push a horse before it is ready can do untold and permanent harm. In the chapter *'there is nothing as pretty as Music in the morning'*, the Glenrowan showdown, I try to describe the feelings passing between Ned and his mare when she comes to him offering an opportunity of escape.

That there is little reference to Kelly and his mare in the literature written about him is not surprising. There are few historical records on the subject. The absolute doyen of Kelly history is undoubtedly Ian Jones. His books especially 'a Short Life' reflect a scholarship and factual knowledge that could only have come about after a lifetime of careful research and investigation. I am heavily indebted to him for the revelation of the historical facts and suggestions he makes as to what may or may not be true. For example, he mentions King, an American, and his possible involvement in the Civil war. He includes a page in relation to the Gang's horses stabled at Mc Donnell's pub during the Glenrowan siege, and sows the seeds of possibility as to whether the sympathisers secreted Ned's grey mare away. I have run with some of these credible suggestions by the learned and erudite Mr Jones and, for lack of a better explanation, given them a dramatic makeover.

The closeness of this relationship between horse and rider is something that is not easy for us to grasp today. Back in Kelly times the steam trains had arrived but not mechanical vehicles. Horses would have been intimately involved in people's lives, being stabled near the home and used for transport almost every day of the week. Of course, some people do have that close contact today such as race trainers, breakers, and various horse sport enthusiasts but generally horses have taken a back seat or should I say back paddock. If you were in the previous centuries a bushranger, outlaw, American Indian, cowboy, in the cavalry such as American Civil war or the Australians Light Horse in the campaign in the Middle East during the First World War, the Boer war, a Texas Ranger, a rider for the Pony Express, a driver for Cobb and Co or even a member of the Mongol horse army under Genghis Kahn, you would have lived day and night with your horse and you would know your very life depended on him. If you were being pursued by Indians or for that matter one or two of the above, and your horse was not fast, or broke down, or lacked endurance, you would have paid a heavy price. If the Indians captured you, you would have been tortured to slow, agonising death. Apart from our own horse experiences, we can draw on the historical records during those times and events to get some insights into a better understanding this dependence. Using all the above sources, I have tried to put the horse back into the Kelly story in a way that might, I hope, assist readers to see him as the elite horseman he clearly was, and to give deserved praise to his grey mare who appears, even on his statements alone, to have been his strongest emotional attachment apart from his family. If you are interested, I have a comparatively lengthy list of books in the bibliography which will provide you with years of enjoyable reading on horse related literature and historical records.

In my book I have used a number of themes which are horse based but like every story there are those universal themes of love, lust, adventure, disappointments, tragedy, humour, injustice...all those things that come to most people invited and uninvited in their life's journey. I have at beginning of the novel, used George King, who was an American about whom little is known and who married Ned's mother after his father died, doing a runner from General Custer's battle of the Little Big Horn. The historical dates are close.

As a teenager in Naracoorte, I would go with friends to the big cave [at Naracoorte caves] to booze and carry on. In the large underground chamber was an alcove where they found the petrified aborigine. Having been shot and wounded by the settlers near Hynam, where I went to school, he hid in the big cave and died there with the water drip preserving and calcifying him.

> 'The blacks, in addition to the destruction of the sheep spoken of above, committed murder and so many acts of violence that the settlers resolved to be avenged. They assembled and set out with the magnificent motto, 'Let not your right hand know what your left hand doeth.' The natives resisted desperately. Some were shot in every part of the country. One wandering near these caves was seen and brought to the ground by a rifle-ball. Badly wounded, he managed to crawl away unobserved; and thinking that he would be sought for as long as life was in him, crept down into the lowest and darkest recess of the cavern, where he rightly judged few would venture to follow. There he lay down and died.' Woods 7th April-1858

I think the steel bars were still there when I visited as a teenager but he was stolen rumour has it by an American showman. I now know who stole the calcified aborigine

Gong, a rebellious girl from the Chinese mining camp, is taught to ride by one of the Quinn Boys and adopts a hard riding style like her Mongol forbears Here is a short excerpt from my chapter 'when I grow up, I want a pony.'

> 'Somewhere in this China girl's genetic material dwelt Mongolian blood and the spirit of Genghis Khan, the legendary Mongolian ruler, who with his army of peasant horsemen conquered the then known world. With her black and white pony given to her by an admirer, the stuttering Tennessee Quinn, she was determined to conquer those incessant and obsessive desires that beat upon her foreign heart day and night, and told her she was not the meek, obedient, colorless daughter her community demanded her to be. Because of his color and her heritage, she called him Panda. But he was no lumbering bear.
>
> Before long, Gong and her piebald pony, Panda, would sweep across the flat Australian plains erratically changing direction, circling and looping the loop, rolling back to return from whence she came, stopping, stalling and going into a spin, pirouetting like a prima ballerina; whatever took this unconventional china girl's fancy she did; she accelerated Panda towards a large, ancient red gum with spreading limbs in which a flock of noisy, plump breasted, sulphur crested cockatoos nested and disturbed the mid-summer country solitude with ear piercing, high pitched

screeches that rattled your brain. On nearing the big tree, she slid from the saddle her feet lightly touching the earth in a graceful, seamless fluidity of movement between horse and human, skipped a little bird dance around the enormous rough barked and pitted trunk with her arms raised mockingly like wings, and singing her delight to her noisy, white feathered, fun loving friends.

After a respectful bow to the tree Gods, she stepped back into the saddle and with a swing of the leather reins the enterprising couple rocketed off ascending into the wild and spectacular Ranges bordering her camp; climbing to the craggy mountain tops touched by wispy clouds, yawing on the slippery rocks, and looking down on her people toiling like ants in their garden patch and gold diggings below; and as though with a parting coup de grace to the stunning display of reckless, imaginative horsemanship, the two hurtled down the ravines, skidding and crashing through the bush, leaping over fallen logs, and startling the grazing kangaroos into flight with Gong riding fast behind and overtaking them like a demonic Indian warrior on a buffalo hunt.

Shortly they burst out of the scrub, the trees, the bush clearings and soft-landed back onto the open plain. Gong, with a smile as broad as the big, blue sky above and as bright as the hot Australian sun, leaned forward over her worn and tatty saddle, and embraced her gallant, little horse around his neck with her loving arms. She dismounted on the wrong side as was her wont, and the two rested in the cool shade of the river gums. She cast a careful eye over her game pony checking him for any cuts and bruises but he there were none to see except for a haze of steam rising from him like early morning mist and a glistening sweat.

For the first time in her short, dull, frustrating life, the rebellious Gong was overcome with the adrenaline charged excitement of headlong, howling speed and stultifying danger her pony so gleefully and unhesitatingly gifted to her in the stunning beauty of a pristine Australian bush. Gong had heard her Chinese community mockingly referred to by the Europeans and Australian miners as 'the Celestials'. She didn't mind. As she and Panda slowly ambled their way to the cleansing, gently flowing waters of a nearby steam to bathe this unusual china girl knew she was in Paradise.

We, mortals, have an innate desire to fly. I saw it the other day in the pure, unadulterated joy of my little grandsons, Harry and Archie, bouncing their hearts out on the trampoline and wanting to go higher and higher towards the sky. Somewhere in the past, we lost our wings. A good, fast pony will give you those wings as Gong intuitively knew, and take you to high, rugged landscapes both physically and emotionally. Photos have shown that a horse in full gallop will have his 4 legs suspended off the earth- literally flying.

There are some fifty or more chapters in the book and they are all named after well-known song titles. It begins with an old favourite of mine - *'please Mr Custer, I don't want to go'*. Because the book has as its focus Ned's horse, Music, I thought it only right that the chapters reflected this in their titles. At the end of this preface I have a photograph of my maternal, great Grandfather, Charles Dougheney on his horse taken in 1895 at Digby in Western Victoria about fifteen years after Ned was strung up. It is a classic photograph and he looks a proper dandy but smart, the same as Ned is described at Glenrowan with his flash clothes and Cuban heeled, leather riding boots. He would have known of the Kelly Gang as a topic of animated conversation. So would have my paternal great, grandfather, Patrick Heffernan who came out from Ireland in 1850 as child with his Mother and brothers, his father having died in Ireland maybe from the illnesses created by the famine. The Irish were of course were badly oppressed in their country by the English who through Cromwell had taken their lands and impoverished them,

> In the seventeenth century, England introduced a code of penal laws intended to humiliate, impoverish, and reduce to ignorance Ireland's nearly one million Catholics. Catholics could not hold political office, practice law, own weapons, or own a horse worth more than £5. Catholics could not operate schools nor send their children overseas to be educated. Catholic bishops were outlawed; any who were apprehended would be hanged, drawn, and quartered. A Catholic who owned land could not leave it all to his eldest son, but must divide it among all his children. Marriages performed by Catholic priests were invalid. Most members of the Irish aristocracy and the merchant class could not imagine life without property and status, so they joined the Protestant Church. The Meagher's, however, remained Catholic, scraping along in County Tipperary until the 1760s, when Thomas's grandfather immigrated to Newfoundland where there were no restrictions on Irish Catholics. There, Grandfather Meagher founded the commercial shipping business that made his descendants rich. Yet in spite of the privileges he enjoyed, Thomas Meagher deeply resented England's occupation of Ireland. After 300 years of English rule, the Irish were among the poorest, least educated people in Europe. "The English left us," Meagher said, "like blind and crippled children, in the dark. The Greatest Brigade: How the Irish Brigade Cleared the Way to Victory in the American Civil War (Thomas J. Craughwell)

His mother remarried a Welsh and later owned and ran the hotel at Harrow. Patrick later became mayor at Edenhope, Western Victoria at the turn of the century and unfortunately died from the after effects of a horse fall in the night on his way home to his property. His wife then took over and ran the hotel at Edenhope. My older brother, Chris, now runs in partnership the hotel at Beachport. Pubs have been a regular part in the family as well as country.

The second photograph is of my piebald pony [gifted to me by the power of prayer!] looking a little fat and me looking a little dreamy at rear of my siblings who are perched rather precariously on top. I said to mum before she passed away - it's a rather contrived, cheesy photo. She replied, 'I'll have you know, Michael, he was the best photographer in the District.' He was I think the only one too, Mum.

I'll finish with a true story my Grandmother told me. She was a Kelly. She told me as a child that when my Grandfather purchased one of the first cars made, a model T Ford, they made their first trip to Naracoorte from the farm near Kybybolite in the South East of South Australia. On the way, they had to negotiate a steep hill called Red hill. Unfortunately, when cautiously steering his way down, Pop kept his foot firmly on the brakes and burnt the pads out. The car started to run away and he and no doubt Grandma were terrified at the gathering speed and what to do. In desperation Pop did what any respectable horseman would have done – and reverted to instinct. He stood up, said Grandma, pulled back hard on the steering wheel yelling, 'whooo boy, whooo.' I hope the unruly iron horse stopped for you, Pop...or that you went back to your horse and buggy. Unfortunately for Pop you could not speak to a car in those times but now you can, and it will speak back! When the model T's first came out in America the people thought it would be a passing fad and they would soon go back to horses. Well, things have certainly moved on from then. I was born on the cusp of these changes and remember rummaging through a lot of the discarded saddlery in the feed shed and seeing their replacements the first tractors like the little Ferguson and the big, old International W.6. which had to be hand cranked in the machinery shed. When you think that horses had been the main form of transportation and farm use for possibly several thousand years, their passing was a momentous and defining event in history. Having lost that close daily contact with a horse, I like to think we are the poorer for it. I leave you with old Mongol proverb from the mists of time,

> 'when a Mongol is separated from his horse, what is there left for him to do but die.'

Michael Heffernan
mheffern01@gmail.com

Boy General.

The boy general looked so pretty and effeminate, so unlike the stern realities of war, that he was certain to be quizzed and ridiculed unmercifully, unless he could compel the whole army to respect him' - Custerology - The Enduring Legacy of the Indian Wars and George Armstrong Custer - Michael A. Elliott.

Worst record at West Point

graduating in 1861 with the worst disciplinary and academic record in his West Point class to a decorated major general just four years later. Of course, any soldier who survived such a deadly conflict-especially one who put himself in harm's way as frequently and deliberately as Custer did should be considered fortunate. But Custer's true fortune may have been in his being thrust into a time and place that called for his flair for the dramatic, for the extroverted gesture in the performance of duty. His early career is filled with feats of derring-do.

Custer's dress

One Union colonel pondered Custer in a letter to his family: "This officer is one of the funniest-looking beings you ever saw, and looks like a circus rider gone mad!"
Generals of his time could dress according to their own taste, Custerology: The Enduring Legacy of the Indian Wars and George Armstrong Custer (Michael A. Elliott)

I dream. My dreams tell me things. They warn me. It's called a premonition and I'm not about to ignore what I see. I am young, I have a beautiful wife and two adoring kids, and I want to stay alive. I want to stay alive for myself and for them. I have a photograph of us all under my pillow, a family photograph, and I proudly show it to the other troops. My dreams tell me I am about to die, a horrible, tortuous death, unless I prepare. I have ventured out into these Bad Lands and joined Custer's Seventh Calvary to provide for my family; to experience new country at the Government's expense and see what opportunities there may be for a young family. I was born just before the Civil War in the bible belt states of the South to a Preacher father and a polite god-fearing mother. We were poor with no home, staying in church basements, Pastor's homes and cheap lodgings. At the tender age of nine I learnt the piano and how to sing the old gospel ballads but more than anything, I harbored a desire to preach. My dad was an uninspiring preacher – he had no fire and fury like I had seen in the best orators who were more actors than men of God. We did the backwoods churches – small log cabins with congregations numbering no more than a handful, mainly black slaves and dirt poor. They could sure sing, clap, hollow and dance, and generally make a great ruckus which I loved and joined in with great gusto for a kid. Sometimes my parents had to physically restrain me much to the disappointment of our small congregation who gave me no end of encouragement. My Dad turned traitor to the Johnny Rebs because he thought slavery an abomination. Our wagon was loaded with our few possessions and we hot tailed it to New York City and was that a revelation to me. My Dad gave much strategic information to Union Army and he was made Chief Pastor of the Army. His status in the world rocketed upwards with influential friends and money. We became part of the New York establishment. At the end of the war there were many ambitious military men looking for opportunities in the Government. The people's favorite was the boy General, George Armstrong Custer, and although I had married well, I was advised to join Custer's Seventh Calvary, cultivate his friendship and when he becomes the President... well the gravy train would roll into my life.

In the short time I have been here I think I have made a big mistake. The desolate, unyielding landscape bakes in a permanent heat haze during the day and freezes at night. I am amongst the riff-raff of society. I have learned that you get advancement and better pay if you do foolhardy things. Some call it courage. Take Custer for example, bottom of his class at West Point, a bit of a pansy they say with his long locks and girly clothes and with a few blood curdling, demonic charges into the gray coats he's promoted to General. And he is only aged twenty three years. The boy General they call him. He sure is one cocky-arsed son of a gun but now he is the darling of the all them gentry back home. And do the Press and the ladies love that peacock dressed in buckskin, long boots and feathers. The Indians are a formidable and frightening foe, and I don't think Custer with his social forays into New York society, with his regular monthly columns in the Press, and his grandiose plans for the Presidency is the sort of leader under whose command your welfare takes up much of his valuable time. Never the less with those thoughts I hope for the best.

At night in the troop dormitory, I have nightmares. I see painted faces, streaked and daubed, on colored ponies swirling about me They whoop, yell and jip like a pack of marauding dogs and blow a deathly high pitched shrill from their eagle bone whistles. They carry weapons made lovingly out of natural materials and steel tips taken from the white man. Their culture is one of war. It is how they are made worthy of respect and adulation, and their ponies - so tough, scrawny and enduring - they are worthy opponents on these vast, desolate prairies that stretch on and on like the endless sea. We troops are soft and lazy. And our horses are not much better. They appear to say 'look out paleface - the dark, swarthy Indian is riding hard to avenge the slayings of his peoples, the thefts of their lands and the wholesale killing of their buffalo herds'. Our horses are in a blind panic; rearing, plunging, pulling at a tangle of reins, breaking free and stampeding off. Through the haze of smoke and dust, I see throats slit and bellies crudely opened up like so many carcasses in a butcher shop. It's gruesome. I want to retch and vomit out the fear and revulsion that consumes me. Young men dressed in their regulation woolen, sky blue trousers and grey shirts scrambling frantically up a hill with horror and fear clamped on their terrified faces. Keogh's and Calhoun's Companies are cut off from the rest of Custer's command on the bluffs above the river. The painted devils are slaughtering them alive as they scramble to reach their legendary, maverick leader as if he has the magic to save us from our terrible fate.

It's going to be a blood bath.

I see myself slumped over my dead horse.

I have arrows embedded in my chest like candles stuck in a birthday cake. Their sharp, barbed points have hooked onto my vital organs. I'm choking on my blood. It dribbles bright red from my mouth and nose and I am surely dying. The pain is like a red-hot poker inside me. My kneecap has been shot off. I can barely crawl to save myself. There is no point. They are everywhere. I can see my friend. He cravenly hands his gun to a brave and cries, 'John! John! Oh John!' He is sobbing. It is a pitiful sight. He thinks his abject surrender will save his miserable, white skin, but it only brings a sneering contempt. They show no mercy to those who plead, who beg for their life, who weaken. His skull is cleaved in two like a split melon by a hatchet wielding Indian. He falls dead. His brain spills onto the rump of his quivering horse, and slides down the poor animal's flank. I wonder what fearful thoughts are now coursing through its sausage like contents.

A young brave rein his pony up next to me. He looks down from his gaudily painted horse with a look of contempt and trades an eager and knowing smile with his compatriot who stands by as if to say, 'this one is yours'. He reaches for his knife couched menacingly in its deer hide pouch. I can see the intricate beadwork woven onto his calf length moccasins and the reddish hue of his smooth, sinewy legs. The brave sees only my luxuriant locks. It's my scalp he wants. Maybe it is his first one - one he can proudly show to his tribe and they will acclaim him a warrior. He throws his right leg over his colored pony's neck and effortlessly slides off like a child down a slippery dip. He is not much older than a boy, sort of underdeveloped in his upper torso but lithe and graceful in his movement. I wish to hell I'd made a run for it before my horse was shot dead. He grabs a yank of my hair and pulls stretching the skin from my skull. His knife blade glints in the fierce sun. It is bloodied. He has his foot in the crook of my back whilst my head is arched back and my neck exposed like a sheep about to be slaughtered. For a reason I cannot explain, I know his name. He is called 'Kills at Night'. I want to say to him,

'Look John...for Christ's sake...it's daylight.'

I am fucking scared and will say anything stupid to save my life. I want to live. How did I let myself get into this mess? I should have done runner months ago, but it would have meant never seeing my wife and kids again. The brave deftly slits a neat circle around my scalp and yanks the skin and hair clean from my skull making a rapid, popping sound. I am alive, and yet he stands there proudly with my bloodied scalp in his hands. My head feels as though it has been clamped to block of ice. The warrior ties my scalp to his pony, wipes his blade and then returns to me to finish his work.

I awake from my nightmare. I scream, grab at my head, and sit bolt upright in my bunk. Sweat pours off me soaking the stained, threadbare sheets. I am shaking uncontrollably and my startled eyes stare into the cold, dark, rat infested dormitory for General Custer's raw recruits of the seventh Cavalry. Other troops are woken abruptly from their deep sleep. An exhausted sleep brought on by hours of drill and long, boring expeditions into the desert looking for outlaw redskins. They curse me and toss and turn, fisting their thin, uncomfortable pillows. One says, 'fucking Darrington having his nightmares again,' and they go back to sleep. Only I stay awake. I can see the moon clear through the dormitory window and this bright orb with its caressing rays' bathes only my bunk as though it is selecting me as the anointed one – the one who will learn from his nightmares and survive. The others slumber and snore in the dark and half choke on their ignorance. They will surely die. Their dreams tell them nothing of their impending fate. They scoff when I tell them of what I have seen in the middle of the night. They are a bunch of felons, criminals, drunkards and layabouts. With desertions nearly matching the new enlistments, the army takes in trash with no questions about their past.

I am Lieutenant Henry Darrington of Tom Custer's Company. He, along with Boston Custer, are the brothers of General Custer. The General also has his nephew and brother-in-law under his command. Talk about keeping it in the family. We are part of his Seventh Calvary; the best Indian fighting unit in the West, or so it is said. It is really only the bragging of Custer that gave us that reputation. His wife, Libbie, will come to the Fort too when he is not messing around with the young, redskin girl, a Cheyenne captive, he's supposed to be keeping as an interpreter. Why - she is only a teenager, but who wouldn't want to bed her with her long, black tresses, the soft, dewy, deer eyes and dark, slender limbs. She has learnt to interpret his other not so public wants apart from the words of her kin. His reputation goes before him - handsome in a carefree way, impulsive, and to add to the intrigue he looks at times feminine, girlish, and wanton. I heard he was called 'Fanny' at West Point by his mates. I am in real danger here being led by such a girl-man, erratic and publicity seeking in his success.

He takes with him his two hunting dogs when we go looking for hostiles. He and his hounds take off after antelope galloping full steam across the prairie like he's on one of those cavalry charges. Two mangy, wolf dogs and a lunatic in buckskin and a big white hat racing across the flat, featureless plain until they became a mere dot on the horizon. We shake our heads in disbelief. An Indian hunting party would find him easy prey but his mind is glued to the fleeing antelope and he has no fear. I think for a moment that just maybe he dreams he's charging the Johnny Rebs again. Some say he gets that glazed look in his eyes, a heady, intoxicating excitement sweeps over him and he hears and feels nothing but the excitement of the chase as he bounds across the landscape pot holed by the burrows of the prairie dogs. Why only a few weeks ago he takes off in the middle of the night, across the Indian infested country mind you, to the neighboring Fort; thirty miles at a flat gallop all the way in the dark of night. Maybe it was too dark for the Indians to take him, but I bet they sure knew he was there. There isn't nothing that moves, sings, yells or dies out there that they don't know of. Custer is a homicidal, thrill chaser addicted to reckless adventure.

At the end of the Civil War, when the leaders were signing the surrender treaty, where do you reckon the son-of-a-bitch was...scrapping and fun wrestling with a couple of Confederate Generals behind the ceremonial tent. Can you believe it? Although he cut and shot them to pieces, I think he liked them Johnny Rebs and their rag tag army of misfits more than his own. I know for sure he hated Ole Lincoln, and wanted no part of nigger rights what with his uppity wife and social aspirations, and letter writing to the Eastern papers. He tempts fate like nobody I know. He's as mad as a polecat, and one day his foolin around and his unbridled ambition will be the finish of him. And me.

My dreams tell me not to be there when it happens.

I want to return to my family. Your life is cheap here on the plains - dirt cheap- more so if it means Iron Butt Custer getting his name on the front page of the Eastern papers. He has political ambitions - he wants to be the President like Ulysses S Grant. Grant was a bankrupt shop clerk before the war so why cannot a blacksmith's son like pretty boy George get himself a ticket to the number one act too. He figures there is one good battle left on these plains before the Indians are wiped out for all time, and he doesn't want anyone to take that honor from him. The tribes have abandoned the miserable reservations near the Forts and have joined up near Rosebud creek and the Little Big Horn. It's in the Badlands. Land where the hellfire's have died out and desolation and waste cover the landscape. But a cooling stream splits the dry, desolate country and that is where the many Indian tribes have camped dreaming of the old days and drugged by the hypnotic ghost dance. We are on our way there to finish them off and for Custer to be the glory of the nation.

There has already been a big skirmish near Rosebud and I have heard the Indians have changed their fighting tactics. They are not circling anymore but riding smack into the soldiers and fighting hand to hand. Half our horses are green broke and many of the men cannot ride a difficult or panicky horse. The Indian is born on a horse; he can ride like the devil; he can roll off the back of his horse and land on his feet; he can hang off his neck; there isn't nothing he cannot do on a horse. His horse is battle hardened, and fit. They are desperately seeking to defeat the white man so their Indian customs can be revived and their youth have respect. If victory comes, they will claw back another few years on the plains they love. They don't want to live as dogs on a leash, fenced in with handouts of sugar, weevil infested flour and whisky rotting their teeth and guts. They wish only to roam the prairie, undisturbed and free, hunting their buffalo or what's left of them after the hunters have almost shot them into extinction. They say it is better to die with a bow and arrow and tomahawk in your hand than beg for handouts in some clapped out reservation lands.

Already a new spirit has come over them at the Little Bighorn now that they have left their reservations near the Forts and joined together on the banks of the Little Bighorn. There is much celebration and dancing. The boys race their ponies in the hills all day and cool off in the clear, fresh running river, unlike the foul, polluted waters near the Fort reservations. The old men talk of days gone and their exploits while the squaws cook and clean. The tipis are lined up for miles along the river. The strutting, young braves parade on their brightly colored ponies in their battle gear eager for contest and to count coup. They soak up the admiring glances of the young squaws. There is much courting and blanket wrapping. The ghost dance tells them they are invincible and they will drive the white eyes back off their lands. Their bullets will not hurt them. Sitting Bull has had a vision. He sees the blue coats coming to his camp in disarray, dropping from their horses like leaves from a tree in the fall. There is much excitement in the air. They are happy to be back in their old ways.

Not far away blue coated and one buckskinned Generals are plying for their name to be written into history. Custer is asked to take men, cannons and find the hostiles. He is overly ambitious and preening. He says dismissively that six hundred men will do. He does not want artillery or a regimental band. It would slow him down. We cover thirty miles and see the unmistakable signs of a large camp of Indians on the move. The grass is cropped short by their ponies and the ground is ploughed by the poles of their travois, carrying their tipis and possessions. The signs show they are heading towards the Little Big Horn. Custer gets restless and orders his soldiers to saddle up after midnight - go without sleep to be the first to engage the enemy.

During the day General Custer leaves the front of the column and rides back speaking to his troops. He wants to keep them keyed up for the battle but the lack of sleep, the dust, the heat, and miles have made his men weary and their horses sluggish. As he passes, dressed in his fringed buckskins, red scarf and wide brimmed, white Stetson, I want to pull back his flowing locks and yell into his ears,

'please Mr. Custer, I don't want to go.'

But he trucks no cowardice. I have seen him chase deserters and have them shot. Men who had had enough of hot, baking rides across the dry wastelands, stale bread and slops dished out in the Fort camps, and the constant fear of agonizing death all for his glory. They want to leave for the goldfields where the gold is said to be as close as the grass roots. America is the land of opportunity and the free. The Army provides none of this. In my craven heart, I want to go with these cowards, these deserters, these opportunity grabbers.

I sense the Indians are watching us. We had campfires last night to starve off the biting cold. I am sure they would have seen them. The scouts argued with Custer. They sense the foreboding in the air. I can feel the red skin's shadowy presence near as we ride on. Their hairless, smooth, oiled bodies merging with the desert landscape; their eagle eyes peer out from every bush, every tree, from behind the rocks and on the ridges. I want to say,

'General, they are all around us...waiting. Can't you see...we are riding to our certain deaths? It will be a massacre. Let us turn back before it is too late'.

But he sees, hears and feels nothing, except his God given destiny to be famous. My dreams tell me there are several tribes - Cheyanne, Hunk papas, Oglala's, Sioux - their names roll off the tongue of peoples who inhabited this wide, open country long before the avaricious, white man ever knew it existed. An army of at least three thousand horse warriors, excited by the scent of battle and wanting revenge on the white eyes. Revenge on those who swarmed like a plague of locusts across their country, shooting their buffalo and killing and maiming their men, women and children in their lust for its natural and abundant riches. But I was warned, given a vision of what is to come. I do not sit idly by. I needed two things to save my miserable neck - speed and endurance. Both come in the form of a horse - Blue Doggy.

I have traded, argued and cajoled for the best horse in the Regiment, and I have got him mightily fit. He is of mixed Appaloosa breeding reputed to be the toughest in the West. Not really a steel dust type with wide jaws, and powerful hindquarters. He has a running W brand which I am told is King Ranch breeding. Blue Doggy is more loosely coupled - a dash of the thoroughbred which I like cus he stretches more and is ground covering at the lope and gallop, a bit like Iron Bum's wolf hounds. Too much muscle will impede his staying capacity but I sure as hell need a horse that can accelerate, and maintain speed. He is a blue-black with white marbling, and when fit, he sure looks a picture. I wouldn't be surprised if he doesn't have bit of Arab or mustang breeding in him. He has a pretty head for an appaloosa. A lot of these horses came from the conquering Spaniards and ran loose onto the vast American plains to breed and feed naturally off a sea of grass. His hooves are as hard as flint. As well as his turn of speed, I want him to learn to run long and easy - real long like days and nights. I want him to cover distance and to breathe effortlessly, and that I know will take a lot of practice and training. The Indians have their lean, little ponies bred on the plains and they just keep running while our big, grain fed horses pack it in. When they get close, their arrows will whistle and whirl past your ears and one will surely find its target and split your fast beating heart in two. It will bring you down, tumbling from your horse and rolling over and over in the dirt where they will slice you to pieces like a pack of blood crazed dogs or take you back to their camp for a slow, tortuous death. The stories we hear do not bear repeating.

When the other soldiers sat about boozing on their days off, I have loped Blue Doggy about country near the Fort. At first five miles - then ten - then thirty, and now we can do fifty, long miles in bit over three and half hours. I will soon have him doing a hundred miles in a day. There ain't no horse around here that can match that. I get off and feel for his pulse just behind his pastern or under his jaw. In time it got slow and solid...loud, firm beats and real healthy like there is some giant engine with big pistons quietly sliding back and forth sitting in his chest. I had a reservation squaw make me a soft pair of boots out of the best deer hide she could get and plenty of cushioning in the soul because of the rocky ground. To rest Blue Doggy without stopping, I have learnt to run alongside him hanging onto the saddle and sometimes the stirrup. Sometimes I tie a branch to his tail to wipe his tracks. I need to plan methodically and carefully if I am to escape the Indian. The exercise has made me fit - fitter than I have ever been - and for the first time in many years I like the way I am feeling. I'm thinner, lean and breathe better and deeper, and my energy seems endless. I avoid the boozers and gamblers in the Fort and eat good tucker when I can get it. Before my premonitions, I was lazy and fat but the desire to live has disciplined me. Blue Doggy and I have worn out a track in the bush with our regular training runs. Custer doesn't mind. He allows me the freedom. He knows that to do extraordinary things you must have physical strength but he knows I am missing something he has high regard for.

'Keep it up, Darrington,' he says, 'but it won't do you much good because you got a pea heart... all the training in the world doesn't make that bigger.'

His lackeys laugh heartily at my expense but Custer has nailed me right. I have no heart for being butchered in a wholesale massacre. I've taught Blue Doggy to move real easy and relaxed like - long, energy saving strides that never appears to tire him or make him blow hard. I have also learned to move with him in the saddle so as to not interfere with his natural rhythms and balance. I have after many miles of riding become a better rider and close companion to my horse. The regular work has relaxed and calmed him down, made him easier to control and in the heat of battle, I need him to listen to and trust me and obey my commands. He and I must be as one or we will both surely die. I have traded for an Indian whip. They are long leather strips tied to bone handle with a wrist strap so it is not lost in battle. I have learnt to swing it side to side in rhythm with the horse's stride like the Indians do. I do not like wearing spurs, and I need to run. In the cool of the evenings I wash him down and let him graze by the Fort with hobbles to stop him running off. I paste cooling, river mud on his legs to reduce any swelling from the hard ground and long miles. I want him to adjust to the natural pasture and not to be bloated by grain for I know I will be hunted for days, and he and I will need to get his sustenance from what grows naturally on the land - simple, honest, life giving grass that grows abundantly along the creeks and rivers.

The troops are amused at what they see. I tell them,

'I'm ridin and runnin for my life,' and they laugh.

They mock me. 'Poor Darrington,' they say, 'The heat and being away from his family is driving him plumb crazy... the poor bugger is riding around in circles.'

But how else can I save my life. I plan minutely everything that I need to do to escape when the battle starts. How can I break through the ranks of Indians that I see in my dreams? I practice flying through the bushes hanging low on Blue Doggy's neck. I have braided a loop in his mane like the Indians do to hold me in that suspended position along his neck hidden from their bullets and arrows. But I worry that it is not enough. Having practiced on their buffalo hunts, the Indians are quick to engage a fleeing horseman and cut him to ribbons. I heard a scout talking about one of their ceremonies and the answer came to me. The Indian has a simple, childlike belief in the supernatural. They see spirits everywhere - in the wind, moon, stars and the animals they hunt. He told a story of the evil spirit, O-kee-hee-de, the figure he said was without clothes and painted completely black with small, white circles on its body and white teeth near its mouth. It ran, he said, in a frightful zig sag motion down the hill and into the Indian camp with a wand of about nine feet in length and a red ball on its tip. He said the poor Indians, watching the devil figure descend to their village, fell over themselves shrieking with alarm and fright, trying to get away from this hideous monster. I listened intently. That night I got out a piece of cloth and made a full-face mask which I painted black, and put in large, red, canine teeth. Even I got a fright when I looked at myself in the mirror. I took one of my bed sheets, dyed it black and made a gown. I even made a matching hood for Blue Doggy bright, cherry red with black painted circles cut out for his eyes. I tested the devil costumes on a group of young braves from the Reservation who happened to be riding by on their ponies. I walked Blue Doggy out in front of them from behind some bushes, and stood there staring at them through the eye slits in the mask. They shrieked in terror, and rode for their lives not even daring to look behind. I have not seen an Indian near that place since. I have put the mask and costumes in my saddlebag in readiness and tell no one. I am not prepared to go to the slaughter like the proverbial lamb.

Some nights I stay out late. I tell the Sergeant I will reconnoiter about the Fort for rogue Indians and he says simply, 'it's your scalp'. I sit hidden by the bushes in the dark. I look at the stars and listen. I move from spot to spot sometimes by the stream. The stars tell me where I am. If Blue Doggy moves or whinnies, I scold him. I want him to stand silent too. We stay there sometimes for hours until we melt into the very fabric of the country and the blackness. I hear the animal sounds that pierce the silence of the night. The night speaks a language if you listen carefully. It's the alien sounds that I listen for - that of a human moving, a horse snorting, a twig or branch snapping. These sounds intrude and do not belong to the bush and for me they may mean death. I also watch Blue Doggy closely for any reaction. He can hear much better than me.

His ears continually scan about picking up alien sounds that may spell danger. His animal senses honed from generations of being predator prey tell him things long before I become aware. One night I saw a party of Indians checking out the Fort. They did not see or hear me and Blue Doggy merged into the bush. We are getting good at disappearing into the landscape. I have put extra saddle bags on Blue Doggy containing food and a spare set of ready shaped, steel shoes. I have learnt to put on my own horse shoes cold, and have a micro set of tools. And now that our Company is nearing the Indian camp, I know I am ready. I know I am prepared to do what is necessary to save my life. My preparations have brought me closer to my horse so that we understand each other in ways the other troopers could not ever comprehend. To them a horse is simply an animal of conveyance. To me, that blue Appy is my dearest and closest friend in this harsh, desert country which really belongs to the savages; we speak to each other in our language of touch and low sounds in the dark of night and in the day under the hot, scorching, relentless sun. I look after him like a mother. Although I push him to his limits, I will not see him hurt or ill-treated. Sometimes I will sleep in his stable yard so that we lie together and know the rhythm of our breathing. I rejoice in his company and movement, and I can see small signs that he likes me...not effusive joy like you see in a dog but subtle signs, nuances, eye expressions I have come to understand by spending all our time together. I see it in the way he eagerly strides out in our rides about the country, the lightness in his step and his boundless energy. He too relishes his new-found fitness the same as I do mine. He likes the variety now in his life. Before he would be stabled for days, and was bored. He enjoys most the cooling waters of the desert streams which refresh him, soothe the muscle soreness and wash out the dirt and sweat from his coat. We are partners. We depend on each other, and soon our long and arduous preparations will be put the the test. We are ready for it.

Our Indian scouts tell Custer the Indian numbers are large and there is movement in their camp. They advise Custer to turn back. He does not heed their advices. He thinks the Indians are escaping. He divides his column into three sending Major Reno to cross the river to the south of the Indian camp and block their way out on flat land. Custer intends to enter the Indian camp from the hills and carve them up in pincer movement. An officer asks is it wise to divide when the Indians have so many. But Custer is full of Wrest Point schemes and maneuvers. He wants to show himself as a master tactician like moves on a giant chessboard in the manner of the old European Generals. The simple logic that escaped him is that we could be outnumbered ten to one if the Indians attacked en masse, with his men dangerously tired and their horses exhausted and hungry from lack of feed. Oh God - how stupid can he be. The reality of their vulnerability is not lost on the troops, and they are uneasy with his orders.

We march in the dead of night through the Badlands. An eerie feeling envelops me. We are in file and the moon is hidden by clouds racing across the midnight sky. The night clouds are hurrying and so are we. I cannot see anything except my horse and the faint outline of the troops and horses ahead. I hear the jangle of our weaponry, and a horse, now and then, snorting, clearing its nostrils, from the rising dust. Steel shoes strike the rocky ground and give off small, bright sparks. They break for a moment the gloom of the black silence that surrounds us. We stop at two am and rest. The scouts go on ahead to find the Indian camp. Some men slept, others huddled around in small groups talking about fighting Indians. At daybreak Custer rode off bareback with the scouts where they had seen the smoke rising from the Indian village. He returned and immediately gave orders for us to advance slowly to within five miles of the Indian camp.

I know my time to leave is about to come, and I am nervous. I will hold out to the last moment. I don't want to be shot in the back by my own troops. The confusion of impending battle will, I hope, give me the opportunity to make good my escape and maybe - just maybe - if I leave when the battle is lost, then it will not be so bad for me. Blue Doggy seems to sense my treacherous intentions and unlike the others he is pulling on the bit, and flipping his head up and down. I try to relax him. I speak to him and stroke his neck. I say quietly,

'There's a good boy - settle down now - save your energy - this is what we have worked so hard for.'

I stoke his fine, muscular neck and talk soothingly to him. He responds to my reassuring words and caresses. He lets go, settles and drops his head. He has come to understand me in our long hours together. We are partners in crime - the crime of desertion with intent.

We came down from the hills intending to cross the river and charged into the Indian camp. We were met by the Indian Chief Gall and a thousand Hunk Papas who had already crossed the stream, and were waiting hidden in the trees. They fought fiercely and we had to retreat. Custer ordered us to climb a hill from where he hoped to bunker down and defend ourselves. He sent a message to Banteen to come quickly. The Hunk Papas were overpowering the stragglers, cutting, hacking and disfiguring writhing bodies. Like my nightmares I could hear their screams as the savages swarmed onto them like locusts in a mad, frenzied attack. The blood lust of the savages had been excited to a fever pitch. The dreams I had experienced back at the fort was unfolding in front of my very eyes.

Crazy horse and his braves, who had been holding Reno down on the other side of the Indian camp saw his opportunity. He and his Oglala's and Cheyenne raced back through the camp, whooping and knocking pots and pans flying. The women yelled their names as they lifted in their homemade saddles and drove their little ponies faster with their leather quirts and their war bonnets streaming in the breeze. In a mass of color and screams and their savage hearts bursting with pride and vengeance, they surged north crossing the river behind Custer. As we were climbing the hill on one side being pursued by the Hunk Papas, Crazy Horse and his men were racing up the other side of the hill out of our sight. He and his braves would beat us to the summit. Soon we would be caught in pincer movement and hopelessly trapped. I wanted to yell to Iron Bum,

'Where are your fancy plans and maneuvers now? What lessons did you learn at the famous West Point and your heroic charges in the Civil War that a mere savage cannot sweep away with a bit of native cunning?'

Custer looked up and saw above him to his great shock and dismay lances, feathered bonnets and several hundred brightly painted ponies and their excited riders cresting the top of the hill before them. He knew his fate was sealed. We were closed off on all sides and Crazy Horse and his braves had taken the high ground. There was no escape for the unprepared. Custer yelled to us to shoot our horses, and make small circles from where we might be able to bunker down and defend ourselves until help came. Our carbines were jamming. I looked down and saw soldiers with their heads cut open and crushed, arrows spiked into blue uniforms and spine-chilling screams from both the assailed and their attackers. It was a scene out of hell.

I had to go. If I stayed any longer, I too would be dead meat. Bullets were hissing overhead and cutting the grass around me. How I wasn't hit, I do not know. Arrows were raining down on us from below and above. I was a horse holder. I had four horses but they were being stuck with arrows and hit by bullets. They were panic stricken, out of control and I had to let three go. Blue Doggy true to his training stood firm in the middle of the tempest. He was my only hope for salvation on that hill of death and utter confusion. I saw one trooper make a run for it. He was on a fast horse and seemed to outpace the five Indians hotly pursuing him. Then a strange thing happened. He pulled out his pistol and shot himself in the head. He knew his horse would not last the distance, and a quick death was preferable to slow torture. Another powerfully built brave rode hard onto a fleeing soldier, pulling him from his horse across the front of his saddle, and deftly tomahawked his skull discarding his lifeless body like a piece of butchered mutton. It was time to run...I then saw a trooper put his colt to Blue Doggy's head.

I said 'What the fuck are you doing?'

He replied, 'General Custer's orders...shoot the horses for our protection.'

Before he could pull the trigger, I thrust my six-inch army knife into his heart. He said as he collapsed, 'You will hang for this treachery, Henry.'

It was done in full view of the General and his men. They started to shoot at me. I quickly took out my devil costumes. With the battle smoke and dust hiding me, I pulled the black and red hoods over Blue Doggy and myself. I took a smoke bomb I made from gunpowder, lit the fuse and tossed it about forty yards in the direction of the Indians who by this time were about three deep blocking my escape. As the smoke bomb exploded, I hurtled Blue Dog into the mushrooming screen. Billy Hughes followed me.

He was a good lad and loyal but it was too much for him to consider staying. I heard Custer voice ringing in my ears as I kicked Blue Doggy into gallop,

'Darrington...you yellow bellied bastard...I'll see you hung by your neck, you murderin deserter.'

I thought no way Iron Butt. You got us in this mess now I'm getting myself out. 'Go little Doggy, go.' Out of the smoke I exploded, like a demon from hell and standing full in the stirrup revealing the true horror of my art work to the savages. They froze in their tracks, their eyes gaping, and stunned by the flowing black apparition bearing down on them. The impact was mesmerizing. They dropped their weapons, drew back as I made good my escape through their lines. Only I had one follower. Billy - and he was right up my clacker. As I steadied, he drew alongside.

'That was the smartest darn thing I ever did see, Henry. Where did you get that gear? He then gave a nervous chuckle unable to contain himself.

'Did you hear Iron Butt hollow, Henry? I sure as hell don't want to die so if you don't mind, I'm coming with you.'

'Save your breath Billy. You're going to need it before this is finished...there's about six of them on our heels already...they have woken up to my guise and are hoppin mad, I'll bet.'

The braves were tailing us like blackbirds after a hawk. We raced through bushes, over fallen trees and across a shallow bend in the river. I looked behind. Our pursuers were waving their weapons and keeping us in view. They knew from past experience our horses would not last. Billy's horse was tiring, and he went pale. We had covered about fifteen miles at a fair pace and Billy's horse was breathing loud, hard and rasping. Its flanks heaved and it was covered in a sticky sweat. The poor animal slowed to a walk. I reined Blue Doggy to a halt.

'I'm a goner,' said Billy, 'don't stay Henry...otherwise it will be the end of the road for both of us.'

He was a brave lad.

'I will keep them holed up for a while to give you a break on them...I reckon you'll be needing it.'

'Here take this,' I said as I threw him my colt and belt of ammunition.

I felt bad about leaving Billy but we both would have died for sure if I stayed. Me and Blue Doggy kept on going until nightfall - must have covered over hundred miles. It was hot but we were fit and didn't stop. The country was sparse desert plains coming on to rugged cliffs, ravines, and washed out and dry, stony creek beds. It was what we had trained for over many months. After we had ran for about thirty miles, I got off and ran. My feet sure as hell didn't touch the ground. I put soft leather boots on Blue Dog which I had made and fitted to make his tracks difficult to see and recognize, and at times I tied a branch to his tail. When night came, we rested on a high peak amongst the stony ridges. From there, I could scan the plains for Indians. In the distance I could make out dust gently rising from the landscape. I was shaking but not from the cold. I prayed for my life 'Jesus Lord' I said, 'let me live and I will become that preacher I wanted to be when I was young, and Lord, if it is not boasting, let me say to you I can get converts because I do have the gift of the Holy Ghost, the gift of languages and a ringing vocabulary steeped in the words of the good book that will have them rushing from their pews to the baptismal waters.' After my earnest pleas I felt invigorated, mounted Blue Doggy and rode into the moonlit night as I had done about the Fort. After many miles, I rested for couple of hours by a creek pool and let Blue Doggy drink and pick on the fresh, sweet grasses that grew by the water. I didn't sleep at all but listened as I had done in the dark by the Fort. The sounds were night sounds. That is the closest to death that I ever want to come. As scared as I was, inside me was a smugness for my planning and my trust in God had saved my skin. I did not think the Indians would travel long distances after me when they would be celebrating their victory. I washed Blue Doggy to clean the sweat from his coat. We rested...I knew I had some distance to cover to get to the Californian gold fields but the worst of it was over. I was a deserter and I survived whereas the rest would have died horrible deaths. I heard later the Army could not identify the badly mutilated bodies and listed me as one of the dead. I wasn't about to change their ideas on that. The Indians fortunately did not talk about the trooper who escaped and outrun them not wanting to admit to failure. But they might talk if I revealed myself. My plans are to start a new life in the Californian gold fields. I am going to reinvent myself - be a risk taker, and not take orders from anyone. After all, I am living on borrowed time.

Me and Blue Doggy...that colored hay burner surely saved my life. If that wasn't enough, I raced him a few times in those dusty, one street towns on the way to California, and he won me a heap of money. At the gold mines, I decided to try something different. You had to be lucky to strike gold. I would look for gold in another way that I figured didn't have as much risk. I had enough money from the street racing to set up a quick tucker house for the hungry miners and invented a meat patty called the hamburger. It was brilliantly simple being easy to prepare, nutritious and tasty. And cheap to make. I got the idea from the Indians where they dried and ground their buffalo meat mashing wild berries into it for flavor. I mixed in natural herbs, fried them in buffalo oil and put them between a sliced bun with onions, lettuce, a slice of bacon and an egg. I wrapped them in a fold of buffalo skin for a bit of selling gimmick and called them buffalo burgers. I had long lines of customers outside my shop and had to put on extra staff. I expanded into entertainment bringing the best actors and singers from the East Coast. I brought in wagons of booze and gambling facilities. When a miner strikes it rich, he spends a bundle in my saloon buying up big for everyone and putting a heap on the cards and tables. Then there are the girls; and my cut from them can be better than all the rest. If a miner wants a woman, and he has money, the cost will not deter him.

Talking about women, I miss my wife and kids something bad. I sent a parcel of cash anonymously to them. She probably thought it was a benefactor who read about her plight. I even went back to New York City and sat in the park next to our home using a disguise. I had to see them again - to see their faces or I would have gone plumb crazy. I watched them walk by from behind a newspaper - my loving wife and two little, adorable girls. It was hard - by Jesus it was hard - only a few feet separating us and there wasn't a thing I could do but peek out from behind my newspaper. The little one dropped a ball that rolled behind my seat. She ran to get it. She saw my disguised face and sensed something in her innocent, little heart. She stopped in her tracks and stared hard at me. She was about to say something when her mum called her to come.

'It's rude to stare at strangers, dear,' she said and came to take her hand.

I buried my head in the paper so that she couldn't see me.

'I apologize for my little child if she has been bothering you, Sir,' she politely said. 'It's just that has not been behaving well for some time... lost her Dad at the Little Bighorn, she did.'

I mumbled from behind my paper, and they left. I swear the darling child recognized me. She tugged at her mother's arm as they walked away wanting to say something but my wife took her hand and walked on. The child twisted to look back and gave a half wave. I lifted my hand in response...for the life of me, I could not stop myself. The little girl, seeing it was pointless to persist, turned and walked with her mother and sister slowly into the distance, and out of my life.

That night in the Hotel, I wept openly for what I had lost. I wanted desperately to gather up those kids up into my arms - to tell them I had come home and I would be there to look after them but the thought of the noose kept me rigid on the park bench. I later read my wife wandered the desolate hills of the Bighorn by herself in a black dress. She had not forgotten me. I've learnt the love of a good woman don't come by too often. I try not to think about for it will surely send me insane. I try to convince myself to leave well enough alone. I still have nightmares about Custer and have to be careful about the women I sleep with. Most of them are bar girls and too drunk to know or suspect anything. I tell them nothing about my past. Money is making me brash and arrogant, much like Iron Butt. I even started dressing like him what with those fancy, tasseled buckskins and a ten-gallon, white Stetson. Instead of chasing deer and antelope like him, I've started drinking heavy and chase loose women. The looser they are the better. I now like the life and wonder why I was so serious and respectable before. But lately I have with the grog become careless and talk too much. I should have enough sense to cash up and leave the country before my luck runs out. Do another runner. After all that's what I am good at.

Me, Blue Doggy and a mate called Virgil are going to Australia. It's the buzz about the fields now that gold here is getting hard to find. They say Australia is the new

Eldorado. The chinks are leaving by the boatload to get there before the gold disappears. It's a long, long, way away...other side of the world...across a wide, blue ocean, the Pacific... they tell me it stretches on forever. The biggest ocean in the World and that suits me and Blue Doggy just fine. I sure am not leaving him behind after what he has done for me. I owe that horse - plenty. Virgil's getting on in years, in his late fifties I reckon, but the ole crooner has spirit and wants one last adventure before he drops off the perch. He was Stonewall Jackson's right-hand man and messenger. He had to ride day and night through wind, rain, bog, swollen rivers and Union bullets. He learnt much from Ole Stonewall, a devout Protestant, who rode small sorrel pony, sucked a lemon and made battle plans of such imaginative scope and daring that had the Union Army in complete disarray. He liked Custer... reckons Custer would have made a better General for them than the Unionists. Virgil went broke after his slaves left his plantation and joined the Yankees to help do him in...made a stable out of his big home they did, and took his land to give to them Negros, buffalo soldiers. But them negro slaves of his gave him something too – a voice to sing those ole sorrowful ballads. He's broke now, stone motherless broke, but the old bugger can croon. He sings them soulful, southern songs that his slaves taught him as a kid...strange that...but my customers like it and I like it too. The songs are sad, lonely, just like life is for the miners away from their families. The more depressed they get the more they drink. And the more they drink, the more money I make.

'Sing on, Ole Virgil...fill them dirty miner's ears with your sad tunes, and fill my coffers. We don't want no honky tonks busting up my bar.'

Virgil's a good drinkin buddy too, so I'm going to look after him. He's my only family now. I don't have many friends, but you know I might even pick up a pretty, little wife in them English Colonies...peaches and cream like...now wouldn't that be dandy. Change my name again too...and those greasy, meat patties look like fort slops to me now. I've become accustomed to good tucker in fancy restaurants and the cost doesn't worry me one bit. Call myself Roy, Roy Kingsly...go down well with the locals over there what with royalty and all that. Money don't buy you love but it sure helps to make life easy...sort of makes you appreciate the lighter side of life...having fun I suppose. Yeah that's it. That's what life is all about. You need to almost lose your life to understand these things. It's a bit like the bible says. The rich man had to give up his money and become poor to save his life but I figure it works the other way too. If you are already poor, like I was, then you need to get rich to save your life. The trick is not to lose your life, and I managed that pretty well, I reckon, what with the help of them spirit Gods. Perhaps that's why I drink so much of the stuff now...here's to the spirit of ole rot gut whisky, General George and Austria...no...that's not right...it's Australia...ahhh...what the fuck...you know, that God forsaken convict hole stuck out in the ends of the Pacific ocean just waiting for me and Bobby McGee, Virgil Robert McGee, the Second, the Third or whatever...Jesus, they go on with some crap, them

Southerners. All I know is them Southern elites with their fancy plantation houses and black servants come a poor second after the hiding we gave them but now I got myself some loot - well - I'm rather partial to them big, luxurious houses and servants to do all the hard slog. I will get me-self a big plantation house and land a plenty in the far away, English Colony...maybe they call it a castle...they even have darkies too I've heard to do the hard work. It will give me something new to do. Help me stop this drinkin and whoring I have become accustomed to.

In his drunken stupor Henry begins to mumble to himself,

And Blue Doggy...git along little doggies

I'm ravin again...the craven ravin... Lieutenant deserter of the Seventh Calvary reporting for duty...Sirrr...just got a bit lost Sir...back there at the Little Big Horn...and I've been too horny and drunk ever since to find my way home... Sirrr.

'That's ok, Henry...we always knew you would return. We have a surprise for you Henry... report for scaffold duties, will you trooper Darrington And while you're about, just try the noose for size. It should be a good fit...especially made for yellow belly's like you...who wantonly and disgracefully abandoned our national hero, General George Custer, and his good men to them murdering savages in their hour of need. And if that is not enough the rumor is going around that you knifed one of our courageous men in your cowardly attempt to get away. Hanging is too good for the likes of you...Henry Darrington

A bat out of hell

Comanche are extraordinary horsemen.

The Comanche are the most extraordinary horseman that I have seen in all my travels and I doubt very much whether any people in the world can surpass them - the Comanche are in stature rather low and in person often approaching corpulency. In their movements they are heavy and ungraceful and on their feet one of the most unattractive and slovenly-looking races of Indians that I have ever seen but the moment they mount their horses they seem at once metamorphosed and surprise the spectator with the ease and elegance of their movements. A Comanche on his feet is out of his element and comparatively almost as awkward as a monkey on the ground without a limb or branch to cling to but the moment he lays his hand upon his horse his face even becomes handsome and he gracefully flies away like a different being. - North American Indians - George Caitlin.

Riding faster than a bullet

The Indians were coming not more than a half, mile away. They chased us to the fort, shooting and yelling. When we were within a few miles of the fort we looked around and saw a band of Indians going for all they was worth. When we got there some of' the folks asked Dad if' they'd shot at him. He said, 'Yes, we heard the bullets twice, once when they passed us, and again when we passed them.' Texas Cowboys - Memories of the Early Days - James Lanning and Judy Lanning.

They waited. Harry would soon arrive. Harry was a bushranger who put fear into the Establishment and his rewards were not, at times, inconsiderable. So were the risks - execution by hanging. But what could a paunchy, middle aged man who had no education to speak of, no inheritance and a less than enthusiastic desire for regular work do to earn a quid. He was a bit theatrical, but there was no theatre that would employ him. He found it difficult to take orders. He had no land or house. He could ride, and he liked the open spaces and Ranges. He had Irish friends. They did not like the Police or the Squattocracy who ran the Government. It all led to one conclusion really. To the establishment Harry was an outcast - but to his own he was a larrikin hero, a mate whose exploits they talked about with pride. What Harry liked best of all was that his name brought a smile to their open, rustic faces and a rollicking laughter to their belly's. He could take it up to the law makers and their police lackeys with a style and aplomb that made those oppressed feel good about themselves. The Irish settlers knew they had a chance, an opportunity to make good in this new world unlike old Ireland where the British had taken everyone and everything with an iron fist and the penal laws. They didn't want to lose the small liberties they had with an open rebellion which was sure to fail but a lone rebel like Harry - well, that was another matter. Harry truly liked his work and excelled at it. He was not violent. He did not seek to kill or injure. He would cajole and bluff, and to his surprise, it worked a charm. When he was on the big stage, Harry performed like a seasoned actor, and his audience loved it.

The horse Harry was riding was tiring and his pursuers, the Traps, were making ground on him. Harry was riding hard, digging his spurs into the horse's sweaty flanks, and his big face was red with exertion. He was riding hard for the fresh horse he knew would be waiting, to help him evade capture another time. He paid handsomely for the service of having ready strategically placed horses about twenty miles from his hold up.

Ned was enjoying the company of his younger sister Kate as they lazed about in the shade of the giant river gums that grew by the river. She was a mature fifteen years. Young girls grow up quick in the country and with the responsibility of caring for many siblings and work about the house and land. She was a game rider, every bit as good as her brothers and cousins. It was tradition with her mother's family, the Quinn's, that women ride as hard as their menfolk. There was none of this side saddle caper for them, propped awkwardly on the side of a horse, putting on airs and graces. They rode astride, flexed, balanced and easy on the horse's spine the same as the men. They valued a sensitive mouth and a balanced, natural way of riding. They detested the clumsy yawing and yanking of the reins seen in those riders of little ability or understanding. They respected their horses, and knew their idiosyncrasies. Every horse is different from the one before and an astute horseman will be aware of those differences and work with them to make improvements. The weak, mean and unthrifty horses were culled and sold to Police or Government.

Ned hobbled the horses and let them graze on the short, sweet grasses growing near the stream. He could hear them eagerly snapping on the juicy stems as he sat against a tree listening to the flow of the river and chattering bird life of the scrubby hills. The sound of horses eagerly eating relaxed him, almost like a drug. Kate had taken off her boots, rolled up her trousers and was wading in the shallows throwing a line and hook. She had already caught a fish scooping it into a small net she carried, and wrapping it in some paper. It was a typical slow summer's day, but in that peaceful scene an air of expectancy hung in the cooling breezes wafting across the stream's glimmering surface.

All of a sudden, one of the horses lifted its head from grazing, pricked its ears and looked across the stream. Ned could just make out the sound of a horse travelling fast. A red faced, rotund horseman crashed out of the bush, going, to use a well-worn phrase, like a bat out of hell. He was a big man with a shaggy beard, dishevelled long coat and knee length boots almost like a cavalier of old. In his hand he held a leather string quirt strapped to his right wrist which he switched left to right on the animal's hind quarters in an easy, rhythmic manner. Untidy as he was, he balanced his bulk superbly, poised over his horse's wither, giving it every encouragement to extend its stride and grab the earth as it powered forward from its strongly muscled hindquarters. The animal literally flew into the stream, and pounded across, spraying water into the air as it went. A small rainbow formed in the reflective sunlight of the water spray and circled Harry like a multi coloured halo as he churned like a paddle steamer to the other side. Ned was transfixed by what he saw as though he was witnessing a religious apparition, but Harry was not by any means heaven sent. The big, fat man was riding for his life. The hard-driven rider bellowed,

'Young Kelly...don't stand there dreaming like some air headed sheila...get that horse saddled and ready for me...pronto.'

Ned sprang into action quickly unsaddling Harry's horse and lifting off the two saddlebags which felt heavier than usual. Harry blurted,

'The Traps saw me some few miles back and have taken chase. They have a blacktracker with them and begorrah...he's good. They're bloody tracking me at the gallop! Kate, my little, raven haired beauty, wash that horse down for me, love, and walk him around until he's breathin normal...he's a mighty good horse...one of the better ones your Grand Poppy bred. He should be right in few minutes. Put him back in the paddock for a few months. He needs a rest and a bit of company for a while...a bit like me.'

Kate was unruffled. She casually took the reins saying,

'I have got a fish for you, Uncle Harry,' proudly showing him the fish she had caught.

'You are a cool one,' said Harry sweating profusely, much like his exhausted mount.

'One of these days, Kate, if you're lucky and keep up the good work, I might take you for me bride.'

Kate giggled scanning Harry up and down with a quizzical eye. She saw a wide girth propped up by legs bent from years of hard riding in the saddle and looking much like the twisted trunks of two wind blasted snow gums.

'If it's not too rude, Uncle Harry, you're not exactly what I had in mind for a boyfriend.'

'Jesus, young Kate, you know how to hurt a man,' said Harry giving her a friendly cut with his string quirt across the bottom.

'It's experience what you need Kate...not some whipper snapper green behind his ears...I could teach a girl like you a lot of interesting things about life.'

'Yeah...I bet you could Uncle Harry and some of them might land me in jail from what I've heard. I'm too young to go to jail, Uncle Harry, but you...well that's a different matter.'

'gaol...gaol...bloody gaol...they'll never catch me...Jesus Joseph and Mary... that reminds me...where's Ned and that new horse he's got for me.'

Harry hobbled off stretching his sore back and rotating his shoulders trying to loosen up his stiff, arthritic joints.

'You had better clear out as soon as I go if you want to avoid the Traps,' warned Harry.

Ned quickly saddled the fresh horse and handed the reins to Harry adding,

'I hope you like him Harry. I've got him pretty fit riding in the Ranges over the last few months. Do you want me to take those heavy bags of yours to lighten your load a bit?'

'Not bloody likely, young Ned, those two bags are the reason for my hurry today but your Dad will get something. It's made to go around and I do my bit to keep it moving from those who have more than their fair share.'

Harry swung himself into the saddle, kicked his horse into a gallop, yelling,

'Take care, my lovelies.'

The stiff, old fox, refreshed by his break, raced down the shallow stream bed to hide his tracks then back across the river to the other side. Kate couldn't help but admire the old bandit as she watched him disappear out of sight.

'You know, Ned' she said 'Harry sure can ride. He looks a different man on his horse. I might take him up on his offer even yet.'

Ned was in a hurry to leave before Harry's pursuers arrived. They washed, towelled and dried Harry's horse, remounted and were about to depart when riders in uniform appeared across the stream.

'He's gone into the water here, Boss,' said the blacktracker.

The Sergeant saw the two teenagers on the other side, and called out,

'you kids...stay where you are...there's a dangerous criminal on the loose.'

Ned said to his sister 'It's too late to run now, Kate...we'll have to take our chances and bluff our way out.'

He moved the horses over Harry's tracks to confuse the trail. The riders waded across the stream looking intently at the young girl and boy waiting nervously for their arrival. As they got closer one of the troopers, Fitzpatrick recognised Ned and his sister. He said,

'It's the Kelly kids, Sarge, nothing but trouble they are. Their mother's a Quinn, you know, drunkards, horse breakers and thieves. She hitched up to that ex-con, Red Kelly, and bred a litter of brats...bog Irish to the core.'

It's a strange coincidence thought Sarge to himself that they should be here at this time with an extra horse.

'How come you kids got a spare horse?' he said to Ned.

'He's been crook...now that he is better, we are just giving him some light exercise without weight on his back. I thought we would wash him in the river. The cool water should do his legs some good,' Ned quickly answered.

'Have you seen a big, fat, bearded bloke on a bay horse like that one come this way, travelling pretty fast?' asked Sarge somewhat suspicious.

'A bloody, fat wombat of a man,' said Fitzpatrick with a smirk.

'No...seen no one...and you lot have scared off my fish,' said Kate.

Sarge nodded to his blacktracker to inspect the spare horse held by Kate.

'Have a gander at that bay, Soapy.'

Soapy was aboriginal. He was shy and reserved. He had a slim build, spare and sinewy, with long, thin legs that hung gracefully from the saddle and a skin the colour of coal. With a laconic ease he swung gracefully from his horse, and walked to the bay held by Kate, his dark, soft eyes modestly downcast.

'Excuse me, miss...boss's orders,' he said apologetically.

'No need to say him sorry to that white trash, Soapy,' said Fitzpatrick staring Kate down.

'You're the only rubbish around here, Fitzy,' quipped Ned.

'You insolent, tar haired mongrel, young Kelly. I'd give you a hiding here and now if I knew Sarge would let me, but you'll keep. Your lot are no better than them black bastards...savages...that's what you and your lot are.'

Soapy winced at Fitzpatrick's words. He ran the white palms of his dark hands over the horses back and down the front leg, lifting its hoof, and inspecting the metal shoe. He then placed his hand on the animal's girth line near the point of the elbow testing for the pulse. He could feel the pulse still racing. He bent over studying the confused pattern of tracks on the ground for a few seconds and stood upright, looking directly at Kate. He then walked to the river where Harry had left hoping to hide his tracks. Kate sat impassively on her horse but inside her heart pounded fast, beating more rapidly than the horse she held, and that Harry had galloped almost to a standstill. Fitzpatrick, impatient, broke the silence,

'Come on you black bastard, Soapy... is that the horse or not? We haven't got all day for you to gawk at the whitey sheila...if it's a root you're after, she's probably already got a coon lover, maybe a tribe.'

Sarge and his trooper mates laughed. Ned shifted in the saddle biting his lip knowing they would take any excuse to arrest him. Soapy looked away, hiding his embarrassment at the crude remark. Kate's temper rose.

'If I did have a blackfella for a boyfriend, he'd be a better man than you bunch of rotten, dingo bait,' she shot back glaring at the loud-mouthed Fitzpatrick.

'Well whatta ya know...the little she-devil has some spunk,' said Fitzpatrick.

'Should I book her for making lewd suggestions to State authorities, Sarge?'

'Hang on a minute,' replied Sarge looking at Soapy, 'we might fry a bigger fish. What do you say about that horse and them tracks, Soapy me boy?'

Soapy drew a deep breath.

'No Boss...them not the horse or tracks we bin lookin for.'

'Let me have a look, Sarge,' bellowed Fitzpatrick upset with Soapy's verdict.

Kate pulled her fish out of her saddle bag and flung it at Fitzpatrick smacking him squarely in the side of his head, and knocking off his new, blue regulation cap.

'That's all you catch today, Fitzy ...a dead fish,' said Kate admiring the accuracy of her throw. Now the troopers were laughing at one of their own.

Shaking his head and putting his hand on his horse whip, Fitzpatrick dismounted.

'Grab your cap and get back up, Fitzy,' bellowed Sarge. 'You wouldn't know the difference between flamin kangaroo or horse shit let alone their tracks. And put that fish in your saddle bag too. I could do with a good meal of fish and chips tonight. Thanks for the meal, young Kate...your lucky day, kids,' said Sarge, and they left.

As Ned and his sister rode home, leading Harry's horse, Kate remarked,

'That was close, Neddy...I think Soapy's one of us.'

'Fitzy made sure of that...didn't he,' said Ned as he slapped his horse into a gallop trying to imitate his Uncle Harry. Kate giggled, and took off after him.

'Come back here...wait for me Ned ...you white trash...trash, trash, trash,' she yelled and her high pitched, joyful voice echoed loudly into the distant hills as clear as a church bell.

'Trash...trash...trash,' it went as it tapered off into the wild recesses of the uninhabited bush.

Fitzpatrick heard it and cursed, 'I'll get that young Kelly bitch if it's the last thing I do ...you hear what she is calling us, Sarge?'

'I've been called worse than that, Fitzy,' replied Sarge in matter of fact way.

'Sometimes I deserved it and sometimes I didn't, but I reckon she only gave back what you gave her. You wanna learn to keep your big mouth shut sometimes. I reckon that boy Ned was about to give you a hiding until you were hit over the head by that flying fish.'

'Oh yeah, Sarge...him and what Army?'

'The Irish army,' said Soapy who usually said nothing but listened.

'Yeah...they did a fat lot of good against Cromwell...didn't they? to busy going to the pub and races to fight for their country.'

'Who dat Cromwell fella?' asked Soapy.

'He's the fella who took all them Irish homes, land and country and made them slaves,' said Sarge impressing the others with his education.

'Well...I don't know or have heard of him,' said Soapy, 'but I reckon his son is running the country over here.'

'Why do you say a damned silly thing like that, Soapy? Whose side you on anyway?' piped in Fitzpatrick.

'Cos we poor buggers lost everything...how come you take our country...we here first.'

'Because we are bigger and stronger than your mob, Soapy but perhaps Sarge can explain, or maybe give you his big, fancy law book from the Mother country,' quipped Fitzpatrick.

'He cannot read,' said Sarge.

'Only hoof prints,' said Soapy, 'and your foot prints are all over our bloody country.'

The others laughed.

'Good on yaa, Soapy...you can always go back to the reserve on the river. Plenty land there for you to fish and catch goanna,' said Sarge.

Harry heard Kate's yells of 'trash...trash' too as he was counting his ill-gotten loot in a secluded cave overlooking the valley. The canny, old outlaw muttered to himself whilst counting his money. Putting the legal tender down, he did a bit of an Irish jig in his worn, horse sweat stained boots that carried him to yet another equitable distribution of this new country's wealth. He tripped on rock, fell and lay there until sleep descended over his tired and stiff limbs like a cloak. Soon his loud snoring would reverberate and echo along the dark, damp tunnels, past the aboriginal ochre drawings of long extinct marsupials and abundant wildlife, and fade into the depths of the virgin earth they inhabited for thousands of years. As the weary bushranger snored, scurrying rodents nibbled on his worn, leather boots and the white, canvas money bag of Her Majesty's Government stuffed with coin, notes and a little gold bullion. Now and then aboriginal spirits hovered above him, spying on him as they would an intruder, then speeding off along the cave ceilings and flittering out the rock crevices into the dark night, through the tree tops, skimming the swamp surfaces and roosting in the sheltered bulrushes. There they rested and listened to the corroboree chants of a nearby tribe camped for the evening and feasting on fresh kangaroo and possum.

I want a lover with a slow hand

A young Irish girl's opinion on migration.
One night after an exhausting bout of lovemaking, as they lay on a haystack staring up at a sky filled with stars, he'd said to her, 'Moira, do you think there's a better life somewhere away from here?' He might as well have asked her if she'd fancy flying to the moon on the back of a pig. She sat up and, leaning on one elbow, snapped, 'What kind of talk is that, Michael Ranahan? Tis here we live and we'll do like our das and mams have always done. I don't like it when you talk queer like that.' - In the Time of Famine - Michael Grant.

The Irish famine and potato plague.
Men sprinkled holy water on their potatoes; they buried them with religious medallions and pictures of Christ and the Virgin Mother. Nothing worked. God had turned away. - The Graves are Walking - John Kelly.

on getting names
'Where did Buffalo Piss get his name?' Star Name laughed, a bubbling sound of pure joy that Naduah had come to love above all other sounds. 'On his first buffalo hunt his horse fell and a bull buffalo wet him as he ran by. And a bull buffalo pisses like a waterfall. It made Buffalo Piss so mad he mounted his horse and killed that buffalo and another one with the same arrow. Drove it right through them both. Everyone knew then that the buffalo piss was strong medicine, and he's been called that ever since.' - Ride the Wind - Lucia St Clair Robson.

Red Kelly had a shock of ginger hair. His family like many others dispossessed by the English lived on the knife-edge of starvation whilst their invaders lived in manorial splendour and excess. When your siblings and parents were stick thin and sickly pale, and meaty bird life flourished in the Lord Kingston's park nearby, a young boy worth his salt was not about to sit and watch his family starve to death. The English Judge slotted him seven years transportation for taking a fat bird off the fat Lord. He was only seventeen, a mere slip of a lad. The Judge did it as though he were swatting a fly and called for the next case. He seemed amused by his sentence.

'You can steal all you like in that country, laddy,' he said, 'from what I've been told the wild life over there will probably eat you...it's a land of prehistoric monsters.'

He laughed while Red's parents wept at the rear of the court. His crime was to take a pheasant that belonged to Lord Kingston, or at least it was on his private hunting land. There was no food and the staple diet of potatoes that had kept the native Irish alive had rotted in the fields. What food was grown was sold to the English back in their own country. Irish families starved to death in their bare stone hovels, and nothing was done. The English landlords evicted them from their small acre allotments so they had to either live in the ditches or seek admittance to the work houses.

Red was sentenced to be taken by convict ship to the other side of the world. There was no appeal from this harsh penalty. His Parents could do nothing and were grief stricken. Red was placed in chains with other convicts, and delivered by horse and dray to the coastal City of Cork. There they boarded the convict ship for Van Diemen's Land. His father, with tears in his eyes, ran stumbling along the banks of the river that led from Cork to the sea waving to a son that he knew he would not see again. His numb and terrified son could see him through the porthole of the prison deck, and his heart split in two with the anguish of separation from his family and country. The image of his loving father's last desperate and futile attempt to save him from transportation seared into his memory and remains there today coming to him in his restless sleep and dreaming. The other prisoners took pity and did their best to console him but they too had their own problems.

The ship coursed its way down the African Coast amongst the lush, volcanic islands laden with banana plantations, tropical fruits and vineyards. Red gazed at the abundance of food and fruit growing naturally in the semi tropical climate as they slid silently by and thought of the famine back in Ireland, and how countries could be so different in what they offered their inhabitants. The ship was dumpy, made to carry goods and not suited to transporting passengers; it leaked and rolled dangerously in stormy seas with waves reaching some thirty-six feet in height; the head space between decks was a low four feet and six inches so that the convicts would have to walk hunched over and bent. Their living conditions below deck were cramped, dark, and wet from mountainous waves sweeping over the deck and cascading down the hatch soaking the bed clothes. A cubicle was six feet by six feet for four persons so they had to sleep head to toe. There was no privacy. The Captain allowed the convicts to take off their shackles, and when conditions permitted, for them to get some fresh air and exercise on deck but there was little room to move. Animal pens and the crew working and maintaining the sails took a lot of the deck space. The stench from the animal pens and the cramped and unhygienic living conditions below deck made you want to retch. The convicts had to wash with sea water twice a week for the fresh water kept in barrels was scarce and precious. Salted meat, oatmeal and biscuits were their only food but the meat would soon become putrid, the fresh water slimy, and weevils infested the flour. Cockroaches, bugs, and rats inhabited the living quarters spreading disease and death.

They had barely crossed the Equator when the ship was becalmed in the doldrums and the ocean was flat and still like a painting. After seven days the wind stirred and pushed them out into the vast expanses of the South Atlantic Ocean. At times the vast sea looked like swallowing the small ship and its cargo of human suffering as it tossed and turned on its long journey. Those who were not strong enough to survive the onslaught of disease, sickness and despair became ill and died. Their emaciated bodies were dropped into the glassy depths of the ocean without as much as a prayer to accompany their sad, bereft souls.

Having neared the Cape of Good Hope, the ship struggled to stay afloat in the raging storms and fogs rolling in from the Antarctic ice lands. The gigantic waves swamped the decks and tumbled in a white froth down the hatches filling the lower compartments so that the men had to pump furiously to save the boat from sinking. Having miraculously survived the storm, the ship set out across the Indian Ocean taking advantage of the Roaring Forties. Red was told the trip would take three months and the ship would travel about twelve thousand miles, half way across the World to a country about which little was known. The Captain headed south to take advantage of the stronger winds and shorter distance. With the southerly course the cold came in. The skies and stars were markedly different from the northern hemisphere. The Milky Way dominated the heavens. Icebergs with cliffs hundreds of metres high drifted ominously by. The southern light played upon their crystalline surfaces creating a kaleidoscope of colours that amazed the uneducated and little travelled Red. Life had always been agricultural and encapsulated within a fifty-mile radius but their imaginations fed by years of stories, fables and myth knew no such boundaries. Red in two months saw many strange and fascinating sights that aroused his curiosity and sense of wonderment giving him a will to survive his troubles. He saw the immense array of birdlife that lived upon and inhabited the seas, and craggy islands; He saw the marine life; the flying fish, the playful, frolicking dolphins, the aggressive, man eating sharks, the huge, inquisitive whales, the hunting packs of orcas in their glossy black and white uniforms patrolling the ocean diving, surfacing and flapping their tails. He saw things he could never have imagined he would see in his lifetime of digging potatoes and reciting Hail Mary's, and the wonder of all God's creatures sustained his will to live.

After several weeks of heading due east, land was sighted and he felt the rhythms of life begin to stir within him. He could smell the earth in the breeze. The bracing fragrances and land breezes of a pristine bush aroused him as it wafted across the sea and filled the ships sails. He shortly gazed upon land like nothing he had imagined. There were no parks, no hedges or fences or expanse of manicured country - yet it was strangely beautiful. Dense, impenetrable scrub covering the landscape as far as you could see. Rows of blue, green Ranges folding one behind the other until they disappeared into the horizon; trees with limbs protruding in angular shapes that defied gravity; furry marsupials that ran, hopped and snarled their way about the scrub; birds, weird and gloriously pretty, who sang, laughed, twittered and seduced and deafened you with their myriad of calls and sounds stretching from the musical to an ear piercing screech; poisonous and deadly reptiles slithered and crawled over the landscape and warmed their cold blood on exposed rocks ready to strike if disturbed. And amongst all this glorious and hideous variety, for fifty thousand years dwelt a shy, slender race of black aborigines that wandered the length and breadth of their home in small family groups, but that you hardly saw as they merged into the undergrowth.

They disembarked at Pt. Arthur, a rugged bay where there were huge, rocky cliffs at the entrance and encircled by thick scrub. Red was put to work constructing roads through the bush, but when they saw his talent for carpentry and stone, he was upgraded to work on the rows of imposing, stone buildings that housed the prisoners and their guards. His work and the Australian bush gave him a patience and acceptance that hitherto he had not known. Red did his time without incident. He saw many injustices given to his countrymen; solitary confinement in small, dark and dank cells; cruel whippings that stripped the flesh off their backs; starvation diets and deprivations unspeakable. Despite his cooperation, there was still embedded in his heart a deep-seated rancour against the British that would never be erased, but for the time being it was biding its time.

Slowly in that hell hole of a prison he grew to love the surrounding bush and its offerings of stone and timber which he fashioned into buildings that gave him pride and eased the hurt in his soul._He was being slow baked by the hot Australian summers, sloughing off his old skin like a bush snake and invigorated with the prospect of a fresh beginning. Others not so blessed died, broken and wasted men. Some went raving mad in the isolation and loneliness of it all. Those who escaped the prison ran to the bush and thought they would eventually reach China. Instead they died of hunger, lost in a maze of endless scrub, or on the end of a barbed spear from a hostile native. On his release, Red crossed Bass Straight to the mainland looking for a new beginning. Not wanting to remain in Melbourne City, he headed for the hills and high country of north-east Victoria with cool streams, swamps and open grasslands that could support a farm, and a new beginning. He would seek work and leave himself open to chance. It came in the unexpected form of old Paddy Quinn at a country pub. Paddy took him home where he had a wife, one daughter and three wild sons. He owned a lot of horseflesh and cattle on twenty thousand acres of near virgin country that was too rough for the Squatters to grab. His youngest boy was afflicted with a gross stammer and inability to converse. When he was mounted on horseback speech miraculously returned to him. Paddy named him Tennessee, having given his older brothers the names of Boston and Colorado. Paddy admired the Americans for getting rid of the ruling English class, and forging a country of their own built on equality of opportunity. He consented under protest for his wife to name the girl. Her name was Elly, and she attracted much admiration in the district with her healthy, good looks and robust personality. She had an earthiness about her and preferred the outdoors and the plain speak of men to the genteel customs of her own gender. Her brothers were tall, athletic men prone to crude enthusiasms born of bush origins. They were impulsive lads given to heavy binge drinking and scrapping with their friends and enemies alike.

Paddy made his living out of trading horses, cattle and other activities that had much to do with his outlaw friend Harry. But his first and only love was the horse. He could sit for hours in the shade of the gums studying their behaviour, movement and habits. He didn't have written records of their breeding for he had it all in his head, and they were as familiar to him as the members of his family. Paddy was blessed with a good eye and could instantly recognise what was good or bad in the temperament and conformation of a horse. He also instinctively knew what mares would nick well with his stud and the offspring were expertly handled by his sons who spent long hours in the saddle practicing their repertoire of trick riding. The silent beneficiary of all this horse knowledge and expertise was Harry Power, the notorious bushranger, and few, apart from close and trusted friends, knew of the profitable partnership. Harry knew his welfare was intimately bound up with his capacity to have access the best horses in the country. They needed to be cool, fast and rock hard if he were to continue to enjoy the panoramic views and cool breezes of the mountain Ranges he inhabited.

Paddy thought he could take advantage of Red's carpentry skills and offered the reserved ex-convict work on his property. Red was lacking in horse skills, but he knew how to build with timber from the scrub, gravel from the creek beds and rocks from the craggy outcrops. His craftsman's eye soon wandered from his tools to Paddy's pretty daughter. She was popular and for good reason. Young ambitious men dressed to impress and mounted on smartly groomed horses invited her to go riding with them hoping to win her favours, and she played them like a deck of cards. Red could see them together when repairing Paddy's buildings and roofs. There perched on rafters and busily thatching the dry reeds, he could observe her playful manner, her hearty laughter and repartee, and her dark, flashing eyes and luxurious, black hair. Red was a modest man with little to offer such a much-admired girl. He did not think he would feature in her bright, imaginative thoughts. Sometimes during his work, she would cock her head, look up at him and say,

'Red...that is a beautiful roof you are making to keep me warm in winter.'

He wanted to reply I have other ways of keeping you warm but he was too polite, too dull, and too ordinary to win such a girl with rude and suggestive replies. Other suitors could do it and she would laugh but he was a worker, and he didn't want to risk Paddy's anger when he was so good to him. As he waited for the next sheaf to be thrown up, he stood and felt the gentle breeze coming from the Ranges. It refreshed him in his labour on a hot day. He looked down. She was still looking at him, and smiling with the sun's rays reflecting off her luxuriant, dark tresses. Could it be...no...don't be silly...but then perhaps–

'Gentle breeze, confide in me, what her idle thoughts may be'.

The wind seems to be pushing and egging him on.

'I would build you a bed of straw upon which to lay your pretty head, Elly me darlin,' he said. 'And what would we do on that bed of straw?' she cheekily replied.

Red went crimson and quickly returned to his work. He was thirty and she was eighteen. Despite her ability to pick and choose Elly came to appreciate Red's calm, tradesman-like qualities. The buildings he made were measured, exact and beautiful unlike the rough, tumble down sheds crudely and hastily constructed by her Dad and brothers. He was not handsome, exciting or even adventurous but there was something slow and methodical about him that she sensed would be good for her. Soon there were stolen glances across the room and the brief clasping of hands under the dining room table when no one was looking.

On the pretence of checking the stock, they escaped on horseback to the swamps that abounded in the rugged, spectacular country and where those coy attempts at romance under the table ran to passionate embraces and reached a climax of sensual pleasure that Paddy would definitely not have approved of. On a giant, fallen red gum, half-embedded into the earth from whence it grew, Elly would stroll like a brazen temptress, tossing her garments, one by one, at the doting, convict carpenter whilst the bright Australian sun, her first lover, caressed and warmed her Irish born, white skinned body. There on that makeshift altar in that faraway country, Red made illicit love. Enmeshed in her vigorous, imaginative lovemaking and his shy, stolid reticence, an awkward embrace would send the two lovers toppling from their elevated stage like two sparring eagles held by their talons, cart wheeling from the log, and thudding to the earth below.

She was nature's child, born into a wild land without guilt or guile, without being stifled by the hell damning rigours of a primitive, catholic religion that pervaded her parent's minds and their native Ireland. In a high-pitched protest, her yells of fucking pleasure spooked the bird life high into the clear, blue sky, chorusing their shrieking approval to her rebellious affirmation of life, and then settling back again onto the mirror surface of the still swamp, like so much multi-coloured confetti. Exhausted and satisfied, they rested on their saddle blankets and watched at the array of bird life parading before them; the tan and black mountain ducks, the plovers, the grey teals, the shovelers, the black winged stilts, the white-faced herons, wading in the shallows and feeding on the insects, larvae and crustaceans.

'This is true happiness, Red' she said as she gazed at big swamp surrounded by red gums, dotted with clumps of tall, wavering reeds, nests and the myriad bird life gliding peacefully on its shimmering surface.

Maybe Red thought, he had to suffer in his early life, as he had surely done, to be worthy of the love that Elly gave him above her many suitors. Paddy would not hear of their desperate pleas to marry. He wanted better for his daughter...someone with property and an ability to know and ride horses which the humble Red did not have.

The couple eloped to Melbourne and married in Ballarat, returning only when her brothers told them that Paddy's anger had abated, and he was reconciled to their union. Thereafter, they had seven children in quick succession. Red found peace and purpose in his brood, and rested in the thought of seeing his children into adulthood in a far-off land that he had grown to love. When he was least expecting it and content with life, God delivered him a thunderbolt and packed him off on another journey to an unknown land.

Red sails into the sunset

Surgeon's thoughts on the brain
'I often have to cut into the brain and it is something I hate doing...The idea that my sucker is moving through emotion and reason, that memories, dreams and reflections should consist of jelly, is simply too strange to understand.' Henry Marsh -The Weekend Australian magazine.

Red's thunderbolt came in the shape of a horse's hoof. It hit him fair square in the forehead when he was not watching for the warning a horse will give if he or she is about to strike. To a horseman these signs are unmistakable like the snorting and foot stamping of a bull or the rattle of a snake. The difficult mare lashed out with her hind leg, and dropped Red. Dropped him as surely as a bullet to his brain. He fell silently into the dirt and horse shit of her yard. He was putting some hay in her bin, a simple enough task that he or the kids had done many times before. It was hardly a death-defying act.

Some people think all horses are dumb animals without intent good or bad. The truth is, sadly for Red, that some horses harbour evil thoughts like Cain to his brother Abel. They have memory and can hold a grudge. This mare had it in for Red and waited her time. She had patience as well as memory for treatment she didn't like. Red's sin was to be a clumsy rider, and she refused to cop it. She thought it unjust to suffer the ignorant jerking of his hard pull hands on the reins. Often the horse would jack up, and run away with him. Red didn't realize he was doing harm - he just pulled harder on her sensitive mouth like she was some stubborn mule. People like Red shouldn't mess with horses. He should have chosen to ride a more even-tempered horse - a forgiving slug.

Red was physically uncoordinated. He had no rhythm or balance. He didn't have that feel or intuition which makes a horseman. Some say you cannot learn these things and that you either have it or you don't. In Red's case they were right. He was a tradesman. He used his strength to force materials together, slamming nails into hardwood, and pulling them out if he made a mistake. What he didn't know was hit on a sensitive mare at the wrong time and it was a mistake that you could not easily fix, or the mare forgive. The nail stayed buried, festering in her memory somewhere between those pointed ears that rotated, listened and heard everything that went on about and around her.

The time came when Red was squarely in the vengeful mare's sights. His head was down, dropping hay into her bin. A horse can see both in front and behind. As he lowered his head within kicking range, she let him have it. She would teach him that it was dangerous to pose as a horseman, be dumb about reefing the soft flesh of her tender mouth about with crude, iron bit, and bouncing on her sensitive back until the muscles in her spine ached and rubbed sore. She smacked him solidly with a lightning, fast kick of her hind leg. Red's head exploded. His eyes rolled back, and he laid deathly still where he fell. The brute force of the kick left a neat horse shoe indentation in the shape of a u to his forehead, just like a horse brand. Man hot brands the horse to claim ownership, and she branded him with lethal, blindingly fast kick to satisfy a grudge and to disown him.

Having hit her target, the mare stood over Red's prostrate body, chewing her hay while his damaged brain swelled like a balloon. Electrical impulses ran awry never to find their paths again. Ned found his Dad an hour later. Together, he and his Mum carried him to the house and placed him on his bed. He was breathing heavy. He was dying.

'What's that horseshoe mark on his forehead,' said Elly.

'He's been kicked,' said Ned full knowing the culprit, 'it was the mare...she's a thin-skinned mare...very sensitive. Dad shouldn't have meddled with her. You know he couldn't handle difficult horses, Mum.'

'I told him, son, but he wouldn't listen, and now this. He don't look good, Neddy...it don't look good ...I've heard of this killin people being kicked in the head like that...he's bleeding from his right ear too.'

'I don't know Mum. I will go and get the Doctor.'

The Doctor arrived two hours later in his trap looking worried and exhausted. Elly took him to the bedroom where Red was lapsing into and out of consciousness. Wet towels were placed on his head to reduce the swelling but it did little good. The doctor prodded and felt his weak pulse but could do nothing. He saw the signs, and knew there was no medicine to cure a scrambled and swelling brain.

'His brain is too badly damaged, like jelly,' he said. 'If he survives, he will be a vegetable.'

This son of Erin was about to take his last ride into the sunset and the doctor said that if he awoke the family should say their farewells. The local priest would be too drunk to come. Red would not have wanted him anyway. He was indifferent to Church affairs, and had forged his own spare philosophy on life. He would go unannounced into the next world. The family pushed aside the spare hessian divider and filed into the dim, slab walled room, silent and afraid.

Red's eyes opened for a moment. His senses were stirred by a gentle breeze filtering through the small roughly hewn window, lightly billowing the plain cotton curtain in a manner that beckoned his imminent demise. The eucalypt fragrances of the Australian bush that he had come to know so well comforted and reassured him...a sort of poor man's benediction or final rights. He knew life was ebbing from his worn-out body and he didn't want to blame the mare, preach to his kids, or worry his family with a lot of dying requests. He would have a dull death much the same as he had a hard, dull life apart from marrying Elly.

The image of his Dad running and stumbling along the Cork River flooded back to him. He looked so helpless and foolish, Red had the urge to laugh but the energy was not there. He looked at his eldest boy, Ned.

'Ned,' he murmured, 'help your mum look after the kids ...I know you can do it.'

His breathing was slowing. In this wholesome, spare limbed, black haired boy, the dying father saw much that he loved. He had inherited his mother's good looks and athletic ability whilst at the same time going deeper in his thought processes and more analytical than the Quinn's. In this young boy's head thoughts were spinning but the overwhelming one was of sadness. Sadness for Dad who had just about beaten the odds having been ripped from his family in Ireland and imprisoned in wild, untamed country on the other side of the Earth. He was saved by love of a good woman and family of horse nuts, raised a brood of his own only to realise that now he would be shortly be losing that too. As Red's sight dimmed, he could hear his old Dad's trembling voice call out to him when he foolishly stumbled along the shore that fateful day his young boy sailed out of the Cork harbour in chains. A tender boy sent down for the crime of trying to feed his starving, skeletal family. Was his father calling him, showing his boy the way to a new world as a last gesture of love for a son he had not seen for what seemed a lifetime. Did his father feel an immense guilt that it should have been him as he watched the ship's sails disappear over the horizon with its cargo of human sorrow and misery. Does anyone know what thoughts, what visions, or what recriminations come to your bedside when we take our last breath.

'What's he saying, Mum?' asked Ned.

'Shush son...I think it's 'do not be afraid... I'm sailing home... Dad, don't worry... I'm coming home.'

'What a strange thing to say,' said Kate.

'No Kate,' said Ned, 'He came here by boat, and now he is sailing home, to be with his Mum and Dad back in Ireland.'

Red's heart stopped, and the doctor placed a sheet over him as the family wept and filed from the room. Little Gracey, the youngest, wrote a poem for her Dad. It went like this–

> 'Here lies my Dad, Red Kelly,
> The doctor said our mare kicked his head, and made it into jelly,
> I will miss my dad, he was bold and game,
> and I told mum I am not going to eat jelly again'.

She handed a little bit of scribbly paper to her mother. The little poem startled her mum at first. She cried a little, and then smiled.

'You're a strange one, Gracey.'

She drew the child close giving her a hug.

'It's beautiful, funny and sad little poem Gracey, but true...just like life...but it will give Dad and the others up there a good laugh. We will drop it into his coffin. He'll like it for sure, when he wakes up and reads it in heaven but don't show it to anyone. They might not understand like we do.'

'Understand what, Mummy?'

'Well Gracey...life, death, heartache, love, pain, humour...all those things you'll learn about soon enough but some of us only see pain. I don't ever want you and the others to end up like that my little dove so keep writing your poems...no good comes of being miserable all your life.' Then she added, ' even if things are, and you know what little one, our Ned can ride that mare, he can do anything, and he is the man that is going to look after us, now.'

'But Ned is still a boy, mum, so I will l help him look after you...just you wait and see.'

Spirit in the sky

Johnny Reb writing home about girls and the way one rode.

The girls were pretty he said but decidedly fast. The younger about sixteen speaks of giving the dogs hell and slaps our faces when we kiss her; this same gal climbs trees for peaches, rides to the mill on a horse bare back and not with both legs on the same side but one on each – astraddle. The life of Johnny Reb - B. I. Wiley.

How the Indians taught a white captive boy to ride

After this they taught me how to ride races. I was tied on the horse the way I was expected to sit, nearly straight, leaning a little forward, with my knees clamping the horse so as to cut the wind. After they quit tying me, I fell off several times. The horse would sometimes fly the track and would have to be run down on the prairie, with me swinging under his belly when I was tied on. Nine Years among the Indians - Herman Lehmann

The relatives and friends came to Red's Funeral in large numbers. The Irish stood together in times of trouble. They came in buggies, Traps and carts, some flash and some dilapidated; others rode their horses; the kids rode their ponies and some even walked, hoping for a lift to the cemetery which sat on a high hill, a short distance from the town. The naturally rebellious Irish girls preferred to ride astride their horses, like the boys, contrary to the accepted genteel fashion of side saddle. Over their riding trousers they wore a smock to accommodate their desire to ride as vigorously as their men and still maintain a touch of feminine charm and allure. Their names of the families read like a roll call at a Catholic church on Sunday morning mass...names like Quinn, Kelly, Ryan, Lloyd, Nolan, Murphy, Cassidy, and O'Neil; displaced persons looking for new beginnings, and a future for their families where back in Ireland they had none.

Red was carried in his coffin to the waiting hearse. It was more a plain dray painted black with some gold coloured carving for a bit of show. It had a rail and step at the front for the driver and a long seat with grip rails either side of the coffin for the family and priest to sit. They assembled congregation left in single file, like a rag tag army, to pass through the town to the cemetery. On their way through, they stopped to collect the local Priest hoping that he would be sober enough to say a few words for Red. The townsfolk watched as the long, slow caravan rolled into the main street. The barking dogs woke the mostly inebriated man of God asleep in his bed and hung over from his repeated binges on the bottle. He coughed, and stumbled out of bed. With the help of Ned and his cousins, he pulled on his frock, grabbed his crucifix, bible and whisky bottle, and groggily climbed aboard the cheaply constructed hearse to accompany the deceased's family. He seated himself at the base of the coffin to the acclaim of the mourners gathering around.

'Good on yer, father,' they yelled, 'we hope we didn't take you away from your prayers.'

'As a matter of fact, I was saying a few prayers for Blue...no...that's not right...Red,' he said without battering an eyelid.

'What's in the bottle Father...altar wine?' asked one.

'May God forgive ye for makin such a heathen statement, me boy...medicinal only...for me crippling arthritis...pains brought from been on me knees praying for the lost souls of my flock like you lot.'

With a customary wave of his whisky bottle he gratefully acknowledged the assembled crowd's appreciation of his presence and blessed them adding,

'Dearly beloved, I have been praying all night long for the deceased, and I am weak from lack of sleep. The spirit is strong but the flesh is weak. I will sit with Red a while on our last journey to prepare his soul for its departure to the good Lord.'

The grateful audience clapped. He then swallowed another shot of whisky, and shook his weary, alcohol sodden head as the unforgiving liquor burnt its way down his inflamed gut. His flock remembered him as a sympathetic and generous man in his sober years, and loved him despite his present indiscretions. He didn't hide his failings under a bushel. They were there for all to see. They would protect him as he had, in his better days, protected and supported them.

The local police watched the long procession with condescending smirks thinking that would be one less to have trouble with.

'Look at this bloody circus, would you...a rabble of horse and cattle thieves, accompanied by their Irish whores and son and daughters of bitches...and a drunken preacher to lead them...God forbid...the women don't even have enough decency to ride proper like.'

'That's not all that spreads their legs,' said an uncouth youth.

The young trooper leaning against the door opening to the street laughed mockingly and let out a high-pitched whistle at the young girls on their horses. They rode close to him trying to smack or whip his cheeky face, and gave him the finger. A bit of fun and idle abuse never worried them... they liked the challenge.

'I'm going to nip that flash, young Kelly lout in the bud if it's the last thing I do,' said Sarge. 'He thinks he can run the show now that his old man has kicked the bucket.'

'Yeah...and I'll deal with that Kate Kelly, Sarge,' said Fitzpatrick as he saw her pass by. Her dark, openly rebellious stares aroused his basic passions in a way that made him wish he could get her alone in the scrub without her brothers to contend with.

'I'd keep well clear of that one,' said Sarge, 'she's got the devil in her.'

Paddy trotted his horse up to Ned. 'Which horse did poor Red in?'

'It's the mare I'm riding, Pa,' said Ned. 'I'm not sure what happened although I have some idea.'

'Perhaps he spooked her from behind,' replied Paddy.

'Maybe,' said Ned, 'But you don't mess with her. You work with her and when she is ready you can ask for more. I can get along with her but she's thin skinned and a sensitive mare...unforgiving too...bump her wrong and she'll jump over the moon. You know Dad was no horseman. He should have left her alone like what we told him. I am frightened to leave her around the house now in case she knocks someone else off. She's a one-person horse, but a real smart one if handled right.'

'Give her to me, Ned. I'll breed her to my Stud...he's got a real quiet head on him and you can have the foal. Sometimes breeding quietens them down,' said Paddy thinking the young boy needed consolation in his grief.

'You never know, the foal could be a good one. It's them quirky mares that sometimes drop a foal that is outstanding.'

'Ok with me, Grandpa...I'll bring her over after the wake.'

The congregation followed a narrow road leading up a steep hill that gave a view over the whole valley. On the top of the hill was a small cemetery, unkempt and overgrown, but pretty in a natural way with wattles blazing bright, yellow flowers, little stands of sheoaks rustling in the summer breeze and roses climbing on the half fallen down fence. The lead riders dismounted and threw a long rope from tree to tree pulling it tight. As the riders dismounted, their horses were tied to the rope and they moved to form a circle about the coffin and freshly dug grave.

The short ride in the fresh air sobered up the old priest from his alcoholic haze and like a witch doctor absorbed in his rites, he went about his duties.

'His spirit is rising to the heavens, dearly beloveds...I am watching it now...can ye not see it, dear brothers and sisters.'

They all shielded their eyes, and looked upwards. To their amazement, they spied a wedge tailed eagle directly above spiralling on the hot and cold currents that waft in the stillness of the blue, cloudless sky. The big bird stopped abruptly in mid-flight as though it hit an invisible wall. The believers who witnessed this spectacle gasped.

'It's Red's soul to be sure...shooting like a cannon ball to Paradise, dear brothers and sisters...just about knocked that big bird sideways in its haste to meet its maker.'

'Them birds can see the bullet coming miles away,' said another who had shot at several and missed.

'The bird surely saw Red's soul being spirited to its maker, dear mourners, and didn't want to get skittled,' said the preacher nodding his head and confirming the wondrous power of the Lord.

'Amen to you, father...we saw it with our own eyes,' they replied and looked down at the coffin half expecting to see a hole in Red's coffin where his soul burst forth on its urgent, heavenly journey.'

Encouraged by the divine intervention, the preacher cleared his throat and said,

'Red came to Australia a victim of British justice. He now leaves a free man. He also leaves a wife and young family. That family, brothers and sisters, is our family. Here in this god forsaken land, we live, struggle and die together. What happens to one happens to us all. It will only be through this commitment to each other that we will survive and hopefully prosper in this harsh country. Poor though we may be, you are all precious in the sight of God. But it is not enough to sit back and trust that the Lord will provide. We must fight the good fight; we must run the good race.'

A few began to yawn having heard the familiar biblical phrases many times before but this was a Quinn and Kelly affair, and this time the old, devil priest had a glint in his bloodshot eyes.

'And a race it will be...the first horse or buggy back to Paddy's for the celebrations, sorry wake, will be blessed by me and given a prize. Paddy and I have worked out a handicap...the kids can leave first, then the oldies in their buggies followed by the rest of you...and remember no short cuts or cheatin.'

As the congregation eagerly lined up, the priest grabbed a stockwhip and let out a resounding crack sending the kids scampering for their ponies. They left in a cloud of dust and excited yells. He cracked the whip a second time, and the elderly hobbled and scrambled to their buggies taking off after the kids.

'Tommy, get that dray...we are not going to miss out on the fun. The others can go as soon as we are a mile down the track.'

The kids kicked their ponies into a flat gallop towards the town. The elderly drivers urged their buggies and carts into the contest, jostling for position, and pursuing the kids not far ahead of them. The young men and women took up the rear, and with their natural speed and agility soon overtook the buggies.

Meanwhile back at the town, the folk were leisurely strolling up and down the main street still talking about the funeral procession a few hours before when a sound of thunder and distant whoops and yelling began to assault their ears. They looked nervously down the street to where the sound was coming from and saw a large cloud of dust build ominously over the horizon. The commotion awoke Sarge from his afternoon sleep. He grabbed his hat and ran into the dusty street not knowing what to expect. The distant thunder was getting louder.

'Sounds like a storm brewing,' one said.

'It sounds like a stampeding herd of cattle,' said another straining his ears.

Sarge pulled out his telescope and levelled it to the dust storm on the horizon.

'It's not a bloody herd of cattle,' he yelled "It's a herd of galloping Irish gits...clear the streets...they are going like the clappers.'

They scampered in all directions emptying the street, and waited nervously for the first of the barbarian hordes to appear. Way out front was a game nine-year-old, Grace Kelly, on a fast-little pony. She galloped into the street alone. The little girl saw the audience lining the street, and the show-off in her could not be held back. She had seen her older brothers and the Quinn boys practice their trick riding. She catapulted off her pony, holding onto her saddle, and then vaulting back onto her pony, then did the same the other side and galloping off working her pony with her legs as she disappeared out of sight. The spectators clapped and cheered her performance. No sooner had the kids left the street, and then the adults, men and women alike, burst onto the scene in a frenzy of speeding horse flesh, animated whoops and high-pitched yells. At the front was Tennessee, pursued closely by Kate and her sisters. Behind them came Ned standing on his horse in a feat of horsemanship that made the townsfolk gasp. A riderless horse galloped up the street to have Dan suddenly appear from under his mount. One of the Quinn boys lay back on his saddle as though it were having an afternoon sleep. The rag tag circus swept through the town like a summer whirlwind, and was gone before Sarge could gather his senses. When the townsfolk thought it might be safe to venture back onto the street, the third wave hit, buggies, drays and coaches, with Ma Quinn having pushed the driver aside, climbed onto the driver's seat and taking over the reins. Elderly faces were thrust out the coach windows yelling encouragement to their drivers and friendly abuse as they fought to gain the lead.

Sarge had seen enough, and stormed indignantly into the street only to be knocked over like a skittle by the speeding hearse. On board was a drunken preacher hanging on for grim death to the side rail with one hand, his whisky bottle in the other and reciting the Lord's Prayer. All Sarge could hear as he hit the dirt was,

'Though I walk through the valley of death, I shall fear no evil.'

'I'll bloody give him and his lot some evil,' Sarge spluttered as he emerged out of the dust. At this last spectacle the townsfolk burst into fits of laughter. The event was talked about for months later except in hushed tones when Sarge was near.

Gracey, a clear half mile ahead, kept a watchful eye on her pursuer's progress. She cantered into the homestead as easy and pretty as you could imagine, dismounted, and stood there waiting for the others. Her small, hardy pony looked on disinterestedly. Ned cantered in, stopped and studied her for a minute without saying a word. She smiled and giggled a little, embarrassed at having beaten the adults.

'Amazing little Gracey...eh,' he said as he swept the child up into his arms.

'It looks as though I taught you too well, little one. Don't you have any respect for your Elders?'

Stayin alive

True ballerina and a fine horse.
*'They can be too bummy, too titty or too short in the neck. They don't
have that line of leg and that slimness and elegance of body. A true
ballerina is much finer, much longer. The best are like thoroughbred
racehorses. They are exquisitely fine, like china. They are the rarest thing
in the world.'* Derek Deane - Chief Executive and Artistic Director of
the English National Ballet talking about English ballerinas.

Owning horses and their care.
*NAT-AH'-KI was the proud owner of a little band of horses, some of
which had sprung from mares given her by relatives at various times. She
loved to talk about them, to describe the colour, age, and peculiarities of
each one. A Blackfoot who was horseless was an object of reproach and
pity. Horses were the tribal wealth, and one who owned a large herd of
them held a position only to be compared to that of our multimillionaires.
There were individuals who owned from one hundred to three and four
hundred. Were the owners sonless, each employed some orphan boy to
herd them, to drive them twice and thrice daily to water. And they liked
to sit out on the plain or hills for hours at a time to be among them and
gloat over them as they cropped the rich grass.* My Life as an Indian:
The Story of a Red Woman and a White Man in the Lodges of the
Blackfeet by James Willard Schultz

The motley collection of competitors spilled into the open paddock near Paddy's
farmhouse. There amongst the crude, timber tables and in the cool shade of the
spreading gums, a typical boisterous Irish wake was about to take place. It was their
time-honoured custom to see their own off in a robust style. The tables were
overflowing with food, alcohol and all sorts of cakes and sweets for the kids. A fiddler
strolled amongst the crowd, and every now and then, couples danced on a wooden
floor hastily put together by Paddy's boys. Paddy had done pretty well with his stock
dealing. His property stretched over twenty thousand acres of untamed Ranges,
mountains and boggy swamps. The low lands were a lot like Ireland he thought but it
was the Ranges he loved. The avaricious Squatters passed over the grant thinking it
too untamed, too rough, too steep and rugged to do anything with. In the far-flung
corners of the large property, Paddy and his boys built makeshift yards out of the bush
timber where they herded the wild cattle, roped them down, and jabbed red hot pokers
onto their leathery hides.

'Just so we don't steal our own cows by mistake,' joked Paddy.

Paddy used the cows to make a living but his pride was his sleek, refined, horse
flesh. When he woke in the mornings, he thought about them; during the day he
walked amongst them; he touched them in loving ways running his hand over their
smooth necks and rumps, lifting their legs and eyeing their conformation; and when

he went to bed at night, he dreamt about them. When the young ones were weaned from their mothers, they were taken from the protected home paddocks to the large areas of mountain country to harden their hooves and tendons, to teach them to be sure footed, and to give them plenty of space to roam and run free. This developed their lungs, gave them stamina so that they had the capacity to cover long distances with relative ease. When they turned two years, they were herded back to home yards for breaking in by Paddy's boys and young Ned, and then turned loose again to mature until three or four years of age when serious training would begin. Paddy had his theory on horse breeding.

'I like a bit of the racehorse for its veeee...locity,' he said hanging on the word and swelling it out as though it was too sophisticated for his uneducated listeners. 'But only reliable, proven blood...not crazy hot heads,' he warned. 'And a good dose of hardy Arab on the dam's side. Hard, dense bone and staying ability...that's what them pretty, girly Arabs bring to the union...and some contrariness too, darn it,' he added adopting the airs of a Professor. He paused waiting for his words to sink into his captive, puzzled audience. Paddy, and his family in Ireland before him, had learnt a lot about the breeding of animals. Their lives were intimately intertwined, and their knowledge came from hands on experience and what was handed down orally from one generation to the other, and not what was read in books. In any event the books were not there, few could read, and the Irish did not trust formal, bold, black lettering such as the English used so effectively in their penal legislation. He remembered only too well his Father telling him it was legislated an Irishman could not own a horse worth more than five pounds.

'Now I have proven, good lookin stud in that paddock over there for a price which you lot would do well to use. It's not difficult to understand. Why look at weedy man or woman with funny set face – they don't breed well, their workin ability is half that of a well-built person, and they often because of that physique, have things goin wrong in their head... you know whining, always complaining and making excuses, breakdowns with weeks in bed. You know what I am talking about.'

The assembled group looked at each other with a little embarrassment.

'Why even just today I have organized with young Ned here to put his flighty mare, the one that did poor Red in, to this stud, and you mark my words, the foal will be a good one.' Paddy was a born preacher, and was warming to his task when something very unusual and alarming happened.

Not far away, in the dense bush, a heavily built, solitary figure on a horse waited. The darkened figure peered through the leaves and branches of the thick, dense bush like a wily, old fox waiting for his opportunity to grab an unsuspecting hen. His horse moved, gentle and light like a big cat, amongst the scrubby trees and undergrowth, stopping for a moment whilst its rider intently studied the scene, then creeping closer, stalking the funeral gathering. It was Harry. He was well known to Paddy's and Red's friends. Around his ample girth were two holstered and silvery barrelled revolvers partly hidden by his tattered, knee length, black coat. His trousers were tucked into long, well worn, riding boots and his weather-beaten and ruddy face shaded by a wide brimmed hat. Under the hat grew a luxurious, beard mottled with streaks of grey. Harry lived frugally and alone high in the Ranges not far from the Quinn's homestead. His abode was a little whirly, perched like a eagle's nest on a high peak where he could see all that moved about and under him. Like his close friend Paddy, he loved those Ranges and they returned that love by secluding and enveloping him into its deep ravines, valleys, and misty peaks away and safe from his pursuers. His continuing freedom depended on his vigilance and the inherent alertness of a few animal friends. Paddy's dogs would warn him of approaching intruders. But what he trusted best was a skinny peacock that nested on Paddy's homestead roof. Nothing got passed that strutting bird without setting off its shrieking alarm. On the floor he had possum skins sown together to make large, warm blankets to keep him snug during the cold nights. His expensive rifle was held by string tied to the branches above his head. It was a carbine which he stole from a flash Yankee travelling to Bendigo for Australian gold. This rifle had a short barrel and could be more easily used when riding hard in the saddle, and Harry treasured it. It was his only piece of furniture apart from some basic cooking utensils.

When he was dozing in the middle of the day, the narrow shafts of sunlight piercing his whirly through the gaps would glint and sparkle off the carbines silver embroidery built into its hardwood casing. In his half dreamlike state, this gun above his head looked to be bathed in a heavenly light assuming supernatural powers and promising eternal salvation. Often at night, like a lover, he would raise his rough, calloused hand and caress the silky, smooth, rounded timber stock made of polished walnut and ever so carefully, ever so gently, enter his right forefinger onto the hair trigger and momentarily hold it there. He practised this movement so he could do it blind in the dark if he should be ambushed by the Traps or bounty hunters. He remembered only too well Mad Dog Morgan who the Traps blew apart while he slept. It was this piece of hardware that was the deal maker in his trade. All he needed was a good horse, a good gun, and he could make a good living.

Today he had a stash of cash in his saddle bag to give to Red's family. Help the little lady and her brood of pups in their time of need thought Harry. She was Paddy's daughter and family. It was only a few weeks ago that her kids, Ned and Kate, had helped him by the river. Family has to stick together if they were to survive. When he was sure there were no law men at the wake, he pulled his broad hat over his face, exploded one of his six shooters into the air, let out a piercing howl like a demented dingo, and kicked his horse into mad gallop towards the assembled crowd. It seemed that Harry was always going hell for leather which wasn't far from the truth. He liked speed or what Paddy called veee...locity. It was easier on his stiff, arthritic limbs than that damned, uncomfortable trot. He well understood that it was the hard riding that both risked and saved his thick neck, and the more he practiced it, the better he got, but it was hard on Paddy's horses. The last one he gave to Ned at the river was still recovering in the paddock.

The crowd turned and looked. The children's eyes bugged out of their little heads. The women and children clustered together, falling over each other as they recoiled in fear of the large, menacing figure bearing down on them on a speeding horse, and brandishing a silver pistol in one hand. As he parted the crowd, Harry came to long, skidding stop with his horse almost sitting on its bum. But as the horse went down on its haunches, something every rider fears happened. His worn, leather girth snapped under the immense pressure of Harry's bulk and the horse jerking to shuddering halt, and the momentum of the rapid speed rocketed the outlaw, his saddle and bags through the air like an elephant with wings onto the dance floor with loud thud. There in a somewhat untidy and dishevelled heap, Harry lay very still. The mourners gathered around him in amazement of what they had just witnessed.

'I think he has broken his neck,' said one.

Another said 'He is dead for sure.'

Harry heard what they said. He was a bit of a ham actor and fooling them. Not that the horrific fall didn't hurt, but he was not about to show it. With a elasticity and spontaneity of young man, he snapped quickly to his feet and yelled,

'I'm stayin alive, you lot.'

As if it were a rehearsed gig, the fiddler and his musicians broke into an invigorating, life affirming Irish reel that had the mourners and Harry jumping about on the floor boards like fire crackers. Harry's antics were well known to them, and they loved him for his devil may care attitude to life. With sweat pouring off his jovial face, the big outlaw jigged about in his jangling spurs with his hands held firmly to his sides and head erect. He then bent down to his saddle bags, pulled out wad of notes, and with a grand flourish, threw a huge bundle of notes into the air for all to share.

'Sweets to the sweet,' he said grinning from ear to ear as the freshly made notes floated lazily to the dance floor.

'There's more of that where it came from,' he yelled above the din.

The crowd broke into spontaneous cheering, and the festivities took on a new vigour. Now and then, there was the occasional speech about the deceased Red and the handing out of prizes for the funeral race. Tennessee tried to speak but he could not progress beyond a painful stammer. The people looked decidedly embarrassed for the boy.

'It's a damn pity that stammer of his,' Paddy confided to a friend.

'Off a horse, his tongue is tied in knots...when he was born, Mum got caught at a flooded creek, and popped the lad out real natural like ....and the first thing the boy saw was her old mare...had its head down licking him like a new born foal...damn, strange thing that...he sort of became one of them...somewhere in his scon he thinks horses are his true kith and kin. When he's on them calmness comes over him and he can speak...that's just the way it is... I can't explain it. We've even put a wooden horse in the house...put wheels on it and all and even a saddle. Red made it with his carpentry skills. Sounds a bit silly, I know, but bugger me, he jumps on it and he can talk like one of them Greek orators...can't shut him up. The local school teacher gave him one of those dictionaries...you know with all them fancy, big words in it, how you say them, and what they mean. He reads it day and night hoping it will help him beat his stammer but sadly, although he has a thousand words in his head, he still can't speak one normally like you and me. It drives him mad, it does. He gets that frustrated he bangs his head against the wall hoping all them fancy words will spill out.'

When the speeches were ending Ned left and, in a few minutes, re-emerged from the barn mounted bareback on a stunning, black mare whose looks made the audience gasp. The mare stood a bit over fifteen hands, showed a good wither, long sloping shoulders and strong hindquarters. A balanced body that wasn't bulky. Harry stopped his jigging about the dance floor, and cast a discerning eye over her. She had a nice length of neck, set right on the shoulder too, and not a ewe necked stargazer. He admired her strong rear end, like a washerwomen's backside, as he slapped her on the rump. This mare should stop dead in her tracks, swivel and gallop off in opposite direction from standing start he thought. Her hocks were low set with good width of bone for durability and she had a deep, heart girth which promised stamina over the long chase.

'Pretty good,' he said as he ran his hand over her silky coat that glistened in the mid-day sun. A large, calm eye promised a cool mind that wouldn't come undone in the heat of the chase. A nice cut of a mare he thought - make a man proud to ride her. All these things Paddy knew instinctively but Harry had learnt through hard necessity. The crowd gathered around the mare admiring her. Harry looked down and saw four flint hard hooves of symmetrical shape, not flat and misshapen. He took hold of her tail and freely moved it about without the mare pinning her ears back.

'Temperament good too,' he said. If the mare had instinctively clamped her tail down, Harry would have had second thoughts. He next examined the windpipe running down the front of her neck. It was loose and well defined capable of sucking down gallons of fresh, energising oxygen.

'Don't want much do you, Harry?' said one of the men.

Harry fixed him in his stare. 'It's my ticket to stayin alive, mate. Pick a wrongin and I'm a goner.'

Paddy saw the opportunity to get onto his soap box again.

'Listen you mob...let me to say a few words. I'm bloody embarrassed every time I see one of you in the town street on them heavy bred, cart horses. Leave them harnessed to the ploughs. Let the Traps ride them. Here in this big country you need a better horse to get you about. I'm prepared to give you a free service to my stud but only one, mind you, to get you started. We Irish have to get smart to survive in this Protestant land or we'll end up the same as back home...bloody tenants to the British owning nothing but doing all the work to feed their fat, toffy faces and us livin on nothin but hand me downs and slops. Being smart means being quick, and being quick means a good horse. If one of us is being chased by the Traps, you know we are not going to get justice in their Courts, so we need to outrun them. That's the only way to get ahead. Ain't no one better at demonstrating the value of good, fast horse than Harry here and my boys and young Ned here aren't too bad at it too.'

Harry flourished his hat, and took a bow.

'If you ridin one of those old bone heads I have seen you on, you don't have a chance in hell of getting away. They will have you caught and strung up before the old mutton head can break into a trot. And you deserve to be caught and strung up if you can't see the value of a good horse.'

'Pop ...give us a break. Some people love their big, cart horses. They have pulled them around faithfully for years, don't buck and kick like some of your high-spirited ones need I say, taught their kids to ride safely, and ploughed their fields,' said Elly as she sensed her Dad was intending to go on with his not too diplomatic lecture. Paddy reluctantly heeded the good advice and retired to the bar.

That evening Harry spoke to Elly before he left.

'Get a pub with the money, Elly. Ned and the boys will help...we've discussed it a lot before and now you've got the money to do it. You'd be good at the job. Always liked the company of men, you has, and it will be some income for you and the kids.'

'And a place for you to stay and have a decent bath and plate of tucker,' said Elly.

'And that too,' replied Harry.

With that practical advice he vanished, riding into the dark scrub like a wombat disappearing into its dark hole, and trotting beside him was his newly loaned, black mare.

Elly looked at the wad of notes she held in her hand. It felt good. No longer did she have to worry about raising her big brood, at least for a while. But with a pub she had the means to make her own way in the world. She remembered Red and how hard he had worked and suffered during his life through poverty and oppression. Over all those long, lean, arduous years with her, he didn't earn a tenth of what she now held in her the palm of her hand. She reflected for a moment. Harry got it in a day's work, and gave it away just as quickly. Her ambitions to own and run a bush pub would now be realized. As she looked at Ned, the sorrow at the loss of her husband lifted, and she smiled hitting the lad lightly on the head with the wad and saying,

'Don't ever let them tell you Ned that Uncle Harry is a bad man...no man as generous as Harry can be bad...the spirit of the Lord dwells within him I say and bugger the other kill joys, the Traps and their mean, boring, law abidin ways. If you turn out as good as that old reprobate, Ned, I will die a happy woman.'

'I'll do you proud...Mum,' said the young boy looking admiringly at his mother.

'Why does Harry dance with his hands held tightly to his sides...Mum?'

'That's the way it's done back in Ireland, son.'

'It's not to hold up his pants up over that big belly...is it?'

Harry has a touch of the 'Je crois attendre encore'

A Civil War General of humble origins talks of his unease in genteel company.

'An' I don't know nothin' now," resumed the mountaineer sadly. 'When I go into a parlour, I'm like a bear in a cage. If there's anythin' about to break, I always break it. When they begin talkin' books and pictures and such I don't know whether they are right or wrong...An' I'm out of place in a house,' continued the General, 'I belong to the mountains the fields, an when this war's over I guess I'll go back to 'em. They think somethin' of me now because I can ride an fight, but war ain't all. When it's over there'll be no use for me. I can't dance an' I can't talk pretty, an' I'm always steppin' on other peoples' feet. I guess I ain't the timber they make dandies of.' - Before the Dawn - A Story of the Fall of Richmond - Joseph A. Altsheler.

The pub was built out of logs cut from the hardwood forests in the Ranges. Ned ran an adze down the trunk on both sides so that the logs would sit flat. The ends were notched with an axe. A rectangle was cut out where the doors and windows went. Joe said it was important to have batwing doors and bought some heavy-duty hinges from the town hardware store. With the doors installed he would swagger in leaving them swinging as he slouched on the bar and banged his fist down for service. Elly slid a glass of whisky the full length of the bar without spilling a drop,

'I read about it in one of them dime western paper backs,' she said 'and I could hardly wait to do it.'

Mud was used to fill the gaps in the logs. Rough sawn planks were cut for the floor and hardwood shingles made up the roof. The warmth of the varnished and oiled timber made it homely. The long bar made of red gum planks displayed their many honey, reddish, and yellow hues taking up one whole side of the saloon. Behind the bar, sparkled glasses and bottles of alcohol of every variety and taste one could wish for. Taking up the rest of the large space were tables and chairs for the customers. On the walls were exhibited large, colourful paintings done by Valerie, Paddy's adopted daughter, a studious and bookish girl. Paddy asked her to paint scenes of American history; paintings of wild west horses, Indians chiefs, Confederate Generals like Jeb Stuart, an impressive eagle, and one of Custer's last Stand. Harry insisted on a painting of one of his favourite female Italian opera singers to take a centre position over the bar. It was a pub made in the good American tradition of a saloon with discreet facilities for gambling. At the rear of the large building were shady horse yards for the customer who wanted to make a day of it. Out the front was a sturdy hitching rail for several horses, and steps leading to a wide, shady porch. The building sat comfortably on fat stumps about two feet high allowing a cool breeze to whip underneath in the hot summers that blighted the landscape. Occasionally mongrel dogs would lie in the shade of the breezeway half asleep with one ear cocked and would jump up barking and growling on hearing raised voices. Elly had a large wood stove put in an annex behind the bar from which she would prepare simple but honest food if the mood took her, maybe an Irish stew mixed with a few boiled vegetables from Dan's garden.

The boys all helped in the work. Dan shared his time between his garden and the work on the bar. He liked flowers - roses. He kept his hobby quiet for fear of ridicule by his male friends. He had cultivated several varieties although he did not know their botanical names. He was attracted to their bright colours; the creams, soft yellows, deep reds, lemony yellows, mild pinks and the clear, immaculate whites; and their sweet, unique fragrances diluted the tobacco smells and smoke haze that soon became a permanent feature of the saloon. The hardiest varieties he collected from specimens growing wild in the local cemeteries. He would ride all over the district collecting cuttings. He tended them with the horse manure from the yards of which there was plenty, constantly enriching the soil, pulling the weeds, and mulching with straw to retain moisture and an even temperature. Dan was different from the others, more subdued and sensitive, a little withdrawn but his ways were accepted by his family and relatives. Somewhat spare, thin you might say, and boyish in looks. In his daily existence he wore a permanent, dreamy expression, much like the sober, arctic white rose sitting quietly amongst its robust, brightly coloured cousins. Music was another passion of Dan's and shared by his friend Steve. Between them they could play several instruments in a manner of sorts.

Steve was sinewy, whipcord like, with a passion for fast horseflesh. He worked as a jockey at the local racecourse. It was through the horses that he met the Quinn's and Kelly's. Together they would run the swamps and scrub chasing kangaroos, intoxicated by the speed and agility of their horses, and whooping and yelping like a pack of wild dogs. Steve knew a good horse and he knew the Kelly's and Quinn's had them. They admired his horsemanship. He was a game rider who would jump and push his horse where most hesitated.

Joe was Ned's friend. He was older, about twenty-three, and of solid build. The most dominant thing about Joe was his curiosity. He was endlessly curious about life and could not be enticed by his parents to apply himself to the monotonous, farm duties. He did well at school through natural aptitude and not discipline. He wanted to roam, and be different. In that way he was well suited to the Quinn's and Kelly's who set the agendas for those who were adventurous. Joe's curiosity led him to the Chinese mining camp and their thousand-year-old culture. The ways of the celestials, their food, their demure and pearly skinned daughters, and their magical, white powder held him in endless fascination so that he practised their language until he could speak it as fluently as English. The European miner feared the vast hordes of Chinese who would descend like a plague of locusts upon the Australian shores and dig and fossick for their gold. Joe knew differently. The Chinese reworked the diggings that the Europeans had abandoned for new fields in their frenetic search for a quick fortune. They worked hard, kept to themselves, grew their vegetables and sent most of their earnings back to relatives in China. In the evenings, they smoked opium and tried to forget the isolation and prejudice, the racist taunts that surrounded them. Joe learnt their customs, sat at their tables, ate their food, and stole furtive glances at their demure, dutiful and obedient daughters. These shy China girls had femininity, a quiet dignity and poise that he admired. They wore sensible, wide-brimmed hats with cotton trousers and plain, leather sandals on their small, delicate feet. They ate brightly coloured vegetables raised in their gardens and little slithers of meat mainly chicken and pig. They walked everywhere always in a group for their own protection. On arrival on the Australian shores they were soon assaulted by the locals tossing their belongings into the sea, and leaving them stranded in the swamps of the South East of South Australia. They walked with their wheelbarrows in long lines from Robe, where there was no tax, to the gold fields some four hundred miles away to be attacked again by the miners. They withdrew for their own preservation and spoke only to a select few who they knew they could trust like the large, amiable Joe.

Whilst the building of the saloon was taking place, Ned took his errant mare to the Quinn's to be put in foal. He had a band of about twenty mares he had carefully selected for their endurance, temperament and speed. He was interested to see what the union of this wayward mare and his grandfather's stud would bring. They let the mare loose in the paddock. The stud ran noisily from his mares trumpeting his robust maleness. Ned's mare promptly booted him in the chest for his trouble. He booted her right back to establish himself at the top of the pecking order, but copped another one this time to his front legs causing him to hobble about with his pride somewhat confused and hurt.

Paddy yelled, 'Shit...he's going to get gelded with her next kick.'

The stud's amorous intent was now mixed with fair amount of discretion for his own safety so he contented himself with chasing her around the paddock a couple of times to regain his self-esteem, but at a safe distance out of her firing range. If he had known how she dispatched the last male, he would have done well to stay with his mares and give her due respect. Better still, if he waited his time letting nature play her role, she would chase him without her former, malicious intent.

'We'll leave them to it, Ned,' said Paddy not bearing to watch his stud getting further injured.

Harry was planning a big job. For such a job he needed help. He would get that Kelly kid. His mum owed him a few favours. He prepared for the long trip and told Ned to bring his best horse and be ready for hard riding and a bit of excitement. Harry did not want to talk much on the way to Bendigo. In addition to the horses they rode, each led a spare. The spare could carry some provisions and money bags. If they were being pursued and their ridden horses were tiring, they could swap to a fresh horse. Harry had learnt his trade well. When the price for lack of preparation was to rot in jail for rest of your life, there was no detail too small. At night they camped on a ridge, lit a small campfire for warmth and had some tea and stew that Elly had prepared for them. Ned could see the dull light of the kerosene lamps of the homesteads, sprinkled about the countryside, as he ate his camp tucker and wondered if Harry ever wanted to retire with a family. His life seemed a lonely one fraught with risk and few comforts. He built up the courage to ask. Harry was about to tell him to mind his own business, but restrained himself for a minute or so, reflected and said,

'I have little choice now...there is a reward on my head and if caught it will be the end of me. I'm fifty years old and that would be a life sentence ...I've had a taste of it and there is nothing worse than rotting away in prison. The way I see it, Ned, I may be lonely at times but the bush is my home, it protects and provides for me. I get my tucker from the kangaroos, good meat that, fish from the streams and wild fruit from the bushes. In the mornings I wake, feel the warmth of the morning sun and look around me and I see for miles. It's my kingdom, miles and miles of bush going up to the snow and I've been there too. There's barely a soul about. I don't have a little woman to keep me warm at night but, you know, I am happy when I am free to wander this great land. It's like the horses we ride, Ned... put them in a small yard and they die.'

He stopped and fell silent thinking he had already said too much, and then began again.

'I like to think, Ned, that I am an artist in a way...not just a crude law breaker,' said Harry looking directly at Ned, and hoping he would not laugh at his apparent earnestness.

'I do like them arty things, opera and the theatre but I don't talk about it to anyone because it's sort of sissy in the circles I mix. I did try once dressing up smart like and going to the opera in Melbourne would you believe. Took me girlfriend and five hundred quid I did; paid for her to doll herself up in one of those fancy Paris type beauty parlours; and I got fitted out at the tailors in a smashing three piece suit with the clock piece, fine hat and all that regalia; Purchased the best seats in the theatre-you know one of them private boxes overlooking all the action much like my lair on the mountain above Paddy's place; but I got excited and carried away when that Italian tenor hit the high notes in Bizet the Pearl Fishers...my favourite song 'je crois entendre encore'; be Jesus, that Ito sent shivers up me spine...I imagined meself gliding across them beautiful Ranges on a winged horse swooping and soaring like with the ebb and flow of the song, and I just had to get up and join in. The Ito stopped, looked up at me and walked off the stage in disgust. I knew the words and kept going. The audience loved it, but I got escorted out and spent the rest of the performance listening by the window. Damned shame that when I was just enjoying meself. Back in the pub, me lady friend said, 'Don't worry Harry. That lot don't know how to really enjoy themselves like you. You were only helping that Ito singer and that was no reason to chuck you out like they did. I thought you sang better. I give them a mouthful too. You can have your revenge when they are travelling to their grand estates, and make them talk your lingo at the end of a gun barrel. Now give me another rendition of that sexy French song you like so much.' So, I did, and it brought tears to her eyes until someone banged on the wall and yelled, 'will you shut the fuck up...we are trying to sleep.' Well, that was enough trouble for me for one day...after all I was a wanted man but they didn't recognise me all cleaned up and looking like an Earl from the old country. I couldn't get out of the big smoke quick enough in the morning, and haven't been back since.' Ned, almost asleep, nodded his head. He did not know anything about opera and the theatre. Harry may as well be talking to the young boy in a foreign language. Ned opened a sleepy eye looking at the big framed bushranger sitting forlornly in the dim light of the camp fire staring at the dying coals. Harry went silent.

Ned had his own problems to think about. A young man does not easily contemplate daylight robbery, guns and the real possibility of things going badly wrong. He may get shot; somebody else may get shot; he may get arrested and spend his life in jail if not sent to the gallows. These were not matters to be contemplated lightly. He liked his life, and didn't want for it to end before it had really begun. He needed to have a lot of trust in Harry and for now he did, but he did not trust himself. This job needed experience, and for that Harry was your man. With that comforting thought the young apprentice dozed off.

His Honour does the soft shoe

Elvis Presley on his dancing style.
Some people tap their feet, some people snap their fingers, and some people sway back and forth. I just sorta do'em altogether, I guess.

The Shamrock Hotel, Bendigo.
One of the great institutions of Sandhurst is the "Shamrock," a capacious and comfortable hostelry that, notwith- standing its aggressively Hibernian title, has been the head-quarters of visitors from every nation under the sun, and a favourite resort of successive generations of gold-diggers. Its founder, Mr William Heffernan, was an Irishman of extraordinary enterprise, who made fortunes and lost them again with equal rapidity. To him Sandhurst is also indebted for a beautiful theatre and a commodious public hall. In the palmy days of gold-digging, he spared no expense in bringing up to Sandhurst all the musical and theatrical celebrities who crossed the equator into the Southern Hemisphere. - The Irish in Australia - John Francis Hogan and Georgia Keilman.

'Ride and hide,' said Harry. 'We'll ride to that steep hill about twenty miles south of Bendigo and hide in the bush. Climbing the hill will slow the coach down and they won't be able to see us waiting just over the top.'

Harry knew it was a Cobb and Co. Their coaches had leather braced chassis and were lighter, reliably quick and more comfortable than the heavy, rigid coaches from England. They used only the best horses and talented drivers to deliver businessmen and goods to the goldfields from Melbourne in fast time. Because they were efficient and popular, it did not escape Harry that they carried the valuable cargo and their passengers were well heeled. Harry saw it as fitting that he should match his wits against the best.

Harry went about his preparation making sure to check the girths, stirrup leathers, bridles and buckles. He knew from recent experience broken gear could be fatal in a hot pursuit.

'Never forget to check your equipment laddy,' he said. 'These strips of leather can save your scrawny neck so look after them...soap and oil them...make em supple like your horse...you sure don't want anything rubbing if it's miles you have to do.'

Harry took out his guns from the saddlebag. He had three colt revolvers and a rifle.

'Ain't nothing like these little beauties to engender a bit of cooperation, Ned,' he said handing him one. Ma Quinn had made up two belt holsters from kangaroo hide. Harry slid a colt into each pouch, practiced a few quick draws, fired off four shots blasting the bark from a gum tree, and nonchalantly blew the smoke from the silver barrels.

'I don't know what the Wild West was like, but I reckon I'd give them a run for their money,' said the old braggart.

Ned studied his silver colt. He liked the way it fitted snugly into the palm of his hand. He ran his fingers up and down the cold, steel barrel and lifted it shoulder height to check the sights and balance. He spun the chamber looking to see if it was loaded. He did up his belt, and walked up and down a few yards to get the feel.

'It's a beauty Uncle Harry...can I keep it?'

'No bloody way, boy...you is only an apprentice and an apprentice don't get the master's tools...took me years to get them six shooters and I won't be letting them go to some amateur.' Ned listened and nodded.

'Now before I forget boy...put the folding money in my saddle bag, understand...and cover your mug with a handkerchief. You don't want to advertise the fact that you are my offsider.'

Harry looked over both horses checking their legs, shoes and strapping on the gear securely. They rode at an easy pace to the hill, and rested in the shade of the scrub waiting for the Stagecoach to come into view. After waiting for an hour, they saw a speck in the distance coming at a good pace. The driver pulled his six horses back to a trot as they neared the hill, and began the slow climb up towards two very interested spectators mounting their horses and moving to the middle of the road.

Inside the coach were five passengers including 'the Hungarian Nightingale', Lima de Murska, who was booked to sing at the wildly popular Shamrock hotel, Bendigo. She was a flamboyant, full bosomed woman confident in her ability and popular with the miners. She was accompanied by her violinist, a polished, elegant man of European origins, with dark swept back hair and of theatrical appearance and dress.

Next to them was an elderly, dour Scottish Squatter returning from Melbourne to his property who spoke little during the long trip and held tightly onto his carry bag. He had made a rare and special trip from his property to visit the head office of his bank and personally negotiate a cheaper rate of interest than his local manager was prepared to offer. On the opposite side was a tall, thin man whose skin was the colour of parchment and exhibiting that studious, academic demeanour that often comes from having your head buried in books from an early age. Judge Bell-Chambers of the Victorian Supreme Court no less; educated at Protestant Trinity College, Dublin; a few years as magistrate in Ireland; and now a promotion to a judge in the Australian Colonies. His appointment was arranged by mutual friend, Judge Barrington, the hanging judge. The law's complexity was his life's joy and each new case visibly excited him almost to the point of spilling and tumbling over his words.

The travellers made polite conversation as the coach rolled on across the countryside sometimes into deep ruts in a road then gliding across a flat plain with grass that high the horses could barely see their way.

'I'm going to Billy Heffernan's Shamrock hotel at Bendigo, Your Honour...those Irish miners pay me handsomely to entertain them,' replied Lima on an enquiry from the bookish Judge.

'These Irish are a wild, ignorant and savage race capable of the most heinous crimes, Miss Murska,' he said.

'I know from my time as a magistrate. I suppose they are worse in this outpost of civilisation. In my opinion, they constitute a threat to society driven by their drunken passions and desire to rebel. The worst of them, I hear, have become bushrangers terrorising the community...why I'm reliably told it's not safe to travel these roads for fear of some brute holding you to ransom. I don't mind telling you Miss Murska, I and my brother judges intend to deal a firm hand to these law breakers. I presume you have little to do with such uncouth ruffians, Miss Murska?'

'On the contrary, Judge, I enjoy their company very much. They love life with a carefree passion I rarely see amongst those with money. The dour Scotsman interposed, 'there no much good, lassie, being happy if ye are broke and penniless.'

'Maybe there is not enough money in this world to make a Scotsman happy,' replied the entertainer.

Addressing the Judge, she added, 'you and your pretty secretary should come along and be my guest tonight and see for yourself.'

'Thank you for your kind invitation, Miss, but I have important papers to read tonight.'

Next to the Judge was his secretary, a slender girl of about twenty years, soberly dressed in formal black attire. She displayed quiet manners, and listened carefully to the conversation unwilling to interrupt the Judge unless asked for her opinion. Her eyes lit up at the invitation of Miss Murska, but realised it was a forlorn hope to expect his Worship to become one of the human race and accept the invitation. It would make a wholesome change from endlessly transcribing judgements of wherefores, whereto's, hereinbefore's, and placitums roman numeral [1], [11] etc. in some stale, musty chambers or court room she thought. She would have to satisfy herself with a little conversation with Miss Murska's sullen violinist if his artistic temperament could be coaxed to say a few words of English. Her life was as much a prison as the inevitable destination of the poor innocents who appeared before the English judicial imports.

Harry put his hand on his holstered revolver. Ned was still hidden in the scrub watching. The horses were almost walking now and he could make out the driver talking to his partner. They seemed to be laughing. Ned could see the driver's mate had his rifle across his lap. He was beginning to feel nervous. He had stolen horses before but that was under the cover of night. This was a direct confrontation in broad daylight. It was plain to him that one side have to give otherwise blood would spill...it could be his. What the hell am I doing here he thought. He looked at Harry. He was dead calm in the middle of the road. Even his mare seemed as though she was going to sleep with her head hung low. Ned's horse began to fidget. He touched her with his spur, growled, taking the slack out of her rein. One minute the driver and his guard were laughing at a harmless joke...the next moment they were staring down the barrels of two six shooters with the words 'bail up' booming into their eardrums. They startled, and half stood in amazement. The offsider lifted his rifle. Harry let a shot whistle by his ear, and shook his head disapprovingly. Ned heard muffled screams from inside the coach. The offsider's courage visibly drained from him, and he slumped back in his seat. They complied. Ned moved out into the open.

'Don't shoot,' the driver said as they handed their guns to Ned, and got down from the coach. One or two recognised Harry from the wanted posters. Harry asked them not to do anything stupid. They would not be harmed and that he bore no grudge against working class men. Harry dismounted, walked to the coach door, opened it and with a dramatic flourish of his hat requested the passengers to disembark. They nervously complied, and filed out.

'My humblest apologies, dear traveller, but I fear you are in need of some refreshments and a little exercise after such a long and arduous journey. Allow me and my kind assistant to unburden you all of a few possessions, worldly goods you might say, and lighten your load. Its the least we can do in view of our impecunious circumstances.'

He ordered Ned to get the trunks off the coach and open them up. The first trunk revealed a sparkling array of theatre costumes.

'Please do not take those ...I need them tonight,' said the Hungarian Nightingale.

'Where pray,' asked Harry.

'The Shamrock,' said Miss Murska

'Well...well...well,' said Harry "give Billy my regards won't you...no better pub in all Australia. A lot of my cobbers drink there, and I'll not be disturbing their entertainment...mind you they will not miss that expensive bracelet you're wearin my love...please drop it in the bag, my dear...there's a good girl...I will leave you your ring but it will cost you a song or two.'

'I'm much obliged to you,' chirped the Nightingale.

'Your Latino friend can keep his violin but his wallet is needed.'

The violinist with a delicate flourish of his manicured hand casually dropped his wallet into Ned's bag.

'Your contributions are much appreciated and I can assure you they will be used for a good purpose if that's any consolation,' said Harry.

'Now what can you offer to our cause, Miss,' he said looking at the young secretary.

'You can fuck off you dirty, thieving bastard.'

Harry stepped backwards in astonishment at such a response.

The Judge blushed.

Ned stifled his laugh.

'You're a bold, little firebrand, aren't you Miss. You think old Harry too much of a gentleman to give you a hidin for such unladylike and intemperate language...well you are right...my good assistant can do it. Put her over your knee and give her a good spanking,' he said to Ned.

Ned sighed, but didn't want to interrupt Harry's flow.

He took the defiant girl by the arm, sat on a trunk and bent her across his knees and lifting her dress to reveal white frilly underwear and long black stockings.

She yelled more profanities.

'She must have been a daughter of an Irishman with a vocabulary like that,' said Harry somewhat in admiration of her spirit. Ned administered several whacks to her pretty rear end. This strongly built youth, whom she had only seen for a few minutes, stirred her emotions in a way that she could not understand. What he did hurt a little but she didn't mind it at all. In an odd way, she enjoyed the close physical contact with the well-built youth. Getting a hold on her thoughts, and regaining her composure, she stood up, dusted her dress down and gave Ned a quizzical look which suggested she was not too upset with Harry's discipline. Without warning she slapped him fair across the face almost dislodging his disguise. Harry laughed and said,

'that little indiscretion will cost you, my dear.'

He snapped her brooch from her slender neck, and dropped it in Ned's bag.

'That's an heirloom,' she protested, 'given to me by my Grandmother...give me another spanking if you will, but give me back my brooch.'

'We all lose the things we love,' said Harry philosophically ignoring her pleas and opened another trunk looking for the Government money.

'Jesus, Mary and Joseph,' he said as he saw a long flowing black gown with blood red markings and elegant horse hair wig. He looked at the two remaining men. It couldn't be the one in a kilt...it must be the other cove he thought. He saw the softness in his white feminine hands and the smug arrogance of learning emanating from his personage.

'And what be your name and business?' he said glaring at the lean figure.

The Judge remained mute, frightened for his welfare. Harry donned the robes and placed the impressive wig on his head.

'Mute eh...refusing to recognise the authority of my Court?

Let me answer for you...it is me, Your Honour, who wears these ridiculous robes...now you repeat it or I may have to consider punishment for contempt.'

The Judge feebly replied 'It is me, Your Honour, who wears these ridiculous robes.'

'That's better, now tell me defendant, how do you treat the common folk in your Court?' queried Harry.

'Everyone is equal before the law,' said the Judge careful not to mention his strongly expressed sentiments about the Irish.

'What a load of fucking, flying duck shit if you will excuse my French, Miss Lima,' said Harry.

'You should be cited for perjury...what about bushrangers?' asked Harry.

'How equal are they before the law?' placing his hand on his revolver.

The Judge was beginning to feel the strain. Beads of perspiration began to form on his learned brow. He didn't know how to answer this last question without ending a promising career.

'Providing they are not cold-blooded murderers, then I am sure that things can be said that may favourably influence the Court.'

'I might be in need of such things as you call them,' said Harry. 'I hope you do well in your career, my friend, and treat those less fortunate than you with understanding and mercy. But I add those without pity or heart, you should deal firmly with, and that includes members of your own little close-knit fraternity.'

The Judge heaved a sigh of relief. Harry moved to the Scotsman.

'Got your mum's dress on, have we Donald?'

The Scotsman forced a nervous laugh and again looked directly at the ground avoiding Harry's gaze.

'What are you holding so firmly in your hands, crafty Donald?'

'It's my purse,' he said 'and I'll not be parting with my money.'

'Your Honour, if you please,' Harry said.

'I beg Your Honours pardon,' he said with nervous smile hoping that his new-found humour would take Harry's attention off his hard-earned money.

'You are holding up our entertainment,' said Harry becoming a little impatient.

'Come with me Donald and we'll discuss this in private, in my chambers, here in the bush.'

They walked a short distance away.

Harry said, 'Look... I can't let you get away with this...it will not be good for my business if it gets around...your choice is to hand it over or me and my assistant will deal with you more forcibly.'

'I told ye I'll not be partin with my hard-earned money.'

'Come here, my boy,' said Harry to Ned, 'and deal with him.'

Ned walked to the Scotsman who looked nervously at him. 'Hand it over.'

'No...no...no...do ye not understand...I'll not be giving my money to the likes of you.'

He foolishly tried to push Ned away. Ned grabbed him, put a rope noose over his head and threw it over a branch, and pulled so that the determined Scotsman had to stretch to his toes and grab at the noose with both hands but still not letting go of his money bag.

'Drop the bag, or I will lift you off the ground by your scrawny neck,' demanded Ned.

'Go on then,' said Donald.

Ned pulled, the Scotsman began to choke, and go red in face. With what little breath he had left he yelled stop and dropped his money bag at Ned's feet. Ned released his pressure on the rope.

'Your meanness for money will do you no good, Donald, but I'm pleased in this case you have seen the benefits of spreading it around...that's what it's meant to do you know,' said Harry.

Ned searched the remaining trunks and found one thousand pounds neatly folded. He slipped the secretary's brooch back into her hand when Harry was talking to the others. She squeezed his hand affectionately.

'Well, ladies and gentlemen, whilst our Donald is getting his breath back again, let us have ourselves a little entertainment before the show closes,' said Harry.

'Liven up that bow, maestro, and Miss Murska, let your sweet melodies sweep over these grand hills.'

She bowed, looked at her violinist who was strumming his violin, and sang like the song bird she was rumoured to be. Her strong, melodious voice rang out into the bush, around and through the stringy barks, by the black boys standing like motionless sentinels, and into the valleys and along the shallow creeks.

'Now for a few Irish reels,' said Harry.

The violinist gave a deprecating glance, but complied. The mood lifted with energetic rhythms of the violin.

'Please be my guests,' demanded Harry.

The secretary saw her chance and grabbed Ned.

'What about you?' said Harry to the Judge.

'I'm not a dancing man,' he protested.

'Don't you give me strife like our niggardly Donald...I'll show you how, Judge,' said Harry pulling his silver colt and firing off a few well-placed rounds near his Honour's feet.

'I'm a quick learner, Mr Harry,' the Judge said as he jigged about in a pathetic, uncoordinated way...I'm a real natural don't you think?'

With a little practice and a couple of well-placed shots from the colt, he soon came to pick up the rhythm and to their surprise became quite adept.

'I'm getting the hang of this,' he said with a smile to Harry, 'please don't stop Mr Violinist and if you don't mind, Mr Harry, I'll not be needing any more of your encouragement.'

The coach driver and his mate, not wishing to miss out on the fun, joined in. The secretary drew Ned close, smiled, lifted his handkerchief mask slightly, and kissed him gently on the cheek. She could taste the invigorating scents of the mountain fragrances and trees on his smooth skin, the strength in his masculine arms, and in her mundane academic existence, she longed for more. She wanted to suck it out of him whatever it was. It made her feel alive and she wanted to steal it from him like he and Harry had taken her valuables; to drive out that stale, fetid air of the Judge's stuffy chambers and court rooms that suffocated her day in and day out listening to peoples pathetic, whining, menial problems. But it was a dream...things like that do not happen to a Judge's secretary...she had to satisfy herself with a spanking, a stolen kiss and her Grandmother's brooch.

Harry joined in the dancing wearing his gown and swinging his long wig as he twirled to the music. It was a very happy, little scene that took place on that solitary hill in the middle of the scrub. Ned thought this is what Harry meant the other night...he really is an artist. He's taking their money, and apart from the Scotsman, they are all enjoying it. The music stopped. Harry and Ned mounted their horses and left. The victims waved goodbye. Harry was still wearing his newly acquired outfit. The Judge lifted his hand for a moment, and appeared to say goodbye to the two robbers but quickly dropped it on seeing the Scotsman glare his disapproval. On the way to Bendigo he politely asked,

'If you don't mind, Miss Murska, I would love to come to your performance this evening. Incidentally, do they have dancing?'

The Hungarian Nightingale smiled.

'They sure do Judge, they sure do.'

'Good, good...I'll look forward to seeing you there,' replied the Judge enthusiastically.

'Maybe I can teach you a few extra steps, Your Honour.'

'I would like that very much, Miss Nightingale,' replied His Honour. 'I hope not with the sort of encouragement Mr Harry so kindly offered me.'

Harry bites the dust

A good horse

Great care was taken by the Blackfoot in selecting and training a buffalo hunting horse. This animal was the man's primary charger, ridden only in hunting, to war, and on dress occasions. Informants named five qualities sought in a buffalo runner: (1) enduring speed (the ability to retain speed over a distance of several miles); (2) intelligence (the ability to respond instantly to commands or to act properly on its own initiative); (3) agility (ability to move quickly alongside a buffalo, to avoid contact with the larger animal, and to keep clear of its horns); (4) sure-footedness (ability to run swiftly over uneven ground without stumbling); and (5) courage (lack of fear of buffalo). Usually a man selected the horse he wished to train as a buffalo hunter on the basis of its demonstrated swiftness and alertness. The horse in Blackfoot Indian culture, with comparative material from other western tribes (John Canfield Ewers)

'What did you think of that,' said Harry as he chucked off the gown and wig.

'It takes experience my boy to do a job like that. Did you notice how them drivers stayed out of it. I took nothin from them. They're workin men like you and me, Ned, and workin men stick together in this world. You don't have to be bright to see how them squatters and Judges stick together. Well we working class can do the same.'

Ned was silent.

Now we have to cover distance. This is where a good horse will save your neck. They know me so it doesn't matter where I am but they don't know you. You see...if you are back home soon, they will say he could not have covered the distance in that time on a horse so put yourself around when you get home...let a lot of people see you.'

Ned still remained quiet.

'What's the matter with you laddy? That sheila and her brooch got you upset has it? Well, don't let it...them type will have nothin to do with the likes of you and me. In their eyes, we're dirt, boy...the filth and grime of the earth washed up here on the shores of Australia so take what you can get I say and don't let a pretty face git in your way. They only give their favours to their fancy men...not you and me, boy. Why I would rather give back to that tight arsed Scotty...at least he probably worked for his lot...but I'll grant you, she did have some spirit.'

'She was alright Harry...she had a job and the brooch was given to her by her Grandmother.'

Ned wondered how he was going to explain to Harry that he had given the brooch back to the girl. He would blow his stack for sure. They rode without speaking for some twenty miles along the hidden scrub tracks avoiding contact. Harry headed for the creek beds using the running water to wash away their hoof prints. Every ten miles or so they slowed to a walk for a mile or so to let their horses recover. As the night closed in, they sought a hiding spot in the dense scrub to rest preferably with a view of the surrounding countryside. Harry made only a small fire and then set about counting the money. In notes there was about a thousand quid...a tidy, little haul for a few days' work he thought. Ned watched him place the money in ten bundles hoping that at least one or more of the bundles would be given to him. Harry asked him to get the jewellery. Ned went to his saddle bag, took it out and handed it to Harry. Harry took the necklace and two watches stolen from the passengers. He stopped, and stared at Ned,

'Where's that cheeky sheila's brooch?'

'I gave it back to her.'

'You fucking did what?'

'I gave it to her...for Christ's sake Harry, it belonged to her Grandmother.'

'I don't give a fucking fig about her Granny...mine died hungry and broke ...I warrant her's didn't...nobody gave a damn about my Granny except me so excuse me if I decide to be a little provident now,' yelled Harry losing his patience.

'If you want to be a do gooder, don't do it at my expense,' he added.

'Take it off my share,' said Ned hoping to finish the argument.

'That was your share,' said Harry.

'I don't believe this,' said Ned 'I have risked my life to help you with this and I walk away with bugger all.'

'You an apprentice,' Harry muttered. 'I shouldn't have to tell you what apprentices get paid...they get experience...it's worth much more than money.'

'Stuff you, you old goat ...I'm going now before I knock your block off.'

'Come on then,' retorted Harry, 'I'll rip you to pieces and feed you to the crows, you insolent pup.'

'Yeah,' said Ned 'I'll punch a hole in that fat gut of yours.'

Harry's hackles were up and he squared up to his young opponent like an experienced pugilist. He jabbed the air in Ned's direction with his left fist a couple of times and then let go with a right uppercut all the time blowing and grunting like an old bull stamping his feet before the charge. Ned stood his ground singularly unimpressed with the show of bravado going on in front of him.

'Cut it out Harry...your play acting will have no effect on me...I don't want to hit an old man.'

'Bloody old man am I...we'll see about that,' said Harry as he advanced on his defiant, junior partner. 'We'll see who will hit who.'

He telegraphed a wild swinging right at Ned's head which if it connected as intended would have stopped the argument. Ned ducked as Harry's huge arm whistled above his head.

'Back off, Harry,' warned Ned.

Harry went for a body blow but Ned deftly skipped aside and he punched the air a second time.

'Stand still and fight like a man,' yelled Harry puffing and out of breath.

'Come on...ye fight like a sheila...dancin away all the time.'

Harry had hardly finished his words when an iron fist exploded on his jaw and stopping him dead in his tracks. He stood dazed with his head spinning. He swayed a little forward, and then sideways taking a few unsteady steps to stay upright, and losing the struggle, he toppled over backwards.

'The silly, old bugger,' said Ned as he covered him with a blanket and packed his gear to leave. He took a hundred quid for his efforts and rode through the night until he reached home the following morning. It was a marathon effort and he managed it only by getting off and running beside his horse giving it time to recover its stamina. Ned had flat soled shoes which he kept in his saddle bag and made of soft canvas sown together by his Gran to be used specifically for running. Harry woke that morning with a sore head. He called out for his offsider but he was nowhere to be seen. He noticed Ned's horse was missing. He rushed to his saddle bag to count his money.

'One hundred quid short,' he said to himself. 'One hundred fucking quid and what has he done for it...king hit me while I wasn't lookin. It's bloody daylight robbery, it is... someone should do somethin about it...the young ones, I tell ya, they have no respect for the law or their elders these days.'

Harry took out his whisky bottle and sat down by almost dead camp fire. The bastard could have put some wood on the fire before he left, he thought. He felt lonely drinking by himself but soon the whisky began to ease his troubled mind. I will count my money again he thought and maybe I won't feel so bad. He did but the missing hundred quid made him unhappy again.

'And to think I gave his mum a bucket of dough too... that's the gratitude of the young for you,' he muttered to himself.

'That was some holdup back there even if I say so myself,' he said. 'I really excelled myself. Pity the kid has no appreciation for my ability. I thought he would turn out better ...impudent, rude, little git...barely fifteen but he can pack a punch...I'll grant him that. But he got no imagination, no stage presence. Just a sucker for a sob story by pretty face...fancy giving the foul-mouthed bitch back that expensive brooch...Jesus, wait til I see his mum. I'll tell her a few home truths about that no-good boy of hers.'

If Music be the foal of forgiveness

Texas Rangers and their mules.

And I cannot here forbear mentioning the useful little pack mules that served the Rangers so long and so well. When the battalion was formed in 1874 a number of little bronco mules were secured for packing. They soon learned what was expected of them and followed the rangers like dogs. Carrying a weight of one hundred and fifty to two hundred pounds, they would follow a scout of rangers on the dead run right into the midst of the hottest fight with Indians or desperadoes. They seemed to take as much interest in such an engagement as the rangers themselves. These little pack animals had as much curiosity as a child or a pet coon. The Texas Rangers by Walter Prescott Webb.

Amy Winehouse and her music.

She's tattooed. She wears whatever she feels like including the beehive. And she is a powerhouse! Her voice has an undeniable depth and undeniable strength. She sings from her gut, from her heart, and from some place very, very real. – Alexander Billet August 9th 2007.

She warbles like a magpie – comment on u-tube.

Ned was exhausted. He had taken Harry's advice and ridden day and night to get home and be seen. He hoped their disagreement would be the end of their working partnership. In the boy's mind, Harry was a liability with his theatrics. One day he would get shot in the back with all his carry on. Years on a horse and cold winters in the scrub had made the old fugitive arthritic and eccentric. He had been too long on his own and could work with no one or nobody. He was like a fox that hunted alone and returned to his lair at night to sit in the dark and contemplate his solitary existence. When Paddy asked how young Ned shaped up, Harry shook his woolly head, muttered a few inaudible words, and changed the subject.

It was near Christmas when Paddy passed on some good news to Ned.

'Your mare, Ned, is about to give birth...can you come and give me a hand with her? I don't want the flighty bitch to kick me while I'm helping her foal...she seems to trust you.'

Ned rode to his Grandfather's barn. He had been waiting for this moment for long time. He had persevered with the difficult mare when others would have put her down. He went to the stable. The mare was in a terrible sweat pawing the dusty floor and looking agitated. They bunched up some clean straw so to make a comfortable bed. The mare lay down and the birth contractions began. Inside the mare's roomy abdomen, the foal rotated with its dainty head and legs tucked preparing itself to exit...a neat swallow dive and out into strange and bewildering world. The placenta broke. Two tiny front hooves like ballerina shoes peeped into view. Ned and Paddy smiled in anticipation. The head could not be seen. It was bent backwards at an awkward angle. Paddy went to work. He slid his hand in, felt for the small head and gently repositioned it to its correct place between the forelegs. The mare was heaving trying to expel the foal and in a lather of sweat.

'Do not try to pull it out...let it come naturally,' Paddy said as two small hooves and pretty, little muzzle appeared through the translucent wrapping. With giant heave by the mare a little, wet slip of a thing that seemed to be all legs flopped onto the soft, straw bed like a pack of cards hitting the deck. Almost immediately the foal began to breathe air into her delicate, pink lungs enervating her spindly frame. Little lungs that Ned hoped would one day suck in a sky full of oxygen as she propelled herself at breathtaking speed over the plains, and up into the steep Ranges. The young, imaginative boy was excited at the prospect. The mare, despite her contrary ways was surefooted and a beautiful mover. The miles seemed to disappear under her and she rarely tired when asked to cover long distances. She ate and drank well, and knew how to look after herself even if that meant dislodging an impatient rider.

'Get the feel of her, Ned...rub her all over...she needs to smell you and feel your touch...breathe into her nostrils...put your breath into her and she will know and remember you all your life.'

Ned did as his Grandfather said blowing deeply into the filly's lungs and rubbing her all over. The human scent of his breath entered her moist lungs never to be forgotten. The foal struggled to upright herself. At first pushing on her spindly forelegs, and then trying to position her hind quarters to balance and steady her weight. Standing on all fours she tottered, wavered, almost falling back to the straw floor, but then gaining confidence and gingerly moving one or two steps. The umbilical cord, that pipe through which all sustenance passes and joining the foal to the mare, broke. The mare raised herself, gently nuzzled the foal and gave a soft whinny. With its gummy little mouth, the foal driven by instinct found its mother's milk bag and began to suck. The sucking noises were reassuring to young boy and his Grandfather. Now they could let nature and her instincts do the rest.

In the morning, the mare and filly were taken out of the stable and led into a paddock next to the homestead. In the homestead paddock there was company of other mares and foals, shady trees and a small stream to drink from. Ned watched the filly scamper in rapid circles about her mother. She was chestnut but would go grey. He couldn't help notice how balanced and symmetrical she looked. She fronted right up to them bold and inquisitive. She sniffed and seemed to recognise Ned's scent. She showed no fear. She had four dark hooves and a bushy, little tail. Ned rubbed her on the bum which she seemed to enjoy. He playfully pulled her tail about. She pushed back against him. I wonder if she can kick like her mother thought Ned moving discreetly to her side. Her bright, dark eyes were taking it all in with her cute ears flicking this way and that to whatever was attracting her interest.

'Bugger me...look at that would you,' exclaimed Paddy as he pointed out a whirl on her neck. When God produces the best, he marks them with his fingerprint.'

Having lost interest in her admirers, the filly accelerated off, bucking and whinnying as she went. She was full of personality, curious about everything, often alarming herself by forgetting where her mother was with her independent, little forays into the recesses of her paddock, and bossing the other foals. If she wanted to suckle, and the mare was not compliant, she would impatiently pin her ears back and shake her head at her mother until she was forced to stand and surrender her bag of white, nourishing milk.

'Look,' said Ned, 'she's bailing up her mum...a right, little bushranger's horse... she is Pop.'

'What are you going to call her?' asked Paddy.

'Music...Pop.' Ned just opened his mouth, and the name popped out.

'I feel as good watching her as I do when I hear music, Pop...good music like a stirring Irish reel and also sad, ballad music too...it all moves me and I go into a different world. And the way I feel now, Pop, looking at that foal cavorting around the paddock... well, the feeling inside me is much the same. I'm at peace with the world, I'm inspired and I am... am...' He struggled to find the word, and then he said 'happy.'

'Yeah, and I am happy too, lad,' replied Paddy nodding his head in approval. 'I have not seen such a promising foal as that one for a long time, Ned...she will do things that will make others gasp and shake their heads in disbelief.'

'I don't have your experience in these things, Pop, but something tells me you are right... but I hope it's not like what she did to Dad.'

'Yes, that did shock us for sure, but I was thinkin good things for this filly. Forgiveness has its own rewards, Ned.'

cry me a river

How Kate Cebrano, a north Baldwyn girl, would travel to City.

there was a creek connecting all the suburbs...on a hot idle summer's day you could almost float all the way into the City on a inner tube – there were just a few parks and suburban blocks that needed crossing on foot.

horse swims for the joy of it

I rested my horse only a few minutes before taking the water again, but Lovell urged me to take an extra horse across, so as to have a change in case my black became fagged in swimming. Quarternight was a harsh Segundo, for no sooner had I reached the other bank than he cut off the second bunch of about four hundred and started them. Turning Nigger Boy loose behind the brush fence, so as to be out of the way, I galloped out on my second horse, and meeting the cattle, turned and again took the lead for the river. My substitute did not swim with the freedom and ease of the black, and several times cattle swam so near me that I could lay my hand on their backs. When about halfway over, I heard shoutings behind me in English, and on looking back saw Nigger Boy swimming after us. A number of vaqueros attempted to catch him, but he outswam them and came out with the cattle; the excitement was too much for him to miss.

The Log of a Cowboy by Andy Adams.

The small holdings held by the Irish selectors could not support their stock during the dry months and it was their habit to graze their animals on the roadside. The Police, at the urgings of the Squatters, impounded their stock and placed exorbitant fines on their release. The Irish selectors were often denied land grants so as to increase their holdings. Ned and his friends would hit back in the only way they knew how. A stealthy, rapid circle of the squatter's paddock and with hardly a sound and the horses would be rounded up and run to a yard high in the Ranges. Their method was simple; one rider in front of the pack, one each side, and others to take up the slack and rein in runaways. There they altered their brands, and drove them on through the scrubby back tracks to cross the River Murray and be sold in New South Wales. It did not happen often and usually only to those who had wealth and displayed an arrogant attitude to the struggling farmers. This time, Kate wanted to go with the boys. She could ride as well as any man, and had good instincts in herding horses and cows.

The moon shone bright in the night sky. Kate waited with Steve and Dan, while Ned and Joe circled the paddock. Thirty horses came out of the semi darkness through the fence opening with little noise and fuss. They took up their positions, Ned placing Kate at the rear where she could see for any breakaways. They moved the horses quickly to the high mountains, and corralled them for the night. At dawn the following morning their brands were altered and the mob driven to creek bed which they rode along for miles to disguise their tracks before coming to the swollen waters of the River Murray. It was not possible to use the bridge for fear of detection. The horses were held overnight on a section of land that jutted into the river with a natural gateway of about thirty feet. Ned said they would cross the river early in the morning. The crossing would not be easy because the recent heavy rains had swollen the normally quiet flowing river. They rose early that morning to see a misty fog hanging low on the gums, and bulk of swift flowing water.

'Loosen your girths,' said Ned, 'the water makes them swell.'

Dan went first into the river as the others pushed the mob from the sides and rear. The horses balked, jumping from side to side, and then followed the lead horse into the swollen river. The herd swum, snorting as their heads cut neat triangular ripples in the surface of the water. On coming to the middle of the river, Dan felt the strong undertow taking his horse downstream. His mount was a powerful swimmer and broke its grip. Dan called out to the others,

'Watch the undertow... it's got a lot of grab out here.'

The undertow hit the mob of horses, and pulled them apart as the weaker ones were swept downstream. Panic set in. Kate tried to push the ones in trouble across and out of the undertow. Her horse got into difficulties, and rolled. The river like a deadly, silent predator saw its opportunity and grabbed her. Kate's struggling horse surfaced snorting with the look of panic in its bulging eyes. Its coordination lost, it rolled over again and again taking Kate with it. Kate appeared to be ensnared in the saddlery. They were both now out of control, and in a death roll struggling to stay afloat as they were being taken rapidly downstream.

Ned let go of his horse, and swam with the tow towards Kate. Two horses swept past him. He got to Kate but she was caught up in the frantic struggling of her horse. She was choking from mouthfuls of water, and caught in a stirrup leather. Ned was able to pull her boot from the stirrup and drag her free of her horse but her weight was taking him down. He would not let go. He would go holding onto her forever even if it meant they both drowned. Out of the corner of his eye, he glimpsed a figure on horseback working his way into the river up ahead of him.

He heard a voice yell, 'grab the rope...take it now, Ned...grab for Christ's sake...grab.'

Ned thrashed around with his spare hand whilst holding Kate with the other. He felt the rough texture of the rope and took hold wrapping it around his waist as best he could. Joe, with his horse standing in chest deep water and facing towards the bank, kicked his heels into its flanks encouraging the animal to brace and take a firm hold of its muddy footing. The rope sprung out of the water and snapped tight as it took up the weight with Joe urging his horse towards the river bank. Ned felt the life line slowly pull them from the clutches of swirling river. As soon as he could touch the bottom, he stood, lifted Kate into his arms and stumbled to the river's edge. Joe dismounted and they both set about trying to force the water from Kate's lungs. Bent over his knee, Joe slapped her back trying to punch the water from her listless body. She spluttered, spewing mouthfuls of Murray water, and kick starting herself back into life. Ned relieved fell exhausted to the ground. Joe massaged her weak limbs bringing warmth to her cold, damp body. He put a blanket under her head and made a fire. Kate looked at her brother and gave a faint smile.

'Thank God for you guys...I thought I was finished out there.'

She began to cry and salty tears rolled down her pale cheeks. She was not crying for herself but the heroism of her brother and quick thinking of Joe.

'Don't cry me a river, Kate...Joe saved us both,' said Ned placing his arm around her shoulders and giving her a hug.

'All in a day's work,' said Joe pulling out a fag and lighting up. Dan and Steve rounded up the survivors downstream. They even found Kate's boot washed up on a sandy bank. Relieved they rested and bedded down whilst the angry river roared its protest all through the night.

A bog up in the pan

Natives nightmare.

The natives believe that the night-mare—a subject likely enough to give birth to superstition—is caused by some evil spirit, in order to get rid of which they jump up, seize a lighted brand from the fire, and, after whirling it round the head with a variety of imprecations, they throw the stick away in the direction where they suppose the evil spirit to be. They say the demon wants a light, and that when he gets it, he will go away.

Australia - its History and present condition - William Pridden.

The country across the Murray opened into wide sparse plains spotted with wildflowers sprung from the dry, infertile soils by summer storms, and a sky of listless, pale blue. It was the Mallee. The riders drifted across the still landscape in slow motion interrupted only by itinerant mobs of skinny legged emu's, curious kangaroos silent and staring, and a few ribby cattle whose heads pointed dejectedly to the ground. Now and then, a spiral of dust, willy-willys, zigzagged across the barren, dry land like a solitary dancer on an abandoned stage. Cursed flies, by the millions, swarmed over them coating their clothes and irritating their sun burnt faces.

In the distant heat haze they would sometimes spy an isolated homestead. A lone figure may be seen looking from the verandah and then move out of sight, much like a dingo looking back and then vanishing into the bush. The emptiness and silence of the country made these lonely desert dwellers shy, withdrawn and untrusting of strangers. It was enough for them to exist. In the loneliness of the night, they talked to the desert, the waving spinifex grass, the acacias, the desert oaks, and the wild dingo answered in moans and howls from the drifting, sand dunes and the dry, stony creek beds carved into the unwelcoming landscape. It was a language they understood and had grown comfortable with like a mother's lullaby to its infant child, and in their isolation, it reassured them. The sight and sound of strangers in their land made them uneasy. They peered through their small, gritty stained windows watching until the intruders disappeared over the horizon.

Ned had made the trip across the sandy desert before. By taking that route, there was little chance of being seen by the law. At the small town on the other side of the desert, the railway line from the east coast came to an abrupt end amidst a cluster of hastily constructed and run-down stock yards. It was the only place for stock to be sold coming from the large pastoral leases of the vast, barely discovered interior. But it was a place where canny buyers knew there would be bargains and no prying police to ask difficult questions. Ned calculated their trip across the desert would take four days. He knew the rock pools were where they could water the animals and refresh themselves. At dusk on the second day the weary riders came upon the small oasis. In the hills nearby they could see smoke rising.

'It's the natives,' said Ned, 'you have to be careful...we'll have to keep guard during the night.'

The black-fella knew to keep away from the white men. They had heard bad news from tribes closer to civilization, and were determined not to venture near them. If it weren't for their fire sticks, they would have attacked and driven them from their lands. That evening as Ned and his group set about making camp, they could see dark figures flitting about the rock faces and strange sounds coming from the hills. Agile wallabies could be heard scampering through the bush, and if you strained your ears, you'd swear it was the patter of dark soled feet in the soft sand. The black-fella worked the night shift, while the country and its unrelenting heat took over the day shift in a conspiratorial assault on the unwelcome visitors.

In the late evening and early morning, flocks of little budgerigars, or lovebirds descended on the pool chirping and twittering their urgent messages to each other along with noisy galahs, pretty pigeons with a curled tuft positioned regally on their fine heads, and a wary crow in shiny black. Small numbers of wallabies and sometimes a dingo would venture to the pools edge, sipping the water quickly, and then looking up and about them before taking another drink. Joe bagged a wallaby with his rifle. The shot echoed violently into the surrounding hills sending the wildlife bounding into the scrub. A shy, slender, dark skinned people hid in the caves and rock crevices of their home, wondering who these intruders would shoot next. The boys skinned the furry hide from the little hopper, and roasted the fresh meat on their coal fire. That evening the little group slept an uneasy sleep. Now and then Ned would rise from his swag, grab a burning stick and search the nearby bush. He saw nothing, but he was being watched by eyes that saw his every step. If he was foolish enough to venture too far from his camp, a long-barbed spear would have penetrated the darkness, and silently taken him down.

On the fourth day a few shanty buildings and a railway siding came into view. They drove their stock to the yards and waited for the market the following day. Buyers and sellers ran their eye over the stock and filled the street and the ramshackle pub with their animated chatter. Deals were done with few questions and money pocketed. That evening they settled down to a hearty meal having purchased some tucker from the town. Kate set about making an Irish stew which her mum had taught her.

'What's this?' asked Dan looking at the meat stewing over the open coals.

'Smells nice,' said Joe who always had an appetite.

'It's mum's bog up in the pan,' said Ned.

'Better than that Chinese chook food Joe goes on about,' said Kate.

'Look...lets go to the China camp on the way home,' said Joe, 'I'll show just what the celestials can do with food...you will be amazed.'

'Yeah...dog and cat stew,' said Ned.

'I mean vegetables, spices, oriental sources, small slices of meat, and of course rice. It's unbelievably tasty. I should know...you lot gotta try different things...we can learn from them...they're an ancient culture with a lot of history.'

'Yeah...goanna like the black-fellas,' said Steve.

'I don't see you living out here too long,' replied Joe.

The others were curious. Joe had befriended the Chinese camp whose customs and language he had studied. Most Europeans avoided them like the plague. Ned and the others weren't sure what exactly Joe's interest was; was it the reticent, plump faced girls, their spicy food, or their smoke-filled dens. Maybe it was all of this. Maybe he just preferred their company. Joe had an open, inquisitive mind free of prejudice, and new ways interested him. The small Chinese camp liked their new friend, Joe, because he was polite and respectful, and showed a genuine interest in their culture. He was not like the angry miners who wrecked their tents, chased them into the scrub and assaulted them cutting off their pig tails, and shouting go back to China.

They rode back to the river town crossing the bridge late at night when no one was about. Kate shivered as she looked down on the calm, silvery glow of the great mass of silent water passing below her. It seemed to her the mighty Murray with its waters coursing down from the Victorian high country to the dry flats below and separating the States of Victoria and New South Wales, was sulking.

China girl

Prejudice.

We don't want the flat faces, the pug noses, the yellow complexions, the small feet, and the long tails multiplied a thousand fold amongst us, as they would very soon be if the Chinese ladies came to us as well as the gentlemen [laughter] Considering that there are upwards of 400 million of people in China...it would require only a few years of unlimited Chinese immigration to swamp the whole European population of these colonies...to obliterate every trace of British progress and civilization.
John Dunmore Lang to an audience in Brisbane.

Food.

'Old yellow cats and young black dogs, they're the best to eat.' an elegant and learned Chinese woman to the Author.

The above two quotes are from the 'Sojourners' by Eric Rolls.

Joe led them to the Chinese camp sitting near a creek on a gold field long since abandoned by the European miners. It was the Chinese way to go over the tailings finding gold that the others had missed in their frantic efforts to get rich. That way they hoped to avoid the racial hatred directed towards them by taking up new leases. The Victorian Government did their best to exclude them by placing a high entry tax on the Chinese getting off the ships in their ports. The Chinese avoided this by going to Robe in the south-east of South Australia and travelling across its endless swamps and scrub for some three hundred miles carrying their sole belongings in a wheelbarrow. The local guides took them to the swamps and abandoned them. To avoid attack by natives and the Europeans, they grouped together walking single file stretched over many miles as they headed for the Hsin-Chin-Shan, the new golden mountain.

The Yellow Peril was descending on Australian shores from the Californian gold fields in unprecedented numbers, and people were feeling nervous. The English, having declared the country terra nullius and taken it from the native inhabitants, were worried lest they too might be dispossessed by Asian hordes. It spelt trouble for the Chinese if they were too successful. They kept to themselves, hid their culture and gold discoveries, grew their own food, and practiced their rituals in private. Mostly they subsisted by being frugal, modest and hardworking.

The small party rode into the secluded Chinese settlement. The women and children were working in their vegetable and fruit gardens wearing their wide brimmed, coolie hats and scarves to protect them from the sun. The men were toiling at the mounds of dirt known as slag heaps that lay dotted about the countryside. Their homes were mainly constituted by large tents with temporary timber structures made for communal activities. It would not be prudent to make anything too elaborate or permanent because with gold fever you had to be mobile and ready to move to new fields.

Joe spoke to the elder, Lim Po, introducing him to the others. Lim as was his custom set about making the visitors feel welcome. He summonsed his wife explaining to her that they would prepare a meal for their friends, and that they should make themselves comfortable. The horses were tethered next to the trees. Tables were set up under the cool shade of the nearby gums and a bamboo grove and Chinese wine made from rice cooled and soothed their dry throats. In a flurry of activity Chinese womenfolk with woks, choppers, steamers, and earthenware pots appeared over small fires and their mysterious mixtures of fresh vegetables, sauces and small slices of meat began to sizzle in their hot pans. Bamboo shoots, bean curd, black beans, Chinese cabbage, melons, wood fungus, snow peas, shallots, sprouts, peppercorns, tangerine peel, water chestnut's, duck, chicken materialized in front of them giving off exotic and tantalizing cooking smells as they were chopped, mixed and fried in their sauces enhancing the clean, delicious, natural tastes.

The group tried to communicate their appreciation with smiles and sign language. Kate moved amongst the women seeking to know what they were doing and pointing to the various spices and vegetables that she hadn't seen before. Joe spoke fluent Mandarin and was engaged in dialogue with Lim probably the others thought over his next month's supply of opium. The Chinese handled the substance with a expertise passed down over many generations. They learned from their fathers and their fathers before them. In the cool Ranges near the camp they sought out the deep, rich, loamy soil needed to grow the addictive, magical plant.

Dan had taken wild flowers from his saddle bag, made them into four or five garlands and presented them to group of curious but shy teenage girls. Embarrassed by the gift they giggled coyly amongst themselves as they placed the flowers on their dark, shiny tresses. Kate noticed that one woman was cooking mashed potatoes and lamb chops much like she had seen at home.

She said 'no.... we will eat your food .... there no need to cook especially for us.'

The elderly Chinese woman looked embarrassed. She said it was for her daughter. In broken English she explained her daughter caused her much embarrassment amongst her people, that she had adopted Australian ways, wishing to wear their clothes, to eat their food and to have their freedoms. She motioned towards a girl sitting by herself away from the others and gazing intently at the horses standing lazily in the shade of the trees. The teenager she pointed to wore a defiant expression quite unlike the submissive demeanor of her kinfolk. She was taller than the other teenagers, sparer of limb, and wore clothes much like the European miner. Tennessee stole glances in her direction. He could see that her attention was fixed on the pretty bay mare with black points, tail and mane he had been riding. She briefly interrupted her gaze to take the bowl of mashed potato, two or three plainly boiled vegetables and a chop in gravy using a steel fork and knife and not the customary chopsticks. She seemed to enjoy her meal chewing on a lamb chop in the manner she had seen

Australians do. On finishing her meal, she glanced at the guests studying them with equal intent as the mare. Tennessee, intrigued by the solitary girl's interest in the mare, got up from the group, went to his horse, untied and led her to the inquisitive girl.

She slowly stood, looked directly at him showing no emotion or attempting to speak. Her dark, determined eyes studied him closely, and moving to the mare she ran her delicate hand down its refined neck, over the saddle and across the broad, smooth polished rump to her finely muscled hind leg. It was a sensuous caress from one pretty girl to another. She was feeling her as though she was blind. The meaning and sensations came to her through the sensitivity of her palms. She then walked behind the mare gently lifting her dark tail, fanning it out and letting it fall over her shoulder and down her back smiling at the similarity to her own jet-black hair. The other teenagers tittered. She ignored them, let the tail drop and stroked the mare's expressive head, lightly running her hands over her ears and brushing over her large, kind eyes. The mare blinked. She put her hand between the mare's rubbery lips feeling the ivory smoothness of her teeth and in the gap between the front and back molars fingering the steel snaffle. Tennessee could see this girl had a natural touch and intelligent curiosity about a horse. Some people push and force when looking into a horse's mouth causing the animal to throw its head and get agitated but this girl's probing was of little discernable concern to mare. She again placed her left hand in the mare's mane, and without any warning or indication, sprang lightly into the saddle in one graceful movement. Her kinfolk were aghast at what she had done and cried out in abhorrence of her unexpected brashness.

Her father, embarrassed, went to reprimand her.

She yelled at him telling him to stay where he was.

Her shrill command stopped him dead in his tracks bringing disapproving utterances and stares of her people. Her father looked imploringly at her as if to say my daughter do not cause me this shame. She felt the soft, pliable leather of the saddle, and the brass fittings. Tennessee smiled and shortened the stirrups. The girl placed her feet in the stirrups, stretching her legs and raising herself above the mare's back. When you first place yourself in a saddle, you can be overcome with powerful emotions, as Gong was. You feel part of the powerful animal upon which you are seated, and there is an irrepressible urge to take flight like a bird. The timid are overwhelmed and want to get off but Gong, as she had shown, was not timid. She looked at Tennessee, gave a discreet half smile, and motioned him to lead the mare so she could feel the movement, the cadence of the mare. He understood. He led her about while her community silently watched. She stood upright in the saddle and twisted her body about as she had seen good Australian riders do as they passed the camp straining their neck to look at the young girls. There was something bold and unconventional in this girl, something which harkened back some 600 years to her distant, fearful, marauding forbears, the Mongols. She jumped off the mare and said to Tennessee,

'Me Gong...you teach Gong ride horse ...yes?'

'y...y...y... yes,' stammered Tennessee.

'You come here with horse next week...yes?'

'S....s...s... sure G...G...Gong. I wouldn't miss it for q...q...q...quids.'

His stutter got bad, and in frustration he banged his head against his saddle. There was much more he wanted to say but the words were stuck in his throat. Gong could see the boy's exasperation and held her finger to his lips, saying 'ok...ok...ok,' and he visibly relaxed. The two sat demurely together and waited for their meals. The community breathed a sigh of relief and returned to their preparations.

Ned's attention turned to a large wooden carving of an ancient Chinese soldier on horseback. It wore a coat of armor standing guard at the entrance to the smoking den. It interested him that you could ride and still wear what appeared to be heavy equipment and he was curious as to how it was put together. Later that evening they watched their host's display of fire crackers and rockets that speared towards the heavens exploding into a profusion of blinding color and lighting up the night sky into cobalt blues, lemon yellows, deep reds, and soft, rose pinks of marvelous, transient beauty. The blinding colors reminded Dan of his roses. Joe had been with the men in their smoking den and was now in a semi hypnotic state sitting in a chair with his head back looking at the glittering expanse of night sky. He muttered something about going to the moon. The others laughed at Joe. Later that night they bedded down in their camp rolls and slept peacefully in the company of the Celestials. Gong kept a watchful eye on Tennessee, attending to his needs. In the morning they thanked their hosts for their kind generosity and left.

Tennessee would later return and teach Gong to ride. He knew she would take many falls to master the art; the art to ride swiftly and with vigor, like her long ago and distant relations who galloped across the plains of Asia Minor and Europe, taking all before them in a giant cloud of dust, fierce weaponry, and on the hardy backs of their small, durable ponies. Gong wanted her dull life to disappear along with the suffocating strictures of her community. A pony would give her the life she so desperately longed for. She wanted nothing to do with the escape sought by her Elders in drugs. Her escape had to be real, to be physical and not brain duped and numbed by a stupefying drug. It was not her nature to be a worker bee, to meekly garden, and obediently serve her men folk. Her mother explained that in Chinese mythology her daughter was a warrior Princess but the others scalded her and said she made excuses for her daughter not to work and to dream of an existence she had no hope of attaining. 'Queen Bee,' they said mockingly and went on with their digging and panning.

Unknown to them the warrior Princess was about to strike her own gold of sorts – a gold that would liberate her from the asphyxiating strictures of her inherited culture about which she cared little and respected less, and introduce her to the dangers and freedoms of a liberal Western society; a civilization, unlike hers, where she could make her own decisions based on her values; and if those decisions involved risk and pain - then that was a price she was more than ready to pay before she suffocated in the regimes of communal demands and obedience to narrow minded Elders.

You are a damned impertinence, Cyril

What Bob Hawke said to the interviewer Richard Carlton when he accused him of having blood on his hands in the Haydon spill.
Harry's description in prison of life on the Ranges.
'ye were never there, sir, you say; well I hope ye'll go someday' said he. It's there ye'll see the finest sights in the world. Ay! It's grand to be on the ranges, and to breathe the beautiful pure air, and to see Mt Feathertop far above ye and down for miles and miles, the beautiful country. There's water all the year round and its always cool and pleasant. That's the place for a man to live; and if I were out and well I couldn't wish for anything better than to end my days there. Ay I've led a bad life but I only wanted a mate to help me make a big haul, and then I meant to go to America and live an honest man.' - An interview with Harry Power' by James Stanley - the Argus and the Age

Sarge was getting cranky. He was under pressure from the Squatters to stop the horse rustling and from his Superiors to catch the elusive and notorious bushranger Harry.

'If we don't do something to stop it, others will follow his example,' he was told.

'I'm at a loss to know what to do,' confided Sarge to his erudite clerk.

'I know it's those Kelly's and his mates that are doing a lot of the border running, and I wouldn't be surprised if they in cahoots with Harry as well. We'll never catch Kelly in the scrub and on those horses of his. Why we have to ride these plugs from the State Supply I'll never know,' he said dejectedly.

'It's because we can't ride the fast ones,' offered Cyril.

'Bullshit,' said Sarge getting riled and pacing the office shrugging his shoulders.

'I might be getting on in years, but I can ride as good as the best of them including that Kelly and Quinn rabble.'

'Listen Sarge,' said Cyril thinking hard, 'I reckon we have to change our thinking. We are never going to get anywhere chasing them. We should set them up, get smart and draw them in like a spider and his web. There are always those who will spill the beans for a few pounds. I know one or two who will be tempted to give me some information if the price is right. Get me a hundred pounds Sarge, and I guarantee I will get results.'

'That's a bit rich,' said Sarge, 'but if nothing else its worth a try. I'll speak to my superiors in Melbourne.'

Within two weeks the ambitious clerk had his money, and soon returned with information that made good his promise. He knew where to get Harry. Sarge was hopping with excitement. Harry's capture would be something to crow about and the publicity...well any struggling Police sergeant in the sticks would like the public acclaim in apprehending Victoria's most wanted bushranger. Cyril told him of his plans.

The following morning they set out before dawn with two troopers and a blacktracker heading for Quinn country. On getting near the homestead they were warned by the informer to dismount and creep silently past the house being careful to be out of earshot and downwind of the dogs. Sarge left Cyril with the horses. The peacock slept contentedly on the homestead roof while the blacktracker threaded them through the bush. The peacock woke and began to strut up and down the roof suspecting intruders. The blackfella told them to freeze. He cupped his hands and made a screeching sound much like big bird about to announce their trespass, and the peacock settled.

'That sure was smart, Soapy,' said Sarge.

'Little trick I learned from my time in the bush,' he replied.

They crept to the base of the bluff overlooking the property, and climbed silently through the bush until they came close to a clearing at the pinnacle of the bluff. Dawn was just breaking over the Ranges, and while he rested and got his breath, Sarge's thoughts turned from Harry to the magnificence of the panoramic view behind him and the awakening of nature coming with the dawn.

'Jesus, this is something to behold,' he said envying his old enemy Harry for having chosen such a delightful place to hide. His attention was then drawn to a solitary humpy made of timber and bark in the style of the nomadic aborigines. The surrounding stillness was disturbed by the loud, regular rumblings of Harry in a deep slumber like a bear hibernating in its cave.

Sarge scanned the peaceful scene noticing Harry's black mare tethered to a tree and saddled for a quick escape if he heard the crack of a stockwhip coming from Quinn's homestead below, or their dogs barked. More often he relied on the peacock whose screeches split the air and invariably warned of unwelcome strangers. That was the signal for him to clear out for a while. He had a lot to thank that big tailed bird for. For the bushranger, eternal vigilance was the password to continuing freedom.

'Don't go putting him on the Christmas table,' Harry told his mate Paddy, 'I'll pay for his upkeep…I'll even build him a nest on that roof of yours if he thinks of moving and find him a girlfriend.'

This time, thanks to the skill of the blacktracker, all three alarms including the strutting bird had failed him. As they were preparing to rush the humpy, they heard loud snoring then a choke followed by a cough and sputter.

'Hang on,' said Sarge, 'stay put for a few moments…he will be armed.'

The snoring stopped abruptly. They heard a few stirring's inside the humpy. They held their breath and looked uneasily at each other. Harry had a reputation that would give even the brave cause to reconsider. Then right before their eyes there emerged from the humpy a big, woolly head like a bear emerging from its cave after a long winter. It was Harry. The three men hiding in the bush visibly whitened. There was a gleaming six shooter poked into his belt. He shook his big, dishevelled head and let off loud, reverberating fart that went on endlessly like a jumping jack cracker and mumbled to himself about drinking too much ginger wine last night. One of the troopers had to pinch himself tightly to stop from breaking into a nervous laugh. Sarge scowled at him. He was excited by prospect of capturing the legendary bushranger, and what it would do for his career. Harry rubbed his bleary eyes and half stumbled to where he could see the whole expanse of the pretty valley below him clothed in a veil of white morning mist. He stood there motionless, admiring the wonderful scene in front of him, and though he had done the same thing many times before, he never once tired of the simple joy it gave him. He broke spontaneously into full bodied song he had learnt from his drunken Irish relations 'take me home Kathleen.'

'That I will Harry,' yelled Sarge as he burst out of the scrub levelling his pistol squarely at Harry's large frame. 'I'll take you home to jail where you belong...don't move or do anything silly Harry or I will be forced to shoot. Get the cuffs on him you two,' he yelled to the two troopers.

Harry looked around and saw that Sarge was about the same distance from him as his mare. The thought raced through his head...the rest of his life in a cramped, dark, stinking cell with hardly a ray of sunshine or to chance death by making a run for his horse. The first was no choice at all and worse than a slow death. He saw the morning sun surfacing through the slender white gums sloughing themselves of the morning dew. He knew he couldn't live anywhere but here in the Ranges.

He bolted.

He ran for what was left of his life.

He ran as fast as his big bulk would take him knowing that life depended on it.

He focused on his black mare and he dearly wished he was on her back flying through the scrub and away from his would-be captors. If he could just get to her, he knew he would be free.

Sarge instantly knew that this was his moment in life too. It was his one and only chance for fame, or, if Harry beat him...ignominious defeat.

'I want this man alive,' said Sarge and the three ran to cut him off.

Sarge ran right through Harry's humpy, knocking it to the ground and diving at Harry's lumbering frame catching him about the legs. The tackle took Harry to the ground but the determined Sarge held grimly to those two great logs as though his life depended on it.

'Beauty Sarge,' cried one of the troopers amazed at his superior's surprising agility.

'Don't stand there you silly git...get those bloody cuffs on him.'

Harry was overpowered within a few feet of his mare.

'I've got money, Sarge,' Harry pleaded.

'I can make you and your men rich beyond your dreams. Can we do a deal Sarge?'

'You can talk all you want, Harry,' said Sarge thinking that it wouldn't be long before his capture would be the talk of the Colony, and his reputation established for life.

'I'm sorry to have to do this to you but you are a cooked goose now Harry, and you may as well save your entreaties for the Beak,' replied Sarge remembering that Harry had not in his time running from the law killed anyone or assaulted women folk.

'Well...if it must be...let me have a few moments more on this lovely mountain,' said Harry rather resigned to his plight, 'I've got some tucker left over here ...eggs, bacon and stuff. Rather than let it rot, would you and your good men care to join me in a hearty breakfast before we journey on.'

Sarge thought for a while wondering what the old reprobate might be up to now but he couldn't help but grant his last wish, and besides, he liked the view and was needing a rest after the effort to arrest Harry.

'Sounds a good idea, Harry,' said Sarge, 'I sure am hungry...being up since dawn...it's mighty kind of you. We'll have to feed you if you don't mind, Harry.

Harry had hoped that the cuffs might be taken off but Sarge was too cautious to allow that. The little group set about making a fire, and cooking Harry's eggs and bacon

'How do you like your bacon, Harry?' asked one of the troopers.

'Well done...nice and crisp if you don't mind, mate.'

'You know, Harry, it tastes better up here in this fresh, cool air,' said Sarge opting for a second serve.

'Too right Sarge...why I have been living a life of perfect contentment in these Ranges and I wish it could continue.' Harry sighed and drew deeply of that pure mountain air that had sustained him in excellent health over the years despite his binges on the bottle. After breakfast Harry and his mare were led down the bluff to the waiting horses.

'Sorry we a bit late,' Sarge said to his patiently waiting clerk, 'our breakfast service was a bit slow.'

'Hell...I could have done with some myself, Sarge... is that who I think it is?'

'Sure is. May I introduce Mr Harry Power no less.'

'Pleased to make your acquaintance,' said Harry.

Harry was helped onto his horse and they all set off for a slow walk back to town. Knowing Harry's propensity to run, Sarge placed a rope around his neck holding the other end.

'Harry...if you try to escape you risk being dragged by the neck.'

Harry just nodded his head and fell into a deep depression thinking of what lay ahead of him. As the small party rode by the Quinn homestead three figures were watching from the veranda.

'What's the fuck the matter with that bird of yours,' Harry yelled at passive onlookers. They were worried about what Harry might say. Would he sing? Harry knew much that could hurt them.

'Who dobbed me in Sarge...I bet it was that Kelly kid.'

Sarge just grinned and replied, 'That's for me to know and you to find out Harry.'

Sarge's clerk knew the answer to that question.

'I'll kill the little bastard,' muttered Harry feeling sure he had been betrayed by those he had helped.

Cyril looked uncomfortable.

'Isn't it always the way,' he said philosophically.

'You can trust no bastard these days.'

'Don't worry Harry,' said Sarge, 'at least you will have four walls to live in...it must be hell living in one of those whirly's.'

'Not at all,' replied Harry, 'I love the open spaces, the sunlight, the smell of the earth, the bush, always on the move, swimming in the creeks and feasting on the bush tucker. I know ten ways to make possum and wombat stew and most of them are edible...ah it's been a grand life, a life on the run, and not to mention the odd stagecoach or two.'

Harry thought for a minute and said,

'You might not know Sarge...I've helped a lot of people in need in my time on the run...it was their kids I wanted to help most...poor little starving mites. I did my bit to put some food on the table and blankets to keep them warm...no good keeping it.'

Sarge couldn't help but like Harry. He was not an ignorant criminal who could only think in terms of themselves and their greed. Passing riders recognised the captive Harry and raced to town to be the first to break the news. When they arrived, a huge crowd had built up, pushing and straining to see Australia's most wanted bushranger. Sarge warned them to keep well clear as they rode down the main street to the cells at the back of the Station. The crowd cheered and joked with Harry. They loved his spirit and sense of fun, and his reputation went before him.

'Let him go, Sarge,' one yelled.

'Take the bastard to the gallows,' said another.

'No way is he leaving my custody,' said Sargent 'Harry is going to make me famous and put this crummy, little town on the map.'

Soon reporters from Melbourne overran the town taking photographs of Sarge and his troopers, and asking to interview him and the prisoner. Important people sent congratulatory telegrams and invitations to State functions and dinners.

Harry did a deal with the prosecution and pleaded guilty to several robberies with others being dropped and a promise that his cooperation would lead to reduced sentence. The English Judge thought differently. He was going to make an example of Harry and put him away for best part of his life. He remembered what Harry had done to his learned fellow Judge. He was a very serious and hardworking man until Harry bailed up his coach and gave him some impromptu dancing lessons. Now he spent his spare time in common dancing halls mixing with the lower classes and is an embarrassment to the Judiciary. His sentences became mercifully short, and were frowned on by his fellow Judges. Harry thought he would get ten years. He got sixteen years. He would be over sixty before he was released. He stood stunned, holding onto the dock rails. He then let out a bellow that echoed through the Court precincts and charged like a demented bull at the Judge grabbing him by his scrawny neck and holding on until His Honour's eyes bulged from his head and his skinny, magpie legs, hidden under his pretentious garb, shook with fear.

'I taught the other blighter how to dance so I hope you won't mind if I give you some lessons in how not to breathe,' said Harry to the red faced, gasping Judge. The police dived on him prising his grip off the terrified Judge's neck. He was bustled from the Court, and delivered into a dark cell to contemplate his sentence.

When back in their office, Sarge said to his obedient clerk,

'And now my smart arsed friend...what about that Kelly boy?'

'Yeah...I've been thinking about him, Sarge.'

'Have you now.'

Sarge warmed to the studious lad in his ill-fitting uniform and glass bottom spectacles. He drew back his comfortable chair, pushed aside the newspapers headlining his bravery in the recent capture, lifted his weary, arthritic legs onto his desk, drew deeply on his cigar, and blew hazy smoke circles in the air which he poked with his finger. Having amused himself for a minute or two, he casually flicked the ash, looked kindly at his four-eyed clerk burying his head in the books of account, and said,

'Tell me all about it, my son - tell the now famous Sarge how to do his job - you little goggle eyed, rat arsed clerk.'

Cyril looked up from his book of figures through his thick glass bottomed spectacles and smiled at the friendly abuse coming from his now smug Superior and said, 'what did I get out of all this, Sarge...it was my idea after all that caught him?'

'Who put his life on the line whilst someone sat timidly at base of mountain holding the horses? who tackled this bear of man bringing him to the ground and cuffing him? who...who...tell me who, Four- Eyes.'

Cyril interrupted him, 'fair enough Sarge...sure it was you...I'm sorry to have offended you with my presumption that I played a part in Harry's capture. I just got a little ahead of myself.'

'If you have any doubt, Cyril me boy, read them papers. I have what all heroes have boy...raw, unadulterated, courage...if you don't know what that is, I'll spell it for you...k.o.r.a.g.e.'

'Wrong Sarge.'

'What's wrong lad? you telling me I haven't got the ticker to take on Australia's most wanted and dangerous criminal?'

'No Sarge...just that you spelt courage wrong. It's a c not k.'

'I'll give you a c and a k...you are a damned impertinence, Cyril.

Now git back to balancing them books, Four Eyes. The head accountant will be coming soon to audit them and I don't want any mistakes or your jobs on the line. And fudge my petty cash expenses while you are about it. I don't want no embarrassing questions...I'm too important now.'

'You missed a u too, Sarge.'

Hold on...I'm coming.

'That Kelly kid, Sarge, you know what he can't resist,' said Cyril.

'What boy?' asked Sarge

'Showing off on his horse...he's crazy about his horses...well, all his lot are but Ned is good with the young ones. He has no fear. You must have seen him riding those half broken, spooky horses into town, Sarge...showing off in front of the girls. He thinks he can ride anything. You saw how easily he gets on them horses of his Sarge. He just steps up and before you know he's on...so smooth like. You know I've tried to do the same on big Bertha but I'm buggered if I can do it...it takes me ages...like climbing a bloody mountain.'

'Yeah...I know only too well...I had the misfortune to see you. Right in front of that girl you keep on talking about...Valerie...the one with the loony Dad. You were almost there until your saddle slid leaving you in a tangle. Jesus...you sure know to put on a comedy when it comes to horses, Cyril.'

'That was embarrassin Sarge...I don't think I can look her in the face her again after that.'

'Don't be worrying about her Cyril. She's a nutter like her Dad.'

'Tell me about your plans for Kelly,' asked Sarge wanting to get down to business.

'Well, it's like this. We get a horse half-broken like, a stolen one. Then we arrange for someone to befriend Kelly, tell him that he has lost his horse and that he has to leave for the City, and if he sees the horse, could he hold it until he gets back. I'll warrant if he finds that horse, he'll not resist riding it into town... then we'll arrest him for stealing the animal.'

'Cyril,' said Sarge 'you, my boy, are truly one of the wonders of the world. I mean the good Lord didn't bless you with handsome looks but you make up for it with them schemes in your head. You're like one of them bloody Supreme Court judges...a mind like a bucket of worms...thinking about everything, always thinking, one day that scheming head of yours will explode right off your puny shoulders. If this works out, I'm going to see that you are in for promotion...chief clerk in one of our Provincial Cities. How does that sound, me boy? I got some influence in the right circles now after capturing Harry.'

'I was thinking about Head Office, Sarge.'

'Well maybe,' said Sarge, 'let's get on with this stroke of genius of yours, and keep it quiet - only you and me, partners in crime like.'

'Sarge, haven't you forgotten something?'

'What,' said Sarge

'I don't like saying it Sarge - it seems indecent like.'

Sarge sighed and put his hands in his pocket. 'Sure, my boy, how silly of me.'

'Sarge, this is more complex and Kelly is more dangerous. I reckon two hundred quid this time,' said the clerk looking slightly sheepish.

'Bugger me boy...you are too smart for you own good but after the last success I'm prepared to back you. I'll get the money. They listen to me real good now that Harry's inside and I'd pay the money myself to be rid of this Kelly kid before he gets out of hand and he sure has the potential to do that. I've got the feeling, you know, that if we don't nip him in the bud, he is going to be mighty popular with his lot in these parts. I don't like admitting it but the boy has spunk,' said Sarge. The wily clerk nodded but he was thinking of pocketing a hundred quid for himself this time seeing Sarge took all the glory for capturing Harry without a word about his efforts.

Two weeks later a stranger rode to the pub when Ned was there. They got to talking about horses.

'I'm only passing through,' he said, 'I lost a chestnut mare with baldy face yesterday not far from here. She only half broken...the bitch pulled away and took off into the scrub... haven't seen her, have you?' asked the stranger.

'No, but if I do, I'll catch her for you,' replied Ned.

'That's right neighborly of you. I'm going to Melbourne for a week and will call in on my way back,' said the stranger carrying out his instructions from Sarge.

'Sure,' said Ned, 'if I find her you won't recognize her when you get back. I'll put some work in on her.'

'I would like that,' replied the stranger, 'I've heard you are the best horse breaker in these parts.' The stranger shook his hand and hurriedly left. Not far out of town, he met Sarge and his clerk coming out of the scrub with a baldy, chestnut mare.

'Have you paid him?' asked Sarge.

'Sure Sarge,' replied Four Eyes looking a little embarrassed.

Sarge turned to the stranger,

'Now clear off...I don't want to see your face here again... understand.'

'Look I'm off... I don't fancy fronting that Kelly boy after he finds out I've duped him.'

'Right,' said Sarge, 'we'll leave this horse not far from Kelly's block and with a bit of luck he will see her when he comes home. The bait is laid,' he said as he chuckled to himself. They rode back to town with his clerk struggling to stay in the saddle. Sarge looked over his shoulder and shook his head in disbelief at the ungainly tangle of arms and legs struggling to stay on the big, feathery hocked and coarse bred mare with a kind face.

'Jesus boy, you can embarrass me sometimes. It's just as well you don't have to earn a livin on a horse's back. You had better get off and walk before we get to town.'

'You smug, old bastard,' thought Cyril to himself bouncing about. He felt the sly hundred quid stuffed in his pocket which Sarge meant to go to the stranger, and comforted himself with the thought that although he couldn't balance on big Bertha's back, he was going to balance his bank account with an extra hundred quid. The next few days Sarge paced nervously up and down his office continually looking out the window onto the street.

'Be patient,' said his clerk, 'he will come...am I ever wrong.'

'I've arranged for trooper Lonigan to be here. He's a big, beefy lad who used to throwing his weight around. We may need his help if things get a little out of hand.'

'Just point me in his direction,' said Lonigan flexing his biceps and doing pushups on the desk.

'I'm pointing to him now,' Sarge said seeing a solitary rider zigzagging up the street on a flighty, chestnut mare.

'Four Eyes, you done it again...I can't believe our luck.'

'He's gotta be arrested yet and that may cause a few problems,' added the nervous clerk. The three of them watched the rider come into view pushing the mare along on a loose rein and sitting light in the saddle as she snorted, jumped, shied and side stepped at the strange sights and sounds of the main street.

'Go get him Lonners. We'll come if you get into trouble.'

'Just watch me, Sarge...he won't know what hit him,' said Lonigan.

The over confident and overweight trooper had grown bold on drunks and layabouts, but the rider approaching him was not one of those. When he had left Cyril added,

'You shouldn't have given him the pistol Sarge - I don't think he has the ability or nerve to handle Kelly.'

Sarge watched Lonigan. The trooper began to zigzag up the street towards Kelly trying to imitate his horse.

'If nothin else the big, fat clown has got a sense of humor...look at him aping Kelly,' replied Sarge.

Ned spied him out of the corner of his eye and began to laugh.

'Looks a pretty wild nag, Kelly,' he said.

'I've ridden wilder,' said Ned 'but she will be a different horse when she gets home tonight...looks like you got the same problem.'

'I like to amuse the town folk...much like you on that nag but you might be lucky to get home tonight,' replied Lonigan.

'Why...up to your tricks again, Lonigan?' asked Ned.

'Well, for a start you might get thrown and injured.'

'The local constabulary concerned about my welfare...I don't think I could handle that.'

'What if I told you that horse you're on is stolen...think you could handle that Kelly?'

'I found it in the bush for a mate who's coming to pick it up in a few days.'

'That sounds a likely story...according to her brand this mare was stolen from Mr. Beaucat's property two weeks ago.'

'That can't be right,' said Ned.

'Get off the horse, Kelly...you are under arrest for horse stealing.'

Ned looked at him, 'if it's stolen, I know nothing about it so bugger off.'

Lonigan pulled his revolver and stood pointing it directly at him.

'Do as I say, Kelly, or I'll blow you out of your saddle.'

Ned dismounted calmly. He could see the trooper's gun hand was shaking.

'Who put you up to this, Lonigan?' he demanded.

'Get down on the ground Kelly, and put your hands behind your back.'

'I'll not get down for you or anyone.'

The hammer clicked.

'You crazy, murderin, bastard Lonigan,' said Ned flying at the trooper and knocking him off balance. He took hold of his arm twisting the gun from his hand.

'We'll see how bold you are without your gun.'

He lifted his large bulk off the ground by the shirt and threw him backwards so that he landed heavily onto the rough corrugations of the dusty street. Before he could recover Ned was on him grabbing his boot and dragging him to the side of the street. The fat, burly trooper knew he was no match for agile Kelly whose strength seemed like three men. He bellowed for Sarge to help him.

'Where the fuck are you lot,' he cried looking in vain towards the Police Quarters. In an undignified retreat he attempted to get away crawling on all fours. Now performing for the street crowd, Ned mounted him and raked his spurs along his meaty flanks so that he bellowed like a scrub cow.

'The way you were walking down the street a few minutes ago, it seems you need the buck ridden out of you, Lonigan.'

He was getting a hiding in front of the whole town, and he knew there was nothing could he do to stop it. Sarge and Four Eyes watched from the window dismayed at what they saw.

'Hold on ...I'm comin,' yelled Sarge out of his window.

He summonsed two extra two troopers, and ran into the street.

'Stop it Kelly...this will not do...let go of my trooper.'

'Come on in Sarge...I'll do the four of you for the price of one.'

The three tried to intervene.

A trooper slammed Ned over the head with the butt of his revolver. Blood covered his face. He fought on landing a right hook on the trooper's jaw sending him to the dirt road. The townsfolk let out a cheer. Sarge circled the fight like an excited, sheep dog barking his encouragement when Ned thudded a sharp left into his expansive gut. Sarge deflated holding onto a verandah post. The blow to Ned's head made him dizzy. Lonigan saw a chance and made a grab for his testicles. The three fell on top of him, their weight pinning him to the ground. The local Justice of the Peace intervened. Ned allowed him to put the cuffs on whilst the others stood back. From there he was taken to the cells to await his court appearance the next day.

His mother came looking for him having heard what happened.

'What have the mongrels done to you, Neddy... your face is a mess. I'll get a lawyer.'

'I reckon I fallen into a trap mum. They say the horse is stolen.'

'Ned it can't be true...weren't you talking to that stranger?'

'I bet he doesn't front mum. I'm not likely to get bail but I'm going to plead not guilty.'

'You won't get a fair hearing son, you know that. Our lot never do from them beaks. They have it in for us. The squatter hates us so he will do what Sarge tells him.'

Ned was philosophical. He had taken horses but not this one. The Judge wanted him put away. He was appalled at the prisoner openly fighting four, upstanding officers of the law. He didn't believe Lonigan had tried to shoot him. He was only carrying out his duty to arrest a felon he said. He went on with his usual prattle about the honesty of the local constabulary. Sarge had stacked the jury with stooges.

Ned sighed. He had heard it all before and wanted them to get on with it. His mum was right.

'Two and half year's hard labor,' said the Judge. Ned vowed they would not do it to him again. He and the other prisoners were clapped in chains and taken by rail to the Melbourne Jail, Pentridge. Harry was not so keen to welcome his ex-partner in crime but he did have one or two things he wanted to discuss with him with help of some of his newly made acquaintances.

Sarge and his clerk rode back to their town well satisfied with their efforts.

'You know, Boy, I think we are going to have a peaceful existence for a couple of years,' said Sarge.

'It would be nice to have some money to enjoy our idle days without Kelly around Sarge and I think I know where to get it.'

Sarge stopped his horse and stared at his clerk.

'What are you getting at now?'

'A bit of horse trading I thought.'

'Yeah...and where are we going to get our stock from?'

'I know where there's a paddock of nags all going for free...I heard the owner is going to be absent for a time...two and a half years to be exact.'

'You have an evil mind, boy,' said Sarge shaking his head again, 'I'll go you halves.'

A short time later Sarge went to the Kelly block and handed Ned's mum with warrant to distrain goods for failure to pay fines. He and his men rounded up the horses and left. In the next few months Ned's horses were sold to itinerant buyers and anyone who wanted a good horse. A buyer from Cobb and Co looking for well bred, fast, coach horses to make the gold town runs from Melbourne bought Ned's favorite filly, Music, who at that time was only halter broken. He was an experienced horseman and coach driver, and much liked what he saw.

'Nice cut of a filly that, Sarge,' he said, 'where did you get her from?'

'From some drunken lout,' said Sarge, 'couldn't pay his fines so I took her...can't remember his name.'

'I can see the initials E.K. on her.'

'Doesn't mean a thing to me,' said Sarge as he winked at Cyril. 'But I do know her name is Music if that is any help.'

Ned's mum did not have the heart to tell Ned about the theft of his horses. His jail term was hard enough. Unknown to Ned, his best horse was soon to be on her way to the big city like him for an education.

Lucille, why doncha come back where you belong?

Woman and mules.

'White-eyes women are no good for bedding.' Old Owl finally spoke up. 'They're only useful as slaves. It's the difference between horses and mules. If you beat a mule enough you can get work out of him, but not companionship. They're too stubborn and set in their ways. - Ride the Wind - Lucia St Clair Robson.

Cobb and Co learned their trade in the gold fields of California, and knew what they were doing when they came to Australia. They moved people and their luggage faster than anyone. It was no surprise they prospered in a Colony where instant fortunes were made by getting there ahead of the mob. Their coaches were imported from America using leather-braced chassis making them light and comfortable unlike the heavy, lumbering, coaches from England. Their advertisements boasted their coaches were drawn by stock second to none. Each team had six horses and they would stream in and out of the main gold towns two or three times a day amidst a flurry of activity and gold fever. Gold was everything. Gold emptied the Cities of workers looking for that lucky find giving instant wealth. With money came speed, acceleration, the spiv, the master of the fast deal, and the yellow hordes with their cone shaped, coolie hats and wheelbarrows. The horses were a thrill to see as they cornered low turning into the main streets and then lifting as they accelerated to the depots in a cloud of legs, spinning wheels and dust. The passengers gripped their seats and whooped as the coach cut a swathe through the blurred countryside. The boss gave strict instructions that all coaches were to gallop into the towns because of the excitement and pride it generated in the eyes of the public. But good horses and speed has need of equally talented and gifted drivers with a deft touch, courage and an experienced and intuitive knowledge of horses and what their endurance limits were.

One such talented driver was Kev Kavanagh from Casterton. A plain man of few words and a admirable work ethic coming from the country where respect was earned by the sweat of your brow and how reliable your word was. He did five years of schooling and worked for his Dad before he was twelve years of age, just tender boy. In time he learned mainly from what he observed and experienced rather than what he was told about how to make a living dealing with good and bad horses. It was not easy work, dangerous, and he learned to read the subtle, warning signs of a horse about to explode in a frenzy of rippling muscle, pitching and bucking, and crashing into the hard wood rails. He knew when to back off, when to go forward, when to reward and when to punish. Horses like people must have relief from pressure, they need to trust and he saw if you pushed and did your block, you could lose a good horse and make him an outlaw. Horses were made mean by bone headed men, men with little imagination or reflection but a capacity for stubborn, cruel domination like that of his Dad.

'Stop pussy footin around and spoilin that horse,' his Dad would yell, and take the horse from him to knock the crap out of it until it stood clamped in by ropes, trembling and soaking in a nervous, dripping sweat. As Kev grew into a man and his reputation as a horseman spread throughout Western Victoria, his thoughtless and ignorant Dad refused to acknowledge his own shortcomings, and his son's abilities.

'Your horses ain't broke, son. You just hypnotize them like a chook. They come unstuck as soon as the owner takes em home. Trickery...that's what it is.'

Kev said 'yeah Dad,' and left to run his own horse breaking business. Why talk to a brick he thought even if he is my Dad.

Cobb and Co recognized the results that Kev achieved with their horses. They arranged for him to do their buying, and sent him on trips to the country. They were prepared to pay good money for the right types. Kev sealed the deal with the local Police Sergeant at Glenrowan, and took the filly to the railway yards awaiting the stock train to Melbourne. After Kev left, the Sergeant said to his clerk with the glass bottom spectacles, 'You know, my boy, I think I am in the wrong job...I reckon I have a flair for this horse-trading business. Too bad that Kelly kid did not have a few more like that filly. It will be a surprise to him doin time in Pentridge that we can steal horses as good as him.' 'It's a warrant of execution for non-payment of fines ...not stealing, Sarge,' replied the studious clerk.

Kev would travel with the filly in the stock crate. He preferred that to a passenger train. Living in the City, its noise and grime, and family problems had depressed the shy horseman. He was separated from his young wife and kids, and he could not accept he was alone with no family to go home to. Recently he began to thinking there was no purpose to life and wanted out of his troubles. Hard work he didn't mind. He had done plenty of that but it was the hard work of a troubled heart that beat him up every night, and gave him no rest. The train took off on its long journey travelling through the night. Kev sat on a stool in the empty rail truck. There was a full moon and he could see well enough in the dim light filtering through the timber slats. He could see the outline of the filly standing quietly in the corner. She too looked dejected and friendless. Images of his young wife, Lucille, flashed into his confused head. He saw her wholesome, country looks; her long, blonde hair, the colour of wheat fields growing on the endless plains of the Western Districts; her smile that stunned a man like a bolt of lightning from the blue sky. Even her name 'Lucille' had a ring of exotic pleasure about it, invoking mystery and risk, something foreign, something French perhaps and everything alluring that might conjure. It was not a common name in the country where formal, old English names prevailed like Gertrude, Rosemary, Deidre or the Colleens and Kathleen's of Ireland. The novelty of the marriage and for a while her kids held her interest but she was not easy to keep happy. In the midst of temptations that always stalk a pretty woman, she would not be hobbled and kicked at the corrals of her marriage. Kev tried his heart out to please her but he knew it was going to end badly. He got into fights and took to drinking but nothing worked. In desperation, he packed up and took his family to the City where he found a job with Cobb and Co as a driver. He worked hard, leaving early in the morning and returning late at night. It would be dark when he left and dark when he got home. He only had time to hold his little ones and hand over his wages to a stranger, his wife.

The big City opened up an Aladdin's cave for Lucille and gave vent to her natural propensities. She adorned herself in the latest fashions and left the children in the care of friends whilst she frequented the restaurants and nightspots. She did not go unnoticed with her regular forays into wealth and society, and when they enquired of her husband, she casually passed it off, saying he was away on business. It was true. Her husband was away – away on the business of hard, physical work of providing for her and their children, and not as they imagined, or how she would like them to imagine. With her flashy, good looks, often bordering on the tart, and playful personality, she began to thrive and wondered why she had wasted the best part of her life in the bush. Her experience had told her there would always be suitors. Men, who would excuse her vanity, cover for her faults and pay her debts. Why couldn't she use her natural, good looks for her own profit the same as others traded their craft or expertise she reasoned. She didn't care to think much on what her destiny might be with the advance of years. Nevertheless, it comforted her that there would be silly, old men around to fawn over faded and wrinkled charms. She had seen these elderly women on her haunts, decked out in their expensive jewellery, unwilling to admit their days had passed and buying the temporary attention of young men with their money. She would glimpse scornfully at them from the side of her eye and exclaim in a less than discrete tone, 'mutton dressed as lamb,' and her young and rich suitors would laugh.

She knew the kids would get by. In any case she wanted to live for the moment, whether it was wrong or right. Proper thinking people, she reasoned, deluded themselves into thinking and planning too much whilst life passed them by. Others gave all to a thankless family that sucked them dry and left them in old age to consider what a waste it all was. 'Open your safe and find ashes,' she would say to her jealous girlfriends. She had a bag of common and trite homilies that both amused her friends and justified her lifestyle. She received invitations to stay out late. She accepted them. Her indifference was soon to end the marriage, and rob the children of their father's intimacy and his only reason to live. He saw their little hearts go cold and their faces sink into passivity unable to comprehend the destructive ways of grown-ups. He didn't want to live. A divorce followed, and separation from his young wife and children. Contact fell to a few desultory and empty hello's and good-byes. The black dog was snapping at his heels, and pulling at his trouser cuffs in that railway van rollicking along the track. When it got him to the ground, the beast would hone in for the jugular. He didn't want to admit it but it pretty well had him licked. Previously he wrote a short note to his wife He wrote simply, 'Love reely hirts without you.' How many times had he said to her, 'Lucille, why don't you just come back home?' He loved her and always would despite her vanity and faults. Lucille mocked his amateurish attempts at reconciliation. She showed the note to her doting boyfriends.

'The dumb arsehole,' she said contemptuously to her admirers. 'Hurt...now that's a word I know a lot about...the hurt that man gave me ...shut up in his bloody hut all day surrounded by crapping horses, dishes, cooking and housework ...he don't know shit apart from bloody horses. I am entitled to life too. I have talents the same as other people. The Professor uses his brain to make a living- I am sociable, I like people and people like me...well, men at least... that much is obvious. They tell me I am beautiful and cannot say enough nice things about me. Kev don't say any of those things...he may think them but he don't say them... he is like a dumb mute. Why can't I use what God has given me to make my way in life the same as the Professor, artist, shopkeeper or whatever...to get the things that I want...to do the things I want to do...with the talents I have.'

Put that way, Lucille made a compelling case for her freedom.

To Kev his wayward wife was one thing, his kids were another. If only he could be with his kids, he thought he might survive the ordeal but he had to work. Two sweet, innocent children - their little minds, too young and hopelessly confused by a loyalty and love for both parents, and the trauma and heartache of a broken family. He could see the hurt in their eyes, and there was nothing he could do to make it go away. When he came home at night, beat up and bruised from battling rogue colts and difficult owners, he would cuddle and kiss them, and the world was at peace again. Now he came home to cold, empty room above the stables at Cobb and Co headquarters, and stared full at the bare walls until he fell asleep in his work clothes. There was no escape from his misery. He was suffocating in it. And he was embarrassed that he was so weak and helpless. He could take it no more.

As the slow, goods train pulled out of the Station, Kev knew what he had to do. There in the rail truck was a halter and rope, his swag, and above him, a cross beam in the roof. The filly stood unconcerned in the corner. Kev went to her and took off her halter and undid the lead rope. In an odd way he wanted to explain to the filly what and why he was about to do, to unburden the heavy load weighing him down.

'I've had enough, little girl,' he said. 'I'm goin to have to borrow your halter for a while...you seem a nice girl...not too much trouble unlike someone I know. She has given me so much heartache, so much trouble.'

He stopped. He did not want to whine and blubber. He took out his pocket knife, measured the halter strap around his neck and made a small hole in the leather. He got his stool, placed it in the centre of the rail box floor and buckled the halter around his neck. He stood on the stool. As the train rocked from side to side on the steel tracks, he could feel his balance tottering. He didn't want to make a mess of the job and half strangle himself to be later revived so he jumped off and took a couple of long, deep breaths to steady himself and regain his composure. He got back onto the stool, threaded the rope over the beam and began to tie the knot. Before he could fasten the rope, a lightening, fast kick out of the darkness sent him reeling off the stool, stumbling across the floor and into the wall.

'Jesus, Mary and Joseph...that was some powerful kick, little girl.'

He looked at the filly. She was looking directly at him. A horse doesn't stare at a man but this one was drilling him with her big, searching eyes. He couldn't move for the pain and started to sob. His tears flowed freely so that they created little furrows down his dusty face much like a sad clown. The filly appeared to sense a deep sorrow. She moved from her corner and stretched her pretty neck placing her soft muzzle next to Kev's head. She began to sniff...trying to comprehend what was so troubling to the man. He felt the tickle of her whiskers and the warmth of her breath. He tried to push her away but she persisted. He began to giggle like a child, and then laugh.

'You sure have got a powerful kick, Music. Why didn't you finish me off proper and give me one in the head?'

She gave a soft, short whinny as he had sometimes heard a mare do when its foal is frightened or momentarily lost. He had never had a horse do that to him before and it made him uneasy. Dotty owners had told him all manner of strange things that they imagined horses had done for them as though the horse was human, but this he knew was exaggeration and wishful thinking.

Now he wasn't sure.

Was he as crazy as them?

The filly nuzzled him again.

Was she trying to say something to him? He shook his head, wiped away his tears and although he couldn't explain or even dare try, he began to feel better. For a while, he thought not about himself but the filly and how she was taken from her home and herd, and how frightening and alien the rail journey would be for her. He could make it better for her. He struggled up, and ran his hands over her smooth, silken coat reaffirming her with the comforting touch of his callused palms. His back still hurt, and he leaned against her sturdy frame for support. He rested his elbows and head on her broad back in a sort of a half, loving embrace. The familiar aroma of a horse was always reassuring to Kev, as though horses were family, and he inhaled deeply. The filly smelt earthy, musky with a sort of sweet fragrance of mountain air that revived him like a dose of smelling salts. He could hear and feel the beat of his sore, bruised heart, weak and irregular, against the strong, regular thump of a big, generous heart thudding away in her cavernous frame, and it felt good. Be resilient was the message that came through like it was being belted out by the tom- toms of an Indian tribe.

There together, the suicidal and desperately unhappy Kev was slowly and gently being brought back to life, being resuscitated, and transfused by a young filly he barely knew His weak, febrile heart began to beat stronger His will to live surfaced, and began to swim, buoyant for the first time in many months, and chased off the black dog snapping at his feet. If he were happy once, he realized he could be again. He should stay in this world and open himself to what life may have in store for him. It might be more of the same, but that's ok he thought. Whatever it was, he was going to embrace it, take it on and ride out the bucks, shies and backflips of life as he had done with his horses.

The two of them, two losers in a dirty, run down stock crate of a slow-moving goods train, winding and threading its way through the moonlit scrub to a big, polluted City, and as odd as it may seem, their two lonely hearts beat as one. They rocked together in that crate like babies in a cradle as the train came down out of the hills, and coursed its way through monotonous array of houses, shacks, factories and suffocating smog. The lights of the Metropolis blurred past. On arriving at Central Station, Kev woke up from what seemed to him a bad dream, placed his hanging noose halter on the filly, took up his swag and walked. The filly stepped onto the platform following Kev, and trusting him to take her to a new world. Together, two lost souls would begin life anew in the big, strange, bustling City of Melbourne. When he woke the following morning, Kev looked into the mirror and turned his back. There it was...a neat brand in the shape of horseshoe. A man brands a horse to prove ownership, and this filly branded him to save him from swinging at the end of a noose. She had booted the shit out of him. He smiled, and whistled as he went to work. He had another pretty girl to love and look after...one he hoped he could keep in a corral.

Chattanooga choo choo

Indian care for good horse.

Buffalo runners of the Blackfoot were given special care. Three Calf recalled that his father, who owned several buffalo horses, would not permit boys to catch, ride, or play with any of them. After a chase a buffalo horse was taken to a stream, water was thrown on it, and it was rubbed down. Some men made a practice of throwing water on their buffalo horses every morning and evening to toughen them and prepare them for hard winters. Before setting out on a chase the hunter's wife carefully prepared his mount for him. She met him on his return, took his horse from him and cared for it. - The horse in Blackfoot Indian culture - John Canfield Ewers.

Cobb and Co had their head depot in the City next to the Railway Station. Kev took the filly to her stable in a complex where they had coaches coming and going at all hours of the day and night. He bedded her down. He lived above the stables where he had his own little kitchen and space to himself.

Kev noticed the filly was not eating. She looked sick and her head hung low. She was not interested in hectic activity and exchange of horses going on around her. Kev changed her food to pasture hay, but she just nibbled a bit and looked away. She didn't want to eat. Kev checked her mouth and teeth looking for sharp edges but everything looked normal. She was losing condition, becoming ribby, and her coat was dull. The filly hated her stable, her cramped confines and the noise. The dust, the acrid, ammonia smells, the older, bossy horses, and the big City pollution. The air that she breathed was impure, and she suffered like an asthmatic. She felt she was slowly being poisoned in a world that bore no resemblance to the horse Eden from where she had been taken.

Kev had to stop her downward spiral before it was too late. She had saved him and he would do his best to save her. At night he put her halter on and led her from her cramped confines. He took her to the railway line nearby where he knew there were clumps of fresh, green grass. The mare put her head down, sniffed and began to slowly chew. She imagined she was back in her paddock next to the Ranges. The grass was fresh unlike the dry, coarse hay in her stable. The air was not as stifled or pungent as in her stable. Kev put some fresh, juicy, crunchy carrots in her feed. She rolled them about in her mouth unsure of what they were but then crunched. She liked the taste and it encouraged her to eat and get some fiber into her stomach.

Kev rose early and walked to the market to buy the best carrots and oil seeds grown by the Chinese gardeners. He travelled back to Casterton and bought sweet smelling, thin stemmed hay and golden plump grain full of goodness. Whatever he could find to entice her to eat more he tried, and slowly she began to improve. He knocked out a wall and put in windows so the breezes would flow in and clean out the ammonia smells. He rugged her when it was cold and saw that she had fresh rain water to drink each day. At night he talked to her in soothing tones as he petted and groomed her, gently combing out the course hair and rubbing her head which she seemed to like. He trimmed and painted her dark hooves and stretched her long, shapely legs feeling and massaging the strong tendons and muscles. All this he did for her, like a doting mother. And her head began to lift, her eyes began to look interested, her coat improved and took on a shine, and her movement became alert and energetic. Wherever she went her pretty ears were pricked and continually turning like a weather vane. She took an interest in all that went on about her, and in a big City there were many things to catch your attention.

She looked forward to her evening outings along the railway line in the dim, sodium glow of the Railway Station's gas lamps, and the shunting of the trains. Although yet not ready to ride, Kev took a long rope during their evening promenades and lunged the mare in circles, taught her to stop, stand still, move sideways, back up, to run with him, to walk on the railway platform whilst he walked on the track below, to jump off the platform and then to jump back up again. He rode her bareback using only a light pressure on her nose. He was educating her as only a good and patient horseman knows.

A drunk leaving the sly grog room of the nearby hotel looked in disbelief at what he thought he saw...a solitary horse walking down the train platform late at night by itself. He yelled out in his drunken stupor,

'Catchin the Chattanooga choo, choo...are you darling?

get your tickets here...choo, choo, choo,

and I am blue, blue, blue,

chew, chew, chew your hay, darling... that's a good girl.'

He couldn't see Kev leading her on a long rope from the railway tracks below.

Kev chuckled. Not able to get a response from Music, the drunk began to slur,

'The old grey mare's not what she used to be, not what she used to be.'

Kev thought he would have some fun. He stopped Music and with a flick of his rope he got her to face the drunk who was eyeing her from a distance and trying not to fall over. Then in strained horsey sound Kev let out a loud neigh and said,

'Well, I have never been so insulted.'

The drunk shook his head. He looked again.

'You talkin to me, darlin?' he asked.

'Who else boof head?' came the reply.

It was getting too weird for the drunk, and he thought he better move on for fear of getting his head kicked in.

'Sorry ma'am,' he said, 'I meant no offense...you are very pretty filly...I used to have one just like you...several in fact...but the drought came and I lost everything. If you will excuse me, I'll be on my way and not bother you further.'

He took off his hat, bowed graciously and shuffled on thinking the demon drink was playing games with him.

Kev took every opportunity to educate and make her life more interesting in the constraints of the City. He put her in large yard where she could move about more freely, see and observe the people, the coaches, the many sounds and activities of big, bustling City. She lifted her pretty head, looked and became interested. The school kids waved, called out to her and petted her through the rails. One little girl would stop every morning, feed her a cube of sugar, and whisper sweet words into her flickering, alert ears. Kev smiled when he saw this. The filly was beginning to like people and go to them without snorting and backing off. She seemed to like the laughter and spontaneity of the children best, and kept a watchful eye for them as they passed to and fro from school. When out on a lead, and a steam train came hissing by, Kev would teach her to stand her ground, not panic, and to face her fears. This would build her trust and nerve to take on bigger challenges. But he did feel a inherent tenseness when he handled her hind legs which worried him a little. Having been nursed back to health, Music would race around her yard and jam on her brakes kicking up a small dust storm, and entertaining the passersby with her antics. The railway precincts, the milling crowds, the giant steam engines, and the care of simple, country horseman had gently shunted this young, ailing filly back to joyful, vigorous life.

When he felt the filly was old and mature enough, somewhere between her second and third year, Kev took her to the training grounds to introduce the harness. Thinking she was accustomed to being touched all over, he hitched her up to the training cart and, after a few preliminary walks, jumped aboard. No sooner had he gathered the reins than she took off, kicking madly at the shafts and cross bar, smashing and overturning the cart. Kev was dumped out of his seat amidst the wreckage. When she was satisfied that she had completely destroyed the creaking predator, she stood still as a lamb as if to say what's next. He had had kickers before and they were dangerous animals to be around. Cobb and Co would sell them early if the habit persisted. He tied her high to a rubber tube and went and got his rope. He circled a hind leg near the fetlock and ran the rope well behind her out of firing range. From a safe distance he played with that leg, lightly pulling, stretching it out and flicking circles to her rear and then the same with the other hind leg until she was thoroughly accustomed to every movement and touch on her hind quarters and legs. Again, she blew up with a series of lightning fast kicks, rears and pull backs stretching the tube almost to breaking point but eventually conceding in a soapy sweat. When she stood quiet and accepted the rope, he untied her and hosed her down putting her back in the stable to think about the day's events and what profited her.

The next day she accepted the cart. Kev rewarded her with some carrots and treats he had in his pocket. In the following weeks they progressed to reverses, sharp corners, figure eight's, serpentines and smooth changes of pace. She excelled and was placed in a four-wheeled buggy to do the same movements over again but different because of the extra set of wheels. Others came to watch her as she performed faultlessly and applauded her remarkable ability to learn quickly. Kev was proud of this now maturing mare he had built up a close and affectionate relationship with. Within weeks she was put in with a team of experienced horses and taken outside to be introduced to the hectic street traffic of a busy City. Her progress was that quick that Kev soon made her the lead horse of his team. However, it was on the open country road her abilities came to the fore. She saw and pushed passed obstacles, holes and washouts that other horses would balk spook or shy away from. She accelerated her team past opposition coaches and led them through flooding creeks and bogs. She breezed through the long grasses of the flat paddocks with a graceful fluidity that had the passengers swoon and clap their appreciation. In the heady atmosphere of the gold rush, competing coach Companies would arrange a race to Castlemaine, but these contests were so easily won by Kev and his team that his reputation and that of his lead mare became well known in the State. In twelve months, the mare was the top horse at Cobb and Co. His team was chosen for the important occasions of delivering visiting dignitaries, and for State occasions. Although he did them, Kev preferred the informality of the gold runs delivering cargo, the Chinese and business men.

Occasionally, on a spare day he would put her in a light buggy and go to see the kids, taking them on a summer picnic in the nearby hills. There, in the shade of the gum trees by a river, he would take the harness off his mare and teach his kids to ride bareback. Music would carry them carefully instinctively knowing they were children until they too could sit comfortably on her strong back and learn to balance to the changes of pace. Kev could not bear the thought of his kids being City raised, and not able to ride a horse. Afterwards they all went in for a swim including the mare. Having cooled down, Kev treated the kids to a fresh, healthy lunch made from the bread, fruits and vegetables he purchased in the Chinese markets. They grew to like the fresh fruit and vegetables unlike the fatty chops and sausages that their mother threw on the greasy pan when she was about. As they lay and tumbled together in the shade, Music grazed happily on the green pastures nearby until it was time to be harnessed and head back to the City. The children grew to love the outings with their Dad and his mare, Music, and in time, an easy peace and acceptance began to descend on this fractured and hurt family from the small country town of Casterton.

Working and running on the chain Gang

Stawell Gift

In 1883 an aboriginal man called Robert Kinnear won the Stawell Gift...he won with ease...he breasted the tape with his hands in the air, well ahead of his nearest rival. This blackfella's victory was received with thunderous applause. He is still honored in towns like Dimboola and Horsham - the Quick and the Dead - John Perry

Ned was placed in the slammer for two years It was twin share, double bunk and a bucket for a toilet. His cell partner was an aboriginal man called Soapy Emu, a lean, sinewy man, spare and loose limbed. Ned thought he had seen him before.

'I saved your bacon down by the river...Harry...remember?'

'Yeah, that's right...you were the tracker. You knew it was Harry's horse, didn't you?'

'I did mate... I didn't want to dob you two in to them Traps.'

'We thought as much...that was good of you, Soapy.'

'That's ok mate. I know what it's like with the Traps ...them doin the work of the Government and they have robbed us of our land .'

'How come you're in here, Soapy?'

'It's a long story. I worked for them Traps for couple years but one day we go to the river to see my mob. I was happy you know...my mob proud what Soapy do, and my uniform but my mob plenty sick, Ned...all bloody crook...that Squatter bastard... he want my mob off our land by the river. The mongrel put poison in the flour he gave em...he kill many of my mob like they rabbits. He told Sarge they were spearing his stock but he chased off kangaroo, wallaby...no tucker to eat...so they take couple sheep. You know what Ned...bloody Sarge not report him...says there not enough evidence for white man's court. Evidence...what he bloody call dead bodies right there in front of him and plenty sick in belly. He just shake his head and say maybe they ate bad kangaroo, Soapy. I go see this bastard who poison my black fella mob. I say why you kill my people? He say piss off you black bastard, and then go to get his gun. I get him good, Ned...bashed him proper for what he done to my mob...and now bloody Traps get me...chase me all over the country for ten days...put me in their Court and say things I not understand. Big boss in white wig...he say you, Soapy Emu, plenty bad black fella for bashin white man...he nearly die, but I say I do it bloody again if I see him. He say to me you not see him for two years where you going Mr. Emu, and they drag me off here. No walkabout in here, Ned...just up and down up and down like them poor animals in white fella zoo.'

'Poor bugger you and me never get justice, Soapy. We have to make our own justice...stand up and fight that's what I say.'

'Big fella Harry in here lookin for you, Ned. I don't think him too happy with you. You better come with me to ship jail. They lookin for prisoners to do sea wall building.'

The next day in the exercise yard, Ned saw Harry lurking at a distance and eyeing him off. Three men appeared around him.

One said 'Uncle Harry wants to see you, young fella.'

Ned went with them to see Harry. He wanted to say it was not him that dobbed him into Sarge.

'To hell it wasn't you ...you slugged me when I wasn't looking on the Bendigo jog and if that wasn't enough flogged my money,' said Harry.

'Listen boy, I've been waiting a long time for this. I'm a patient man. In fact, I have bloody years in this stinking hole to get patient thanks to the likes of you. My boys here and me don't like snitches.'

Two pinioned Ned's arms behind him, and while they struggled to hold him, the third let loose with his fists. Harry saw his opportunity and booted him hard in the balls. Ned buckled but was held upright. Out of the shadows, a dark figure intervened sending two assailants to the ground with a straight right and a left jaw shattering uppercut. It was Soapy. 'We got no argument with you, Soapy,' said Harry backing off. He knew Soapy could fight. He bobbed and weaved around them, and hit hard picking them off one by one. Harry ran and his thugs were not far behind. Ned looking a little bloodied saw the good sense of Soapy's advice and the two opted for the sea wall construction After his unwelcome introduction into prison life, Ned thought it wise to join Soapy on the prison hulk anchored in the bay.

It was an old convict ship, infested with rats, and with cramped and dirty cells. The hulk creaked and groaned at night as the waves slapped against its leaky, rotting hull. There were thirty-two prisoners on board with four guards and four prisoners to each cell. A new head jailer accompanied the exchange of prisoners. He was known to be a fair man. He gathered them for a talk on what they could expect. He said that if they behaved decently, they would be treated decent. That more privileges would accrue as they proved themselves deserving of them. If they were untrustworthy, their privileges would be reduced. It was up to them as to how they would be treated. He would personally see to it that they would get remissions for good conduct. It was his contract with them. He intended to keep a tidy ship, with the decks being washed every day. He organized exercises every morning on deck and encouraged prisoners to keep fit as the wall construction was hard work. The inmates wore a blue and white striped uniform.

In Ned's cell, there was Soapy and two others; Reggie, a dwarf and Giuseppe, a Italian priest defrocked for embezzling the Church funds to spend on his mistress. Reggie burnt down his neighbor's barn in the middle of the night. 'His kids wouldn't leave me alone...always taunting me, making fun of my size,' he said. When I went to their place to complain, he just said 'is that so Reggie.' Without as much as a warning, he picked me up and chucked me into the vegetable patch. 'Come back again, little man, and I'll chuck you in the pig pen.' His missus and kids laughed while I lay there hidden in the corn, beans, carrots and artichokes. I couldn't take it any more...I pelted a few potatoes at them and ran off. Later that night I burnt his barn down...it was easy...just one match. If he had treated me decent and disciplined his brats, none of it would have happened but he wanted to make a big shot of himself, and now I'm here.'

His mate Giuseppe didn't appear remorseful for taking the church loot. His story took a while to come out.

'I'm not sorry I spent their money on French champagne, expensive hotels and a woman who demanded it all. It's gone, no money, no friends, nothing. Just me, you lot, and this shit hole. I don't want to talk about it ...just do my time and then go back to my family in Italy.But the girl I cannot forget.

'Who?' they asked.

'Lucille,' he said 'Lucille Kavanagh from Casterton. Do you know her?'

'No,' they replied.

'Her husband Kev asked if I could counsel her - you know get her back on the straight and narrow. She was giving him a hard time. Up to then I had a vocation. I had led a good, moral, Christian life but she, Lucille, was something else. I tried to teach her to recite the catechism hoping she would mend her ways but she ripped the book up in my face. She said Father there is only one thing certain in life and it is not parroting off all that church crap.'

I said, 'Ok then Lucille...you tell me what is important in life.'

She said, 'Not only will I tell you, but I will show you.'

'She stripped off her clothes and stood there in all her innocence. God help me, I have never seen the female form in such perfect proportions. The girl was absolutely luminous yet wistful, vulnerable and naïve at the same time. She was utterly incapable of concentrating on any important dogma or committing herself to anything or anyone. She craved endless stimulation, entertainment and the company of male admirers of which there were many. I raided the church funds to take her to fine restaurants, parties, the races and the high life. All I wanted was to be in her company. I didn't think that my vows, learning, respect for the faith, goodness, virtue...whatever you like to call it...would unravel as though it had no purpose or meaning in my life at all. How we fool ourselves with our importance and morals. I was in a word besotted. She literally turned me upside down.'

'What did her husband do?'

'He heard about it, and was hoppin mad.

I was preaching from the pulpit that day. It was a Sunday. I cannot forget it and the memory will not leave me. I could see him on his grey mare, cantering towards my church...I saw it through the window, slow and deliberate like he was on a mission. It was difficult to concentrate on what I was saying. I knew I had it coming. Lucille was working her charms on my teenage altar boy in the Presbytery whilst she waited for me to finish the Sunday sermon. That day I was preaching on the evil of sins of the flesh. The irony does not escape me. My fear made me speechless. I began to sweat. Perspiration dripped onto my notes making inky splotches on the white paper. The parishioners looked at each other. When I felt I was about to faint, the Church doors burst open and Kev stood there glaring at me.

He yelled 'you Father Giuseppe are a no-good two-faced hypocrite... preach one thing and do another...an imposter and not worthy of the robes you wear.'

He walked down the aisle. He was calm and determined. The parishioners were deathly quiet not knowing what to expect. Only his spurs gave an ominous jangle as he walked towards me. He grabbed me by front of my robe pulling me head first out of the pulpit. He ripped my black robe off popping the buttons and leaving me exposed, flat on the floor in my underpants for all to see. I tried to push him off but he slugged me one in the head knocking me semi-conscious. The congregation did nothing. They knew I deserved this hiding. Before he could king hit me, Lucille rushed from the Presbytery and fell upon Kev striking him with her fists and screaming,

'Let him go, Kev...he's a fucking priest for Christ's sake. You cannot assault a man of God. He is teaching me how to be good person.'

Kev stopped, held his fist poised above my head, amazed at what she had said. Only Lucille, in all her guile and innocence, could say such a thing he thought and only he would be silly or willing enough to believe it. Kev stared at her, and said,

'To be good at what, Lucille? to be good at what? What you are good at doesn't bear repeating in the walls of this pissy church.'

Kev knew he still loved her, faults and all. He turned and said '...don't tell me you didn't know what was going on and what did you do? Except sit there and sing those crappy hymns about the good lord Jesus. Not one of you came to me to tell me the truth. And you know what the truth is - it is not the bible, the gospel, not attending this church like a herd of mindless sheep. The truth is in the run-down pub across the road where men can have a drink or two...unload their sorrows, mistakes, errors, failures and god knows how many I have had, and not be judged or scorned by his mates. Let he without sin cast the first stone.' Kev was doin a better job at preachin than me. They began to clap and cheer him.

He said 'if you lot are interested, I'll tell you where I am going. I am going right across the road to that pub. And if you like, come with me and I will buy you all a drink. I'll have to do that because there is no money in the Church till. Giuseppe and Lucille have spent it all.'

All my parishioners filed out and went with Kev to the pub. Now I have no Church and no Lucille. She has forgotten I ever existed. She blamed me for the ruckus at the Church. She stormed out saying,

'I should have let Kev pummel you into the floor, embarrassin me like that in front of all those good people. How am I ever going to set foot in a church again Giuseppe after what you have done to me. I don't know what I have done to deserve all this aggro.'

All I could say was, 'sorry Lucille,' as she sashayed out of my church and out of my life.'

'Men always forgive beautiful woman,' said Reggie apologetically hoping to console the unhappy, ex priest.

'Yeah...life goes on,' said Ned philosophically. 'That fella Kev sure had a hard time of it. He sounds a good man. I would like to meet him one day. What work did he do?'

'He worked for Cobb and Co. Their best driver I heard,' replied Giuseppe.

In the mornings, two boats filled with prisoners rowed to the shore. Reggie sat up on the bow and called the stroke. Two guards on horseback marched them single file along the beach to the building site. The prisoners sang as they marched. They learnt to lay stone in interesting and varied patterns. It was hard work and the wall grew solid but slow. At the end of the day Ned would stand back and admire his work. He had inherited some of his dad's trade skills he thought. When the storms came before, as they did, the waves pounded against the soft, white sand eroding the coast line. Now, they pounded against a solid, rock wall which protected the rapidly developing real estate behind it.

The guards enjoyed the company of the prisoners. They were generally a happy lot. The sunny environment by the sea maybe had something to do with it. Soapy liked to run. His lean physique was suited to such an activity. When his team finished their work early, he was allowed to run along the beach back to the boats. Ned would run with him, and although no competition for the lithe Soapy, he got fitter and could stay with him for part of the distance. A guard would follow on his horse. He pulled the struggling Reggie up behind his saddle. 'You, my little friend, can travel with me.' Reggie scrambled up beaming at his elevated status in life. Soapy with his gracefully, tapered limbs and relaxed easy stride loped effortlessly over the sand. Ned struggled when he ran out of breath, but he was not one to accept defeat easily. He took hold of the horse's tail as the guard cantered alongside, and allowed himself to be pulled along. The three overtook Soapy in what appeared to be a strange combination linked by cantering horse. The comical scene was too much for Soapy, and he collapsed in fits of laughter.

Other days, Ned would watch the light rain sweep across the white capped ocean like a low mist hanging over the Ranges. It made him homesick. Ned would lean his head over the railing and look longingly into grassy, green depths of the sea imagining he was back in the Wombat Ranges. Working on the stone walls, they could see people going about the lives in the nearby streets. One day Ned saw a Cobb and Co coach traveling up the street with a grey mare out front. The coach pulled up about a stone's throw away and the driver went into a store. Ned looked again. He had never seen such a smart coach; shiny black with gold trim; and the horses beautifully turned out, trimmed, their coats glossy.

'Soapy,' he said, 'I have a grey filly at home just like the one out front there...bred her myself I did...she looks a beauty, doesn't she...I can tell she's a mare even from this distance.'

'Horses, horses...that's all you think about...me... I can take or leave them,' said Soapy.

Ned's gaze was riveted on the mare. He swore there was something familiar about that horse, the way she stood, the way she held her head. These are things an astute horseman does not easily forget. The mare sniffed the breezes coming off the sea, and turned her head in his direction. There was something in those gentle, cooling breezes that reminded her of her birth place, a human scent that took her back to bush stable not so many years ago. It pricked her ears and alerted her. The driver returned from the store. Ned saw him stroke the mare's neck as he passed her on his way to the coach.

'Did you get me them smokes, Kev?' the co-driver asked.

Ned's eyes were glued to the mare. As if drawn by invisible force, he began to walk towards her.

'What do you think you are doing Kelly? get back to work before I cat-of-nine tail you,' yelled the guard.

'Did you see those convicts building that wall?' asked Kev.

'Yeah,' said his co-driver 'I thought the black haired, young fella was about to do a runner...his attention seemed riveted on your mare.'

'He'd be a good judge of horse flesh then,' said Kev as he looked in Ned's direction. He flicked the reins but he couldn't get his mare to move out in her usual confident manner. She baulked and seemed to want to stay. Kev lightly cracked his long whip above her ears, and she startled back into reality and strode off.

'That's better,' he said.

When Ned saw her baulk not wanting to leave, he instinctively ran towards her but the guard was right next to him on his horse grabbing him by the arm and pulling him back.

'I don't want you to get into trouble, Ned,' he said.

Ned let out deep sigh, thanked the guard and went back to his wall building.

'What's the matter mate?' said Soapy to Giuseppe, 'you look as though you seen a bloody ghost.'

'I reckon that driver was Kev Kavanagh...that fella I was telling you about who was married to Lucille and gave me a belting,' said Giuseppe coming out from hiding behind the wall

'I could swear that mare...no...it was nothing...just dreaming,' said Ned.

'I know all about bloody dreamin, Ned, said Soapy. 'When I get out, I'm going back to my dreamin land. My heart sick of white-fella ways.'

'You will be lucky to have any country left, Soapy...maybe mission house, no more walkabout for your mob.'

'I'll go to desert. My people travel there...many years live in that country...no pesky white fella there.'

When their time came, the prison authorities released Ned and Soapy together. Ned arranged to have two horses to travel home, one being for Soapy. On the way, when they camped in the bush, Soapy left without a sound. His people came for him in the middle of the night. Leading them was King Billy in a soiled, big, white cowboy hat. Ned didn't hear a thing. All that was left was Soapy's clothes, a horse and a note scribbled on piece of paper.

'Have gone with my mob, Ned...one day we meet again and have good time, like white-fella jail.'

'Goodbye, Soapy,' said Ned as he packed his gear for the final leg home but he was glad Soapy was with his people. He was feeling excited about reuniting with his mob but a little apprehensive. Would things be the same after this time away? He felt, when Dan, his mum and sisters visited, they were hiding something. He would soon know the cause of their uneasy reticence.

I'm long tall Texan, I wear a ten-gallon hat

Kit Carson.
Actual events in the lives of Kit Carson, Wild Bill Hickok, California Joe, Billy the Kid and many other western gods and demi gods furnished departure points for wild plotting and violent action. A friend once showed Kit Carson the cover of a dime novel which pictured the plainsman slaying several Indians with one hand while he clasped a fainting maiden with the other. The old scout studied the lurid cover through his spectacles for a long time, finally drawling, 'That may have happened but I ain't got no recollection of it.' The American West – Dee Brown.

Not far from Elly's bar, two riders rode for their lives. Two riders who had travelled the vast Pacific Ocean between the USA and Australia, disembarked on a lonely beach, and took off into the wilderness. Their horses were dropped into the sea from a boom swung off the ship, sinking in a grand splash, and then rising to the surface snorting and paddling to a golden shoreline. The two men, illegal immigrants, rowed their small dinghy leading the swimming horses to the golden beach fringed with dense, green foliage. They chose the isolated coast of eastern Australia for it was unlikely that a deserter from the battle of the Little Bighorn and Custer's 7th Calvary, and his mate, a drink sodden General from Ole Dixie, would have gained official access in one of her Majesty's ports.

Darrington, alias Roy Kingsly had money, and that was all he needed to get them into Australia without having any questions asked. The money was in the form of four solid gold bars, one in each of the four saddlebags. Roy also had in his saddlebag a map of their intended route to the Victorian gold fields, and one memento to his past life, an official Army manual describing the ways of the Indian. He thought it may come in handy in this sparsely inhabited land, and for handling their natives of whom he had heard and knew little. Roy was though a little worried. When they were about to leave from a non-descript port on the West Coast, people lined the wharf waving goodbye to the passengers. In the crowd Roy saw a face he thought he recognized, a distant relative. Their faces met for instant and Roy saw him reach for his bag and take out a spyglass. Before the relative could get a good fix on him, Roy dashed below deck and did not resurface until the coastline had disappeared from sight.

The two immigrants eventually arrived on the east coast of Australia. After rowing to shore with their horses, they would ride due west from the coast along the little used tracks until they hit the Melbourne to Sydney road, travel down it for a short distance, and then across the Ranges to Bendigo. Roy had not been on such a long trip since his days with Custer and as for Virgil...well, he would tell you he had damned well ridden most of States during his time in the Civil war. He rode with General Jeb Stuart, and that man sure could ride. He could gallop into the black night as though it was daylight, ride long distances circling behind the Union Army, and attacking with his cavalry as the Blue Coats slept in their tents.

'We been ridin on bush tracks for days now and not seen anyone except them big lizards and hoppin animals, them hop along Cassidy's, and every kind of bird one can imagine. Those, what did you say, cock- a- toos or cock- a -threes, big white birds... they sure can squawk. Everything is different... the trees, the animals, and I haven't seen any inhabitants...is there anyone living in this god damned country?'

'Sure Virgil. It belongs to the Queen of England. From what I've been told they only sent their convicts out here but the toffs have got interested now that there's money to be made and land and gold aplenty.'

'What about Red Indians, Roy? You got them redskins over here too.'

'I sure hope not, Virgil. I hope I have seen the last of them murderous heathens. There is a native Aborigine I think, but where he lives, what he wears, or what he rides, I don't have a doggoned clue.'

Soon the bush began to recede and they saw signs of civilization. Small farmhouses, grazing stock and travelers came into view. Passing riders stared at them for what reason they were not able to make out.

'Howdy partner,' said Roy but they only chuckled and rode on.

'What's causing them to behave so strange?' said Virgil.

'It's got me baffled,' replied Roy.

'I'm sure I heard them laugh...what's so funny. We don't look funny... do we?'

'Of course not, Virgil' said Roy indignantly. 'We didn't attract any attention back home in this clobber. Why should it be different here? It's probably our horses, I reckon.'

Roy had on his favorite Custer outfit which featured his buckskin coat with long tassels attached to the sleeves, his broad, white ten-gallon hat, maroon pants with a white stripe down the leg; and fancy, expensive buffalo cowboy boots and luminous, silver spurs that glinted in the hot Australian sun. Virgil wore his full-length white dust slicker protecting his black three-quarter coat with tails and a black ten-gallon hat of the same style as Roy's. As they rode along if your eyesight was good, you could spy Roy's silver colt six shooters, peeping menacingly from their holsters. Virgil had his small derringer concealed in his boot. The old habits of the Wild West die hard, and the two did not forget the times where their gun toting ways had saved their lives.

'It looks as though we're coming to a Town so we might cash in one of these gold bars at the Bank and get ourselves some tucker in the local saloon,' said Roy.

'Sounds pretty good to me,' replied Virgil, 'I could do with a few home comforts since we had some fun with them hula hula girls in their grass skirts on the way over.'

As they rode into the main street, Sarge's clerk was idly staring out the office window.

'Come quickly Sarge... have a gander at these two dudes.'

Sarge dropped his newspaper and strolled to the street window,

'What's bothering you boy? You should be balancing those books and not looking at the scenery...Jesus, I see what you mean. There must be a circus coming or something.'

And look at those horses...I've never seen anything like it. They're like ponies but such broad muscled rear ends and the color on that blue-blacky.'

'Like a washerwoman's bum, don't you think Sarge,'

'Don't talk dirty with me, boy.'

'Sorry Sarge, but look at them fancy saddles with that big horn sticking up.'

'I said don't talk dirty, boy. I won't tell you again.'

'Sarge, shouldn't we go out and talk to them... see what its all about. They seem to be attracting a lot of attention,' said Cyril excitedly.

'It's not against the law to wear weirdo clothes and ride up the street on funny looking horses as far as I know my boy. We'll just watch them a bit.'

'Sarge, they pulled up out the front of the bank!'

'I know boy...I've got eyes...I can see.'

'Sarge...they're goin in the Bank.'

'Git them rifles boy...we'll mosey on up and see what's cooking.'

Sarge and his clerk walked up the street to the bank as the townsfolk scurried for cover. Sarge opened the door and saw the bank manager handling over a large bundle of notes to Roy.

'Git em up boys' said Sarge pointing his rifle at the two oddly attired strangers.

'You taken leave of your senses, Sarge,' demanded the Manager, 'allow me to introduce our new and most welcome customers...Texans...all the way from the US of A. Sarge meet Roy Kingsly and Virgil Mc Gee, the Second.'

'I know I can count,' said Sarge putting down his rifle.

'No Sarge, you don't understand... the second...it's part of his name.'

'I'm sorry fellas,' said Sarge apologetically, 'but we have to be careful in these parts. I have only recently arrested our most dangerous outlaw single handed...isn't that right Cyril.'

Cyril didn't reply.

'Sure Sheriff...I understand...no offence taken...I take a few precautions myself,' said Roy pulling his six shooter and spinning it on his finger and deftly letting it fall back into its holster.

'It's not the custom to wear guns in this country, Roy. I'll have to ask you to leave them with me whilst you stay in my town.'

'I'm happy to oblige, Sheriff. We only intend to stay for a bit of a cleanup and feed. By the way do you sell hamburgers in this town?'

'Hamburgers...what the hell are they?'

'Never mind Sheriff...it's a long story. We'll just go to the Saloon if you don't mind.'

'We call it the pub here,' said Cyril.

'I could do with a good soap up,' said Virgil rubbing the dust off his slicker.

'Let us show you the way to the pub,'

'Much obliged Sheriff,' said Roy doffing his Stetson.

The two left the pub the next morning all refreshed but finding a large crowd surrounding their horses. The town Mayor had heard of the Yanks arrival and had brought his committee to meet his new guests. There was handshaking all around and a lot of interest in the unusual looking animals and ornate saddlery.

'What kind of horses are these?' asked one of the townsfolk.

'Mines an appy, and the other is a steel dust horse ridden by my partner.' said Roy, who by now had become accustomed to the curiosity of the inhabitants.

'Whatta ya use em for, mate?'

'Why everything, partner...stock work...they're good with cattle...stop and turn on a dollar they can, racing – nothin around here can beat them. If you like we can have a race down the main street sometime but I have to git a little weight off me hoss.

At that moment down the street came Cyril on his big clumper.

'Mr Kingsly...Sarge has asked me to return these shooters to you with his compliments.'

'Much obliged my good friend. I must say you folk are mighty friendly people and I'm pleased to have made your acquaintance. Where did you get that big hoss from, Deputy?'

Big Bertha stood there – a rough coated, feather legged, ungainly horse with one redeeming feature – an honest face. The big mare didn't bear comparison to the compact, sleek muscled, shiny American horses next to her.

'Sarge got him for me, Mr Kingsly- she's a beauty don't you think?'

'I'll tell you what lad, if you ever want to sell her, let me know.'

'You like her that much, Mr Kingsly,' said Cyril proudly.

'Sure thing lad – I'd get a lot of steaks out of her.'

The gathering audience laughed. Roy the Cowboy slapped the clerk on the back, swung into his big horned saddle, wheeled a few neat blindingly fast spins that made the audience dizzy, reined his horse back on his hind legs, and let off a few rounds into the air from his six-shooter yelling, 'yeeee haaaaa.'

Cyril protested,

'Er, er, Mr King, Mr Kingsly, you are not allowed to shoot a firearm in public place in Australia...firearms act section A. 2 paragraph 5 B I think.'

'What the blazes, boy...it's just letting off a bit of high spirits...who could object to that... none of you lot,' he added waving his shiny, pearl handled pistol towards the admiring crowd.

'Not at all, Mr Kingsly,' they chorused.

Roy galloped off in a cloud of dust yelling, 'hi ho Silver.'

'Ooohs and ahhhs,' came from the gathering crowd of onlookers.

'He might be the Lone Ranger,' said a spectator who was known to read the dime novels coming from America.

'I sure would like one of them big hats,' said one.

'But his mate didn't look like Tonto,' replied another.

'Why didn't you chase Mr Kingsly on Bertha,' one said to Cyril, and the crowd laughed. Cyril blushed and plodded off back to his office adjusting his glass bottomed spectacles and a little confused as to what was so funny about him explaining the laws of Her Majesty to a couple of Yankees.

Ma boomerang did come back in a big hat

The kiley, or boomerang, is a thin curved missile, which can be thrown by a skilful hand so as to rise upon the air, and its crooked course may be, nevertheless, under control. It is about two feet four inches in length, and nine and a half ounces in weight. One side, the uppermost in throwing, is slightly convex, the lower side is flat. It is amazing to witness the feats a native will perform with this weapon, sometimes hurling it to astonishing heights and distances, from which, however, it returns to fall beside him; and sometimes allowing it to fall upon the earth, but so as to rebound, and leap, perhaps, over a tree, or strike some object behind.
Australia, its history and present condition William Pridden

Roy was always the showman. Virgil caught up with Roy about two miles out of town.

'You went on about our horses, Roy. Why didn't you tell them they knock up after about ten miles?'

'Listen Virgil, you have to be a salesperson. Give em bullshit. They're look a bit backward here, you know convict stock, and you saw it...they believed everything I told them. You never know Virgil, I might want to return one day and sell some of these steel dusts to them. It be no good if I told them they are rooted after ten lousy miles...would it. They wouldn't be buying them what with their distances between towns...a man would need five steel dusts to get to the next town. Mind you I'm not talking about my Blue Doggy...when he is fit, he'll give any horse a run for his money.'

'Yeah, but some horses are naturally fit and your horse has got a bit of thoroughbred blood in him.'

'Listen Virgil, when are you going to learn...I hustle and I bullshit... in the end they're happy for me to take their money...they're ripe for picking in this country. You mark my words, Virgil...give up singing them mournful songs for a livin and sell, sell, sell and the world sings with you. I could sell them bottled horse piss for medicine and they would thank me for it. That's why I got money and you got sweet fuck all, Virgil.

It can be anything...hamburgers, Hoss's, livestock, girls. It's the bullshit that wins every time...not telling them the truth whatever that is. That's good ole American entrepreneurship and it works. And it wins hearts and it puts dollars in your pocket...I tell you what Virgil, the next little woman we see, I'll prove it to you.'

'Roy...loyalty, honour means a lot to me...it's in my breeding. Say what you like but I don't feel good if I cheat people ...that's the way I am and I can't change. I don't like what's happened to me Roy; and I don't like what happened to my men during the war; they died terrible deaths and why I survived I do not know. Everything that meant something to me has gone; my wife, my kids, my estate, my workers. Mind you, I said workers Roy, not slaves, because I looked after them well and they wanted to return to me after the war but there was nothing to come back to. They used my grand mansion as a stable and then burnt it down. My land has been divided and sold up and what money I got I spent on booze to forget.'

'Fuck your sense of honour, Virgil...it's just snobbishness...that's all that is...you think it's below you landed gentry from the South to sell, to git out of your big plantation houses with their tree lined drives and all them slaves to do your dirty work...so you pretend to be high and mighty. The world has too many do-gooders, Virgil, and not enough salesmen. Salesmen save the world...they make it go round...they give jobs to people and they advance backward countries like this place here, Austria.'

'It's Australia, Roy.'

'Yeah...whatever Virgil...you hear that bird in these Ranges, Virgil...that's what they call a kookaburra or jackass over here. Listen to him real good, Virgil, because he's got it right. He's laughing at what you're telling me, Virgil.'

Virgil tired of arguing with Roy, let out a couple of rolling yodels that echoed back into the Ranges and silenced the rude, grey and white feathered bird with the long, pointed beak. He just sat in his hollow tree trunk silenced by the alien sound and was looking to swoop on a unsuspecting snake that happened to slither by or a fish that came too close to the surface of the reedy billabong.

'Let's have a rest and give our horses a drink from that water hole over there.'

'Good idea, Roy...I am just about done in and in need of a rest.'

The two dismounted and led their horses to the billabong decked with pretty wild flowers and bright water lilies. Their horses were exhausted and thirsty after Roy's exhibition gallop and drank greedily of the clear, sweet water.

'Old Blue Doggy lost a lot of his fitness on that boat trip,' said Roy as he loosened his girth.

The two visitors studied the dense bush land around them. The ghost gums rose straight as a gun barrel into the sky with their solid and perfectly sculptured trunks of creamy white, while beneath them was a luxuriant growth of green ferns thriving in the shade of the canopy. What held their fascination were several odd-looking plants of an exotic and ancient shape.

They strained their eyes to observe more closely. They saw a spike like figure growing to a height of about six feet and opening out in the top half with grass like foliage falling like hair over the black trunk.

'I ain't ever seen such a strange tree,' said Roy. He looked away but then darted his head back quickly.

'God damn it, Virgil, I thought for a moment I saw one of them trees move.'

'You imagining things, Roy...the heat of this place is getting to you...it's mighty hot under that blazing sun.'

'Those strange plants are coming at us, and they have spears, Virgil.'

'Them black devils look like the werewolves of London if ever I saw one, Roy.'

It was King Billy of the local tribe taking out a few of his young warriors on a hunting party. They were naked except for a loin cloth made of reed. As they advanced the two frightened travellers could see one had a small wallaby draped over his shoulder whilst another carried a dead goanna. At least two or three had long wooden spears and the others carried a mixture of reed bags, wooden artefacts and a waddy. The waddy was a solid stick used to knock their prey senseless. Their slim, dark bodies were decorated with white paint and their bushy, hair sprung out from their heads engendering a fearsome quality that unnerved the two riders.

'Should we make a run for it, Roy?'

'No Virgil...I've had some experience with savages. If you run, they attack...it's the predator instinct in them. Just stay stock still and look brave.'

The small party of aborigines were talking animatedly amongst themselves. The older native being their leader said to his mob,

'See white fella with dat big, white hat and frilly coat...I'm thinking he kill our sacred, white kangaroo to make dat big hat.'

'Maybe frilly necked lizard or porcupine to make dat coat too, King Billy.'

'Bugger the lizard and porcupine...plenty of dem about but not our white kangaroo. Him very rare. Spirit God live in him see...that why he white and others red and grey...you boys should know dat if you listen proper to my dreamtime stories.'

'Too right, King Billy... dem bloody, white fellas show no respect for our beliefs. Want me spear him in leg, King Billy...make him run crooked like a winged cockatoo...teach him lesson he not forget.'

'No...too many white fellas come after us then...chase us into swamps and take our women but I like that dat big hat. Could do proud corroboree with dat hat. Think you young fella who good with the boomerang get me dat hat.'

'No worries, King Billy.'

The young warrior threw his boomerang a good distance to the side of the two men.

'Don't do anything, Virgil... that stick is not aimed at us. I think they are only trying to warn us... it will land harmlessly in the waterhole.'

'I don't think so Roy... it's turning around and coming straight for your head...you'd better duck, Roy.'

'This is no time for practical jokes, Virgil. You're not going to fool me.

'Woooosh.'

Off came Roy's beautiful, white hat spinning its way back to the young warrior leaving Roy stunned and bareheaded.

'That's it, Virgil...let's make a run for it.' They leapt on their horses and galloped off not daring to look back.

The young warrior caught the hat but there was no boomerang.

He was distraught.

'King Billy...ma boomerang didn't come back.'

'Stuff the boomerang...gimme dat sacred hat,' said Billy grabbing the ten-gallon Stetson and placing it on his head.

'We go home now boys. You have done well today...learn many things and we'll have big celebration tonight.'

'Something knocking on my head,' said King Billy 'maybe it's the great bulla spirit trying to tell me something. I'd better take it off and listen.'

'You bloody galah... look here is your boomerang in my hat.'

'Sorry King Billy,' said the boy elated at the return of his favourite weapon.

'Yeah... that was a good throw ...you, young fella, can have first bite of the goanna or possum tonight for dat good work but not the wallaby...dats mine,' said King Billy admiring his big, white hat made of white kangaroo hide or so he thought.

'I think I prefer the witchiti grubs and wild bee honey, King Billy,' the boy replied looking a little sheepish.

'You young fellas always eatin dem sweet things...not good for ya...you gotta eat meat boys...its possum or nothin. Now shut up while I listen to dis hat talkin to me ...maybe it tell me somethin important.'

'What dat big hat tellin you, King Billy?'

'Shoosh you young fellas...have respect for bulla spirit...it will not speak if too much yabba yabba.'

The mob went quiet for a few minutes, stood still and watched King Billy with the hat pulled down over his eyes concentrating.

'It dark in here,' said King-Billy.

He then began to sing and chant and fell on his knees – then prostrate on the ground with his legs stuck in the air and shaking violently. Suddenly as though taken over by a invisible force, he went deathly still and a deep, serious voice seeming to come from the depths of his newly acquired big, white Stetson said,

'Soapy Emu comin back to his mob from whitefella jail in big smoke.'

The young bucks looked at each other in amazement.

'Soapy,' they yelled with glee and did a bit of a dance.

'Tell us more, big, white hat,' they demanded.

The big, white hat replied,

'Dats right boys. He with dat Kelly boy, and dem ridin horses back home after done lock up time.

'Let's go boys, and get Soapy...give him big corroboree welcome,' said King Billy jumping up from the ground and resetting his hat so that he could see daylight again. King Billy really could communicate with the spirits. By this time they had forgotten the two frightened riders fleeing for their lives and riding hell for leather from the werewolves of London, or was that Austria...no...Australia.

Dancing in the dark

Cowboy hoes it down.

The cowboy enters the dance with a peculiar zest not stopping to divest himself of his sombrero, spurs, or pistols... a more odd, not to say comical, sight is not often seen than the dancing cowboy. With the front of his sombrero lifted at angle of fully forty five degrees, his huge spurs jingling at every step or motion, his revolvers slapping up and down like a retreating sheep's tail, his eyes lit up with excitement, liquor and lust he plunges in and hoes it down at a terrible rate in the most approved yet awkward country style, often swinging his partner clear off the floor for an entire circle then balance all with an occasional demonical yell... all this he does entirely oblivious to the whole world and to the balance of mankind. After dancing furiously, the entire set is called to waltz to the bar where the boy is required to treat his partner and of course himself which he does not hesitate to do time and again although it costs him fifty cents each time. The West – Jon Lewis.

The days passed slowly for Elly since her husband died. Elly missed a man she could be close to. There were her kids and the pub and that kept her busy enough. Ned was doing time, and would soon be free. She had plenty to do but she longed for the intimacy of a man in her life. She felt her life to be empty. She needed a man to quell her rising temperature and despondency. She longed to be courted again like she was in her youth. She was grateful for the money from Harry. The pub gave her independence. Without it she would have gone broke. Her customers were miners and itinerants passing between the cities, and a few locals. Many were shady characters; nervous, fidgety men, gulping down their liquor, anesthetizing their ghosts, and riding on into the blue yonder to try their luck. Chance, luck, good fortune...in a pioneer country it seemed that these words were the only salvation for many a gambler as though the land was one giant lucky dip. Up and down and across the wide expanses they rode hoping that fate would deliver them one good hand from the deck of misery, separation from family and brittle existence written on most of its cards. Elly knew what it was like to struggle, and it was that empathy with her customers that made them stay longer to unburden their sad stories. Often, she wished she had remained quiet, but she had to pay the bills and the longer they stayed the more they drank. Years listening to the same endless, sad stories left her numb. It was driving her down and making her lethargic and listless. She began to behave in odd eccentric ways. She longed for the welcoming smile, the firm embrace of an energetic, wholesome man to give the simple joy of male physicality to her life.

Now in her late thirty's, she noticed in not too subtle ways she was losing her feminine allure. Men talked to her but there was no play, no flirting or eagerness in their voice. Just conversation as though she were another man and an empty look across the bar. The ones who were interested held no attraction for her with their hang dog expressions and eternal regrets. Some days she would drink a little too much whisky and drift about in sort of haze listening to sad, Irish melodies and ballads played by the sullen squeeze box player from the nearby town. As the pitiful, lilting tunes ebbed and flowed around her, she began to dance dreamily about the darkened bar and tables oblivious to everyone and everything, and possessed by the intoxicating mood the instrument evoked. Sometimes, without the music, she was just plain intoxicated, bumping into the bar tables, stumbling over and struggling up with the help of a mouthful of expletives. Dan and Steve had seen it all before. They eyed her solitary waltz, despaired, and yet on the odd occasions would out of sympathy join in. There in the half dark of a not very much patronized bar, the sullen man lovingly stroked the pearly buttons of his worn accordion, while two boys danced together, and a lost, middle aged widow waltzed alone dreaming of her youth and better times.

'I am sure I can hear their whoops and horses gaining on us,' yelled Roy strapping his horse from side to side, and plying his fancy spurs to Blue Doggy's hide.

'We must get help...we won't outrun them if they are anything like our redskins...I hope there is a Fort nearby.'

As they rounded a sharp corner on the track, they saw welcome signs of civilisation. It was Elly's bush pub.

'We'll have to make a stand here, Virgil...our horses won't last any longer.

It looks pretty rough but it will at least provide some cover when them black devils start to circle us...grab your repeater and we'll barricade ourselves in.'

The two horses, exhausted, skidded to a halt. Roy and Virgil grabbed their rifles and ran to the veranda, pushing through the swinging doors to the dimly lit interior. Adjusting his eyes to the darkness Roy yelled,

'Anyone home?'

They saw shadowy figures gliding about the room to a slow waltz being pumped out on an old sqeeze box. Elly swept by hardly noticing the two strangers at the door.

'Maam, Maam, begging your pardon Maam, please...there's an emergency. We are being pursued by black indians on their horses...I'm sure they not far behind. I could hear their yells...we'd better bunker down. It will be a fight to the death.

Can someone go for the Cavalry?

Is there a Fort nearby?

They won't scalp us, will they?'

Virgil knocked out a window with the butt of his rifle and readied himself for the onslaught. Roy went pale and his legs began to go weak at the knees.

'My God...I'm not feeling well...I have terrible memories crowding in on me...I can't breathe...I think I'm going to faint...for Christ's sake somebody help me.'

Elly stood there utterly puzzled by the drama unfolding before her. On seeing Roy about to faint she sprang into action laying him down on the bar floor and cradling his head in her lap. The boys poured a strong whisky and took it to him unhurried by his pleas.

'Here friend, drink this and you will feel better. Our natives are not hostile and at least not in these parts, and they don't ride horses. They walk and run. You are imagining things. Now calm down. Everything will be okay,' said Elly.

'You sure Ma'am...you sure that's right...you not foolin with me are ya?'

Roy's nerves were shot.

'Get my medicine...quick Virgil,' he cried. I fear I'm about to die in this God forsaken country. O'God help me.'

Virgil ran to Blue Doggy's saddle bag and scrimmaged for Roy's bottle of pills but before he could return, Roy had fainted. A surge of sympathy flooded into the Elly's breast tinged with a degree of puzzlement in this foreigner with the twangy voice, and helpless in her arms. She cushioned his head in her lap and stroked his luxuriant, shoulder length locks like he was her child soothing his fears.

'Get a blanket and a pillow, Dan,' she called 'and Steve...you get the smelling salts.'

She tenderly sponged the beads of sweat from his troubled brow. Emotions other than motherly stirred in her, some she had not felt since Red had passed away. When Steve brought the smelling salts, she hesitated. Holding and stroking the stranger's curly, shoulder length locks, it was she who was being revived. She looked up at Steve holding the small bottle and gently pushed back his extended hand. Then, as if in a hypnotic trance, she began to hum a lullaby.

'Mum...what the hell are you doing...we don't know these men...they sure sound and act a little strange to me?' said Dan as he snatched the smelling salts from Steve.

'Here give him a whiff of this.'

She acted as though she didn't hear, lost in a world of her own. He shrugged his shoulders looked at the others and retired to a table. In the background the accordion player picked up her mood and began to pump away on his accordion. Virgil too, not able to resist his propensity to croon, took the cue and began to sing.

Dan looked at Steve and shook his head.

'I don't know anything,' he said.

Elly looked at Virgil and smiled. She instantly liked the two men and their eccentric behaviour and unusual accents. Elly took the bottle, placing it near Roy's nose. Roy whiffed the bracing scent and awoke. He did not jump or startle. He just dreamily opened his eyes and looked up. Up into the eyes of love... mature, unconditional, selfless love that beamed down on him, warming him like the rays of a winter's sun. He gently took hold of her hand. He could see although worn it had not entirely lost the bloom of youth. For what seemed like an eternity, they both balanced on the emotion as though on the edge of a precipice. Roy gazed into Elly's kind, benevolent eyes. Incipient love, at first fragile, kicked into life and then slow burned towards their hearts like a long fuse to a stick of dynamite. The middle aged, lonely bar keeper had prayed for this moment. She didn't know when or how it would come but she was sure this was it. Everything in her intuitive, suffering, restless body told her it was right. Even if it was not right, she was determined to make it right.

'Into my arms O'Lord,' she said, and that was how the good Lord delivered him.

The gaudily, costumed Yank literally fell into her ample bosom from another world across the wide, blue ocean. He was no itinerant drunk boring the pants off her with the usual tales of misery and woe. He was mysterious, sensitive, vulnerable and... and... funny...well he spoke funny although she dare not say it. There in the darkness and half-light of a pub made of logs and mud infill, the carefree ways of her youth were resurfacing faster than her foreign visitors rode to escape the local natives, and that was pretty quick in any language.

Roy sneaked a sly look in Virgil's direction.

Virgil looked away embarrassed by a smugness he did not like.

Roy pulled Elly onto him. She pretended to protest and then laughed uncontrollably taken in by the man's impulsiveness, bravado and that nasally accent. Like two kids they wrestled, and it didn't worry her, an elderly woman in front of her son, rolling about the floor in a way that could only be described as lacking common decency and respectability. But they were boring virtues espoused by a morality that played little part in her life. Roy lifted her to her feet, and together they waltzed around the room weaving in between and around the tables while the others watched incredulous. Roy then pulled away and hoed it down like a real cowboy with his boots, spurs, and six shooters all rattling like a steam train belting down the track and his white chaps flapping like a big eagle about to take off. It was a scene the Australians had never seen or envisaged. If they had, the man would have been taken to the nearest mental asylum. Elly stood there watching in stunned amazement, while the music box man began to punch his keys in a mad frenzy to keep up with the frenetic steps of the dancing American. Roy stopped, exhausted from his dance routine, and strolled to the bar real, casual like, and downed a glass of rot gut whisky.

'Yeee haaa,' he yelled and thumped his chest like a big ape from the African jungle. He went for the quick draw of his silver six shooter, fired a shot right at the painting hitting Custer fair square in the head, and clouding it in a veil of dust. He blew the smoke from the barrel, spun it on his finger, flicked it up into the air and landing it safely back in its pouch. He smiled at his small audience who were spellbound, grabbed the whisky bottle off the bar, poured several glasses in a neat row and threw them all down one after the other. He strutted up and down the bar like he owned it, looked at himself in the mirror and straightened his long hair, felt suitably impressed and then turned to face the others with his elbows resting on the counter. His eye caught the Custer painting again. He realised what he had done. He saw General Custer with a hole in his head. Not once but now twice, he had failed his General and let down his country. He felt an immense shame for what he had done, fell to the floor and sobbed.

'No...no...no...am I ever going to be free of this curse that haunts me day and night? I am a sinner unworthy in the sight of the good, Lord Jesus Christ.'

'What the matter? What's he talking about? he's not a bible basher is he?' asked Dan.

'He's not well,' said Virgil, 'them natives have given him a terrible fright what with their spears and boomerangs...and he lost his big, white hat too...specially made from beaver hide it was...the best there is. He was mightily attached to that hat... maybe he got a bit of sun stoke without it... the sun sure is hot in these parts.'

Elly rushed to his aid and with the help of Virgil they carried him to a bed where he slept for a day. When he woke, he saw there sitting in chair beside his bed a woman in love, a dedicated woman.

'Roy,' she said 'Virgil has told me all about you, and I am impressed. Now you stay here for a week or so and get better. I'll cook you some fine Australian tucker and look after you like a loving wife. And I'm going to get you a new hat, an Australian one, Roy... made of rabbit skin, an Akubra, the best there is. You'll see, you will like it as much as the one you lost back there at the water hole.'

'A what?' he said.

'Akubra,' she repeated again

'No need to swear at me, Ma'am,' said Roy

No Roy... it is a hat, an Australian hat like the big Stetson you lost but it's made of rabbit fur,' said Elly

Roy kissed her hand. 'That's right neighbourly of you, Ma'am, but can you git me one made of white, buffalo hide if it's not asking too much - I'm not too keen on bunny fur.'

'I will, Roy...now don't you worry...you are in safe hands now and I am goin to see that you are well looked after.'

As disapproving as the boys may have been, they had little hope of stopping Roy waltzing his way into Elly's life. Virgil stayed at the pub for a few months, but moved on to try his luck in the gold fields. Roy gave him a gold bar to cash and asked him to keep in touch. Though Elly was much years older, Roy made her a young again and put energy into her step, and much needed bounce into her lumpy, feather bed mattress. Elly's girls liked his jaunty, happy-go-lucky manner, and laughed at his flamboyant clothes and weird accent. It would be wrong to say that Roy's love for Elly was superficial. He was in love with this older woman but like his horses, one wondered whether he'd last the distance.

Before long Roy's knack for risk taking and making money led to a resurgence of interest in Elly's bar. With Roy's Yankee 'can do' attitude and his hamburger recipe, there was soon a lineup of customers for lunch and evening meals the likes of which the locals had not seen before. Roy had taken his recipe for the hamburger from his success in America, and it was a instant success. Extra staff including Elly's daughters had to work long hours in the bar to keep up with the demand. Customers came from far and wide to hear Virgil sing his sorrowful ballads in his deep South American accent which they loved and yelled for more. He taught one of the Elly's daughters, Grace, to sing honing her natural skills, adding pathos and poise to her youthful, angelic voice. She responded by hitting the highs and low notes with a near perfect pitch, and hidden in that reedy voice of an innocent child, was a tremulous quaver tugging at the strings of the emotionally charged lyrics that Virgil taught her. Virgil knew what he was talking about. When he sang them sad songs, the customers sat there quietly listening, some with a few, solitary tears rolling down their stolid faces and dropping onto their hamburgers and diluting Roy's secret recipe for a sauce he rather oddly called ketchup. They didn't even notice the money coming out of their pockets and disappearing into the till. That is not anyone except Roy. He didn't even trust the bank to keep it. He buried it in a steel container in the scrub at a spot that only he knew.

'We'll keep it for the kids,' he said to Elly.

What he didn't explain though was that he was a bit of a kid.

'Billy the kid,' he said, and she smiled.

'Well, I'm Annie get your gun, Roy, so look out.'

'Steady on girl,' said Roy.'

'Ride on, cowboy Roy, ride on,' said Elly as she took a firm grip of his long-barreled pistol.

'Hmmmm...needs a bit of greasin...dont you think Annie?'

'What about a spit and polish? Roy.'

'Mother knows best,' said Roy.

Roy, the cowboy from Illinois

Eager to see his mum and siblings, Ned pushed his horse along at a quicker pace. He trotted through the rivers and creeks leading Soapy's horse, along the narrow, dirt tracks that he remembered, and past the small, struggling farms with their ramshackle sheds. Every now and then he would come across the grand homesteads and treed driveways of the wealthy Squatters. Having learnt the art of stone laying on the sea walls, he was interested in the stonework of these large, imposing buildings and cottages often built by Irish tradesmen from stone found on the property. He liked making the decisions of color, size and shape in the laying of the stones, making each one fit and support the other, to see a pattern emerge, to stand back and feel the stability and permanence of the work that would last for hundreds of years. The construction of the sea walls strengthened his shoulders and arms, hardening his sinews and muscles. Stone made a strong building and a strong body. The Ned returning to his family was no longer a boy but matured in body and mind. Prison was not such a bad experience for him and he made friends and occupied his time usefully. The screws were often decent, hardworking men just doing their job but the lack of freedom made him determined not to return.

As he neared his home his thoughts turned to his mum, brothers and sisters. The family was close after his father's death. They depended on each other, and the girls were growing into womanhood and seeking their own identity, their own friends and relationships. He was the eldest and the responsibility of their care and protection fell to him. He was not going to forget his promise to his Dad. He would get regular work and provide for his family. What he didn't reckon on was the new man in his mum's life...Roy. Elly wanted to tell him herself when he came home. She didn't want him to worry when he was in prison the same as she didn't tell him about his horses. She was unsure how he would receive the news of the new man in her life, after all Roy was not much older than Ned.

Ned's excitement rose when he saw the hazy outline of his home from a nearby hill. As he came into view of the pub, he saw the front door burst open spilling out an assortment of human shapes running towards him. He could hear their animated yells carry across the paddocks and his sisters and mum buffet and grab each other to be the first to be embraced by their long, absent brother. Elly had used a telescope, left by Virgil as a gift, to watch the roads that morning and recognised her son on the hill. Ned jumped off his horse, tied them both to a tree and ran to greet the tidal wave of joy and excitement bearing down on him. They flew into his open arms grabbing and pulling him around the neck, swinging from his legs and forcing him to the ground by the pure weight and urgency of their warm embraces and affectionate kisses. Lost in the rush was the youngest, Nell, a little girl of three years, running as fast as her small, plump and unsteady legs would carry her. The others gave her room as she rushed into the arms of a brother she could not have known, but knew instinctively belonged to her large, fun loving brood.

Hidden from view, a pair of foreign eyes peered out from behind the lace curtains at the boisterous and joyful scene unfolding before him.

'Well...I'll be buggered...the prodigal son returns,' muttered Roy to himself, and quickly resumed his seat in what used to be Red's chair.

The front door flew open. Ned halted in his tracks, bewildered by the stranger sprawled over his Dad's chair puffing smoke rings from an expensive Cuban cigar, and lightly fingering his polished, ornate American cowboy boots. Roy casually looked up.

'Welcome Mr Ned...I'm Roy, the cowboy from Illinois,' and laughed at his poetic greeting.

'Nice to make your acquaintance, Mr Ned. Your mum and the girls have told me a lot about you.'

'Who the hell are you?' asked Ned.

Elly moved quickly between them.

'Ned...I need to speak to you alone for a few minutes...I should have told you before but things have changed a bit since you're been away. Roy, I thought I told you to stay out of the way until we were ready to have you meet Ned.'

'I know apple pie,' he explained, but I heard the commotion and figured I shouldn't be missing out on the fun seeing I am...well...er...part of the family.'

'Part of the family,' spluttered Ned.

Ned and his mum went to a room.

'Ned,' she said 'Roy has been with me for some months now. He's a nice American gentleman, Ned, I hope you will learn to like and accept him as much as we all do. He has helped us a lot with the pub. He has some great ideas Ned. Now, I know I should have told you but what with your Dad going the way he did and you to jail. I was scared how you would take it. I didn't want you to do anything silly. I love Roy, Ned. He has some strange ways I'll agree, but he has made me want to live again. I've had a hard time of it since Red went and you in jail. He's a good help about the place, he's been a dad to the girls, and he sure has put this pub on the map. Did you notice the extensions? Well, Roy is responsible for that - he's taught us to make these things called hamburgers, and we can't keep up with the demand. We mince up beef add some secret ingredients Roy got from the Indians, cook it, and add two pieces of bun...'

'Yeah mum...I get the drift. If it makes you happy I'll go along with it. It might take a bit of time to get used to him. I mean he appears to be not much older than me, mum.'

'I know son, but love comes in many strange ways ...I'm still getting used to it myself. You're a darling boy Neddy, and I know you won't spoil it for me. You'll get to like Roy in time after the initial shock. I'm arranging a big welcoming party for you on the weekend...you're cousins, and Joe and Steve will be there...it will give you a chance to see how popular Roy is with the relations. You know Ned, he keeps Tennessee rapt with his Indian stories...even gave him his old Army manual on the Indian ways. And guess what...the boy is besotted with it. She giggled a little 'he's even taken to dressing like an Indian and painting his horse all these weird colours. Sometimes I think the lot of us should be put in the funny farm. My God, there so much to tell you...he's taken up with that China girl...what's her name Bing, Bong or something like that. Teaching her to ride, would you believe...a China girl ridin a horse...now that is something, I would like to see...her idea, too, so I gather. Tennessee sure is a strange one. One more thing before I finish Ned. I've tried to avoid bringing this up but you have to be told. Sarge took your horses. Shortly after they locked you away, they disappeared from the paddock one night. Sarge said he had a warrant for non-payment of fines.

'Hell no,' said Ned, 'Did they take Music?'

'Yes...I'm afraid they cleaned the paddock out.'

Ned slammed his fist down uttering profanities some of the more colourful learnt from his stay in Her Majesties jail.

'Mum, I asked you about her every time we wrote. I had my heart set on them horses Mum - especially that filly, Music. I don't think I'll ever get one like her again. Everyone told me she was coming along well.'

'I know Ned. I told them to do that. I didn't want to worry you and like I said I didn't want you to do something silly and get a longer jail sentence. You're home and you're well...that's what is important to us...forget the past and get on with your life. No more lairising about Ned. I want you to settle down and go straight...remember what your Pa said to you.'

'He didn't tell you to get married again, Mum.'

'Maybe he did, and maybe he didn't, son. All I know is that it is what I want, and if he don't like that...well it's too bad, but that's no reason for you to be disrespectful. Now that's enough of that talk. You're home now...that's all that matters and we're going to be one big, happy family like before Neddy.'

Ned and his Mum hugged and went out join the others including Ned's new step dad.

'Well, howdy do you do, partner,' said Roy blowing cigar smoke all over Ned.

'Have the girls make you one of my hamburgers, Ned...mighty popular hereabouts they are...or would you prefer a hot dog with some ketchup. They taste nice with one of these fat Cuban cigars. We gotta git you strong and well again, Boy. I got plans for you.'

'What is he talking about, mum?'

'It's ok Ned...you will learn his lingo soon enough. We all have.'

The girls giggled. Roy and his foreign ways were an constant source of amusement to them

In the midnight hour Roy yelled 'more, more, more'

General Jackson of Confederate Army and the 'yell'

One thing interested and delighted him. It was the "rebel yell" of his troops. To this grand chorus he never failed to respond. The difference between the regular "hurrah" of the Federal army, and the irregular, wild yell of the Confederates, was as marked as the difference in their uniforms. The rebel yell was a peculiar mixture of sounds, a kind of weird shout. Jackson was greeted with it whenever he made his appearance to the troops, on the march or in battle; and just as invariably he would seize his old gray cap from his head in acknowledgment, and his "little sorrel," knowing his habit, would break into a gallop and never halt until the shout had ceased. The Annals of the Civil War Written by Leading Participants North and South Alexander Kelly McClure and Charles River Editors.

That night Ned settled into a deep sleep when he was awoken by a blood-curdling yell coming from his mother's room,

'more...more...more Blue Dogeeee...run - they are making ground on us.'

Ned jumped out of his bed.

'Holy duck shit...what the hell was that?'

His mum emerged from the bedroom looking a little dishevelled.

'Its okay Ned...its just Roy having another of his bad dreams. Blue Doggy is his horse and it appears he wants him to go faster; somehow its affected him in the head; don't ask me how cos he don't talk about it and we get this side show about once a month. We've got used to it now but it took a bit of time. He gets upset if you talk about it so we say nothing,' said Dan matter a fact like.

'In fact it makes me laugh now...wait till you hear what happens next. The Indians must have nearly got him sometime in his past.'

'Come on Blue Doggy...we can beat them scalping injuns...sure we can. Jesus, is that you Billy up my arse...oh God, will we ever get out of this.'

Elly stepped in,

'Roy, Roy, wake up...you're having another of those dreams...you'll wake up the kids again with all that yelling.'

Roy startled and woke from his nightmare.

'For Christ's sake help me...I'm shakin all over...I got tremors racing up and down me body...tremors in me backbone...tremors in me knee bone...git me my medicine quick.'

Ned could hear his mum rummaging around in the kitchen.

'Am I'm living in a mad house? asked Ned.

'Its a bit like that,' replied Dan.

They could hear the girls muffling their giggles who after the initial shock came to think it as a bit of a joke. 'One of the girls got hold of a military trumpet,' said Dan trying to restrain his mirth and blew it when Roy had one of his dreams. He crashed out the bedroom window and ran to the stable looking for Blue Doggy until mum tackled him to the ground and got the medication into him. It frightened the living bejesus out of her. She didn't want another husband kicked in the scon after what happened to Dad. It's a real circus here sometimes I tell ya.'

'Shut up you girls,' said Elly, 'it's not nice to be laughing at Roy's illness.'

'Roy don't mind mum,' said Dan.

'No, no... I'll get over it in time,' replied Roy taking his medication.

'Oh yeah, Roy...what about all that trembling...you must have got one terrible fright some time ago to be like that...it's not normal and you should see a big City doctor, Roy,' added Elly.

'Just forget it Elly and let's get back to sleep. I don't like making a ruckus especially when Ned here just come home.'

'That's enough now...all go back to bed- do as you are told... it's your mum speaking. Poor Ned, first night back and he has to put up with this hullabaloo. If we are not careful, he will be goin back to jail for some peace and quiet,' demanded Elly laying down the law.

That morning Ned sat at the breakfast table when Roy emerged shirtless in his short pants and fancy cowboy boots. Ned just about choked on his porridge. The girls tittered in amused embarrassment.

'That's Roy's and mummy's bedroom,' exclaimed the three-year-old seeing Ned's look of confusion. The girls laughed at the child's apparent desire to help Ned understand. Ned patted her chubby, red cheeks.

'It sure gets hot about here...scald a cat it would.' said Roy plonking himself down at the table, and wiping the sweat from his brow.

'Margaret, honey, I'll have one of them fat pancakes with maple syrup and lashings of cream for breakfast thanks...none of that boggy gruel for me. Toss on some hot fries from the pan too love.'

'You mean chips, Roy,' said Margaret.

Roy shook his head, 'cheeky isn't she. You lot sure speak a strange lingo over here, but I'm getting the hang of it.'

'Have a good sleep, Ned,' he asked pouring a cup of imported coffee.

'A little restless,' replied Ned remembering Roy's outburst.

'I slept like a baby, myself,' said Roy.

'You sure did,' replied Dan, 'a screaming one.'

'Was I hollowing again, Elly?'

'Yes, just a bit Roy darling – it don't mind, does it kids?

The kids looked at each other.

'Nah mum, Uncle Roy can't help it,' they chorused.

'Too right children...Uncle Roy is getting better but mind you... don't talk about this to anyone, do you hear,' said Roy moving in his chair, looking at Ned and getting a little uneasy.

When I grow up, I want a pony

Genghis Khan fathers many descendants

After analysing tissue samples in populations bordering Mongolia scientists from the Russian Academy of Sciences believe the brutal ruler has 16 million male descendants living today meaning he must have fathered hundreds if not thousands of children...He chose woman of highest rank. He liked them with small noses, rounded hips, long silky hair, red lips and melodious voices...the greatest pleasure he said is to vanquish your enemies and chase them before you, to rob them of their wealth, to see those dear to them bathed in tears, to ride their horses and to clasp to your bosom their wives and daughters. His armies ravished northern China, central Asia and much of far off Russia - Mail online, Christopher Hudson

To ride is to live

Suddenly the world looked totally different to Naduah. She had ridden before, but always old, broken-down horses, and always surrounded by women as they moved the camp. Now she was alone on the plain with the wind ruffling her half-wild pony's black mane and blowing her own hair. She could feel Wind's muscles rippling between her thighs and knees, and she felt herself swaying with the rhythm of her horse's gait. She felt beautiful and wise and powerful and swift. She wanted to kick Wind's sides and tear off across the plain as fast and as far as she could go. To feel the wind whipping past her and to see the ground flowing away under her as though she were flying. To know that she was one with a beautiful, powerful animal. Ride the Wind Lucia St Clair Robson.

Tennessee studied Roy's Indian manual until he could just about memorize every drawing and page. He loved the natural leathers of the Indian clothes and head gear made from the abundance of animal furs, feathers and pelts; the colorful war paint smeared on their lithe bodies and the signs and decorations embroidered on their tough, little horses with their flowing manes and tails; and the simplicity and artistry of their hand made weapons. He saw how they had braided a loop under their pony's neck and into the mane to balance on as they hung precariously from one side to the other during battle. He studied their weapons like the shields made of hide and hardened by buffalo hoof glue to deflect bullets, the tomahawk, lance and bow, their beautifully adorned buckskin clothes with porcupine quills, and their comfortable tipis embellished with the scenes of battle and counting coup. He dreamt of adopting their lifestyle, imagining he was a Comanche brave riding the vast open Prairies looking for signs from the mighty spirit as to what fate lay ahead, camping by the fast-flowing streams, hunting the buffalo and joining in their rituals and dances. He wanted to let go his dull Anglo-Saxon culture and to live in the rich texture and mythology of Indian life. He already spoke their language...sign language, although not everyone understood him.

On the weekends he rode to the China camp to see and teach Gong how to ride. It was her one and only passion much to his disappointment. She was not an easy student, impatient and wanting to gallop before she could sit to the trot. As she improved, Tennessee swapped her quiet, aged horse for a spirited, piebald pony in the style of the Indian horse and took her out of the safety of the bush yard he had strung together and into the wide, open spaces and misty, mountain tops that she longed to visit and explore. The mountains were vast, wild and uninhabited; the place where heaven and earth met or so the Chinese thought. They were mockingly called 'celestials' by the locals so Gong wanted to go there away from the dirt piles, dust and noise of the mining camps. With a determination that was unrelenting, the China girl became a bold and reckless rider. Her abilities soon matched that of her pony and they became a formidable partnership hell bent on taking those excitements she knew would be denied if she complied with the modest and sedate wishes of her community.

Because he was a stutterer, Tennessee would scribble in his note pad 'balance lightly on the balls of your feet,' and show it to her.

She rode her feet full in the stirrup.

He wrote 'relax at the gallop and sit full in the seat of your saddle,'

She shortened her stirrups, stood high in the saddle and yelled and shrieked her joy to the world in strange, staccato high-pitched voice that had Tennessee shaking his head in disbelief.

'Do not use your leather quirt unless needed,' he wrote.

She spanked her pony vigorously from side to side so that he flew at a blindingly fast speed across the earth.

'Somewhere in this China girl's genetic material dwelt Mongolian blood and the spirit of Genghis Khan, the legendary Mongolian ruler, who with his army of peasant horsemen conquered the then known world. With her black and white pony given to her by an admirer, the stuttering Tennessee Quinn, she was determined to conquer those incessant and obsessive desires that beat upon her foreign heart day and night, and told her she was not the meek, obedient, colorless daughter her community demanded her to be. Because of his color and her heritage, she called him Panda. But he was no lumbering bear.

Before long, Gong and her piebald pony, Panda, would sweep across the flat Australian plains erratically changing direction, circling and looping the loop, rolling back to return from whence she came, stopping, stalling and going into a spin, pirouetting like a prima ballerina; whatever took this unconventional china girl's fancy she did; she accelerating Panda towards a large, ancient red gum with spreading limbs in which a flock of noisy , plump breasted, sulphur crested cockatoos nested and disturbed the solitude with ear piercing, high pitched screeches that rattled your brain. On nearing the big tree, she slid from the saddle her feet lightly touching the earth in a graceful, seamless fluidity of movement between horse and human, skipped a little bird dance around the enormous rough barked and pitted trunk with her arms raised like wings, competing with and singing her delight to her white feathered, fun loving friends.

After a respectful bow to the tree Gods, she stepped back into the saddle and with a swing of the leather reins the enterprising couple rocketed off ascending into the wild and spectacular Ranges bordering her camp; climbing to the craggy mountain tops touched by wispy clouds, yawing on the slippery rocks, and looking down on her people toiling like ants in their garden patch and gold diggings below; and as though with a parting coup de grace to the stunning display of reckless, imaginative horsemanship, the two hurtled down the ravines, skidding and crashing through the bush, leaping over fallen logs, and panicking the grazing kangaroos into flight with Gong riding fast behind and overtaking them like a demonic Indian warrior on a buffalo hunt.

Shortly they burst out of the scrub, the trees, the bush clearings and soft-landed back onto the open plain. Gong, with a grin as broad as the big, blue sky above and as bright as the hot Australian sun, leaned forward over her worn and tatty saddle, and embraced her gallant little horse around his neck with her loving arms. She dismounted on the wrong side but the right side for an Indian and they rested. She cast her eye over her game, little pony checking him for any cuts and bruises but he was so sure footed there were none to see except for a steam rising from him like early morning mist and a glistening, golden honey like sweat.

For the first time in her short, dull, frustrating life, the rebellious Gong was overcome by the adrenaline charged excitement of headlong, howling speed and stultifying danger her pony so gleefully and unhesitatingly gifted to her in the stunning beauty of a pristine Australian bush. Gong had heard her Chinese community mockingly referred to by the Europeans and Australian miners as 'the Celestials'. She didn't mind. As she and Panda slowly ambled their way to the pure, cool, gently flowing waters of a nearby stream to bathe, she truly knew she was in Paradise. Drained of energy, she dismounted by a small stream, unbuckled the girth of her saddle, removed his wet blanket, and washed the sweat and dirt stains from his soiled black and white coat. The game, little pony luxuriated in the cooling waters - splashing, rolling about and snorting like a baby elephant. Together the two sauntered lazily back to the confines of her community.

The other China girls were envious. They resented the freedoms she had stubbornly asserted and that she did not work in the gardens as they were obliged to do. The Elders grudgingly made an exception for Gong but they were not about to give into the others. To retain some dignity, they asked her to circle the gardens on her pony every few days with a kite scarring off the birdlife that plundered their vegetables and fruits. But it was a hard-won peace and Gong was seen as an outsider to be tolerated because of respect they held for her mother.

On her many trips to the mountains, she rested by small colonies of koala bears chewing and getting high on their lemon scented gum leaves. She intently watched their behavior and imitated their little grunts, roars and growls so much so that they stopped chewing and pricked their cute, little ears trying to comprehend the odd guttural sounds coming from below their tree. She loved the way the mothers carried the young on their backs and through patience and a little temptation in food bits she was able to befriend one or two and stroke their furry hides and cute heads. Deep in an untouched garden of Eden, she would see the strange, hopping marsupials, the kangaroos, emerge from the bush to graze on the sweet tasting grasses of the clearings. She giggled and laughed at their attempts to box and kick each other in combat. It got her to thinking. She knew that a few young men in her community had taken to learning and practicing kung fu to protect themselves from the drunken Australian and European miners. She joined with them to learn those movements, interpreted from the animal world, which the Chinese had perfected over the centuries. The fighting techniques of the tiger, panther, monkey, snake, eagle, crane, and the insect, the praying mantis, were closely studied and adapted. Gong, in her inimitable style, would add the kangaroo, and when alone in the mountains with her animal friends, practice her firm stances, her impenetrable blocks, and low, snapping kicks.

Whilst passing the hours there one day, she noticed a lone cub wombat obviously not well and its mother nowhere to be seen. She picked it up and knew that unless it got milk soon it would die. She wrapped the furry bundle in a blanket, put it safely in her saddle bag and took it back to her camp. There she and her mother cared for the strange little marsupial and before long it became plump and healthy. It was devoted to Gong and followed her about like a dog. She named him Wally which she thought was a good honest, Australian name. Because she could not bear to leave her new pet, she made a soft cotton and wool pouch strapped to her back in which she carried him on her pony, and he sat there happily peering about like a contented baby.

When she rode into town on her colored pony, Panda, with Wally the wombat strapped to her back pouch, she really looked a picture and attracted a lot of attention. The boys whistled and laughed at her and her bush baby. She smiled back at them, abused them in Mandarin and putting her fingers into her mouth in the manner of the Australian, sheep farmer, let out a loud piercing whistle that stopped them in their tracks and left their mouths gaping wide in astonishment. This China girl from the mining camp had an uncommon pluck for a demure Asian.

When she went into the shops, Wally waddled behind Gong and remained close to her heels. One young ruffian, eager to impress his mates, followed her, and put his boot into Wally. The little, fat marsupial let out a hiss and rolled like a fluffy ball into the dusty street. Hurt, he squealed and ran to Gong for protection. Gong pacified him and glared at the bully. She then attacked like a panther and struck like a snake, swinging her leg in a neat but lethal circle, and catching the assailant squarely in the groin with her boot, sending him rolling into the street bent over in excruciating pain. She was applauded by the townsfolk who soon became accustomed to this unusual China girl, and greeted her warmly for the efforts she was making to assimilate and the character that she was. Soon the wombat would be too big to carry about and dug holes all over the camp like you would never believe... deep ones. The community complained until one said if he can dig like that, we can make use of him. They asked Gong to take Wally with them to their diggings and try his obsessive digging there. Seeing all the loose dirt about, Wally quickly set to work thrusting out tons of dirt behind him as he disappeared into the bowels of the earth. Gong got worried when he did not reappear and entered the tunnel with a rope around her waist. Some yards down she could just make out Wally asleep on what turned out to be a gold nugget. The Chinese miners were ecstatic when she handed them the heavy, precious metal. Gong led them home with Wally by her heels and the miners in single file singing the praises of the couple. There were no further complaints about either her pony or Wally. Although he did not find gold again Gong was unhappy that Wally was away from his kind, and like a good mother, she gradually introduced him back to the wild after she was sure he would come to no harm and had made friends.

Her life was changing in the ways she wanted. In her conversations with Tennessee she now understood how the Indian felt when the horse first came to the tribes. It lifted her to another stratosphere - off the earth away from the soiled cabbages and beans and the mundane existence of daily toil to the intoxicating world of flight and heady, windswept imaginations. She was liberated and became friendlier. On returning from her trips to the Ranges she would carry back in her canvas saddle bags juicy wild plums for her community which they eagerly devoured and introduced into their recipes. She now felt she could talk to the Europeans on their terms and not stay huddled in little groups that look away embarrassed when addressed by strangers. If she came across farmers driving their sheep or cattle she would offer to help. At first taken aback, they nearly always consented and were surprised at her friendliness and willingness to learn. They would invite her to eat with their family, and the mothers and children warmed to her friendliness and individuality. Children played on her knee and marveled at her doll like features.

Her devoted and protective mother cordoned off a piece of land for the pony and attended to his needs. She bargained with the Elders and persuaded them that horse manure would grow better and healthier vegetables. They tried it and saw much to her relief that she was right. She reminded them of the wild plums her daughter brought from the Ranges which they had no hope of reaching on foot. During the hot evenings, whilst the men were in their opium dens, Gong and her mother would go to Panda's yard and brush and pet him as though he were a member of the family. She spoke to him of her ambitions and anxieties as did her mother and the black and white pony listened, or he appeared to do. A good horse in his way is much like the Chinese; hard working, tolerant, uncomplaining, passive; the loveable pony was as inscrutable as them in his seemingly indifferent manner. In this way, the love between this willful and wayward child and her dutiful mother deepened, and shone bright in their faces much like the shine in the pony's colored coat. Her daughter smiled her appreciation of her mum's courage in defending her unconventional ways. The mother smiled back. When she saw the joy in her daughter's face, it pleased her but a touch of regret for an opportunity she did not have when she was young dwelt lightly in her generous, loving heart. If she could have her time again, she too would have loved a pony – any color would do – perhaps a spotted one like she had seen in some of her ancestor's paintings. But life had been ordinary for her and she had to admit she did not have the courage of her daughter to challenge the long-accepted traditions her community had imposed upon its members for centuries.

Cold as ice

Damaged waif

Isabelle Eubank suffered great emotional and physical trauma as a captive, resulting in bizarre nightly behaviour. In Denver, Mollie Sanford, wife of Lieutenant Byron Sanford, was going to adopt Isabelle, but her behaviour was too disturbing and uncontrollable. "I could not stand it," Mollie said "She would wake up from a sound sleep, and sit up in bed with staring eyes, and go in detail over the whole thing. She was scarred all over with the prints of arrow points that the squaws tortured her with." Doctor Caleb Burdsal, a surgeon in the 3rd Colorado became her guardian until military duty called him away. The damaged waif was passed among the Denver townsfolk. One family changed her name to Mary. The frail little girl, with poor health, and emotional problems, died on March 18, 1865.

A fate worse than death Indian captives in the West S Michno and G Michno

That weekend, Roy got into his best clothes for Ned's welcoming home party. A bright, yellow shirt with large, black polka dots and a pink thin strip of leather shoelace for a tie, black trousers tucked into his boots and his silver and golden dress spurs. Paddy arrived with his boys Tennessee, Boston and Colorado. Roy was impressed by Paddy's admiration for American independence and the names he gave to his boys. They greeted Ned and Roy warmly. Staying quietly at the back with Ma Quinn was a rather thin, moody girl with black hair but pushed up on her head in a fulsome bun so that it made her look taller than she was. Ned thought he recognized her.

'Ned, do you remember our neighbour, Valerie? She's living with us now. Her dad got worse and he's, well...to make it short they've taken him to a home in Melbourne by the river, very nice it is, and he's well looked after there...isn't he Valerie.'

The girl shook her shoulders, and looked away.

Her eyes were cold, as cold as ice.

Ned remembered her mother had died during childbirth and that her father had battled with the bottle and his sanity ever since. He remembered her as a skinny, sad, neglected child with a chip on her shoulder and insolent looks.

Ma Quinn wanted to bring Valerie into the conversation.

'Do you remember Ned, Valerie? He's grown into big, strong boy don't you think?'

She gave him casual glance, and said 'if you say so Ma - he looks like any other boy to me.' She knew of Ned and Dan's troubles with the constabulary. She hummed a rhyme that came into her head,

The Traps search and search for the Kelly's - Edward and Daniel.
Valerie wants only her books, - and her cocker wocker spaniel.

Elly's girls laughed, and Ned thought it strangely funny too. Valerie was given to impromptu rudeness, odd, idiosyncratic behaviour and periods of solitary introspection. While some were offended, others were aware of her tragic background and accepted the way she was. Valerie had taken over the care of her spaniel when her Dad was taken to the funny farm. The dog and her were inseparable, she having raised him as a pup. His name was Hercules for his long, wavy, smooth red coat. He was the only strong man in her tragic life. He was a hunting and water dog and liked nothing better than going to the river, and rooting the birds out of the bushes and taking chase. At night in her room, Valerie petted him and run her hand over his beautiful domed head while he looked lovingly into her not so cold eyes. Valerie did have a good relationship with Sarge's bookish clerk, Cyril. They had much in common, especially books, and they talked endlessly about literature, politics, technology and more subjects than you could imagine. The books were provided by Cyril who through his government contacts in the Police Department had access to the relatively large Melbourne library. Each month a suitcase of books would arrive on the train to be eagerly read and discussed by the two outsiders. These books were needed for current investigations Sarge said to his superior in a deal worked out with his clerk, and he received them without cost. Sarge turned a blind eye to the whole business. Cyril was helpful with his broad, general knowledge and bright ideas and the wily Sarge was the beneficiary of this in small and big ways.

Valerie had an abiding interest in the cosmos. Paddy had purchased a powerful telescope at considerable cost so that she could pursue her interest in a practical way and he could use it to see if Harry had returned to his mountain top nest. The funds came from Harry so the generosity really came from the State which is as it should be for matters of educating the young thought Paddy. Valerie with help from Cyril had mapped the sky, and was conversant with the ever increasing discoveries that had been and continued to be made in the unexplored and undiscovered Universe such as the earth was not the centre of the solar system as the Catholics had taught; that there were moons orbiting Jupiter and sunspots on the sun; that to every action there an equal and opposite reaction; that the planets follow elliptical, not circular paths around the sun; that we are part of the Milky Way and that there may be millions of other galaxies. Valerie painted the Milky Way on her ceiling in cobalt blue, yellow and white because she read the aborigines believed it was the place where departed souls fled. She liked to think her mother resided there, and in the quiet of a moonlit night, she would look up at the ceiling and speak lovingly to her about her plans and hopes and her Dad in the funny farm.

Apart from the cosmos, her curious mind extended to the new technologies such as telephone, electricity, and how the steam trains ran. She had analysed the Civil War in America, studied the battles, the debate on slavery, native American rights to land and the operation of a truly democratic State and Socialism. She would converse and advise her adopted grandfather, Paddy, about the American Republic, and how best she thought this could be achieved in Australia. She had an interest in architecture and buildings. She had scaled the shed roofs that Paddy had built by Red and seen they were square within fractions of an inch. She observed the exact mortise and tenon joins, the placement and strength of the hardwood beams and rafters to support the loads. She admired the work that Red had done. She lived in a room built next to Paddy's saddlery shed which was away from the main house. She preferred that arrangement with Hercules sleeping on her bed. The Quinn boys were noisy and robust, and despite the good and kind care provided to her by the family, she did feel more comfortable having her own place where she would not be disturbed. Red had built the room out of hardwood cut from the scrub. It had a timber floor and well-placed windows that allowed for the morning light but was a little hot in the evening. He had built in benches, long desks that well-suited Valerie's academic interests. She would neatly arrange her writing material on the desks so that her pens, notes and files all had a place and order. The Quinn's knew not to move them without her permission otherwise they risked a shouting match coupled with a tantrum.

Valerie was not interested in horses or an outdoor life apart from walks to the nearby river with her spaniel. What she kept to herself was that she was indifferent to religion, and the catholic faith, or any faith for that matter. She saw it as a load of old claptrap, and would have none of the strict and senseless moral censure of the Church when it came to women. In her heart though there was a lingering want to believe in the mercy and redemption that religion offered lost souls. It is clear Valerie had a lively, inquiring mind but many thought she lacked the social skills to develop these pursuits so that she could be profitably employed. If she had to be polite and serve customers, the business would have gone broke. Maybe in a big sophisticated City like Melbourne she would have found a purpose and place in a secluded office away from the public. Due to the problems with her Dad, Valerie left school early and her formal qualifications were lacking. Most girls in the country left school after seventh grade to later get married and have a family but marriage and family had only brought heartbreak to Valerie, and she saw no solace in pursuing those ends.

Ned was in two minds about her the same as she was to him. But he liked her rational and inquisitive mind and her desire to improve her knowledge; that she was prepared to express her opinions fearlessly; and he thought that he could learn from her and they might, if he were patient and she tolerant, have a relationship of sorts. Ned had seen firsthand the corruption of Government and its institutions like the police and law courts. He had seen how the squatters who were pro- British had profited in the large land grants and that the selector's rights were placed at the end of the list or pushed aside. There was privilege and struggle and he and his family, in fact most of the Irish diaspora were firmly in the latter category with a firm determination by the Protestants to keep them there. Valerie would not tolerate that, and neither would he.

Valerie surprised everyone when she said,

'Ned...your Dad built my room at Grandpa's. It is well built by a craftsman. Can I ask if you have inherited his talents?'

'I'm afraid not, Val,' he said 'but I do have basic knowledge of stone laying due to a couple of years forced experience should I say.'

'Would you be interested in making some additions to my room. Looking out the back door in summer I am hit with a blast of hot air like a furnace. A shaded area would make a big difference if it is not too much inconvenience.'

'That I could do, Val...I can lay some flagstones, put up a frame and cover it with suitable reed that I know provides a good cooling shade.'

'It's a deal,' she said, 'and I will of course reimburse you for your time and labour.'

'I would not hear of it, Val. I would like to be part of my Dads work. Building was one of the things he did well and the job will not take me long.'

They all settled down to their evening meal. After they had eaten, Roy gave his well-rehearsed speech on the life of the American Indian and his time in the U.S. Cavalry. He had cleverly adopted his history to be well clear of the Seventh Cavalry. He liked best the Comanche. The finest horsemen in the world he said. Each brave would have many horses and the horse became the source of wealth to the Indian. Brides were bought with horses, the number increasing with her beauty. He noticed Valerie visibly wince at this information. He explained how they got their horses from the plains having run wild from Mexico and the early Spanish. Little horses he said of barb or Arab breeding but very hardy and could exist off the natural grasses. Our horses he said were heavy grain fed European horses that lacked the endurance of the Indian horse and in our initial skirmishes we were carved up by the small roving Indian bands that suddenly attacked and then melted into the landscape. Tennessee was seen busily making notes.

He told them of how they tried to reload their muzzle rifles while the Indian fired off several arrows all before the first landed. He told them about their spiritual beliefs; how it resided in the animals and wildlife about them and their respect for all animal life but particularly the eagle and buffalo. He explained their itinerant life, nomads, and how comfortable were their tents known as tepee made of buffalo skin. They could only compete with the Indian he said when they divided into small bands like the Texas Rangers and technology brought them the repeater colt. They could ride close to their enemy and fire off six shots. The Indian he said could be a fearful enemy often scalping and mutilating their victims, and torturing them alive. Roy was an entertaining speaker using imagination, interesting detail and wit to hold his audience interest, especially Tennessee.

When he finished Roy asked for any questions from his attentive listeners. Not surprising it was Valerie's hand that went up.

'Wasn't that egotistical fool Custer responsible for all his men's deaths at the Little Bighorn?' she asked. She had read widely and knew there were criticisms of the boy

General. Roy went pale. He stuttered. He wanted to agree with her and say Custer cared for nothing except his own glory, but such information might expose him in front of the probing Valerie. He swallowed and looked at the floor. He tried to speak but no words came out. Elly thought he was going to faint again, and went to his assistance.

Valerie persisted,

'Have you been there, Mr Kingsly.'

'Call him Roy,' said Elly, 'Roy is family now.'

'Where?' asked Roy.

'The Little Bighorn,' repeated Valerie. Valerie trusted nobody. She challenged a lot of what she read. Roy piqued her curiosity. He was a recent arrival without much history. She knew from Tennessee that he had some Army experience in the West. He had lent his Indian book to Tennessee to read, and Valerie took it from him for a week. She read it closely making notes. She thought Roy's American Indian knowledge shallow at best with little understanding of their culture. As for the morality or even legality of the wholesale theft of their lands, Roy had nothing to say, or more likely, he had not even thought about it. After all had not history shown the Europeans grab and take what they wanted. Valerie saw the same thing was happening in Australia.

Roy gulped and stammered, 'yeah, Val... I did go there once... n,n,n,n.... no, no, no...I'm mistaken, hell I'm not really sure. Excuse me, friends, I'm not feeling well, must have been something I ate.'

'Valerie, Roy is not here to be cross examined, love. You of all people should know that he is not well, and there are some things that do not play well on his troubled mind. He clearly has had big fright in the past about which he does not want to talk, but with our help he is getting better. Isn't that so, Roy?'

'Yes Elly,' he said, 'if you don't mind can I be excused for a short while. My head is in a bit of a spin but nothing serious folks.'

Elly helped him to the bedroom where he lay down in cold sweat.

'You are shaking again, Roy - what's the matter darl?'

'I don't know what come over me but I'll rest a while.'

Roy didn't come back until he felt more composed.

When he returned, he sat impassively in his seat occasionally staring across the table at the dark-haired Valerie. This brooding, impolite girl had unnerved him. Could she know more than she was letting on he thought. Had she been sent by American spies to have him whisked back to the States? Why was she concentrating on Custer? Or was he becoming paranoid? He knew he should quickly enter back into the conversation to avoid attracting undue attention.

'Partners,' he said, 'I've got a plan which will make us all rich.'

'Tell us more Roy,' they chorused.' You have already seen that my ideas make money but this one's a real porker. It's a license to print the bloody stuff. I've seen it work. You'll make plenty...enough to buy yourselves a Ranch each.'

'You mean a Station, Roy,' asked one.

'No, a damned Ranch...who would want a one of them piddly Railway Stations?'

'A Station is a Ranch, Roy, but go on,' they replied straining to hear his scheme.

'Wait for it...it's called the travellin Wild West Show...we'll all be partners,' added the wily Yank, and peeled himself a long, thick Cuban cigar, and striking a match off the sole of his fancy, cowboy boots.

'By the way Elly...how about another serve of apple pie,' he asked as he blew the thick smoke all over the table and guests.

'Roy, I can't see the apple pie bowl for all the cussed cigar smoke. Why don't you smoke them horrible things outside?' she replied fanning the table while the others choked on the thick smoke. Through an opening in the smoke cloud hanging over the table, Roy could see a big haired, girl staring right back at him as though all his dark and terrible secrets were being rolled out, one by one, on a blackboard for all to see. He quickly lost his appetite for his second helping of apple pie, pushed the plate aside, and hurried back to the seclusion of his bed. And there under the threadbare cotton sheets, Roy took another dose of his medicine and slept.

Ned's welcoming home evening had been a mixed bag. Valerie listened quietly to Ned talk. She saw how well he related to the others; was ready to laugh at himself and had a laconic sense of humour. But Valerie was interested in more than that. She thought there were deep seated values, an honesty and integrity in the boy that stood him out from the others and was strangely at odds with his dubious reputation in the District due to conflicts with the police. She had also heard snippets of information from Cyril and she respected Cyril's opinion because, despite being their subordinate, he was in his private thinking at least independent of mind and not a mouthpiece for their propaganda. She thought Ned seemed to inspire respect from others without seeking or asking for it. Of course, with the Quinn boys he had to be physical and strong and capable of standing his ground in a fight otherwise they would have run over the top of him, but she hoped there was more than this in him. She would investigate it further when he came to do the improvements to her room. They would be one on one and Valerie was always better in relating to someone this way than with an audience.

In any event they were all curious about Roy's new plan to make a stash. Roy with his hamburgers already had a track record for new ideas and making money. Even Valerie thought there might be a place for her talents in putting on such a Show. She would read up about it and offer her assistance to Roy's plan so that perhaps, if Roy agreed, it would be historically authentic as well as entertaining. It would be a welcome change to do some practical work and earn some money, even if only to pay Ned for his work she thought.

Roy's rootin tootin Wild West Show

The thrill and excitement of Buffalo Bill's Wild West Show.
Such dare-devil riding was never seen on earth. When the American cowboys sweep like a tornado up the track, forty or fifty strong, every man swinging his hat and every pony at utmost speed, the roar of wonder and delight breaks from thousands in the grandstand...every day thousands were turned away for lack of seats. 'The American West' - Dee Brown.

Roy lost interest in the bar. It was making money and could run itself. He would leave it to Elly and her girls, and look for new ventures. Everyone was a risk taker in the States and fortunes were made overnight. It bred a commercial man who moved quickly for fear of his idea being stolen by his neighbor. Taking risks had saved his life and made him money. Roy's new idea was a travelling Wild West Show in the mode of Buffalo Bill. He had hinted at his plans at Ned's welcome home party and they continued to question him about it. Its time had come; he had better do it before someone else did. He had seen the beginnings of the wildly successful shows just before he left for Australia. Buffalo Bill put the shows on all over the States and they had to turn people away. They even took the show to England, and made another fortune. Roy figured he needed a cast of Indians, cowboys, stagecoach, cavalry, horses, guns, bows and arrows, trick riders, shooters and whip handlers. That was no mean cast to find in Australia. It was big budget and Roy would have to put a lot of his money on the table to get it started.

Fortunately for Roy in the Quinn and Kelly clans along with their motley friends and relatives, he had a ready-made circus. They were always practicing their riding and shooting skills. He put Tennessee who was now well versed in the native Indian culture in charge of the Indians; Ned as the stagecoach driver; Joe in charge of the cowboys; Steve and Dan to run the cavalry; Elly as Calamity Jane and cast himself in the lead role as Buffalo Bill and compere. The old and the less talented could be coach passengers and ticket sellers. There was a lot of organization. It was here that Valerie showed her talents. She obtained a program from America that Buffalo Bill had used and researched the actors and performances. From this she devised and worked out how long each performance would take, organized a schedule, instructed and saw that the performers had regular training to be able to carry out their acts in competent manner, drew up and had printed the posters and advertisements, and arranged the costumes. Roy was impressed with the efficient Valerie and made her second in charge. Her faithful pooch Hercules followed her about barking at the fierce looking and painted Indians.

The Squattocracy from the town would not lease the show grounds to Roy. They did not like him or his acquaintances, let alone his fanciful ideas. He was less than politely told that it was not suitable whatever that meant and that they were Royal

Show Grounds and not a Circus ground for the drunken and rioting Irish. Roy not to be outdone hired a paddock next to the show grounds on the same day as their Royal Show, and set up in competition. That was Roy; challenge him and his money and you had a fight on your hands. He chuckled to himself to think that he might pull the crowds away from the snobs and their less than interesting collection of well-bred stock, prize cattle, flighty thoroughbred horses, and the dull cake contests and flower arrangements. Anyway, who wanted to see their snooty daughters jumping one-foot hurdles when he could give them all the excitement of the Wild West Show with its large tents, stands, flags, hamburgers, hot dogs, shootin, ridin, Indians, cavalry and thrilling Stage coach pursuits.

'Tennessee,' he said 'that China girlfriend of yours interests me. I always reckoned them Indians come from Asia...you know...dark skinned, almond eyed and dark hair. Do you think you can persuade her to join up and maybe do bit of Indian warpath dancing or something like that? It will add a touch of authenticity to the show, and a real redskin squaw all the way from the plains of America would cost too much. If she's not interested, tell her I'll make an exception in her case and pay her the same as the men. She'd be a draw card for sure. In fact, we'll give her an Indian name, something stunning and crowd catching like 'Morning Star' and I'll get color billboards done and put up around the country. I'll make her a celebrity, Tennessee...you mark my words. Imported from America, the daughter of Chief Sitting Bull... hell...I'm even getting excited myself thinking about it.

And by the way Valerie has asked your Mum to help with the costumes. I'll pay her well. I'm a generous man Tennessee...generous to a fault when it comes to family. What are families for if we can't help each other in times of need. Mind you, we might have to wait until the money comes in before anyone gets paid but it's as good as done. I stand by my word. He knew he would have little difficulty in persuading Gong to join the Circus. She liked the limelight and on her piebald pony Panda...why she was ready made for the part. He set about making his weapons including the tomahawk, bow, knives, lances and arrows. His mum along with the women folk made the costumes for the Indians, cowboys and cavalry. Ned and the other boys practiced their trick riding, whip cracking and roping. Gong left the women needle workers and joined the men in their horse activities. Tennessee and Valerie read up about the ghost dance and taught her the steps. They read that the Indians did it in a trance like state for days thinking it would protect them from the white man's bullets. Gong did it like a professional holding the Irish relatives spell bound by her natural rhythm and the enticing fluidity of her movement to the earthy, muffled sound of the Indian drums. They couldn't stop themselves joining in her dance routine, whooping and hollering, and carrying on like they are want to do. Roy considered her so necessary to the success of his show that on Valerie's advice he instructed the local lawyer to draw up a contract. Valerie had large color posters featuring Gong as 'Morning Star' on her colored pony challenging Calamity Jane with the cavalry and stagecoach in the background, and stuck them all over the countryside.

She had a vigilante posse pursuing a horse thief, and a makeshift scaffold where the hapless thief would be strung up and shot at with real bullets. Only Ned, the horse thief, and a role he had some experience at, had to drop below the stage when a dummy was substituted and hoisted up. Steve and Dan along with a few of their mates dressed in their cavalry uniform and practiced their horse drill. Paddy Quinn's property was a hive of activity in the heady days of preparation.

In two months, they were primed up and ready to perform for the eager public. Roy hired a big tent to house all the actors and horses in until it was their time to burst upon the arena in a frenzy of action and color. He wanted them leaving the tent at a full gallop.

'It's action, action, action - I don't want no one standing around - this is entertainment Yankee style and you people are just going to luv it, I'm telling ya,' he said clapping his hands, doing a little dance and yelling into his loud hailer like an old time preacher. This was Roy at his best – a natural showman if ever there was one.

It took two days to set up the tent next to the show grounds and flying from the several tent poles were flags - the Stars and Stripes of the United States of America - Roy's pride and joy. He took his hat off, held it to his chest and bowed his head when he first saw those flags fluttering in the Australian breeze. Some say they saw a tear or two but Roy quickly regained his composure.

Next door, the Squatters in their tweedy suits looked across from the green turf of the Royal Show oval to the big flashy tent and stands in the neighboring paddock and wondered rather nervously what in the hell this Yank was up to now. It was bad enough that he took the trade away from the town with his common eatery out there in the bush. The big day came. Roy sat nervously in his large tent with a few of his helpers and the trusted Valerie with her notebook.

'Where the hell are the Indians, cowboys, cavalry and Calamity Jane?' he yelled looking at his watch.

'They're over at the town saloon...Morning Star too,' replied Valerie.

'What - the whole bloody lot of them! I told them to be here ten am sharp and they over there boozing. Gimme that shot gun...this'll will get them running.'

Roy fired off two shells booming across the town shops and dwellings and raining buckshot onto the saloon roof.

'Hell, that's Roy,' said Ned looking at the time, 'come on you lot...we're late...skull and everyone to the tent, and don't forget what I said.'

An array of brilliant colored costumes abandoned their drink glasses, ran for the door, out onto the street, along the Royal show oval creating havoc with the animals in the judging ring, and into Roy's tent like madmen let loose from the asylum.

'I won't tolerate this she'll be right attitude - you were all told to be here ten am sharp and where do I find ya all - in the pub boozin without a care in the world,' said Roy complaining. 'What do you think this is?'

'It's a circus, Mr Kingsly, Sir,' said Bobo the clown, and they all laughed except for Roy.

'Wrong Bobo...it's a bloody business...the Wild West business...and businesses don't exist without profit, and without profit, guess who don't get paid. In case you don't get the message, it's you lot who don't get paid and don't come complainin to me because I ain't got no sympathy for slackers. Now git on your horses.

I'll just do a check. Tennessee, are all Indians present and able?'

'Present and able, Sir.'

'The horses painted?'

'Sure are, Roy.'

'Buffalo Bill if you please.'

'Morning Star, are you ready?'

'Yes, Honorable Master.'

'Thank you my dear. I wish they were all as polite as you.'

And down the line he went marking them off and checking their costumes and equipment. Roy already had a decent crowd with his advertising but he wanted more.

'Follow me lads, and hold that Yankee flag high boy... the rest of you stay put until you're called. Strike up the band and let's get out there and give them a show like they have never seen before.'

Looking resplendent in his new Buffalo Bill outfit, Roy circled the paddock on Blue Doggy a few times with his blue uniformed cavalry behind. He pulled up in front of the large Royal show crowd where the bugler made a trumpet call. Roy pulled out his loud hailer, his voice booming across the Show grounds and interrupting the Mayors speech to his Squatter friends.

'Hear ye, hear ye, hear ye... come and see the most exciting Wild West show ever to visit the shores of Australia; Morning Star, the Indian daughter of Chief Sitting Bull - all the way from the great plains of the Americas - see her do the ghost dance. See the cavalry save the stagecoach from the marauding Indians and lots more - trick riding cowboys, and even Calamity Jane and the real life hangin of a horse thief. The kiddies are free, adults one pound, money back guarantee, see if you don't have the biggest and best time of your lives.'

Urged along by Roy, they left in their hordes pushing and shoving to get their tickets and all but deserting the show grounds except for one or two dispirited officials, a few lonely show jumpers, and the Mayor with a handful of complaining squatters. When the masses had assembled in the dusty paddock Roy took out his big cone shaped loudhailer and announced,

'Cowboys and cowgirls of Australia, do I have a rootin, tootin show for you here today. First, we are going to witness some astounding individual feats. There will be trick riding with the Malarky boys, four brothers from Muskogee U.S.A... ladies and gentlemen, give them a big Australian welcome.'

On came Ned, Joe, Steve and Dan dressed as cowboys, catapulting, leaping, vaulting from their horses; one riding three horses over jumps while standing on their backs; another circling under the horse's neck and up the other side as it cantered around; another time two riders going at full pace and picking up a third on the ground carrying him safely across the arena.

Roy loudhailer boomed in,

'These boys bred in the American saddle sure can ride them ponies...don't you reckon.'

The crowd cheered ecstatically.

'Now for a bit of dead eyed dick shootin and who no better for that than your favorite and mine- Calamiteeee Jane.'

On came Elly dressed in her buckskins and sporting a long-barreled rifle.

'Where did you learn to handle a big gun like that Calamity?'

'Shootin them pesky redskins off me Pappy's cattle ranch, Buffalo Bill. Why one day I shot that many of them savages, me gun barrel just about darned melted away so I says Pappy, Pappy get me a long, hard one,'

'Whooo there Calamity,' says Buffalo 'this here is a respectable show. We got women and kids here you know - show us how you can shoot that thing, Calamity.'

'You tellin me I ain't respectable, Buffalo?' said Calamity pointing her gun in his direction.

'I wouldn't dare Calamity - I like breathin this fresh Australian air.'

On ran four cowboys holding balloons. Roy had blanks in Calamity's gun and pins in the fingernails of the cowboys. Calamity turned away from her target shooting those balloons over her shoulder, and under between her cowboy boots.

'Careful you don't set your pants on fire, Calamity.'

'Ahhh, it's nothin Buffalo, git this gun smokin and I'll send them varmints a few smoke signals with a swish of me buckskin skirts.

You wanna do a bit of square dancin with me, Buffalo?'

'Not just now Calamity but talking about dancin I got a real treat for the folks now. Morning Star, daughter of the big Chief, will do the Ghost dance. This is a very sacred performance never witnessed in Australia before and seen only by a few white men back in the States so put away that fire stick Calamity.'

'You sure Buffalo, a few well-placed shots could improve that uppity Indian squaw's footwork mighty good.'

'Now, now Calamity, I'm goin to have to send you back to the tent. We don't want any diplomatic ruckus here today, do we folks - well, least not till the Deadwood Stagecoach comes on.'

The crowd roared and went silent as the Indian drummers and Gong dressed as Morning Star took front stage. She danced a rhythm so provocative and tantalizing to the exotic beat of the drum that Roy sensed he might lose control of the crowd if he didn't cut it short.

'Sorry ladies and gentlemen...the dance is so sacred that I can only let you see a small part of it. Now you'll see the lasso and for a bit of local interest for you stockmen, the stock whip act. This was followed by the vigilante posse and the hanging of the horse thief causing loud boos and protests from the crowd.

'It seems they are darned friendly to them horse stealers over here,' said Roy, 'not like back in the States. There it's a capital offence.'

And when the audience thought they couldn't take any more excitement, on came the Stagecoach for the grand finale chased by a band of murderous, yelping Indians. When the Indians looked to be getting the upper hand, Roy had arranged for the Cavalry to race on and save the day. Only he had not planned on the mischievous relatives wanting their own ending. When the heroic Cavalry burst onto the scene, they were shot from their saddles by the rampaging Indians, and scurried off for their lives back to the tent.

Roy went mad with rage.

'Come back here, you yella belly deserters,' he yelled.

Then he stopped, appeared to choke on his words.

'My God,' he thought to himself, 'that is what I did.'

Not to be outdone he called his last card Calamity Jane to the rescue.

Morning Star gave the big wigged sheila full blast of her shotgun knocking her fair off her horse. The crowd roared their approval.

'This is not scripted,' yelled Roy but by this time the crowds had broken through the cordon and were carrying their heroes, the Indians and Morning Star, around the arena on their shoulders while the Cavalry and Calamity lay dead on the ground.

Someone should have told Roy that Australians always root for the underdog. He made quids that day, but could not see his way clear to forgive the treachery of having Uncle Sam humiliated. He summonsed the disobedient actors into the tent.

'The show is cactus,' he said. 'It's goin to take me a long time to get over this. And you lot, I mean I trusted you and you did this to me. It means only one thing, and believe me it hurts to do it, but my hands are tied.'

'What's that Roy?' they chorused.

'I've taken advices from my lawyer here. He says you have all breached your contract and I should not have to tell you lot what follows from that.'

'What Roy?' they asked.

'My lawyer tells me not to pay you lot a cracker. He says you should be paying me damages. He says you have damaged my pride, and that is no small thing. As you know I can't go against my lawyer's advice but I tell you what...I'm generous man as you all know...Valerie here who is doing all the accounts will pay you fifty percent of what I promised. Now I can't be fairer than that in the circumstances...isn't that right, Val?'

'Whatever you say, Roy.'

Roy had promised Valerie her full pay but she had to sign his lawyer's hastily hand-written contract of confidentiality. On the contract it said,

'I, the said Valerie, hereby agree to remain mute and silent about matters pertaining to the administration and payment of wages of Mr. Roy King's Wild West Circus...'

Roy studied the document for a time and said,

'change them words to include everything she knows about me here or in the States.'

'Why that?' asked the puzzled lawyer.

'Listen,' said Roy 'I'm paying your wage to do what I say...not to ask me stupid questions.'

The scolded lawyer scribbled in,

'not only the Circus but all matters known, read, relayed or discovered by me in relation to Mr. Roy Kingsly's private current or past life, dealings, business, employment whatsoever and whosesoever and wheresoever but more particularly in the United States of America.'

'That's beautifully put,' said Roy mouthing the legalese.

'How anyone can understand it I don't know but it sounds good and tight.'

Roy spoke to Valerie alone and out of earshot of anyone nearby.

'This contract Val doesn't just apply to this Circus business...look here,' he said showing her the scribbled words. 'It means whatever you know about me, and I'm fair dinkum here as you lot say. It means you say zero, naught, absolutely nothing...do you get my drift, young lady?'

'I don't know what brought this on, Roy. I know nothing of your past in America. I should not have to sign it.'

'Well Val- you have been of great assistance to me in setting up this Circus. Between you and me, and you know it too because you have done the books, I have made a lot of money. And I am going to make even more when I cut their wages in half. So, do you want fifty percent and no signing, or double with a signature?'

Roy was the master of the deal. Valerie thought for a few minutes holding the pen in her hand. She desperately wanted to know the truth about Roy and his dark background but she also wanted the money. Her delay made Roy think she really did know something about his past.

'My lips are buttoned,' she said and scribbled her signature on the contract.

'You are a sensible girl, Valerie,' said Roy. 'Money is what sets you free. It is the reality of existence and without it life is short, brutal and nasty and you should know all about that...money is everything Val and that means not burying your pretty head in books, literature, music, and silly theatre dramas...all them fancy things that the arty farty mobs indulge in and Cyril...it's us wheeler dealers that end up paying for it with Government subsidies and the like. I mean big commercial shows like this are good because everyone likes them not just the elite. I tried to tell my mate Virgil about these things but he doesn't listen. You are a good listener Val. You are different from the others. I could do with a secretary like... you're a smart one. You should save up and go to the States. They would appreciate your talents...not like here where you can appear little odd if I may use the expression.'

Roy stopped and put both his hands on her shoulder and looked deep into her eyes. Hercules growled, and tugged at his trouser cuffs. Roy said,

'Sometimes, Val, you can know too much for your own good. You get my drift girl? and call that bloody dog off from ruining my expensive Buffalo Bill outfit.'

'Hercules... stop frightening Buffalo Bill. I am odd girl Roy. There is no getting away from it. I don't think or behave the way most girls do.'

As Valerie went to count out the wages, the pensive, thoughtful girl added under her breath, 'but buttons always come loose, Roy Boy.' Valerie could double deal as good as the best of them.

Roy had good reason to insist on the amendment to silence Valerie. He had overheard from a visiting Yankee, there was a report in an American newspaper from a witness, who knew Darrington, seeing him getting on ship to Australia with an old Southern Gentleman. Roy was comforted in the thought that not many persons in Australia read newspapers or books, particularly overseas. That is not many persons except for the widely read and enigmatic Valerie busily counting out everyone's pay...less fifty percent. But the wily American was always scheming a new plan - well, it wasn't really a plan - more a calling and fulfilling a promise he made not so long ago when he outran the murderin Indians, and to his way of thinking the time and place were ripe for the picking. Roy would go back to his roots in the deep South, to his time growing up as boy in the backwoods churches where his dad preached and he sang and learnt to play the piano. This time he would be be doin the preachin as only he knew how. He had been to the local Catholic church and it was a formal, cold, lifeless affair. The people yawned and looked about - one or two even fell asleep during a monotone sermon from the pulpit that they had heard repeated a hundred times. Attending church in Australia on Sunday was a chore. Roy had seen in America what the old time Revivalists with their gospel blues could do and the crowds they could draw and just like the success of his Circus venture he knew the Lord would smile down upon him and that his rewards he hoped would be more than spiritual.

Athletic but dumb men – Paula Yates talking about footballers.
They're not bright but I like that in a man. I like people who are calm and sleepy because I find it a good reaction against me. It's probably why I don't mind people being incredibly thick. It's quite charming their brain isn't constantly working out how…I make jokes, and they can just stand there and look fantastic. On nights it's just Tiger and me, I switch on the light and read 'soccer hunks. Australian Magazine September 2000.
Frank and Jesse James.
Frank James was tall big boned and quiet. He enjoyed reading Shakespeare and the essays of Francis Bacon. Because of his book learning some people thought he was the gang's strategist - The West - Geoffrey C Ward.
words
words ought to be a little wild for they are the assault of thoughts on the unthinking. J. M. Keynes

Ned worked in the Ranges as a timber cutter. In order to get the valuable hardwood, he had to venture into the hidden recesses of the vast, natural forests, creeks and mountains. He had to arrange for bullock teams to get the giant logs out the boggy forests to the saw mills. It was hard, honest work and it supported his mum and large family. It got him away from Roy. The physical labor made Ned as strong as an ox, and in the hotels and bars of the district which he would frequent with his mates, there were not many who were game to take him on. There was always one exception who held the heavy weight crown - Isiah, a big, loudmouth of a man who took delight in his brute force and was not about to countenance a young upstart or a pretender to his throne as boss bully. He let it be known around the town that he would belt the tripe out of the young Kelly, and before long a challenge was issued for a fight under the Queen of Marksbury rules.

'The kid is turncoat…old Harry said as much and he ought to know. That Kelly kid put the old bugger behind bars I heard with a Judas deal. It will do me good to put him on the canvas, and him some good too,' he boasted to his lackeys while he shadow boxed around the bar. The town gathered for the bare fisted fight. The bookies took a bundle of money on the favorite Isiah. The two pugilists dressed in their flannels eyed each other off from their corners. Excitement buzzed in the crowd. The bell summonsed them to the referee in the middle of the canvas. He told the contestants there would be no kicking, head butting and hitting below the belt, or hitting when one was down for the count. The two contestants nodded, shook hands and returned to their corners to wait for the second bell for the fight to commence.

Big Isiah came out swinging. He had knocked most of them out like this and saw no reason to change his style for the Kelly lad. One good hit and it would all be over he thought. Ned ducked, weaved, and deflected the way Soapy had taught him as

Isiah's punches whistled around and over his bobbing head. After punching the air for the first two rounds, Isiah began to slow and change his tactics, hoping to bring him in close. Then when he let his guard down, he was hit with two quick punches in the bread basket knocking the stale air from his bloated gut and setting him back a few steps. It both surprised and worried him a little. The boy was no pushover like his other challengers. He was methodical, quick and had a real strength in his punch. He was going to be there for the long haul if he couldn't get in a king hit. The old bruiser went on the back foot and began to box defensively. Ned came at him again but this time Isiah was ready for him. He landed one squarely on Ned's jaw thinking that would be the end of it but although stunning the boy momentarily, it did little to put him off his concentration or rhythm. The big man was running out of options and he knew his fitness level didn't match that of his young opponent. Ned saw a fear creep into his face and hesitation in his movements.

'Come on young fella,' he said, 'we all friends here, no need to get serious.'

Ned hit him with a straight right to the jaw. The punch shook him to his foundations, made him groggy and disorientated. He was getting a hiding. The crowd sensed it too and it excited them like no other fight they have seen. The challenge could have ended there but the young pretender played with his opponent wanting his supporters to suffer their embarrassment. After another two rounds Ned tired of the contest and let rip with a bone jarring, upper cut that nearly jerked the big man's head off his shoulders, lifting him momentarily and dropping him to the canvas where he lay still and oblivious to the roar of the crowd. The fight was over. Ned's supporters hoisted their hero shoulder high carrying him to the pub. Out of the corner of his battered eye Ned saw Valerie across the street avoiding the crowd. She avoided him, and went to the Police Station to talk to Cyril.

The following day Ned called at his Grandparents place to visit her, and start work on her room improvements. His grandmother pulled him aside,

'Be careful with Valerie, Ned. Although she is well, her condition is a day to day affair. She is given to long bouts of depression where she shuts herself in her room and doesn't speak or go out for weeks. It's in the family I think... you know her dad went crazy. His condition deteriorated after his wife died giving birth to her. That girl, you know, practically nursed him along when she was no more than a child until he had to go to the loony bin. If it were not for Pop, she would be an orphan. After they took her dad, she ran off into the bush. Pop found her wandering down by the river, and brought her home like a lost kitten. She would spend hours walking by that river alone. Thank the Lord she is getting better. The doctor said she must avoid stress. He thinks she may have some of her Dad's problems. I think he called it doubter's disease. I have seen her open and close her door repeatedly in the time it takes to boil an egg...like she has forgotten something... she can be a strange one, our Val.'

When Ned knocked on her door, she opened it. Without any greeting she said,

'Ned, I am not impressed with what I saw yesterday. Two grown men belting each other up and a blood thirsty mob urging you on. It's a shame and a disgrace. And poor Mr. Isiah...I understand he has been badly hurt by your violence upon his person. I hope you are going to apologize to him for your inexcusable conduct.

Come in and sit down at my desk. I want to talk to you about some things that have been worrying me. I am not against violence if it is necessary in self-defense. I am not a pacifist but I would like you to research and have a deeper understanding about what is important in life. There is more to life than riding wild horses, and drinking and fighting in the pub with your mates. You are better than that Ned. You have courage and an ability to speak well on your feet. You have a good heart. Your choice of words also shows a discriminating mind but your depth of knowledge is shallow. From what I can see you work more on intuition and emotion than logic, Ned. I hope I can change that.'

Ned was feeling a little uneasy that he had been so closely analyzed.

'Ned... understand this... your abilities will come to nothing if you do not have knowledge and learning. Achieving that takes more guts determination and long hours to master than riding and learning about a dumb animal or border running stolen stock. Without it you will be as the bible says an empty sounding vessel.'

'Now look here,' she said pointed to a stack of books. 'I figure this building improvements will take a week. You can work half a day in the morning and the other half you can read a book. I will choose it for you. In the evening we will discuss it. What do you think about that Ned?'

'Val...this might come as a surprise to you but I agree. I do have an interest in what you value...it is just that I have been set on different course and not thought about it a lot, or for that matter had the opportunity to as you say to be reading books. He stopped and added somewhat embarrassed, 'I did start to read a bit on the ship. There was not much else to do but the books were usually discarded penny dreadfuls. What books would you like me to read, Val?'

'First of all, Ned...I like my books stacked in proper order. You see how the spines are matched one way. That is how you are to leave them when you have finished reading in the evening.'

Ned smiled.

'I am not joking Ned. I am deadly serious...just ask Ma or the boys. No one rearranges with my books but enough of that...let's move on. You know Grandpa and I have interest in early and current American history. We have seen how the Americans have thrown off the shackles of the colonial British and organized their own constitution. It's called a Republic, Ned, and both Pop and I would like to see that happen here. After that we will look at the Civil War in America. It dealt with the issue of slavery and human rights. You will like this history Ned... there is lot about horses, riding, battles and episodes of great bravery. Associated with that is book about

President Lincoln. He came from the backwoods Ned and was self-educated. But it is power with words that I would like you to study. He was very succinct and clear. Not verbose and boring like a lot of our politicians. I would like you to read the Gettysburg Address, Ned, and see how you can get your message across in a few simple and elegant words. After that you can read about the art and inventiveness of the Chinese to look at different culture from ours, the Great Wall and the Mongols, Genghis Khan. You know he conquered nearly all of the then known world.'

'What sort of people were they?'

'Who?'

'The Mongols.'

'They were barbarians. All they knew were horses and how to cut throats. The poor Chinese, an intelligent, cultivated people, must have suffered badly when they invaded their country.'

'They must have been good horsemen to do what they did, Val.'

'Whatever,' said Val.

'If we have time we will go to Napoleon and French Republic and finally the Cosmos.'

'The what?' said Ned.

'The sky, stars, the sun and moon, the rings of Saturn and Jupiter; the Galaxy; and if you like, the existence of God. Galileo discovered four moons circling Jupiter in 1610. He was attacked by the Church...your Church Ned...because he believed the Earth circled the sun whereas the Church believed the sun circled the Earth. Under threat of torture he had to recant but really, he was an atheist, someone who does not believe in God.'

'Oh my God, Val...my head is spinning...I have never heard about these things like Jupiter, and I am not sure what you are referring to when you say existence of God. My relations I expect would not like to hear that kinda talk.'

'Ned... please understand this is not just for one week. That would be a superficial knowledge at best. You should develop the habit of reading regularly so as to educate yourself. You don't have to go to University to do that. You can do it with a good library. Ned was intrigued. 'That's a big agenda, Val,' he said 'but I am up for it.'

During the week he worked on the improvements and read books. Valerie did not disturb him. In the evening she prepared a meal for him and they discussed what he had read. These conversations were not placid affairs; Valerie would debate with vigor and not tolerate flimsy or flippant answers. If he gave a silly answer or was too verbose and not relevant, she would slap him lightly about the head with her book in friendly manner. But generally, Ned was an interested and astute student, and Valerie enjoyed his masculine no nonsense approach to the history and topics they discussed at night. Late in the evening he would saddle his horse and ride home in the dark carrying the weight of knowledge not in his saddle bag but in his head.

The relationship between him and Valerie became close although there was no physical intimacy. Ned was unsure how she felt or would react about those matters. She was not beautiful in a classical sense; yet she was attractive in a rather austere and mysterious way that he found compelling. The more he saw her the more he was drawn to her unconventional charms and intelligence. It is probably fair to say that Ned had aroused in her feelings that she had not previously experienced or even thought about. There was an alchemy going on much like Ned had read about China and their invention of gun powder, rockets, and flying bombs crafted beautifully in the form of black crow.

He did ask Valerie if she could find out from Cyril what happened to his horses particularly Music, his grey filly, who he could not forget. Val asked Cyril but he would not say anything. If he did the books may have to be fudged again. She said

'I do not want to involve Cyril in any trouble Ned. He has been a good and loyal friend to me and I could not live without the constant supply of books he so kindly provides to me.'

'I find it difficult to live without my grey mare, Val...well she would be a mare now. I wonder where she is and who is looking after her. She has my brand on her you know Val. A good horse is not easy to find.

'The same as a good man,' said Valerie as she carefully lined up her books with the spines facing the same way.'

'A man with a spine,' said Ned.

Valerie smiled. 'Yes Ned. I see you are a quick learner.'

Every little thing she does is magic

story about Twain in his youth

Because he was sickly, Clemens [Twain] was often coddled, particularly by his mother, and he developed early the tendency to test her indulgence through mischief, offering only his good nature as bond for the domestic crimes he was apt to commit. When Jane Clemens was in her 80s, Clemens asked her about his poor health in those early years: "I suppose that during that whole time you were uneasy about me?" "Yes, the whole time," she answered. "Afraid I wouldn't live?" "No," she said, "afraid you would.'

Thomas V. Quirk Transcript of The Writing Style of Mark Twain "The Adventures of Huckelberry Finn" 1885

Roy began his plans for an old time Tent Revival. It was a calling he knew well from his childhood days in the deep South. He hoped he could make it a national spiritual awakening, a crusade, and he would be the figurehead for the movement- a famous Evangelist from the USA. He could use the massive tent he had from his Wild West Circus. He was not sure about Ned, his mad Quin cousins and assorted friends who undermined his love for all things American, but he made a heap of money and that eased the hurt of their cynicism. One person he could use though was Val. The girl had great organizing abilities and a sharp intellect which he would need. He chose a pleasant shaded spot by the river on Old Man Quin's natural and untamed property in the high country where he would build a basic, wooden structure on long poles that has stairs leading to an open platform, and roof that sort of directed the sound out to the multitudes. It was a simple enough timber construction he could trust Ned and his cousins to do - they could cut the timber from the bush being physically strong boys accustomed to hard work. From that platform on high Roy imagined he would be like Moses handing down the commandments to the awe-struck crowds below. He would have drop toilets and some huts from where food and water could be purchased along with religious memoranda and figurines. A section of the river was cordoned off for baptisms of the newly converted. Roy's favorite installation however was a grand piano which had to be carefully hoisted to the platform, and with Valerie's help he would have a choir of pretty, young girls with angelic voices to get the people in the mood with their favorite gospel songs. Roy would stroke the ivories and he could hold a tune of sorts, not as good as his mate, the old Southern General Virgil, but he would get by. He asked Virgil if he could be there at the opening as the guest vocalist and he gladly agreed acknowledging Roy had done a lot for him in the past bringing him to a Country where good land was relatively cheap and giving him a second chance at life. He had taken it and established a large and profitable farm which he had built with a long-treed entrance, and big columns and spacious porch with swing seats at the front of the house - much like the grand, old plantation home he had before the Union Calvary took possession and made stables in the spacious rooms. This time he farmed merino sheep - a fine wool breed from Spain brought to Australia by one of the early pioneering families, William Wentworth. He would of course prefer to grow cotton, his old stock and trade, but Australia did not have the free labor that once existed in the South before the Civil War he explained careful not to use the word slavery.

Roy set about planning the big event with Val. She had made a handy sum from the Wild West Circus, and although she had reservations about Roy, she liked the challenge involved in organizing a big event, the independence money gave her, and that she could have a few luxuries like adding to her expanding library which she had in alphabetical order in her bookshelves made of river red gum with all the timber's natural beautiful hues. Almost like expensive mahogany she liked to think. Val was not one to follow fashion which she thought ridiculous and impossible to work in like the long, flouncy, billowing dresses, strapped in corsets that cramped your stomach, and frames with stuck out behinds forcing the wearer to waddle like an old hen. Any way, they cost more than she could afford. She would use hand me downs and when the opportunity came buy practical, nondescript clothes much like the Quin and Irish girls used for riding, that is a dark smock over tapered trousers and laced boots with a heel, but not being a rider, she substituted a colorful, beaded moccasin in the style of Tennessee's Indian dress obsession and made by her adopted mother, Ma Quin. She did make a concession for the pretty, floral, silk tunics the Chinese girls wore like Gong which were cool, so smooth against your skin and comfortable. Ned had shown her that she could be attractive in feminine way, and she hoped her slightly different look, perhaps eccentric or unconventional, might add some allure to her bookish personality. On any other girl the clothes may have appeared to discordant but on Valerie, with her black hair combed high in the French, bouffant style, one would have to say it looked independent, resourceful and intriguing.

Like always Val researched her topic, Revivalism. She said 'Roy, people will not come to pray - you need something to catch their imagination.'

'I have that,' said Roy 'singing, the old-time gospel blues - you saw what it did for the pub.'

'Everyone uses that Roy I was thinking more radical - something cataclysmic.'

'What,' said Roy 'what does that word mean?'

'It means, Roy, something calamitous.'

'What does that mean, and stop talking in riddles, Val.'

'It means something earth shattering, that scares the hell out of them and they come running to the Lord looking for protection and salvation. And guess where they are going to find it.'

'Val, your sure are one son of a gun with that brain of yours - - how did you get that way.'

'My Dad and literature, Roy.'

'Well, whatever - the problem how do we get, waddya call it, cataclysmic?'

'Let me think on it, Roy.'

'Ok, but don't be too long I have things going pretty well now that the boys have done my pulpit in the sky. And I have been practicing to get my voice to carry, to project as they say - deep breaths from the diaphragm I am told and pushing pebbles around in my gob to strengthen the mouth muscles. I overheard a old preacher tell my Dad that when I was a kid playing the piano for him and have never forgotten it.'

Val researched the history of Australia for weeks but try as much as she did, there was hardly any earth-shattering events since settlement and even less now. In fact, Australian history was mind-numbingly boring and lackluster. There was only the Eureka Stockade, a few miners at Ballarat getting upset over the cost of the mining licenses and when the mounted constabulary arrived from Melbourne, it was over in a whimper. She thought of giving up the idea until Cyril mentioned to her that the world-famous author, Mark Twain, was about to visit Australia staying in Melbourne for short time and visiting country towns who could afford to hear him speak. His books Tom Sawyer and Huckleberry Finn were best sellers in many countries including Australia, and she had heard he was an entertaining, adventurous man, just the sort to draw big crowds. She methodically worked out her plan. She knew he was going to stay with one of the owners of the very popular and well-known coach transport that dominated the roads of Australia, Cobb and Co, a Canadian Mr. Wagner. After speaking to Roy who was warming to the idea and told her to go ahead and get the detail, her negotiations led to Cobb and Co offering to take the popular American author to their Tent Revival in their grand Leviathan Coach driven by their top driver, Kev Kavanagh. They saw it as great advertising for their business. The Leviathan Coach was an immense timber and leather structure requiring a team of eight horses, and could carry some eighty-seven passengers. Roy was ecstatic on hearing this - he was now hob knobbing with the elites and the publicity of what was probably the largest coach in World would guarantee large crowds he thought to his Revival meeting. He was pleased with Val's negotiations and decided to offer her a partnership. Before he could make the offer, Val interrupted,

'I can do better -what say we have competition for young boys and girls from all over Victoria to write short essay about what they liked best in Mr. Twain's books and the best essays, five boys and five girls, can accompany Mr. Twain on his trip from Melbourne to our river venue, and have the opportunity to speak to him about reading and writing. Every local paper can advertise the competition for free, and it is in their interests to have people reading and writing, so rather than having all the winners come from a big City, we will have democratic spread across the Country. I along with

Cyril will judge the entries and also accompany the winners on the Coach. It has two compartments and Cyril and I can sit with Mr. Twain in one compartment and interview the winners individually and have Mr. Twain judge which out of the ten winners has the best essay. And that person will accompany Mr. Twain to the podium and receive a wonderful gift.'

'Val, I am speechless. If you aren't the darnest bestest secretary and right-hand man I have ever had - every little thing you do is magic. It's time for you to move up in the World, Val - you have been my apprentice and we have made a lot of loot with the Circus - but mark my words, this can be bigger. I don't like to hold onto these businesses very long because before long the interest drops and they become a money pit. But if you sell at the top, you avoid the risk, and cash in on the excitement it can generate in the beginning. I sold my Circus rights to some proper suckers, and the last I heard they had folded with a mountain of debts.'

Val looked a little puzzled by the offer. She said,

'I don't know about that, Roy. I don't have the financial resources or experience you do, and if it doesn't work, the stress could be the end of me.'

'How do you think I started, Val? I was on the bones of my arse and took a chance. Listen girl, opportunity does not knock twice - blink and it is gone.'

'What's the deal, Roy?'

'Sixty forty divide of profits my way because I have the experience and forty sixty divide of debts against you if we fail because your fancy book dude has the larger expenses by far.

'Let me think about it, Roy.'

'No Val, it's now or not at all. I might feel differently tomorrow - remember what I said about being decisive.'

Val quickly ran through the figures in her head - maybe five thousand attendees at say one pound each, kids free. The expenses she was told was six hundred pounds for Twain, a lot, but he was the draw card. Three hundred pound for Cobb and Co which was a discount, say three hundred for labor and some security she was told would be required for Mr. Twain. And he wanted a river boat to be available next to the venue for his departure and to remind him of his time as a river pilot on the great Mississippi - another say three hundred quid. She had the cost of the winners in the essay contest and their accommodation and travel expenses adding to perhaps another three hundred pounds. Say two thousand pounds at the most allowing for contingencies. It meant a three-thousand pound profit. Valerie was interested. She remembered the words of Shakespeare - Brutus in Julius Caesar which she could recite off by heart,

'There is a tide in the affairs of men...

She said, '50/50 profits, and it's a deal.'

Roy winced at the increase, thought for a minute, and said extending his hand

'It's a deal, partner - lets shake on it.'

When the much-lauded author arrived in Melbourne, Val travelled by train to meet and to discuss the arrangements. She caught a taxi from the Station to the Italianate residence of Mr. Wagner, and was taken to a large book lined library by the butler to await the two highly respected men. Valerie was nervous. She had never seen such a grand home or envisaged talking to such well known, wealthy and important men. Her Dad, a schoolteacher, whose mind had left him, had always told her when he was well to do your homework, be prepared and you will have little to worry about. His words gave her confidence as she sat alone amongst the expensive furniture and books which she would dearly like to read. The door opened and in came Mrs. Twain introduced to her by the butler. Val found her a delightful woman in whom she could converse freely. Val talked about her home life, her Dad's illness, the Quin's who adopted and provided her with a home, her interest in literature and women's suffrage, and that she was intending to visit her Dad at the sanatorium whilst in Melbourne although the chances were that he would not recognize her. Valerie looked a little tearful. She was immediately embraced and comforted by her kind host who said,

'I am so pleased and interested to hear about your life, Valerie - you are indeed an intelligent, thoughtful girl. Let me tell you that we are not as we appear - we have lost our home and my inheritance through my husband's stupidity - he has spent our savings on hair brained inventions that have cost a fortune and impoverished us. Ok, he can write a sentence or two, but he is no business man so be careful in your dealings with him and his hangers on. Tragedy overtakes us all - we have lost a child - and illness stalks both me and one of our daughters - I can see that you have had to bear the brunt of misfortune far too early as well but enough of this - let's talk of more pleasant things. I had a privileged upbringing. Fortunately for me my parents were liberal and free thinkers. We had friends who supported civil rights, anti-slavery, and women's rights - not popular in these times. I sometimes think but dare say it that these radical opinions were stolen by you know who in his novels. And I can see that you have developed a clear and rational understanding as well through your extensive reading for one so young. I particularly loved your proposal giving young girls and boys all over Victoria a platform so to speak for their interests and opinions. It was me that convinced him to accept your offer to attend your event. You know my husband doesn't speak too highly of British imperialism or religion and Catholics for that matter. He is a little peeved that Australia tugs the forelock so meekly to the English Crown and is not a Republic like America.'

'I know someone who would heartily agree with those sentiments, Mrs. Twain, my adopted Grand Pop Paddy Quinn - even named his boys after American States.'

'Well, that is good to hear - you know when my husband says Australia is a nation of sheep, I am not sure he doesn't mean the two-legged type as well. But he has so far kept his opinions to himself. We will spending time in the mother country shortly on our world trip and he doesn't want to, how should I say, reduce his earning capacities by intemperate remarks even if true - his financial manager is very strict with him and anything we earn apart from living expenses goes to his manager - so he plays the fool and entertains people much like a comedian or town clown - how embarrassing and he will at times drink himself to oblivion to hide the pain. I have probably said too much and ask that you keep our conversation private Valerie. I hope you will enjoy your short stay with us and I will see if my husband can accompany you on your visit to see your Dad tomorrow because it may be distressing for you. He is good company and likes bright, young girls with thoughtful opinions. I will shortly take you to your room which has kindly been made available by our friend Mr. Wagner, and I assure you it is not a Cobb and Co stable. Mr. Wagner seems to have made a lot of money I hear through his coach business, Cobb and Co - he's a lawyer educated by the best - Trinity College in Ireland no less - so I suppose that explains it but he wants to be a playwright hence our welcome. I can hear them coming so I will do the introductions and we will speak more later.'

'Thank you for your kind words Ma'am - it has been a great relief for me to to have you speak so warmly and frankly.'

The door opened and in walked two men talking animatedly about a play showing in New York.

'This is the lovely Valerie,' said Mrs. Twain. She will be more than a match for you two villains I am sure, and Val, remember if you need any help in putting them in their place, just call me.'

'yes Sir.' said Mr. Twain as she left the room and smiled sweetly at his youthful guest.

'I was not expecting one so young and pretty,' he said. Val blushed and said she hoped that would not impede their discussions. On the contrary it is refreshing to speak to the youth of Australia and the World. - original thought and vigor whereas us oldies are rather complacent and conservative. Isn't that right Mr. Wagner?'

'good things are worth keeping,' replied Val

'Too true my dear, too true - now let us speak about your plans.'

'First, can I thank you for agreeing to speak at our venue Mr. Twain and to you Mr. Wagner for your big stage coach and reduced fee. I am sure they will be a stunning attraction for our engagement.'

'Well,' replied Mr. Wagner, 'it is a big expense for us but it is not all one way. I feel confident the advertising will do our Company good and increase bookings with the country people who are still using their own mode of transport to get to the City - with the big coach we can carry many at reduced fee for more profit- so we are pleased with your proposal Val and impressed by your shall I say commercial instincts.'

'Talking about commercial, I hope you will excuse my rudeness miss Valerie but have you brought the cash,' asked Mr. Twain.

'Yes, it is in my bag here I have counted it out in bundles of one hundred pounds- six for you Mr. Twain and three for you Mr. Wagner.'

'Thank you my dear - ugly but necessary this money business. I hope you understand Miss Valerie that I am ruled over by my manager who doesn't explain but dictates to me about these matters. Personally, I have little taste for it but my dear friend Mr. Waggers here, our kind host, has a gift for amassing the filthy lucre, don't you think.'

'I would not like to comment Mr. Twain but I can say I could very easily get accustomed to it.'

They discussed the remainder of the arrangements such as the travel and accommodation of the district essay winners, the trip to the venue and retired to their rooms for a short rest before formal tea. Val had a refreshing bath, groomed herself and put on a formal dress that Roy, keen to see that she made a good impression, bought for her along with all the other fineries to go with it.

At tea Mr. Twain regaled them with tales of his adventures which were amusing and entertaining. Val joined in showing a wit and intelligence advanced for her years. In truth, for the first time in her life, she felt she was amongst people with whom she could easily converse and debate without appearing too learned or knowledgeable. She had a million and one questions to ask about life, politics, the civil war, science, travel and of course America, the land of opportunity, equality and freedom. Mr. Twain and his charming wife had much to ask her about Australia, how the Irish immigrants were treated, the Church, the squatter's land grab, the aboriginals and what happened to them in Tasmania, the Judiciary which was in the main imported from England and Protestant Ireland to which she gave original insights and in the main diplomatic answers. The less diplomatic her answers were the more Mr. Twain nodded, got excited and clapped his large hands.

One admirer asked if she had a boyfriend to which she replied 'I live in hope - a young man with a good heart and courage like you wouldn't believe. In fact, to the point of being foolhardy but that is the way of the country. I have done my best to develop in him the habit of reading and he is showing some promise although maybe he fakes a sort of interest. I suspect he is more interested in horses and drinking with his mates.'

'What sort of horseman is he?' asked Mr. Wagner looking interested horses being his business.

'The best so I hear. A natural people say who can tame even the worst rogues. He has no fear which I feel will be his undoing.'

'Yes, we have a young man from the country at the moment who has the most amazing horse skills we have seen. Kev Kavanagh from Casterton, and believe you me, we have thousands of horses and not enough good men to handle or wrangle them as our distinguished guest may say. Kev bought and trained a grey mare from up your way that has in eighteen months turned into the most talented horse we have seen - the two of them are inseparable but he told me he would not be putting her in the team to pull the Leviathan - he don't want to risk her legs on something as heavy as that he said. She is a speedster - with her in the lead our company has won all the contest runs to Gold Towns and done our business a great turn in customers. We are mighty proud of him and his mare - his missus is stunner too but there's no way he train her. I see her all the time at the night spots and she is mighty popular with the men. They have separated. Poor Kev took it real bad...don't blame him... she would drive any man crazy with desire.'

'A real Southern belle,' said Mr. Twain 'I have to confess a weakness for them myself. But don't you worry none about your man riding horses, Val. I have written about the Wild West and how it makes our youth strong, independent with a healthy work ethic - not like the big Cities where cads and thieves abound. That reminds me, Val, I will accompany you on your visit to your father tomorrow - it must be a very sad and worrying thing to have those closest to you stricken down with mental frailty.'

'Sometimes he is quite lucid,' said Valerie, 'like he sees or hears something and it comes back to him in waves. It gives me hope. But before long, he is away in a different World, and sometimes a frightening and worrying one.'

'I feel like that regularly,' added Mr. Twain keen to add a bit of levity especially when I am giving talks, but they haven't taken me off yet.'

When they retired to their rooms that night Val was a little lightheaded from the wine, the stimulating conversation and the admiring attention she had received. She gazed out of her bedroom window to see a beautiful, full moon shining down on her – the blessed one at last - and felt she was in different World - a world where there was witty repartee, literature, politics, history, humor, unconventional and radical opinions, all accompanied with fine foods, exquisite cakes, heady wines and bubbly French champagne. The evening was a magical one for a magical girl.

Sway

Jimmy Swaggart- a preacher from the South

It was about four months ago, according to a New Orleans prostitute named Peggy, when a man she believes was Swaggart first became a habitué of the seedy Air Line Highway pickup strip on the outskirts of New Orleans. Peggy, who appeared on a Baton Rouge TV station with her face obscured, said that on one occasion the man told her he was in that dubious neighborhood to arrange an adoption. Another time he stopped his Lincoln Town Car, invited Peggy to get in and asked her to perform a sex act for $10. "I just laughed," she said, "because, you know, here is Jimmy Swaggart, and he has millions he could pay me, or at least thousands. I said, 'No,' and he said, 'Well, I guess you'd better get out of the car then.' "Joanne Kaufman- the fall of Jimmy Swaggart

A white indian is returned to his people

During all this time Herman maintained a haughty indifference akin to Indian stoicism. He had forgotten his mother tongue, and could not speak English. He sought every occasion to shun the company of others, and when assigned to a clean feather bed in which to sleep, he refused, preferring to sleep on the ground with only a blanket for a covering. Oftentimes he would doff the suit furnished him, paint himself, and with leggins, breech-clout and feathers, appear among the hotel guests in all the barbaric panoply of a Comanche warrior. A few weeks after his return, a protracted meeting was being held under a brush arbor in Loyal Valley. Herman viewed the proceedings from a respectable distance, and his amazement was extreme. He finally concluded the whites were having a rain dance, and one day at the 11 o'clock service, when religious feeling became intense, and singing and shouting was at its height, Herman dashed into the altar with his war club, and engaged in a war dance that had a startling effect. His brothers seized him and led him away, and the service closed without the benediction. Nine Years among the Indians (Great Texas Books) (Herman Lehmann)

Val returned enthused by her weekend in the Big City. The preparations were nearly all complete. Roy had put up posters of the Tent revival declaring that he had obtained his degree in theology and God Business from America. He could show lost souls the way to Paradise. In small letters at bottom was the entry fee of one pound but what value do you put on saving your soul he said to customers coming to his temporary office to purchase tickets. If that didn't get them to hand over the pound, he said it would be good value because they had booked at considerable expense the most popular writer in the World, nobody less than the wildly popular Mark Twain, attending in the Cobb and Co Leviathan, and that had them quickly diving into their pockets. They longed to hear the stories about the Mississippi and the backwoods and see the biggest stage coach in the World, and bring grandma and grandpa too whose souls needed a little reassurance of their place in heaven.

Roy sold many tickets and deposited half the funds into in his earthen safe in the scrub without telling anyone. Val read the many essays, chose the winners from each

District, and had the local papers publish an article on their winning contestant and the big revival by the river. It led to much interest and plans to attend from all over Victoria. There was something for everyone. Just before the weekend Val caught the train to Melbourne to organize the winners for their short stay in Mr. Wagner's spacious mansion, and to make the final arrangements with Mr. Twain. She had booked a carriage to take everyone to the nearby town where they would disembark and board the Leviathan. This way Mr. Wagner explained the horses would not have pull a large coach a long way, and the shorter trip would leave the horses relatively fresh for their arrival at the river venue.

That morning they all boarded the train. Val observed Mr. Twain to visit the hotel and have them load for him two large crates of champagne and other expensive alcohol. He looked a little embarrassed when Val asked him about it but said it was needed to entertain guests on the river boat booked for his departure. On the way Val had given the task of picking the group winner of all the Victorian Districts Mr. Wagner. But something had happened. The atmosphere at his grand home was restrained and tense. Mr. Wagner had abruptly left for New York. Mr. Twain was moody and non-communicative. To Val it looked as if they had fallout or a disagreement, and she was worried. She attempted to speak to Mrs. Twain but all she would say was that she would not be accompanying her husband to the Tent Revival. Nevertheless, she busied herself with organizing and talking to the teenagers. They were all given free copies of the two famous novels by Mr. Twain and he intended to move freely amongst them discussing their essays and literature. But remained in his cabin and drank. When Val entered, he said, 'I do not feel well my dear but do not worry I have bought some medicine which will revive me.' He gave her several copies of a single paragraph he had written. He said give each one of the boys and girls a copy each. If I spoke to them for two hours I could not do better than give this advice. It said,

> 'I caution you use plain, simple language, short words and brief
> sentences. That is the way to write English—it is the modern way and the
> best way. Stick to it; don't let fluff and flowers and verbosity creep in.
> When you catch an adjective, kill it.'

Did Mr. Wagner leave with you the name of with final winner of the contest. He said yes. She asked where is it. He reluctantly pulled out a piece of paper with the name Venus Burns from Edenhope in Western Victoria written on it. She knew the girl - shy, withdrawn but a prodigious reader with a rapier intellect She cut a solitary figure with her head buried in one of the two books by Mr. Twain given to the winners by Val. She said-

'I have researched Mr. Twain with what limited materials I have, mainly public libraries and newspapers. I will try to do it in the plain speak that he so much admires. She identified with the kids and the river, a place where they were free. Her town was perched in edge of a very pretty, freshwater lake surrounded by shady red gums. It was a place where kids could swim, dive, fish, play and boat in the hot Australian summer. Freshwater lakes abound in her home and their existence in the conscious of the people and their vocabulary was as common as church, school and family.

She said was racist undertones - the use of the word nigger over two hundred times was used as was the stereotype of the runaway slave. He was portrayed as someone gullible with superstitions and a childlike intelligence. She read further and saw what Twain wrote about the American Indian which was superficial, and from what she had read untrue. Twain attempted to justify his criticisms on basis of reality. She wrote the degradation was as a result of their lands and way of life having been stolen by the white invaders much the same as happened in Australia with the aborigine. Far from being the hero of a new reality writing she thought him of doubtful learning, and a spendthrift and dilettante. She read how he had lost his wife's inheritance on hair brained inventions and publishing and that his talks were not unlike some comedy show with little or no comment on matters of national importance.

About Church matters and the Catholic faith he adopted the usual prejudices without acknowledging the good they do. She was ready to admit she had issues with the Church, but it was at the coalface and doing good things for those in need. And apart from the kindness of a few, it was the only Institution doing acts of charity, and for that it received little support or praise from so called intellectuals who wished only to see theoretical fault. Twain was a free mason and she thought a cupboard, white supremacist. He spent two weeks as confederate soldier and deserted probably she imagined through cowardice than any other high morale excuse like slavery. The Catholic Church was a refuge for the poor and starving Irish in Ireland, and continued its good works in Australia educating and feeding the poor. Without the assistance of her local priest, her destitute mother who was left alone with five starving children would have given up hope.'

That Mr. Wagner had chosen an essay highly critical of the famed author and his character, and left for America, confirmed with Val there had been a radical breakdown in their friendship. The effect on Mr. Twain was to make him uncommunicative, aloof and, and as was becoming alarmingly apparent to Val, increasingly drunk. She would have chosen Venus's essay because it was hard hitting and to her way of thinking accurate in her observations. She said things that others were too frightened to say in public and she probably expected to have it torn up and thrown into the rubbish bin but life is sometimes unpredictable. Apart from diplomatically attempting to have Mr. Twain stop drinking until he locked the door, she could only sit with the others and await the train's arrival at the country town where they were to board the giant Leviathan coach.

She had arranged for Ned and his cousins to be the security for the weekend and purchased them all expensive outfits, hats and boots. They were to accompany the coach to the venue much like a gold escort. She was feeling worried and afraid ...a telegraph had told her a large crowd had paid to hear Mr. Twain speak... and the way things were panning out and Mr. Twain's lack of sobriety increasing with every mile, there would be pandemonium at the Tent Revival. She was anxious to speak to Ned and get his advice. She was also anxious about whether she might have a massive debt if things took a sudden turn for the worse.

Unknown to Val, Roy was preaching as only he knew how – in the ole way – the Pentecostal way, the way he had learnt in the Southern backwoods where he was born. There was clapping, singing, swaying and the speaking in tongues. You could hear loud yelling... hallelujahs and glory be to Gods breaking out like spot fires in the crowd with their arms outstretched. It was fire and brimstone like they had never seen or heard. Roy dressed in his formal black preacher outfit with a fine tail, ranted and raved, strode up and down the high platform holding high his bible, speaking in powerful, evocative, biblical words of redemption and suffering, the blood of Jesus, the fires of hell and damnation...words that he knew well and came to him in inspired sentences that set his audience jumping up and down, swooning, and yelling for more. One moment he would fall to his knees, plead, whimper and cry with the big audience going deadly quiet, hanging off every word from his holy lips. Then loud and clear he would rise to his feet, jauntily pacing the platform up and down with his voice booming across the multitudes,

'like Moses I have been to the mountain, and I have seen the Lord, I am redeemed, I have risen, I have been washed in the blood of Jesus, glory be to God.'
And pointing to the crowd and waving the good book in his hand, he would exclaim,

'and you too can be redeemed, you, and you, and you, come to me, run to me, walk to me even crawl to me, and be cleansed of your sins, come to the alter of Jesus of Nazareth, the savior, and his humble servant and we will baptize you in the cleansing waters of the river'.

The audience spellbound and intoxicated by the powerful oratory of back wood's preacher pushed forward to the alter in a fever pitch. Every now and then Roy would return to his grand piano, and hollow in his deep baritone voice a moving, gospel ballad 'I go down to the river to pray.' Virgil would take over dressed in his fading grey, confederate uniform of a General, much like Robert E. Lee, do a few fancy steps in his long boots and spurs, and break out into song 'I would rather go blind'. The music and the crooning drugged and hypnotized the surging masses. In unison, they swayed like a tall wheat crop in a strong wind, one way then the other with their emotions running wild. The ready to be converted were taken to the clear waters of the river by white suited assistants to be baptized in the faith and to have their sins forgiven. It was all as Roy envisaged...he could not have hoped for better...it was like stealing candy from a baby.

The famous guest was to arrive in the Leviathan in the afternoon with Val and the teenage winners of the essay competition, but all was not as planned. Ned had to jemmy the train carriage door to get to Mr. Twain who was comatose on the couch snoring loudly. They tried to wake him to no avail. Ned said he would have to carry him upright by arm with help of his mate Joe on the other side to get him to the coach. A large crowd had congregated at the Station to see both the impressive coach and famous author who had featured in all the newspapers around the country with his bushy moustache and shock of greying wavy hair. Val placed a blanket over his head so they could not see his inebriated condition and said,

'I am going to need your help, Ned... I have a bad feeling and it's getting worse.'

Back at the river camp Roy had backed off to rest and peace descended on the crowd. They were awaiting the arrival of the spectacular coach and the even more spectacular American. Riders told them they were not far away and they gathered in rows beside the long entrance marked off with ropes. Suddenly amidst loud whoops and whip cracking a coach emerged out of the scrub much like a slow moving house on wheels in the brilliant colors of Cobb and Co. There was much cheering and clapping and waving of the old stars and banners flag.

'Ohhh my God,' yelled Roy,

'brothers and sisters – have I not delivered to you the greatest writer the World has seen – shortly you will see him and he will talk to you in words that unmistakably come from a man of great learning , great wisdom and intellect, and great integrity-mark my words dear and beloved friends this day will forever be imprinted into your heads as the day you saw and heard the best that has come to Australia from the mighty U.S. of A, and God willing, it will inspire you to repent and lead the holy life, a life that Jesus died on the cross for you to experience, a life away from the evils of sin, the hotels and the dead hand of alcohol. Do not let that poison touch your lips, brothers and sisters or you will burn in hell – set the example, be the light on the hill brothers and sisters for your dear little children to follow so that their lives will not be contaminated, be ruined by the sins of a drunken and forsaken man.'

The massive coach creaked to a stop in front of the alter. The teenagers and Val emerged looking a little hesitant. Roy and the crowd looked on waiting for the eminent guest to emerge. Val spoke to Ned.

'It's our only hope that he sobers up when he sees the vast audience. I have been told that he has done this before and spoke well enough to entertain the crowds.'

Ned and Joe entered the Coach. Mr. Twain was standing up a little unsteady. He pushed away the assistance of Ned and Joe and stumbled towards the door. As he emerged into the sunlight with his shaggy grey hair and his famous, crumpled, white suit the crowd pushed forward yelling his name and waving their small American flags. Ned and Joe assisted him up the steep stairs. On getting to the platform he rudely pushed Roy's embrace away, took hold of a rail and inched his way to the front of the alter. There he stood and looked out across the vast expanse of people who went deadly quiet waiting it seemed to hear the sermon from the mount. The ominous silence went on for about two minutes with each staring at the other. They were waiting for his words of wisdom, humor and smart repartee. He took a deep breath and in a raised voice said,

'my dear Australians, I will only say two sentences so listen carefully. Look at yourselves and ask if you have the guts to be independent, to be a Republic, or are you too yella to fight as we have done and forged our own destiny. As to this God business going here with this charlatan, this American dissembler, this God botherer, I say to you - don't waste your time or money because you, like me, are all going to hell in hand-basket. Now repeat after me – going to hell in a hand-basket.'

The crowd obediently repeated his words. They began to laugh. He was a funny man, an entertainer as they had heard, and they wanted more. He stood silent. The crowd began to slow clap. He said,

'clap all you want... you probably all have the clap.'

Another ripple of laughter spread through the crowd although this time they were not sure if he was being funny or just abusive.'

Some of the crowd started to boo.

The renowned author gave them the finger, hiccupped, made a grab for the rail, missed and toppled over the balcony falling from the platform into the crowd..

'He's as drunk as a Lord,' they yelled.

'He drank all the way,' said the teenage contestants.

Mr. Twain vomited, and passed out. Two males entered the Coach and emerged with crates of alcohol and empty bottles.

'This what we paid for,' they yelled holding the empty bottles in the air for all to see. The crowd went into a frenzy demanding their money back and heading for the office tent where it was kept in leather cases. Roy protested but was pushed aside along with his two security men. The crowd tore apart the cases, stuffed their pockets and threw wads of money to the enraged masses. One moment they were born again Christians and there was love in the valley and converts in the river - now there was a bunch of criminals baying for blood. Virgil jumped into action. He was used to organizing men,. Ned and his men rushed the drunken author to his River Boat and told them to stoke the fires and leave immediately while the crowd was still occupied in getting grabbing what they could. The boat rapidly took off with their paddles churning at a rate of knots not daring to blow their fog horns. Virgil, Ned and his men quickly gathered Val and Roy, mounted them, and also took off along the scrub tracks. They had no choice. The crowd would have shortly turned on them seeking revenge and they were hopelessly outnumbered. They rode hard and no one spoke as they threaded their horses quietly through the bush.

Some twenty miles away they stopped to rest and make a little fire to sit by. They looked at each other relieved they had made some distance, and a nervous laughter broke out. Not so Valerie who seemed to be in shock staring blankly ahead. Ned had ridden close beside her watching that she did not fall. She was not an experienced rider. He was close enough to catch her if she fell but strangely her indifference to her fate made her calm. She did not clamp down like a nervous rider or franticly pull on the reins but sat loose in the saddle almost willing herself a fatal injury. The horse responded to her calm and together they glided gracefully through the bush in a almost dreamlike state.

When they halted, Roy looked glum.

He looked at Val and said,

'I kept my part of the bargain – what about you, our girl wonder of the business deal and the darling of the literati?'

Val did not respond.

Ned strangely did nothing. Did he too think Val was getting above herself, and an explanation was needed?

Val looked at Ned.

Ned looked the other way.

Val slid off her horse, walked to a tree, sat down with her back to the others and put her head in her hands.

All she wants is another baby

The death of Indian children.

Children are carried about in their cradles on the backs of their mothers wherever they go. When the children die they are often left in their cradles floating on the water of a brook or pool, which their superstition tells them to regard as sacred. A cluster of these little arks or cradles, or coffins as they may be called of different forms in a lone pool is a very picturesque and affecting sight. - History and manners and customs of the North American Indians - old Humphrey.

an Indian baby talks to the squirrels and birds.

my mother would suspend me from a wild grape vine or a springy bough, so that the least breeze would swing the cradle to and fro. She has told me that when I had grown old enough to take notice, I was apparently capable of holding extended conversations in an unknown dialect with birds and once I fell asleep in my cradle, suspended five or six feet from the ground, while Uncheedah was some distance away, gathering birch bark for a canoe. a squirrel had found it convenient to come upon the bow of my cradle and nibble his hickory nut, until he awoke me by dropping the crumbs of his meal. It was a common thing for birds to alight on my cradle in the woods. Indian Child Life (Charles A. Eastman)

Valerie's short foray into business failed. She would be sued for the debts and would have to go bankrupt. Ned tried to console her but she regressed. Indifferent to her usual conversation topics, she said,

'I enjoyed my ride away from those madmen.'

Ned replied, 'you rode well, Val... the best I have seen you ride... I didn't think you had it in you.'

'Ned, I can do things like you can never imagine...like going broke, bankrupt, a miserable failure...all in one weekend.'

For weeks after Val remained in her room at Paddy's farm, saw no one, and became depressed. Her books were strewed across floor and she barely had the will power or energy to leave her bed. Ma Quin prepared meals and took them to her but she pushed the plate away saying 'I have no appetite for anything Ma'. Her little cocker spaniel, Hercules, sensed her deep disillusionment and stayed close. On Paddy's urging she would take her loyal, little dog for occasional walks along the nearby river, and in time nature, the gentle, flowing water, the breezes, the eucalypt perfumes of the red river gums, the flowering bushes and shrubs, the intricate and vividly colored wild flowers, and all the sweet sounds of the myriad bird life, their calls and animated chirping, healed her wounds and brought her back to a life of sorts. She would take on new ideas and ambitions. This time local and domestic. But the sudden mood changes remained.

One evening she thought to go to the local Church. With her new-found ability she borrowed a horse from one of Paddy's boys and rode into town. She saw on the walls the Stations of the Cross, unbearable and senseless suffering every ten feet of the

Church wall as Jesus struggled with the weight of the cross, the whippings, the nailing of his hands and feet to the timber beams while his mother stood by not able to do anything to ease his plight. The Catholic Church espoused a tradition of silent suffering. It made her even sadder yet she could empathize with the sufferings of Jesus. As a helpless child, she could do nothing when the relationship between her and her demented father disintegrated into blank stares and mad ranting's in the middle of the night while she, a child, lay confused and alone in her bed. There was no-one to help her, the same as there was no one to come to Jesus's aid. Sometimes her Dad would be his old self, lucid and affectionate, but it would not last and he would then be pursued by voices telling him what to do. It was a hell of a life for a kid and she got no respite at school with the cruelty some children show. Now some people had turned against her seeing her as schemer, and an associate to the serial fraudster, Roy. If they spoke to her, she frankly admitted,

'I tried and failed. It was not Roy's fault. It was mine and I accept the blame. I trusted respectable people, was over awed by wealth, celebrity and the City, I should have known better... but life goes on or at least I hope it does. I will get over it although it has taken a toll on me.'

When Ned visited one evening, Ma Quinn said Valerie had taken off unexpectedly. Ned rode into town to see if he could find her. Someone said they had seen her heading to the Church. He walked down the street and entered small timber construction which appeared empty and poorly lit. A full moon shone through the stained-glass windows where he could just make out a solitary female form standing very still in front of the Stations of the Cross. He moved closer.

'Val...is that you?' he asked. The form did not reply but Ned could hear a muffled sobbing. He saw it was her. Without looking at him she said,

'I am not taking this shit anymore.'

She was standing in front of the statue of the crucifixion.

As she sobbed, she hung onto the outstretched arms of Jesus nailed to cross.

'All that remains is for me to be crucified, Ned.'

'Come now, Val ...you are not well...we'll go home.'

His condescending manner irritated her.

'It's Valerie, not Val and home...I don't have a home in case you didn't notice?

I'm a boarder in other people's homes...a boarder in their hearts...not like family, Ned... I don't have family.'

Ned stood there not knowing what to say or do. He remembered what Ma Quinn said about her.'

'I want to have a baby, Ned...we can be a family.'

Ned stood there speechless at what she had said.

'Do I have to spell it out? We can create life in God's little house here, Ned...we'll be doing God's work...go forth and multiply the bible says...with his blessing, I will bear a child. It will be our baby. My last baby was enterprise and business but it was stillborn.'

'You're going plumb crazy, Val...we can't do this in the Church of all places.'

'Ned, be a man ...treat me like a normal girl and not like cot case. I don't need people's charity or their condemnation. I can prevail over my troubles, and I can forge a life on my own terms. I don't have to be lectured to or told how to behave or what is expected of me.'

'We are leaving, Val...I'll take you home...let go of that statue.'

Valerie hung desperately to the arms of the outstretched Jesus and resisted his efforts to pull her away. She gripped him around the waist with her thin legs, and said,

'Nail me to the wall...and then the dearly beloved congregation with their dull, apologetic faces can say their boring prayers in front of me rather than these depressing statues...at least they'll see a smiling face, joy, contentment rather than their precious, eternal suffering, damnation and hellfire.'

Ned relaxed. Valerie was establishing her territory in her normal confrontational style.

'To make love is not a sin in the eyes of the Lord, Ned...it is life affirming...it produces life... and didn't Jesus say I have come so that you may have life more abundantly?'

Clamped together in the cold precincts and dim light of the darkened and empty Church, Ned's mood changed. Valerie felt his resistance ebb away, and her anger subside. They kissed and caressed. Ned was strangely aroused by this unconventional girl, so far different from the girls popularly sought and pursued by the local boys. She always kept him guessing and although he wouldn't admit it he liked her that way. She challenged him to be different. The absolute forbidden impossibility to conceive of two people having sex in a small, country church challenged him in a way that heightened his desire to consummate the relationship. He entered her rebellious softness.

Valerie with her incessant fears, her inhibitions, that crown of thorns in her head left there by the death of her mother and a father gone crazy, let her spine rub up and down against the smooth, alabaster legs of the tortured Son of God as she hung grimly to his firmly sculptured arms. In that small, humble church constructed of hardwood from high in the Wombat Ranges, Valerie felt the purifying blood of Jesus flooding into her, coursing down through her body, cleansing her of her sense of abandonment, neglect and rejection that cruel fate had unfairly placed on her youthful shoulders. Enmeshed in the vigor of their illicit lovemaking, a plaster arm of Jesus strained, and unable to bear the weight of a poor, demented girl, snapped at the shoulder collapsing the copulating couple onto the church floor in a unseemly heap. They lay there too frightened to move or speak. Above them the remaining hand of Jesus, holding his lacerated and tormented torso to the cross, swung slowly on its embedded nail like the pendulum of a Grandfather clock.

'How are we going to explain this...a one-armed Jesus,' exclaimed Ned in some despair. He didn't know whether to laugh or cry. This academic, solemn, book reading girl had run him ragged with her demands, her clandestine sexuality, her ramrod intellect and unobtainable ambitions. Valerie stretched herself out on the floor clasping the broken hand. She was calm. She listened holding her fingers cupped to her ear.

'Shush...can you hear that?' she asked.

'No...what?' he replied.

She thought she heard her mother speak,

'My darling child...you poor, little, abandoned waif...come to me my child...I am waiting and this world is not for you or me.'

'I'm coming mum ...I'm coming...and we will soon be together, together in the that big firmament, the Milky Way.'

'Is it peaceful and beautiful there, Mum... in that bright firmament with all that luminous whiteness surrounding you?'

'Darling, it is paradise.'

'What are you talking about, Val?' asked Ned confused.

She would not tell him. The crazy hear voices...don't they. The two illicit lovers departed from the Church and took with them the right hand of Jesus. They told none of their erotic vandalism in the house of God that evening.

'The forces of evil are at work,' said Father Murphy the following morning when he spied through his alcoholic stupor the desecration visited upon his humble Church in the form of a missing limb of Jesus, and the holy statue hanging askew. Some said vandals and disbelievers were up to no good. 'Methodists, Protestants,' said another. One parishioner said Jesus must have lent a hand to someone in need. 'Sacrilege, blasphemy,' they cried as they quickly ushered him from the Church for his crude attempt to be funny.

'I was just trying to make everyone happy...for once,' he protested as they flung him out the Church doors.

'Be gone, Satan,' yelled Father Murphy as the innocent offender fled the Church grounds wondering what he had done. 'It don't make sense,' he said to himself, jumping the pretty, lime washed picket fence and taking off down the street.

Baby, please don't go

Loneliness [mother's advice to her daughter]

Dear Astrid, Don't tell me how you hate your new foster home. If they're not beating you, consider yourself lucky. Loneliness is the human condition. Cultivate it. The way it tunnels into you allows your soul room to grow. Never expect to outgrow loneliness. Never hope to find people who will understand you, someone to fill that space. An intelligent, sensitive person is the exception, the very great exception. If you expect to find people who will understand you, you will grow murderous with disappointment. The best you'll ever do is to understand yourself, know what it is that you want, and not let the cattle stand in your way. – Janet Fitch – White Oleandor

'Fitzy...I want you to go to the Kelly's and execute this warrant for the arrest of Dan Kelly. That little bugger thinks he can take the place of his older brother. He got into a fight at the pub at Wangaratta and the report here says he started it. That's good enough for me.'

'I hope that Kate Kelly is home...I sure got the hots for her Sarge.'

'Leave that trash alone,' said Sarge 'I don't want any more trouble than I can handle. If you get problems from any of the others, just come back and I'll send reinforcements. Ned's been a reformed boy since coming back from jail. They must have rehabilitated him.'

'It's not that,' said Four Eyes, 'he's got a girlfriend...Valerie.'

'Has he now. I thought you were a bit keen on her, Cyril...what happened?'

'I thought I was doing all right too Sarge till Kelly came on the scene. She let me hold her hand one night.'

'She's a bit crazy in the head I heard. Wasn't that her old man they put in looney bin.'

'She got a good head, Sarge. As you know we share a common interest in books. I even lent her some of my accounting books. She needed them to do the bookwork for Roy's Circus.'

Sarge just shook his head, saying 'the less said about that the better, Cyril.'

Fitzy cleaned up his trooper's uniform, polished his long boots, slicked back his wavy, dark locks and studied himself in the mirror. Having admired himself for a few minutes, he took the warrant and rode off on official business. As he rode along, he swigged from his flask of whisky. He rode up to the front door of the house behind the bar. Elly came to the door.

'Mrs. Kelly...can I come in...I have something I'd like to discuss with you.'

'No, this will do... make it quick. I don't like to be seen fraternizing with the likes of you...nothing personal I hope you understand.'

'Now there's no need to be unfriendly, Mrs. Kelly...I'm only doing my job.'

'If you want my advice you would do well to give up that job for an honest one.'

'Like your boys, I suppose.'

'They doing nothing wrong if that's what you are trying to say.'

'I beg to differ, Mrs. Kelly.'

He pushed past her into the house seeing the girls about their work.

'Hello Kate,' he said, 'I haven't seen you at the dances lately...got yourself a regular man have you?'

'If I have it would be none of your business,' she replied tersely not stopping from her work.

'Spirited little lassy aren't we now,' he said pulling up a chair and grabbing her around the waist.

'Come then and sit on my knee while we talk about it.'

'Get lost,' she yelled trying to extricate herself.

Dan walked in.

'Just the man I want to see,' said Fitzy.

'Let her go, Fitzy,' said Dan.

The trooper saw his opportunity.

'You...you fucking little pansy...have a look at this piece of paper. In case you can't read it authorizes me to arrest you and take you to the nearest prison. Now I'm sure Kate and I can work out a compromise.'

Dan jumped him getting him in a bear hug forcing him to let go Kate. He broke free of Dan's grip and pulled his revolver. He pointed it at Dan,

'Ok... now you do what I say time.' He felt a jarring metal thud on the back of his head knocking him to the ground. Elly clobbered him with Dan's spade. As he stumbled to the floor his gun misfired grazing his wrist. Ned heard the noise from the paddock and ran to the house.

'What the hell's going on here,' he demanded.

'I've been shot,' said Fitzpatrick looking at his wrist graze.

'He's been messing with Kate,' said Dan 'and he says he's got a warrant for me for pinching stock but he hasn't got it on him. He's drunk too.'

'Look we'll bandage the wound,' said Ned It's nothing much. Here is your pistol... you can go back now. There's no need to say anything about your wrist.'

'If you say so Ned...I don't want any trouble.'

'You did your best to start it,' said Kate.

'I was only jokin, Kate...nothin serious.' Elly wrapped a bandage around his hand, and he left. He left to tell a lie that would make him a victim and the two brothers wanted men, wanted for attempted murder.

'Sarge,' he said 'I got that Dan Kelly, but I was shot by Ned and hit over the head by their mum...I was lucky to get out with my life...look at my bleedin wrist.'

'Attempt murder... don't you think,' said Sarge examining the wound and looking at his studious clerk.

'Sarge, you know what a bunch of felons they are,' replied Fitzy. The news of the warrant for attempted murder against both Ned and Dan spread fast. When Ned heard about the warrant, he knew it meant a long time in jail. He had already done two years and he'd not risk a long sentence taking up most of his life.

'Pack your bags,' he said to Dan, 'we heading for the Ranges. I've had enough of these Traps harassing us every chance they get. They're going to learn that we will hit back from now on. I'm sorry Mum but there is no other way...I'll not spend my years rotting away in jail. We'll keep an eye on you and the kids, and Roy will look after you. I hope to God there will be a way of setting this right but in meanwhile we'll hide in Ranges.' It broke Elly's and the girls' hearts to see the boys forced from their home to be hunted like wild animals. Light, misty rain was beginning to fall as Ned and Dan saddled two packhorses and their best mounts. They put on their oilskins, kissed the family goodbye, and rode into the dying, evening light.

'We'll track up the Ranges to a hut I know about from my logging,' said Ned, 'It's pretty isolated and will give us shelter for a while but first I have to call on Valerie and break the bad news. I don't want her to hear it from someone else. She'll take it real bad.' By the time they got to Paddy's place, it was raining heavily and black clouds hung low in the skies. The wind came up bowing the treetops and they could hear the clap of distant thunder and an approaching storm.

'You stay with the horses, Dan...we have to be careful now. I'll just see Valerie on the verandah for a few minutes.'

Ned explained what had happened to his Grandparents at the door.

Valerie appeared, and with a smile took Ned's hand.

Valerie sensed things were gravely wrong.

'I'm sorry...me and Dan have to run for it...I couldn't risk goal for the next twelve years...believe me there is nothing I can do to stop this happening. It will be better for you if I keep clear for a while... the Traps will be watching the place and they will trump up a charge against you like they have done us. I hope you can understand, Val.'

'I understand nothing about you, Ned... nothing...do you hear ...I knew it would come to this. You prefer it this way, I know...out in the Ranges on those bloody horses. It's a big kid's game, isn't it? Answer to no-one. You're not prepared to give it up for the sake of a decent life, a life that I might be able to share. It's not going to come to any good in the end, Ned, you know that, don't you?' She broke into heartfelt sobs. Ned went to console her.

'Don't touch me,' she yelled.

'I feel like sick...sick in my head and sick in my stomach. Left by a mum I hardly knew, abandoned by drunken, crazy father, a failed business and if that weren't enough, now this...led on by a philanderer, an adventurer, who plied me with a pack of lies about how he was going to change, about how we would have a family together, about...about...,

You, Ned, have cruelly built up my expectations and then robbed me of them as though they didn't exist or have any legitimacy. It's nothing but robbing of the worst kind. I should have known you would do that... it's your specialty isn't it...robbing, thieving, stealing... call it what you like. You can steal emotions, Ned, just the same as a horse. To me they are my most valuable possessions...take them ...I don't want them back ever again. It will only stop with you swinging from a noose, Ned, and don't expect me to be a crying, little wife in the background.'

In halting, unconvincing words she could barely speak through her sobs she said,

'I've got more important things to achieve...my books, that's all I need...books, books, and more fucking books...at least they don't piss off in the middle of the night or make dishonest promises. Now please go...I need time to be by myself.'

Ned turned and left. He knew and understood how she felt. He had no answers, no words to pacify her disappointment. She would have to endure as they would. She watched Ned go to his horse and stand silently in the rain for a minute looking at the lightening flashing in the distant Ranges. He then looked back at her as if he wanted to try and explain but stopped, put his boot in the stirrup and swung into the saddle and left. As she saw them disappear into the wet blackness, she put her hands to her face, walked as if in a trance out into the mud and rain.

'Baby please don't go, baby please don't go...' she yelled after them.

She began to flail her arms about wildly and her eyes rolled backwards to the dark, brooding sky. Lightening cracked across the blackness lighting up the countryside. She struggled and fought but something more powerful, more sinister was taking control of her body, drowning her and hitting on her like the pelting rain that splattered in dirty pools around her and deluged the countryside. The Grandparents watched the pitiful sight from the window.

'She's flipped,' said Paddy, 'I'll go get her.'

'I don't think the poor girl will get over this,' said Ma Quinn shaking her head, 'I don't blame Ned cus he has little choice, but she can't take any more, Pop...the shock of her Mum, then her Dad and now this...it's too much for any kid.'

They two boys rode silently into the night bonded by their brotherhood and a common enemy. They didn't notice the rain soaking the earth, turning the roads into quagmire and swelling the gently flowing rivers and streams until you could hear them roar their presence in the distance. Every now and then the lightening lit up the sky above their heads giving glimpses of windswept bush and the narrow tracks littered with broken branches and broken dreams.

In the morning, Valerie left her room, and went down to the stream flowing full and fast at the base of the Ranges. Before she left, she took her mother's old wedding dress from her cupboard and put it on. She briefly looked at herself in the mirror. She then took a box from under her bed and placed on her finger her mother's wedding ring. Without closing the door to her room, she left. No one saw her leave. She strode through the paddocks carrying the right arm of Jesus which she had hidden in her closet. Hercules was at her side but strangely quiet and uninterested in the bushes. Not glancing to the left or right but her head fixed straight ahead, she walked on. The train of the white wedding dress trailing behind her became muddied and wet. She remembered her mother saying the longer the train the more noble the family. That was a generation ago and now with her mother prematurely dead, her dad trapped in an Infirmary with a feeble mind and incapable of looking after himself, and she having blitzed what little respect the family had left with ignominy of her failed business venture, and finally the loss of settled life with Ned, she knew there was no hope or future left for her. Val walked through a herd of skittish horses that leapt this way and that and raced up to her snorting and curious. She walked on scattering the sheep as though she had not seen them until she came to the river's edge where she stood frozen and passive. There she contemplated the powerful torrent of water swirling past her, and longed for her mum.

Not far away a solitary rider approached.

It was Roy.

He had given up wearing his brightly colored American clobber not wishing to attract more attention than he thought necessary. Valerie had spooked him. He thought maybe he had been too careless to boast about his time in the Cavalry. He had recently been told she had borrowed his book on the American Indian from Tennessee. He had heard that Valerie had been writing to the States and he needed to know what she was up to before events overtook him. Without being too obvious he sought information from Ned but that only got Ned and the girls curious. He knew he would have to front Valerie when she was alone. He knew that their relationship had cooled after the Revival failure and although he had taken sufficient money to keep himself in the clear he had abandoned Val to the debt collectors. Would she now have revenge on him and reveal his true identity. Roy also knew she had the habit of walking the river by the Quinn's property so he took to having regular rides in the area hoping to come across her. With the river in full flood, he guessed she might be there. Now the opportunity had arrived, and he was unusually nervous about what the confrontation would bring.

Valerie patted her dog, told him to be a good boy, held tightly to the hand of Jesus, and began to wade into the stream when she heard Hercules bark and sensed the presence of someone directly behind her, watching her every step.

Tell me the things you never speak of, Roy

Kate Kelly

folk law has it that in the 1890's a touring stage company playing in Forbes included a brief Kelly pantomime in its repertoire. Kate was in the audience and at the conclusion of the sketch a cast member pointed her out and said 'there's the real heroine of the story'. Kate immediately ran out the theatre. The incident seemed to trigger a deep melancholy within her. A few days later her body was found floating in the river. Glenrowan - Ian Shaw.

dog companion

Wabeda, the dog, the companion of my boyhood days, was in trouble because he insisted upon bringing his extra bone into the teepee, while Uncheedah was determined that he should not. I sympathized with him, because I saw the matter as he did. If he should bury it in the snow outside, I knew Shunktokecha (the coyote) would surely steal it. I knew just how anxious Wabeda was about his bone. It was a fat bone--I mean a bone of a fat deer; and all Indians know how much better they are than the other kind. Wabeda always hated to see a good thing go to waste. His eyes spoke words to me, for he and I had been friends for a long time. When I was afraid of anything in the woods, he would get in front of me at once and gently wag his tail. He always made it a point to look directly in my face. His kind, large eyes gave me a thousand assurances. When I was perplexed, he would hang about me until he understood the situation. Many times, I believed he saved my life by uttering the dog word in time. Indian Child Life Charles A. Eastman.

'It's a little cold for a swim, Val,' said Roy seated on Blue Doggy. She turned to see him. He and Blue Doggy were as still as a stone statue except for wind flapping the tails of his long coat. She had not heard him come up behind her because of the roar of the raging river.

'And what's that you wearing – are you goin to some fancy-dress show?'

'I'm not intending to swim but to sink, Roy, or whatever your name is.'

'Now Val, I mean no offense. What do you think my name is, Val?'

'I don't think ...I know...I read far and wide, Roy. As wide as the vast American Plains or even that place you know well, the Little Big Horn.'

'To tell you the truth I suspected as much - go on, Val – tell me more.'

'You tell me, Roy.'

'What?'

'The things you never speak of.'

Roy kept his cool, but inside his heart was beating as fast as when he deserted Custer.

'Let me tell you, Roy... your name is Henry Darrington, second lieutenant in Company D of the Seventh Cavalry...the only body they could not find or identify after the massacre.'

That was the first time for many years that Roy had heard someone address him in his real name. It shocked him to hear it but it also came with authenticity and a desperate feeling of homesickness.

'Go on, Valerie. I am listening.'

'You did a runner, Henry?'

'Me – do a runner?'

'I think you did. There was no Roy Kingsly in the US Seventh Cavalry or the US Army. I have checked the records. Your Indian book you gave to Tennessee has Company D stamped on it, not clear but under strong magnifying glass it is there, and would you believe that was your Company, Henry. I have studied all the reports of the Little Big Horn but one Indian statement which was officially discarded interested me. The witness, an Indian brave, said the blue coat holding the horses let them go except his which was an Appy and stabbed a trooper who appeared to be confronting him. He then threw a smoke bomb and rode for his life. He says three braves including himself pursued him and another trooper just behind him. He says the other two stopped to scalp one whose horse had given up but that he followed you for a day and half and then gave up because your horse was too good and outdistanced him.'

Roy smirked, and patted Blue Doggy's neck.

Valerie went on- 'He described that horse and the description exactly fits Blue Doggy. Not many horses that color, Roy. The Indian didn't want to admit his failure in the post battle celebrations and lied saying he overtook and killed you. That deserter was you...wasn't it, Henry? The Army couldn't countenance such cowardly conduct and filed it away never to be shown to anyone because it was only the word of one Indian who had told two different stories, but secretly they have been looking for you, Roy. Your file has never been closed, Roy.'

'I am not a coward, Val.'

'How does it feel, Roy, to have deserted America's greatest hero?'

Roy sighed and gave up his denials. She knew too much.

'You are a smart girl, Val. I can fool all the others but not you. Have you told anyone?'

'No...I have kept it to myself. I didn't want to upset Ned and his family...but for how much longer...well maybe that's up to you,' She had no fear of death. In truth she wanted it when she knew there was no prospect of normal life with Ned. But she would for a while exploit what she knew just to see how Roy would react.

'Roy...I have had a shit of a life as is too plain to see. You will have to pay to keep your dirty, little secret safe. I wouldn't mind a few luxuries in life like a cottage, books and music...you know the sort of things you can afford.'

'How much?' asked Roy.

'Big money, Roy... and the consequences if I sing don't bear considering...do they? I mean extradited back to USA. I don't think they would even give you a trial Roy when they hear what you did to their hero Custer and his brothers.

Let's see now; your hair would be cut off; if not hung you would be imprisoned for long time; and I heard they even brand your face with large 'C' or 'D' for all to see.

You know what that means Roy? I'll tell you.

'C' for coward, Roy... did you hear clearly, Roy?

Or would you prefer 'D' for deserter? You can have your choice.'

Roy shook in his saddle. Val was right. Although there was something about this astute, smart girl that he admired, he knew then he would have to shoot the know all, snooping bitch. Not being sure he could get a clean shot with her in the stream, he said,

'I've got the money in my saddle bag, Val. I knew this time was coming and I have prepared for it.'

He placed his hand on his silver barreled colt hidden in his bag. It fitted snugly into his palm. Valerie knew instinctively what he was about to do. She did not flinch.

'If you are going to shoot me, Roy, don't bother because someone else has done that much better than you could ever hope to do- shot to the heart.'

'Who?' he said as he slowly withdrew his hand from his bag.

'I'll take that secret to my grave,' she replied as she waded further into the deep torrent. With all the lucidity and honesty Valerie was capable of, she said,

'Come with me, Roy. You are living a lie here in Australia, and it will come to no good in the end. I don't blame you for doing a runner although many would. I would have done the same myself. Custer had it coming to him. He was out to make himself a hero and if that meant massacring the Indians, he would have done it, woman and children too. Come Roy...come on...we can both leave this world together...consider it the last of our business deals, a free pass to eternity...or are you going to do another runner...which is it, Roy?'

Roy moved uncomfortably in his western saddle, and gripped the horn looking around for some solace. Her taunting yet encouraging words echoed in his head, and though he would not admit it, they made sense. His emotions were in turmoil. His eyes moistened. For the first time in many years since he had run disgracefully from the Battle of the Little Big Horn, he had not been able to reveal the truth and unburden the terrible guilt that weighed him down and followed him everywhere like a menacing shadow. This guilt that kept him looking back and over his shoulder, day and night, that made him hyper vigilant such that he developed a nervous twitch and uncontrollable shaking that came and went without explanation no matter how many doctors he saw or what medicines he took. A guilt that made him hollow and scream in the middle of the night, and wake in a cold sweat feeling for the imaginary noose around his neck. Valerie, this neglected and tortured girl, was defending him, and he was about to shoot her down. He was conflicted. Would he accept her invitation and stop his running, his nightmares, his isolation in foreign country or would he look the other way.

'I can't do it, Val...I want to go home, back to the States. I want to be reunited with my wife and kids...Oh Jesus, I miss them kids - my loving, faithful wife and my home in America...I have no real family here in Australia, Val, and I don't much like the place or people for that matter. I want to go home to where I belong.'

'I understand, Roy,' she said, 'it's ok ...I understand. I think I too will go back to my family.'

She waded into the deep, strong current. Roy hesitated. He wanted to say 'don't do it, Val...come back and I will care for you and make life better...buy for you all the things you have ever wanted,' but the words did not come. He noticed that Valerie was carrying a broken plaster arm. He had heard of the vandalism at the church.

'What's that you are carrying in your hand, Val?'

'It's the hand of God, Roy...the mercy of Jesus of Nazareth has come to me in my final moments. And he will guide and lead me to my mum in the Milky Way.'

Poor child...she's gone stark raving mad thought Roy, but her words resonated to his deepest emotions, and his moved his cheating heart.

'In a different world, in a kinder world, things could have been better, Val...' Roy choked and bit his lip. 'I mean you did such a good job with the Circus, and...'

Val intervened having heard enough.

'Keep your love, Roy...try shoving it up your star spangled, Yankee arse where everyone else's shitty love can go,' she said and gave a sad, little laugh.

With eyes as cold as ice, she waved a gentle goodbye to Roy, and with a wan smile she entered the surging water. It rose about her, tugging and pulling her thin, yielding body draped in her mother's heavily braided wedding dress with its mud stained train swirling behind her. The strong tow lifted and swept her downstream. Roy saw the alabaster hand of Jesus break the frothy surface of the fast-flowing river as though calling, trying to summon help, and then there was nothing.

As the river took her under, words like bubbles of air tumbled over and over in her head. They said 'Mum, I'm coming home to you.' Hercules ran up and down the river bank barking and howling, and then leapt in, swimming strongly towards the bobbing Valerie. They were both sucked down the raging river, and out of sight. Perhaps Hercules thought he could take her in his soft mouth as he would take a stunned or shot bird from the river, and carry her to safety but it was a task too difficult for little dog in such a strong current. Valerie went from a world that gave her nothing but anguish and heartbreak to a place of contentment and peace. She took her life to another place with no fear as though she were simply boarding a train.

Roy sat there in the saddle for a while unable to comprehend what had happened. Without even thinking he took his lasso and swung it above his head several times so that it made a strange whirring sound as though it were some odd funeral rite. All the time Blue Doggy did not move a muscle. Roy turned Blue Doggy and rode down the river for about a mile or two, looking and calling for her, but he found neither Valerie or her faithful dog. 'Val, Val,' he yelled but he could hardly be heard above the roar of the angry river. Was Roy hoping for a miracle, to find her swept onto a bank gasping for breath, or clasping to a half-submerged log for dear life. And would he have taken her home, made her warm, talked to her all night, and convinced her that life after all was worth a dime? And with his money, would he have made her life comfortable and surrounded her with expensive and interesting books? Or would his intentions be more sinister? Valerie never gave him the chance to know.

The wind came up, and the clouds went dark and foreboding. Roy turned up the collars of his long, dust coat to protect himself from the cold, pulled down his wide brimmed hat, turned Blue Doggy again to face the wind and rain, and trotted home. He did not want to be recognized. As he rode through the sleet and darkness of the enveloping bush, Roy ears were pierced by the eerie sounds of the barking owl. It sounded like the desperate screams of woman or child, and it chilled him to the bone. Was it a harbinger of death he thought, and whose death was it heralding - Valerie's or his? That night alone in his bed Roy wept. He cried for a girl that exposed his hidden identity, and took him back, back to a person he now hardly knew or recognized. A person who was in love with his young wife and two beautiful children, and who only thought of doing good, until the fickle hand of fate stepped in, and spun him onto another stage where he had to reinvent himself to stay alive.

They found Valerie's limp body snagged against the gnarled tree roots of a big, old, river red gum like an abandoned, rag doll, her muddy trains washed to a dull white and ensnared on half submerged branches. Hercules was there guarding her like the strong man he was, and holding in his soft lips, not a duck or wounded bird, but the stolen right hand of the Son of God. Her Dad loved those giant, weirdly angular, brittle red gums, the spreading roots in which Valerie lay. They reminded him of a country lost in time and forgotten on the edge of the world. In his better days, he would proudly point them out to her as they strolled hand in hand along the river. One moment strong, massive, and unassailable and then, in the still heat of the day, a loud rip rendering the silence, a gaping, splintered red scar, and its limbs scattered and broken on the earth below. Their burden like Valerie's was too heavy. There on the sheltered bank, she looked at peace. There, wrapped in the tangled roots of the ancient, red gum, like the comforting arms of her demented father... waiting...waiting to see a mother she was too young to really know, but whose distant memory she held as the only precious thing in her sad, troubled heart.

Roy said nothing of their meeting. This man from the U.S. of A led a charmed life. Valerie's life had little charm right to its bitter end.

Johnny, won't you come on home

An Indian child comforts a white child, Cynthia Parker, taken by Indians.

The Indian child crawled up next to her and pulled the robe back. She wrapped her arms around her and rocked her gently, smoothing the snarled, dirty yellow hair and wiping the tears away with the side of her palm. Star Name was dressed in a breechclout and was as brown as saddle leather, polished smooth. "Ka taikay, ka taikay, Tohobt Nabituh, don't cry, blue eyes. It's all right." It was the first warm, human contact Cynthia had had since the attack on the fort. She huddled in the lean brown arms, inhaling the sweet, smoked smell of Star Name. She clung to her like a baby squirrel to a tree limb a hundred feet above the ground.
Ride the Wind (Lucia St Clair Robson)

Ned felt responsible for Valerie's death but he had no choice. He could either rot in jail and come out an old man with his best years wasted or make a stand. The Police kept a close watch at her small funeral, taking a low profile and hoping to at least get a sighting of Ned and Dan. Elly was arrested for aiding assault with intent to murder and the trial was listed before Judge Barrington at his request. He knew of the Kelly's and considered he was the one to sort them out. Fitzpatrick was a plausible liar. The drunken trooper made himself out a hero who barely escaped with his life from the lair of violent and desperate criminals whereas it was he who groped the young Kate and threatened her brothers. Barrington described him as a courageous and honest witness who had no motive to lie unlike the defense witnesses. Having got his verdict, he sent the hardworking mother down for three years saying he would have given her son Ned fifteen years if he were in his Court. It made no matter that she had the care of young children. When Ned heard the result, he said he would hand himself over in return for the release of their mum. The Authorities wouldn't hear of it. They intended to get all of them with no deals. One injustice was heaped on another forcing Ned and Dan to go on the run.

It was not long before Joe and Steve joined their two friends in the Ranges. Whereas Joe and Ned were tall and strongly built, Steve and Dan were almost the opposite; younger, lightly built boys, soft faced and agile – just kids really. Steve's enraged father did his block when he finally left to join the Kelly's. Steve had longed for the day when he could walk out the door and turn his back for good on the bickering and the misery of two depressed and ugly humans who pretended to be his parents. As Steve rode from his home, he heard his Father yell,

'You fucking, little queer...I hope you rot in the bush with those other mongrels. Don't ever come back here, so God help me, I'll choke the life out of ya with my bare hands.'

Steve pulled his horse to a halt.

'Queer,' he said, as he spun his horse around and glared at his Dad, red faced from his abuse and spitting venomously from the slit in his brick face. He stopped. He knew that although not strong, the lightly built youth carried in his head something he'd best not meddle with. But meddle with he had. The boy spurred his horse in the flank and bore down on his abuser at a rapid pace. His Dad turned and ran for the safety of his grubby house calling desperately for his partner. She watched from the kitchen window, and smiled. The bastard had bashed her too often for her to answer his craven call. She drank herself stupid, and the boy could no longer help her. The grog made her brain feeble, and the two of them when not fighting each other, turned their malignant abuse on their boy. They would not call him by his given name.

'He's a Johnny come lately,' said his Dad. 'We didn't want him, I don't like the name you gave him so his name is Johnny.'

The boy neatly slipped his stirrup leather from its anchor and swinging the weapon, he closed in on his fleeing target. The heavy, iron stirrup gave a satisfying thud as it hit the back of his Dad's skull dropping him neat in his tracks, and just as he was nearing the safety of his dilapidated verandah. He lay on the ground writhing and wishing he had kept his big mouth shut. The boy dismounted, picked up one of the many rubbish bins overflowing with refuse, cigarette stubs and empty whisky bottles, and tipped the rotten contents over his cowering Dad.

'That's a farewell present from Johnny shitcan.'

He looked up at his Mum peering out the kitchen window.

She pleaded 'come home Johnny...things will get better...I know they will.'

'Take him to the rubbish dump, Mum ... that's where he belongs, and where you will end up if you don't leave him.'

'I'll call the Traps on you,' she said, 'you are not our son anymore.'

'I never was or wanted to be, you silly, old cow.'

The boy left without as much as a backwards glance. The wife walked to her husband lying and groaning in the rubbish denying him any assistance. She laughed.

'You cranky, drunk bastard... you had that coming didn't you?'

He lay there staring at the wispy clouds hurrying along in the clear blue sky.

'Don't worry love,' he said 'life will be good now that violent, little weirdo has gone...and git me my whisky bottle before I suffocate in this shit.'

Sarge had two men follow Kate when she went out riding. She hid in the scrub as they passed and then left to take supplies to the boys. Sarge and his men were getting nowhere. The brash, country girl laughed at their amateurish attempts to apprehend the Gang.

'You may as well catch the wind,' said Four Eyes, 'those Irish are just as much part of those Ranges as the trees, sky and earth. They know every crook and cranny like the palm of their hands and it make no difference if it's day or night.'

'What sort of wordy rot is that Cyril? You're going as crazy as that Valerie sheila you had the hots for. Too bad what happened to her.'

Ned and his boys needed money for themselves and their supporters. Ned remembered when he and Harry did the Stagecoach run. Alone in the bush they made easy pickings. They rode stealthily through the night and waited for when they knew the coach would be returning to Melbourne from the goldfields. Cobb and Co were known to carry gold and money to and from the mining towns. They saw the six-horsed coach in the distance, shiny black with gold trim, a sure sign that it was one of Cobb's. The vigilant driver saw a glint of shiny steel in the distant scrub and knew there was danger. He told his partner to hold on, and cracked his team into a flat-out gallop. They sped past the stunned Gang. The driver turned in his seat and with a cheeky grin gave a finger salute to the shocked outlaws.

'This is not the way it's done,' exclaimed Ned to the others, 'he don't think we can catch him but I'll show him something different.'

'What went wrong,' said Joe looking at his colt.

'I'll go cross country...I know a short cut down the hill...you lot follow me,' yelled Ned. He plummeted headlong into the scrub crashing through the undergrowth and shortly appearing on the road further down. He threw his rope around a log and with his horse pulled it into the center of the road just as the coach came around the corner and screeched to a halt. At the same time the other three riders appeared from the scrub. The driver could see that they were blocked and raised their hands.

'Much obliged, gentlemen,' responded Ned, 'we are not out to harm or take from honest, working men so I would appreciate your co-operation.'

Harry had taught him how to get the drivers onside. The passengers were ordered out and the luggage searched. Joe and Steve with masks covering their faces collected the money bags and two gold bars which they loaded onto the packhorses. As they were about to leave Ned spoke to the driver,

'I like the way you handle your team, driver, you sure had them going a pace...what's your name?'

He replied 'Kev, Kev Kavanagh.'

'I've not seen a team go that fast before...without that short cut you would have got away from us. Tell me...how do you do it, Kev?'

'The secrets that lead mare in the front there...I wish I had a paddock full like her...' he stopped in his tracks, fearing he had said too much.

'I know, Kev...good horses come once in a lifetime.'

Dan walked down the team of horses casting an eye over the gray mare standing quietly at the front of the team. He looked a little closer. He couldn't believe what he saw on the mares near shoulder.

'I think you should come and have a look at this mare, Ned.'

Ned dismounted and walked to the mare. 'What is it?' he asked.

The brand read 'E.K'. and gave year of birth.

'My God,' said Ned running his hand over the mare's back and rump.

'It's my mare Music...Christ, I thought I would never see this horse again.'

Kev was beginning to regret he had opened his mouth at all.

'Where did you get this mare, Kev?' he asked.

'I bought her from a Trap...up the country and his clerk, a guy with thick spectacles.'

'What part of the country?'

'Glenrowan way...why?'

'Kev...I want to have a private word with you...can you come over here for a minute.'

Both men walked a short distance away and talked in a huddle.

'Kev...that mare is mine. I bred her... you can see she has my brand 'E.K'. I'm Ned Kelly and the local police stole her when I was in jail. I'm telling you straight Kev because I respect a man who looks after a horse well, and I can see you have done that.'

'I beg you not to take her, Ned. I'm very attached to that mare...we've come a long way together. She's part of me. It would break my heart to lose her.'

There was a pause as both reflected on the tense dilemma.

Kev's knew the mare rightly belonged to the bushranger, and he would have to part with her. Ned felt sorrow mixed with kindness for this honest, simple, horse-loving man about to part with a mare that was part of him

'Look,'said Ned 'I will pay you well for the way you have looked after her,' pulling out a wad of notes.

'No...no money. I don't like the stuff but promise me this...if at some time you are not able to keep her, remember me...that's all I ask.'

'I promise on my life I will do that,' and they walked back to the coach together.

Kev teased her mane through his hands and took a carrot from his pocket. His eyes moistened again as the mare's soft muzzle rubbed his callused palm taking the carrot and slowly crunching it. The memories of how the two sustained each other in their time of need flooded back, and he broke down. Teardrops streaked down his weather-beaten face and his whole body heaved as he sobbed. Since that fateful day in the railway crate, Kev no longer bottled things inside himself where they would like a slow creeping cancer eat his heart out, but he let go of his emotions and was not frightened of what people thought or that he was not acting like a man. The four, intrepid bushrangers looked at each other, and the sight of the distressed driver made them uneasy. Ned handed his colt to Dan, and put a comforting arm around Kev. The Gang was moved, and they joined together and hugged him. The confused travelers did not know what was going on; was it a hold up or was it a love in like they were beginning to see in the arrival of the new Pentecostal churches from America? Ned said 'we are handing back all the money and possessions we have taken from you. We have never done that before and you have Kev to thank for that...we doing it because we respect, Kev, and not because we don't need your money.'

Kev unhitched the harness, slipped a halter on the mare and gave her to Ned. Kev watched them disappear into the scrub with Ned leading the mare. There was no rancor in his heart...just a gut-wrenching emptiness of having lost a part of himself. He bore the bushranger no ill will. His mate getting impatient said, 'come on Kev...she's only a horse...there are others.' Kev glared at him.

'Only a horse,' he said rubbing his eyes, 'what would you know...that mare was my life.' His mate shrugged his shoulders. 'Sorry Kev. I should have kept my big mouth shut.' He began repacking the coach, and placating his customers now complaining about the complicity shown by Cobb and Co's talented driver. Kev went for a walk in the scrub to regain his composure. When the passengers complained a further time, the co-driver said, 'shut your fucking faces up...you got your money back so what are you complaining about?' Kev got up from the log he was sitting on, climbed the ladder to his seat, took up the reins, and drove on not speaking to anyone.

The following day his boss called him into his office.

'I have a letter of complaint here, Kev... asking why we employ crybabies.'

The loss of his mare was too great. Kev looked distressed again. His Boss told him to take the day off.

'He would have to take our best mare,' he said.

'The mare belonged to him,' said Kev as he left the office.

'I'm worried by the strange way you have been acting lately, Kev...Lucille hasn't come back and upset you again, has she?'

like a virgin

Indian love for his horse.

Comanche esteem for his horse knew no bounds. Each man had at least one favourite horse, although his personal string might run to dozens, or even hundreds, of animals. His favourite horse was kept picketed close by his tipi while the remuda grazed on the open plain. He tended it, petted it, and adored it. Some men loved their horses better than they loved their wives said Post Oak Jim. Favourite horses were emotional objects like people. Comanches – Wallace and Hoebel.

riding

Feel her gait with your calves and knees and thighs. With your seat and your hands and your heart. Feel every twitch and slide of her muscles. You should know what she's going to do and what condition she's in with your eyes closed. Look at her ears. They'll tell you things. When she's trained she can warn you of danger with them and tell you if the danger is man or beast. She will be your best friend. You will know her as you know yourself, and you will care for her as well as you care for yourself. Maybe better."
Ride the Wind (Lucia St Clair Robson)

The Gang rode back to their hideaway high in the Ranges.
'I didn't feel good about Kev. He seemed pretty upset,' said Ned
'Yes, he did,' Steve replied.
The boys were a little shaken up seeing a grown man cry.
'I want you all to remember my promise to him, men. If I go, then he gets the mare...no ifs or buts,' said Ned. The mare trotted obediently beside Ned's horse.

He kept stealing glances at her as they travelled along. He could tell a lot by her willingness and effortless movement. He felt her studying him when he was not watching her. Did she remember her early past back at Glenrowan he thought to himself? Were images, sounds and scents flooding back somewhere in the recesses of her pretty head, and if they were, what were they telling her. The mare had maintained a respectful distance from Ned as he guided her along with the halter lead. She then moved her head close to his boot. He thought for a moment she might bite him but she hung her head there as though interpreting his scent as they trotted along the narrow, bush track. Was this mare from the City remembering his calm, reassuring tones when she first came into the world back at his Grandpa's stable; his firm, soothing caress over her wet, spindly frame; his warm breath going deep into her newly minted, pink lungs as she struggled to get to her feet and find her balance; did she recognise his slim, muscular features, the sound of his voice, the way he moved and the small house paddock where she frolicked as a foal with the other colts and fillies, and fed from her Mum.

All these things are impossible to know.

The horse is a mysterious, inscrutable animal thought Ned, a bit like the Chinese Buddha at the mining camp he visited with Joe. The don't gush and jump all over you like a dog. You have to observe closely and minutely to know a horse. It is not information easily obtained for those whose understanding and observations are superficial and shallow. What he did know is that he sorely missed this filly. She was intimately involved with his family, and he had dreams and hopes about what sort of horse she would turn out to be ever since he was a young boy. He remembered the prophecy of his Grandfather, a man who knew horses intimately. Now he would soon find out.

Ned rose early in the morning, boiled some tea, and went over to the mare who was hobbled and grazing quietly. A feeling of anticipation built in him. He was keen to ride her, and see how she handled. He released the leather hobbles, slid his bridle over her ears and placed the blanket and saddle on her back. The saddle appeared to fit not pinching the movement of her shoulders. It was still half dark when he mounted. Grabbing a handful of her mane he pulled himself up into the saddle. He sat there getting the feel. His reins were loose. He thought how good it was. Some backs were too wide, some were too thin and others felt just right.

The mare stood quietly with her ears twitching, waiting for a cue.

'Let's see what you've learnt down there in the big smoke, Music,' he said.

He clucked, and lifted slightly in the saddle. The mare went into a smooth relaxed trot - not bumpy or short but ground covering. He clicked again and she extended into a relaxed canter with a light feel on the snaffle bit. It was smooth and she was listening. There was no pull or excitement, no sourness, no throwing or flipping of her head which she kept level and relaxed. Ned could not have asked for more and admired Kev's skills in producing a well behaved, balanced and responsive horse. Ned gently pressured her side with his right boot and the two went into a circle to the left on the correct lead. Testing her balance, he pushed her with his outside boot and did a flying change as he turned across the middle of the circle and went the other way on the right lead. He had ridden horses that would almost tangle their legs and fall over in trying to find the right lead. Others like this mare did it naturally and with poise and balance.

So far so good he thought to himself. But quite a few horses have those abilities and something extra was needed for an elite, riding mare – speed, agility and endurance. Ned turned the mare from her circles to the steep descent from the plateau. The mare didn't balk at the steep descent and plunged down the ravine grabbing and swallowing the earth with her powerful hind legs. Ned gave the mare her head and stretched back in the saddle with his feet pushed forward into the stirrups. He yelled exuberantly as the landscape flashed past in a greenish blur but he quickly stopped her not wanting to overdo the exercise with a new horse he did not fully know.

The short burst of the mare's brilliance and sure footedness had mightily impressed him, and he got off and led her down to the bottom giving short whistles of incredulity, shaking his head in disbelief and looking at the mare.

'Ok... downhill is one thing... how about uphill, girlie.' Aware he didn't want to over exert her without knowing her true abilities, and having seen foolish, headstrong riders seriously lame a horse with a pulled or bowed tendon, and he was not about to do the same here. He rode carefully up the steep mountain but feeling for the way she used her hind quarters, and how she negotiated the obstacles like the rocky ridges, bushes, trees, holes and fallen logs. A horse too had to be observant and discrete in the way he or she covered the ground, and negotiated the many obstacles that mountain and bush riding presented. Half way up the mountain, Ned slipped out of the saddle, joined her reins into one long rope and took a hold of her tail, urging her up the steep incline. It took her little time to understand what he wanted, and using her hind legs like two pistons, she pulled him back up the mountain almost as quickly as she descended. Pulling is something she knew a bit about in the last two years with Cobb and Co.

The others were having breakfast over the open fire. The sound of the two coming through the bush alarmed them so that they ran for their guns. Suddenly the mare burst into view and onto the plateau with Ned gripping her tail and being pulled up from behind. The other three stood there relieved it was Ned but somewhat curious as to what he was doing.

'How she going,' asked Steve.

'Pretty good,' said Ned in the understatement of his life. 'Kev has done a great job with the mare... she is everything I had hoped she would be...sensible, sensitive, alert, and unbelievably, comfortable gaits. I haven't really tested her top speed and endurance yet but I am going to be real careful with this mare. she is just so, so...' and he looked for the right word as Valerie would have insisted, '...sort of fresh, untouched, not spoilt, not bungled or messed up, and ready and willing to learn. Kev really did a top job on this mare.'

'Like a virgin,' said Joe.

'Yes, that's the word, Joe' said Ned 'and no one is to ride her except me...understood.

In the following weeks a close union built between the grey mare Music and Ned. The mare felt an inner strength in her new rider, a sensitivity, a respect in their partnership that spoke to her as though she had returned to the embrace of a loving family. Ned felt the dreamlike lightness of the mare as they flew through the bush on a cushion of air, her athleticism and balance in the way she accelerated, stopped, spun on her strong haunches, stood silently on command in the bush, and outran any horse that challenged her. The miles drifted by and the mare's endurance and stamina was such that she hardly took a breath, or noticed that her outlaw rider and her were not joined by some invisible umbilical cord that made them one like the fabled centaur. The words of his Grandpa as they watched her as a filly romp and play in the paddock came back to him - 'let not the sins of the parent be visited on the child'. The filly's mother had driven her hoof into the skull of his Dad. Forgiveness and belief along with a canny and intimate knowledge of horses by an old man would repay them with a horse of spectacular ability, kindness and understanding just as he had prophesized.

When Ned slept at night in his tent he remembered what Roy had told him about the Indians – how a Chief would tie a rope to leg of one of his wives in a tent nearby so that he could summons her with a gentle tug – when searching parties were known to be in the area at night he would tie a rope to Music as she grazed running it back to his tent and looping it around his wrist so he could get to her quickly if bounty hunters or the traps eluded their lookout. He chose his favorite rope, one that had a good feel and weight and made the end into a halter so the feel would not be hampered by another material. In that way through the feel of the rope and the subtle vibrations he became associated with her movements during the night. If she was spooked and suddenly lifted her head by something alien in the bush, Ned would be instantly alerted. These smooth, rope fibers were like a telegraph line that passed messages to the two in a strange kind of Morse code that only they understood and brought an intimacy of touch and feel like two lovers in their bed.

The banks of the Ohio

Stringybark.

Kennedy never uttered a word after he was brought down, except "God forgive you." "I shot him," continued the outlaw. "He kept firing all the time, running from tree to tree, and tried to kill Byrne until his ammunition went done. Ned Kelly - Extracts from the Argus - William Kerr.

Skating

A man learns to skate by staggering about and making a fool of himself Indeed he progresses in all things by resolutely making a fool of himself. George Bernard Shaw

Ned's enjoyment with his newly found mare was short lived as they heard the echo of several rifle shots coming from across the valley.

'I have seen four Traps yesterday. The word is they are armed to the teeth and have bragged to bring us in dead or alive,' said Joe. 'I didn't realize they were so close – probably at Stringybark creek down the hill a bit.'

'Wanted dead or alive, is that right …we'll go down and introduce ourselves,' replied Ned. 'We are not going to skulk away from them if that's what they are intending to do.'

The four crept silently down Stringybark creek and hid in the tall reeds not far from the camp. They readied their guns, looked at each other and then leapt from the tall grass yelling 'bail up' to the startled men sitting by the tent.

Lonigan grabbed his pistol and ran to a log. He aimed and fired as his mate surrendered raising his hands. Lonigan's bullet grazed Dan's cheek. Ned returned fire from his pistol, an old one that had the barrel taped to the hand piece. It was old but Ned had practiced for many hours blasting away at a gum tree by their camp. Lonigan slumped to the ground with a neat bullet hole drilled into his brain. Death was almost instant. Ned recognized him as the trooper he had fought with in the street not so long ago.

'It's a pity he had to do that' said Ned, 'it was not my intention to shoot anyone but seeing that it was Lonigan, I do not regret him his piece of lead. The bugger would have shot us if his aim were better.'

Joe and Steve did not expect this to happen. They had joined the other two but they didn't count on being included in a murder charge. Their position had changed dramatically with a corpse laying there in front of them. Ned said he would take the blame if there be any in defending yourself.

'We didn't have any choice,' he said again, 'he was given the option to surrender.'

He turned to the other prisoner.

'As long as you do as you are told you will come to no harm - where are the others?'

'They have gone out searching,' he replied looking around nervously.

'For us I suppose,' said Ned looking directly at him.

'Yes, I'm afraid that's right - we have a warrant for your arrests.'

'And rewards too.'

'I think so,' he said.

At that time Joe came out of the tent with ammunition and rifles.

'There's enough for an army in there,' he said.

And he carried out the leather, body bags.

'Did you come to shoot us like dogs or arrest us?' demanded Dan sponging the bullet graze to his face.

'Only arrest,' said their captive.

'Give me a look at the warrant,' said Ned.

'We didn't bring it with us,' he said with a look of despair.

'Why are you not in your police uniforms?'

'Don't know, I don't give the orders.'

'What's your name?' asked Ned.

'McIntyre,' he replied.

'When are the other two due back?'

'Anytime now - they may have heard the gunshots.'

'We will hide in grass. I want you to tell them to give themselves up - you will be covered - don't do anything rash or you'll get the same fate as your friend, Lonigan.'

In a short time, two riders appeared out of the bush.

McIntyre left the campfire and went to them.

'Throw down your guns... you are ambushed.'

Kennedy smiled.

'I'm not jokin - on my life please do as I say - surrender.'

Ned came out of the bush, 'you are all covered – bail up.'

The others emerged from the spear grass with their guns levelled. Scanlon began to dismount but went for his rifle. Kennedy pulled his revolver. Scanlon swung around and fired. Joe fired and Scanlon dropped from his horse. He struggled to rise, faltered and fell dead. Kennedy jumped from his horse putting it between him and the others. He ran for the cover of a tree firing as he went. McIntyre saw his chance to escape, grabbed Kennedy's horse, pulled himself into the saddle and galloped off clinging to its neck, and crashing through the scrub out of control. The panicked animal threw him off about a mile away. He rolled, picked himself up and ran for his life. When night fell, he hid in a wombat's hole until the morning when he built up enough courage to run for help. Ned and Dan pursued Kennedy through the trees. They exchanged shots. 'Give up man,' yelled Ned but it was to no avail. Ned's next shot hit him in the arm and he looked to be lifting his other hand for another shot when a bullet hit him in the chest knocking him to the ground. He groaned. Ned went to him, kneeled and placed a coat under his head.

'Why didn't you surrender – you left us no choice but to defend ourselves. I want you to know Kennedy because I know you to be a decent man, we had no intentions to shoot you. If you surrendered, we would have taken your horses, guns and ammunition...you had plenty of it along with body bags for Christ sake. You know that we had no choice but to go to Ranges – that Fitzgerald is lying mongrel as you well know. What chance do you think we would have had before those pompous English biased Judges on attempted murder? Barrington would have locked us away for life in those stinking jails. Look what he did to our mum and she had absolutely nothing to do with it. And the bastard even said what he would do with me if I was there and he that without even hearing my evidence.'

Kennedy was in deep pain and his breathing raspy and labored.

'I know – it's too late for regrets now – I don't blame you Kelly and it is true what you say about Fitzgerald and Barrington– it was a fair fight and we have lost. I'm sorry for my wife and kids. I wish I could see them one more time. Hell, the pain in my chest is like a red-hot poker – do you think I am done for Kelly?'

'I'm afraid so Kennedy. You are losing a lot of blood. We have to leave as you know and I don't want you to suffer a slow painful death here in the forest. What do you want me to do,' said Ned feeling immense compassion for the dying man.

'Do what you have to do, Kelly,' he whispered.

Ned pulled the trigger and his pain stopped.

He covered him with a blanket and they left.

The stakes now were dramatically raised. McIntyre would be a witness to the State's allegation of murder of three policemen. It did not matter that they came with ammunition for a small army and armed to the teeth; it did not matter that they boasted about bringing the Gang back dead and had the body bags declaring their intent; and it did not matter that they were given the opportunity to surrender and chose to fight. The Gang were now marked men with large rewards to be put on their heads and could be shot on sight – in their bed asleep or out of their saddle when least expecting it.

'We must leave this area quickly. It will soon be swarming with Police,' said Ned.

They packed up the police ammunition and guns and rode hard to the Murray. The weather came in bad and the river was in flood and impassable. Police were riding everywhere looking for them. They hid submerged in the reeds of the muddy swamps as Police rode by. Ned decided to head for an isolated cabin in the snow line where no one went. He knew of the place from his work felling trees in the hardwood forests. On their way up the mountains, the fog and mist lifted for a moment, and there to the side of the snow-covered track, was a small timber cottage overlooking a frozen lake. On the lake a young couple were skating. The Gang stopped and rested their horses in the scrub careful to remain hidden. They watched the young skaters at work. It soon became apparent they were observing an astonishing display of ice skating that helped ease their troubled thoughts. They knew that to become good horseman, or any athletic and artistic endeavor for that matter, took much time and training as did trick riding. There was danger and risk and one needed courage and discipline. The couple oblivious to their small audience hidden in the thick scrub put on a dazzling demonstration of daring, imaginative and graceful skating - circling, leaping, twisting and spinning on the glassy surface - and sweeping by them with her perched on his shoulders, another time perilously suspended above his head by his hand, her body poised delicately like some sacrificial offering to the Gods. The display was breathtakingly beautiful to the boys and made even more so by the distant sound of old man singing an American ballad of rejected love and death accompanied by the accordion, a guitar and mouth organ. The soulful music seemed to resonate with their easy, languid movements across the ice, and the emotion and sensuality of their art. To Dan the music coming from the cottage sounded melancholy but oddly charming. It occurred to him the distance of the sad strains drifting faintly across the lake has something to do with it. He had ridden past cottages in the dark of night and delighted to the sweet sounds of someone playing an accordion. If he were in the same room, he knew from experience he would not be similarly moved. The distance and the dark added a magical call and tugged on his heart strings. The uplifting event taking place before them soothed their hurt and showed them that although they were fleeing from mayhem, hate and death, there was good on the Earth. They were moved to clap and cheer but Ned would not allow it. Dan asked to dismount and leave a blood velvet red rose on the lake which he had kept carefully wrapped in his saddle bag. He said,

'These roses do not last long. I picked it on the way up and wrapped it in damp cloth. I want to give it to her before it dies.'

Dan's garden was now neglected and overgrown, and he had taken to plucking a blossom or two growing wild by the roadside or a garden when the opportunity arose. The others were intending to pluck coin and pound notes from the Town banks. Ned agreed. Dan quickly placed the rose without the couple noticing his presence making sure to cover his tracks. They left travelling higher into the white, virginal snow whilst a pretty girl skater held a blood red rose close to her nose, inhaled its heavenly scent and felt it's velvety skin. She scanned about the lake's edge and pondered.

'We need to practice the death spiral,' she said to her partner in a manner of fact tone.

'I was having so much fun I forgot it,' he replied. 'Where did that rose come from? It couldn't have grown here. Maybe you have a secret admirer.'

'Maybe I do, maybe I don't...I felt we were being watched and put in an extra effort. This new International form of skating from America is really something...it liberates me...the moves are like ballet and the adrenalin pumps me like you wouldn't believe...in those scary lifts I feel like I am flying but I sure don't want to fall on my scon.'

'Yeah,' he said, 'it would be like hitting concrete. One crazy day darlin if you keep getting roses, I will take you down.'

She smiled, placed the rose neatly into her dark tresses and glided away with her thoughts scurrying to keep up. She went faster and faster.

Her partner pursued and grabbed her hand. Slightly annoyed at her indifference he said,

'Do it now shitface, or are you my yella rose of Texas?'

He braced himself to take her body weight. She went down with her arm fully extended and anchored to his into low, rapid revolutions around him like a windmill spinning in a storm; with every sinew strained to near breaking point, and her taut body stretched, parallel and dangerously close, only inches, to the unforgiving ice. Her skate dug into the glassy surface on an almost impossible angle, the cold ice grinding and hissing at her boyfriend like a demented, jealous lover. The music stopped, a deadly silence prevailed and all was dark.

> In the beginning, God created the heavens and the earth. The earth was without form and void, and darkness was over the face of the deep. And the Spirit of God was hovering over the face of the waters.
> And God said, "Let there be light," and there was light. And God saw that the light was good. And God separated the light from the darkness. God called the light Day, and the darkness he called Night. And there was evening and there was morning, the first day. Genesis1

Buffalo Soldier

Famous last words of Union Major General John Sedgewick before being killed by confederate sharpshooter.
Why- they couldn't hit an elephant at this distance.
The Whitworth rifle.
The Whitworth's deadliness was well known to the Union officers with one Colonel noting when we were within one half [880 yards] or three fourths [1,320 yards] of a mile of the enemy, the effect of their sharpshooters was terrible - Sharp shooting in the Civil war Major J.L. Plaster - both above quotes.

The Government knew that the Kelly Gang had support amongst the poor farmers of the North- West. These farmers needed land. Large tracts of good land were tied up by the wealthy Squatters who fought moves to have it divided. The Government had been warned that Kelly might provide a focus for the selectors which may galvanize into a political force to oppose them. They sought to manipulate the press to alienate this support. They gave extra funds to Police and to Sarge to get results. He had caught Harry Power and put away Kelly's mum. Their supporters were put on trumped-up charges, thrown into prison without bail, and their trials delayed so their farms and crops went to waste. The battle lines were becoming more defined. Sarge sent his troopers out into the Ranges in their starched blue and white uniforms to ride in circles, and return home empty handed. What happened at Stringybark gave them good cause to reflect on their possible fate, and they didn't stray too far into the bush for fear of coming across the Kelly Gang.

'This is not working,' said Sarge to his clerk 'and it's costing heaps of money to keep them search parties out in the hills. I'll need a bloody miracle to get that Kelly lot. What do you think?'

'Look, said Cyril, 'there's a bounty on their heads. Why not employ a Bounty hunter, Sarge, and a good one. The best are in the States - it's the experience their sharpshooters have what with their Civil war and the Indians. They are battle hardened and smart and their gun technology is good, much more advanced than ours.'

'I reckon you have nailed it again Cyril. Where did you get that idea?'

'I read it in one of those books you get for me Sarge.'

'Well, I'll be buggered. They are of some use after all. I'll get onto it straight away. The hierarchy are running out of ideas to catch Kelly and I reckon they will be cock-a- hoop over this.'

'Don't forget to tell them it was my idea, Sarge.'

'If I remember, lad. My memory is not so good these days with all the responsibility I have.'

A urgent request was sent to the U.S. Army in America coupled with promises of large rewards for the right person who could get results. They had the man for the job.

Sarge would have to negotiate with him over price but they let on that they had given him a contract as well so he might be prepared to discount a little.

'What is the contract Sarge?' asked the inquisitive clerk.

'I will tell you later but it involves someone who disgraced them at the Little Bighorn. They have suspicions he is here in Australia. But it is strictly confidential. Only me, you, them and the President know,' said Sarge having gone up a notch or two in his important and powerful friends.

'The President of the United States,' exclaimed Cyril. 'You sure move in important circles, Sarge.'

'Now you forget that, Boy. I want to concentrate on the job at hand and that is getting Kelly and his cohorts. The Government here is getting pretty impatient with our lack of success. Kelly is making fools of us.' Cyril was about to add that wouldn't be too difficult in your case Sarge, but he liked his job.

Not long afterwards Stagger Lee strolled into Sarge's office. His face was broad and pockmarked, with thick lips and his hair in dirty dreadlocks touching his shoulders. He was a negro with white blood– a mulatto. He had a light brown skin and green eyes. He nursed a long, narrow box that he pulled on a set of iron wheels behind him. He stared at Sarge, and sat down in the chair in front of his desk. Sarge looked at him for a short while. He had not seen a man like this before. Neither party spoke. The stranger despite his grim facial features was dressed rather like a dandy with expensive clothes tailored to a perfect fit, and decked in jewels of a showy, flamboyant taste. Gold earrings dangled from both ears and on his calloused hands and fingers shone numerous diamond and ruby rings and gold bangles. He wore all black– black tail coat, black pants and boots, long enameled and jeweled spurs, and a flat, wide rimmed, black Stetson hat

'Stagger's the name,' he said.

'So' said Sarge.

The stranger took out a small silver case from his coat pocket, plucked a cigarette and lit up, blowing a neat puff of smoke in Sarge's direction.

'I have come on Government business - are yoose the man to see?

I gather you want the Kelly dude dead or alive,' he said without changing his expression. Stagger Lee was one cool, confident assassin.

'What's your qualifications, Mr. Lee?'

'I have the one thing your men do not have,' he said. 'It's called experience. And I have the eyes of an eagle, a steady hand and slow beating heart... slow like a swamp crocodile from Louisiana. And I wear this pretty silver badge here,' said Stagger pointing to his lapel.

'And I know guns. There's nothin I don't know about guns and weapons, Mr. Sarge, and there are many in Lincoln's army six feet under to prove it. I can take a rider off his hoss about a mile away. You probably can't even see that far Sarge. And by the look of your clerk's spectacles, he would probably have problems seeing out the front door?'

'I can see far enough to suit me, Stagger, but you are right about Cyril here...too much readin I say,' said Sarge with a little laugh at his clerk's expense.

Stagger lifted the narrow, long case onto Sarge's desk.

'This long, barreled baby is one of them Whitworth rifles,' he said as he opened the case to reveal several rifle pieces and a long barrel which he methodically screwed together. He then took out an elaborate telescopic sight, unwrapped it from the soft cloth and attached it to the barrel with all the poise and expertise of a master craftsperson. The rifle extended about six feet and looked menacing. Sarge and his clerk marveled at the construction, length and the workmanship that had gone into the making of the weapon.

'English handiwork honed by world's best manufacturers,' said Stagger lovingly stroking the polished timber. Stagger smiled and said 'I'm not finished yet. These death dealers are damned heavy and need some support. Mind you I wouldn't use them if I had to ride hard. But for setting up and waiting for a target, you cannot beat them. They were like gold during the Civil war. They need to be cleaned out well because of the black powder residue in the edges of the hex barrel otherwise they are difficult to reload. Let me say though, Sarge, I usually only need one shot to do the job.'

Stagger took out a stand which he extended to about waist level, and with confidence of an expert attached the long barrel and swiveled it around like a small cannon. Sarge jumped back as it pointed in his direction.

'Careful,' he objected 'I hope that thing's not loaded.'

'It has cost me a packet, I can tell you. It can take the wing off a butterfly over a mile away or blow a prairie dog's head away like an exploding water melon. There's nothing here to compare to it. Look at the barrel...it is called octagonal rifling and it has a twist inside the barrel to rotate the bullet. A rotating bullet goes faster and longer and is more accurate. Look at the bullet, Sarge. It has six sides and is three times as long as it is wide ...it's a javelin shaped bullet and it spirals and cuts through the wind. Only .451 caliber but that is enough if the bullet is well placed like a head shot. You and your lot will never catch the Kelly Gang with what you are doing now, and your toy pea shooters. He's too smart for you lot - he's like one of them red Indians the way he creeps about the country. Even if you see him you can't catch him but this baby will even the odds. A hill top, a good view and I can blow Kelly out of the saddle before he knows what hit him. Without him, the others will soon give up. It's like shooting an Indian chief - the others lose spunk and run.'

Sage looked impressed.

'Now about the contract price.'

'Two hundred pound,' replied Sarge.

'Six hundred pound...half up front and you have a deal.'

'Two hundred and fifty,' snapped Four Eyes as quick as a card.

Stagger glared at the clerk sitting at the desk.

'Who the fuck is you?' he asked.

'I'm the accountant,' he said in a faltering voice.

'Well stick to counting beans boy and don't meddle in men's affairs.'

'Money is my affairs, Mr. Lee...I'm the accountant. I hear you also have a contract with your own Government so two for the price of one.'

'Two for the price of two, Mr Bean counter. That's none of your business, boy...but I may need some help from Sarge here after I do his job.'

'Tell me a bit of your history and experience, Stagger, and then we'll see if we can come to a price.'

'Well, I usually let my rifle do the talking Sarge, but as you ask, I was born in the deep South; raised by a good family of cotton pickers on one of those big plantation homes in Virginia. The Master was good to us. My mum was half white and darned pretty. She worked in the big house and I was allowed to accompany her. I played with the master's children...me and his boy got on well. We were like brothers...very much alike in our thinking...we rode and roamed over all the forests and mountains...sure was beautiful country in them hills...God's acres they were... a garden of Eden. I didn't like the way the other plantation owners treated their black workers...you know work all day, fed little, locked in like a prison, families broke up and sold, children taken from their mothers. It gave me a cold heart Sarge. The only way I could combat it was to better at everything they did and respected...you know fight, shoot and ride. Then came the war...I went with the Master's son to look after him. He was a good shot and was enrolled in the sniper brigade. I would cook, groom the horses and oil and clean his rifles. I got to know them rifles real well - better than most of the soldiers. They would bring them guns to me fix and to align so they shot straight. Them country boys didn't take the time or have the intelligence to understand the mechanics of a rifle and I did because I was pulling them apart and putting them back together. They wouldn't let us fight...said they couldn't trust us what with the war and slavery but none of that worried me. My master got shot...he was jus eating his porridge and smack... his head split and his brains fell into his plate. I was mad. I got his rifle and knew where that assassin was hidin...a puff of smoke in a tree gave him away. The others were pleased with me when they saw that union sniper drop out of the tree like a shot bird. They tumble, over and over and hit the ground with a dull thud. I was a better shot than all of them in that sniper brigade, and when they put me on as enlisted member of the Grey coats, many blue boys fell from their horses. Sometimes I got them just walking around talking to each other like at a picnic or something... One moment there was peace in the valley, and then boom and bedlam. They would look around, puzzled about where the shot came from, but could see nothing. I have more experience than anyone on this earth, I'm the best there is and I am for hire. I am known to use common talk Sarge as a Buffalo soldier. You two have probably never seen a Buffalo. The name came because bullets bounce off our heads like a buffalo. We have a skull like steel. It's only a stomach bullet that may do me harm.'

'I'll remember that.' said Cecil.

Stagger glared at the scrawny clerk giggling to himself.

'I have killed people for less than that so keep your mealy mouth shut and your book eyes open my friend.'

Not wishing to break his sales pitch Stagger continued.

'I like them big hulking wooly animals. Now thanks to them white hunters they have been shot out of existence, and most for simply target practice. Even the red skin don't do that. He only takes what he needs to exist and then pays homage to his spirit Gods. But enough of that. I am not here to give you a history lesson.'

'I agree with you Mr Stagger,' said Cyril.

'Well there is hope for us yet, replied Stagger.

'Listen Sarge, give me a contract, I will do the job, and you pay me. Nothing is simpler than that. Why I am better than anyone you can find to do the job is I know the hardware and I have good eyes, steady heart and hand. And I am curious about how things work. I could take my rifles apart, adjust, fix, and make em better than when they were spanking new. I took down General Whipple from the longest distance ever, about eighteen hundred yards, over a mile. I needed telescopic sights but I did it. They thought it never could be done at that distance. The answer was long heavy, octagonal barrel... it dampens the vibration and gives accurate trajectory. The gases are tighter and propel the bullet further... I'm not getting too scientific for you, Sarge ...am I. They gave me a medal for knocking that General off his horse. Ever heard of that, Sarge? - a nigger fella slave getting a medal.'

'Not around these parts, Stagger...we usually give em a piece of lead.'

'And take a gander at this piece of American pride, Sarge... it tells ya I come with the authority of USA,' and he pointed to his lapel where shone a silver Marshal's badge...six stars and an eagle.

'Is that badge genuine?' asked Cyril.

'What the fuck you talkin about, Boy...you think I would wear something dodgy...come here all the way across that damned big ocean just to tell you a pack of lies,' yelled Stagger.

'No, Mr. Stagger, certainly not ...no disrespect meant...it's just that we have had a little experience with American entrepreneurs. I think that would be the best way to put it.'

Sarge shifted in his seat, and was getting very interested in what Stagger was telling him. He was either very good at his job or just about the best salesman he had listened too except perhaps for one living not far away and in whom Stagger would have been mightily interested. Cyril was busily taking notes as he spoke.

'Well after the war, Sarge, I joined the Texas Rangers. Normally they would not take a nigger but they knew my war record and that I would be very useful to them in combating the cattle rustlers, outlaws and especially those cunning Indians. They were hard men, them Rangers. They asked for no quarter and gave none. There was no other way in the Wild West. I rode day and night, lived off the land and hunted like an Indian. When we rode into town the people ran and hid and they had good reason to. Do not mess with the Texas Rangers. Give me a drink Sarge...my voice is getting a little husky.'

'Pour him a whisky from that drink cabinet of mine, Cyril, and me one too. There some cordial there for you.'

'After about three years with them I had more experience than most at huntin and killin, and how to survive. But I had not much money. I had seen how much loot some of those outlaws had and how easy they got it and what luxurious lifestyle they had and the pretty woman. I wanted some of that. I left and became a bounty hunter and the work flowed in. Really, Sarge, who has a job history like me. I do private and government work but only big jobs for big money. For my type of experience, you must pay. The job has many dangers as you have found out with them three marshals shot by Kelly. I hope you are not going to put any more of your good men at risk, Sarge.'

'Certainly not, Stagger...I am a right-thinking man - isn't that right, Cyril?'

Cyril barely nodded and said 'The best there is ...is our Sarge.'

'You little, bum licker,' said Stagger.

'Let me add this,' said Stagger, 'I can go out with me pack horses and gear and look for him and do the deed. That may take two to three months ...could be longer. That will cost six hundred and fifty quid in your terms, not dollars, but I want it converted to dollars when I go home.'

'That's a lot more,' said Cyril.

'Too right it is but look...if you know where he is likely to go I can camp out on a hill overlooking the track, and take him down from there with my Whitty here. That is cheaper... say four hundred pounds because it is less work.'

Cyril was peering over the rifle.

'This is a muzzle loader?'

'Yeah- so what?'

'And it has a percussion cap?'

'What are you getting at, Four Eyes?'

'It's old technology...bit like a flintlock...you know Davy Crockett and the backwoods.'

Stagger stood up and walked over to Cyril standing over him in threatening manner. 'You make me plumb crazy you do, Four Eyes...with all your supposed learnin.. all out of books and books. Well they tell you nuttin... it's real experience in the field, in the battle, at the coal face, whatever, you know what I mean.... it's that what counts in this World and not readin and writin...that's for lay-abouts and girly men. Now Four Eyes, for your benefit I have had this barrel lengthened. The original was thirty-six inches. It is now a two foot longer. I'm working on making it a breech loader but I'm not an engineer like Mr. Whitworth. I wrote to him in what they call the Mother Country...now what was I talking about... the rifle...yeah, this rifle here is not a fighting rifle - it's a sniper's rifle. That is, you take your time and set them up. As I was saying before you rudely interrupted, I wrote to Ole Whitty in England asking him to make me a sniper special. He agreed for a price and I had the money. I wanted a longer, heavier barrel and the sights on top of the barrel and not to the side as the originals were. The original Whitworth rifle was not so heavy because he wanted a bigger market for the Army but for accuracy you have to sacrifice portability. He made it for me and called it the Whitworth special S.T.G, but it was a one only model so that is why I protect this gun with my life. Nobody goes near or touches my rifle without me knowin...get it.'

'What does the S.T.G stand for?' asked Cyril.

'Stagger - what else? The original Whitworth could kill at fifteen hundred yards but this will kill at two thousand yards, and probably the only rifle in the world that can consistently do that. We could only get three hundred of the original rifles from England because of the blockade and they cost over six hundred dollars. With telescopic sights they cost twelve hundred dollars. They cost big money and I paid two thousand dollars for my model with modifications. So Sarge, as you see a lot of research and cost has been built into this death dealer, not to say my own practical experience. That is why when you employ me you have to pay a fair price cus you are getting the best there is and my life is on the line.'

'Ok,' said Sarge jumping in before Cyril replied, 'four hundred pounds on second option, Stagger. I reckon I know what tracks Kelly will take. But if you don't mind, Stagger, I would like to see how that cannon of yours works. We can take a little ride out of here to nearby hill top and we'll see if what you say is true.'

'I got the preliminaries all written out here, Sarge- perhaps Mr. Stagger could sign before we go?'

'Put that piece of scribble paper on your notice board there Four Eyes...up high.'

Cyril did what he was told. As he was pinning his notes to board above his head, Stagger drew his hunting knife and with deft throw skimmed Cyril's head and stuck square in the middle of the carefully prepared notes.

Cyril froze.

'Them little pins hold nothing,' said Stagger.

He walked to the board, pushed Cyril out of the way, snatched the note from the board and tore it into pieces.

'My word is my contract,' he said putting his hunting knife back in its pouch. 'Fair enough with me,' said Sarge.

Stagger did the deal and shook hands but ignored Cyril's extended hand.

Stagger tied the equipment to his pack horse, and the three of them rode to a nearby hill. Stagger dismounted and set up his buffalo gun. When he was happy everything was right, he looked into the sunny horizon shielding his eyes. There was not a cloud to be seen except pale moon in a blue sky. He could make out a speck circling in the distance. He studied it with his spy glass and then took out a metal plate with a slide that closed onto the target with an estimate of distance in yards set out like a scale. The figures intrigued Cyril who was rudely told to mind his own business by the dark-skinned operator.

'See that big buzzard circling above the hill over there. I'll put that bird into a nose dive if you just watch.'

'I'd like to see you do just that...it's a moving target,' quipped Sarge.

Stagger chose a long, thin conical bullet, with six sides the same shape as the barrel and wrapped in paper with the powder. Then he went through a set of priest like procedures oiling inside the barrel, using the ramrod to drive the bullet snugly into the long barrel and adjusted the sights and cap.

Cyril yawned.

Stagger saw it, and stopped, looking a little embarrassed.

'One day, Four Eyes,' he said 'I am going to drill you with one of these nuts, and he held the lethal piece of honed lead and metal bullet to Four Eyes face such that the clerk blinked, and went pale.

'Anything worth doin takes time. Them repeaters fly metal all over the place... everywhere except where they are supposed to go. Me... I only need one shot, one of them magical bullets and the job is done...no mess and no waste.'

Stagger then pointed the deadly weapon to the heavens. He held it still for a moment looking into the gun's sights took up the tension on the trigger and then moved barrel ever so slightly tracking the near perfect circles of the majestically winged bird in the distance.

'Boom.' The rifle kicked but Stagger stood firm.

The eagle jerked in midair as the shot echoed through the Ranges. A whitish puff of feathers burst about the big bird, its wings went limp, and it dropped like a lead ball from the blue sky into the scrubby trees below. It was both a remarkable and sad sight.

'Kelly is dead meat, don't you agree Sarge,' said Stagger with smug look on his face.

'I've seen enough. You have the contract,' said Sarge.

Cyril went to put his hand on the rifle that was clouded in blue smoke and shimmied in the bright sunlight.

'Don't touch it,' yelled Stagger losing his cool for a moment, and pacing excitably up and down drawing on a cigarette.

'Nobody touches my gun, and I mean nobody,' he said staring right at Cyril who was studying the rifle with keen interest.

'How do you feel about shooting a man in cold blood. I mean Kelly don't have much of chance, does he, with that rifle?' said Cyril taking the high moral ground.

'I don't give a damned shit about that,' Stagger replied. 'Life is cheap and we all have to die sometime. I've got used to it and I like my work. It's a job and pays the bills the same as yours, I expect. The difference is Mr. Clerk, my life is in the balance. These crims I chase will one day get me and it's that danger that makes my work expensive...not sitting on my arse like you peering into books and payin others to do their dirty work. I can only hope that when my time is up it comes as quick as you have just seen for that big buzzard.'

'That big buzzard is a wedge tailed eagle, a sacred bird to our aborigine, Mr. Stagger...you shouldn't have shot it,' said Cyril getting a little bolder, 'according to legend you have just earned yourself a painful and certain death.'

The emboldened clerk didn't know this, but tossed it in because Stagger had riled him with his abuse and demeaning his office work which he took seriously.

'What a load of mystical mule shit, but listen you scrawny, little, pen pusher, I don't know what your game is, but you're half too darn smart for them glass bottom spectacles of yours. The only sacred thing in life is this here fancy shooting iron. It's sacred because it has the power of life and death at a distance not known before, and because it earns me a much-needed quid. If you are so damned concerned about that big buzzard why didn't you say something earlier,' snarled Stagger.

'I didn't think you had a hope in hell of hitting it at that distance and what being a moving target,' said Cyril.

A cynical grin swept over Stagger's smug face,

'Well, ain't that a shame, Mr. Four Eyes...are you going to make a report in one of those lily white, little note books of yours that I have broken the law?'

'It's not an offence...it's just something a right-thinking person wouldn't do,' offered Cyril not letting up. Sarge looked at Cyril shaking his head disapprovingly.

'Well I'm not a right-thinking man. I hate the word and everything it stands for.

So called right thinking people make me want to puke...and don't you forget it... do you hear?' said Stagger getting animated and his attention fixed on the troublesome clerk. 'It's only you lot on the Government tit every week that can afford to be right thinking... me ...me...I am the poor nigger who has to hustle for a living. Of course, you know nothing about that. Two weeks of your right thinking and I would be starving. If I hadn't shot that bird...no contract, no food. It's that simple Mr. Book Clerk. You and all the rest of your lot can sit on your bums all week, all year for that matter, and still get paid. I don't get a single dollar unless I get results.'

'Come on,' said Sarge fearing for the welfare of Cyril and trying to change the subject. 'We 're all friends here.'

'He ain't my friend...that's for sure,' said Stagger and made out to swing a jaw breaker on the slightly built Cyril who peddled back that fast that he tripped falling over losing his spectacles. Stagger gave a scornful laugh, turned, packed up his impressive shooter and left on his horse.

'I'll be waiting for your call Sarge.'

'No worries Mr. Lee,' said Sarge,

'I'll come down for that advance this afternoon, Sarge. Give that right-thinking clerk of your something to do...earn his living for once,' he said.

On second thoughts, come to my hotel tonight. I have some important and confidential business to discuss with you. I have orders direct from the President Ulysses E Grant and confidential means you don't bring that note scribbling clerk with you.

'He's bloody rude if you ask me,' said Cyril picking himself up, adjusting his bent glasses.

Sarge looked with admiration at the rider disappearing down the hill with his timber box firmly strapped to his pack horse, and placing a steady hand on his valuable hardware.

'We have to do business with all types, Cyril. There's no need to take offence... Stagger comes well recommended. He almost won the war for them Southern Rebels with that fancy shootin iron of his. He sure is a plum shot with it...that big buzzard didn't stand a chance, did he?'

That night in the confines of the hotel room, Stagger told Sarge that he had met the President for his secret assignment, and began to tell him the whole story word for word. The President said he had heard of him during the Civil War as one of the best sharp shooters in the Confederate ranks. He said he did not bear any grudges and that each person fights for and defends his beliefs. I wanted to say I didn't have any beliefs but stayed silent. He then told me a interesting report on the Little Bighorn. Custer was one of my Generals he said, and although foolhardy at times, he was a fighter until the end. The disaster of the Bighorn he said was in effect a victory because our citizens now believe we should fight to the last man rather than the endless lists of desertions we have been plagued with. 'You know Stagger,' he said, 'I fought many battles in the Civil war...battles in which thousands of brave men died horrible deaths...death and courage on scale ten times greater than what happened at the Little Bighorn, but that tragedy for what reason I do not know has burnt itself into the national psyche like no other. I need not tell you, it has done much for engendering a spirit of courage and loyalty in our fighting men and we have been the beneficiaries of that. But he said, and a frown enveloped his face, 'we have a report from a young Indian boy who was there who says he saw one of our troopers stab one of our men and ignore Custer's orders to hold his horses and stay. We have reason to believe that trooper got away. We also have reason to believe this solitary Indian's witness statement to be true. Those that did run were going to get Benteen, and didn't make it before they were cut down. This one went in the opposite direction, out into the badlands. A trooper followed him and his body was found about four miles out. He was shot in head too and it appears it was with one of our own revolvers. Suffice it to say it doesn't look good. A lot of questions need to be answered. This man was the only body that was not formally identified. We have reason to believe that he has sought refuge in Australia after spending some time in the gold fields in California. We want that man, Stagger, he said. We want to bring him to justice because if we make an example of him, and I'm talking about the noose here, it will have a salutary effect on reducing this big list of deserters we have.' He further said, 'I have studied your background. You are the best man for the job and we will pay you well, Stagger. We have the names of all the Americans in Australia over the last few years ...there are not many...registered that is. This fella went there illegally we think with one of your Johnny Rebs. Our further inquiries reveal he is probably in Victoria somewhere, north west I am led to believe. Here's a photo of him in his uniform... not very good one but good enough to recognize him. I am told he rode a blue appy with King Ranch brand...they say he was mighty devoted to that horse having saved his life. Now you don't see many horses with that coloring so that bit of information might help in your searching. Our sources say he took his horse with him on the boat. We want that traitor to face justice Stagger and you are the man I hear to do the job. We will make you a deputy Marshal for this purpose, but only until the job is done and to give you some diplomatic protection if you get into trouble because them English Colonies are good at making rules to protect their interests. The President then reached into his drawer and took out a large silver six-star badge with a magnificent eagle perched on top and dropped it onto the desk in front of me. I pinned it to my black coat. 'You cut a fine figure of a man,' he said.

'You want him alive, Mr. President?' I asked him.

He replied, 'I do, Stagger. We want to see him swing. My secretary will give you the details and the warrant to apprehend him. Good luck and may God be with you. I owe it to that gallant Boy General of mine to see this matter cleaned up and history put right.'

'By the way, Mr. President,' I said 'where exactly is this place, Australia?'

'It's a convict colony of our old enemy, England. But we are on good terms now, Stagger, and I don't want any diplomatic ruckus with her Majesty, Queen Victoria, after she welcomed me so warmly at Buckingham Palace recently.'

'Did they name that place after her, Mr. President?'

'I reckon they did, Stagger. They seem to be a pretty compliant lot over there and like all that regalia...tipping the lid, bowing and scraping and aping their toffy ways...not like us plain speaking men, Stagger.'

'I have told you all this, Sarge...word for word... so you know the importance of my assignment. I have a photograph of him in Seventh Cavalry. It is not very clear but his horse sure is a stand out with its markings...a marbled blue.'

'Give me a look at that photo,' said Sarge.

Sarge studied the tattered photo.

'My God ...I think I know your man, Stagger. His face is not too clear but that horse is a dead giveaway. You don't see many like that horse especially here in Australia and it caught our attention when he first arrived. Tell you what...he comes in tomorrow to get his American newspaper he has on order each month. Don't know why because they are three months old by the time they get here, but he doesn't seem to mind. You can watch from your hotel window here, and while he is in the store, you can check the brand. Now I don't want him taken before you get Kelly. Kelly would go underground and we would not see him for long time or he may go crazy robbing more banks and making us look stupid. Kelly first, Stagger...your man is not likely to go anywhere...he has family here...do I have a deal?'

'You sure do, Sarge. I don't want to have to hold this man for months if it takes that time to get Kelly, so I'll do him second, and I'll do him slowly cus he's a traitor to our Stars and Stripes...a deserter and a coward... there aren't more stronger abuse against a man than that, Sarge. I'd be watchin close that four eyed clerk of yours if I were you, Sarge. He looks proper traitor material with his head in them books all the time. Never trust them readers...they are full of wild and weird ideas.'

'Cyril's alright, Stagger...he just gets a little ahead of himself at times and he can be a bit thin skinned and sensitive, but me and him have a good working relationship.'

The next morning Stagger kept a keen eye on the store in the street from his hotel window. Sure enough he saw a western looking man canter down the street on blue marbled horse. Excited he ran down the stairs and out into the street. He waited until Roy went into the store, and quickly walked to his horse. He looked for the brand. It was a bit hard to see with Blue Doggy having a winter coat but he trimmed the hair over the brand with his razor-sharp buffalo knife and there it was – a running 'W'. Blue Doggy was a King Ranch horse from Texas that had been sold to the Army and delivered to the Seventh Cavalry. His heart jumped – here was his man – here was the man the President of the United States of America wanted - and he was the man to do the job. He walked to the store and looked in through the large, street window. There he saw Roy seated at the table, puffing on one of his Cuban cigars, his flash cowboy boots on the table and laughing at a humorous article he was reading in the New York Times. Roy was a patriot, through and through, and he loved nothing better than reading the news about what was happening back home. He looked up for a brief second and saw in the window a tall, dark figure dressed in black staring right back at him. His eyes were drawn to the large, gleaming, silver Star on his coat lapel with the words 'US Deputy Marshall'. Roy quickly drew the paper up to cover himself from view. He waited nervously, listening for the jingle of the spurs of the lawman walking slowly back to his hotel. He rushed out the shop, mounted Blue Doggy, and galloped down the dusty street and back home. There he saw the shaved brand. He was a hunted man.

'You look like you have seen a ghost,' said Kate as he hurried into the bar.

'I have seen something worse than a ghost,' he said. 'Get me a whisky quick Kate...make that two, and my tablets.'

This traitor could wait thought Stagger. Sarge wants this Kelly job done first, and would not tell him much about their enterprising American citizen. He has a wife and kid he said. He didn't tell him his wife was Ned's mum and that she was in jail. 'No need to complicate matters,' Sarge said to his wily clerk. Roy made enquiries about the lawman but was told little. Sarge kept his plans involving the President of USA secret...at least for now. In truth, he would not have minded the locals knowing that in addition to capturing Harry, he was now associating with the top brass in the States. But he wanted Kelly more. Kelly was threatening his job, the whole police establishment and even the Government. Meanwhile, Roy was a worried man. He wondered if that interfering know it all, Valerie, had something to do with it. He knew from his circus venture, she was an information gatherer of unusual persistence and talent, and like that spaniel dog of hers, she would course the countryside, rummage around and sniff the bushes, and spook the hidden birdlife into the open where their deadly fate awaited them.

Mum, I have a dream

Fools Crow tells of a vision.

'Frank Good Lance started to sing again and, in the blackness, I could feel something flying around the room. Then I began to hear bird noises; loud bird noises. I knew immediately what kind of bird it was. It was the chirping of baby eagles. Many times, I have found their nests, and heard them make this same sound. Then outside the house and above us I could hear the most wonderful and clear sound of screaming eagles. It was really something marvelous to experience.' Fools Crow - T Mails.
the impatient, restless soul.

the soul was not made to dwell in a thing; and when forced to it, there is no part of that soul but suffers violence. Simone Well - the Iliad poem of might.

Tennessee stood by as the hunt for his friends went on about him. The Kelly's were his relations and he wanted to do something to show his support. Sympathizers were being arrested and held in custody without trial. They were held long enough for their crops to go to seed, stock to go missing, and the bank to repossess their land. Ned's sisters rode the night run for supplies and on occasions he went with them as a lookout. The State rewards made him suspicious of new friends.

As he rode through the scrub that day, he could feel hidden eyes watching his every move. Spies, informers and opportunists were eager for the reward, and thought Tennessee may lead them to the Gang's hideout. His relationship with Gong waned as he became tense, and withdrawn. He had shown a devotion to her, but as much as she liked his company, she did not give over in ways he would have liked. They would hold hands and kiss a little but it was measured, restrained. He left it at that. He resigned himself to allowing the relationship take its natural course, or to falter and fade as many do. But in a way he felt cheated. He had taught her to ride, and she rode off. Maybe she wanted to be chased down, her affections earned or fought for, or maybe the time had not yet come. Today, on one of his solitary rides in the bush, a depressing weariness overcame him and he dismounted to lie down and rest against the trunk of a large red gum. The sun's rays beamed down on him through the tree tops, warming and slowly sedating him, so that he soon fell into a deep sleep. As he slept alone in the bush, worried about his friends on the run, he dreamt. In the dream he was walking by himself by a hilltop cemetery where they had buried Red no so long ago. When walking about, his attention was drawn two headstones close together in a clearing in the bush, away from the other graves. There perched on top of one of the headstones was a solemn, wedge tailed eagle staring with its beady eyes having a determined fix on him. The big bird aroused his curiosity. He wanted to read the names on the headstones but try as he may he couldn't get close enough to read the inscription. The eagle did not take flight as you might expect but kept its steadfast, serene gaze as he approached. As close as he got the words remained blurred. He was about to give up when the bird spoke to him in high pitched, nasal sound, an American drawl you might say. The bird said,

'Tennessee, Tennessee, do not come any closer. It is not for you to know the names on these headstones. I am soon to leave these Ranges in a permanent way and my spirit will be set adrift. It is a temperamental and willful thing. If it is not happy it will flit away across the seas in search of a home. It roosts only in the hearts of those who exhibits rare strength and fearlessness.'

Tennessee was intrigued.

'I think you know such a person. But, but...how am I to ...' implored Tennessee but before he could get the words out the big bird flapped its wings and flew high into the sky until it became no more than a speck.

A loud, rifle shot startled Tennessee from his sleep.

'What the hell was that?' he said to himself as the shot echoed through the Ranges and ravines. Then came a sudden rushing of wind, and a dull thud that made him jump. A wedge tailed eagle hit the ground next to him in a mass of fluffy feathers mushrooming into the air. Tennessee stood up and looked around. Way in the distance on a hill top he could just make out three men and some horses. One man dressed in black looked to be handling a long-barreled rifle on a mount. He went to the wounded bird and cradled it gently as its wings made a desperate, agonizing attempt to raise itself and then fell dead in a limp bundle. Tennessee could see that a bullet had smacked into its soft, warm, pulsating breast so that it fell like a lead weight from the clear, blue skies. A sense of rage built up from within him that anyone should shoot such a majestic bird, and in his rage it was revealed to him what he should do. He remembered Roy's book and the magnificent buffalo horned war bonnet with its elegant trailer of eagle's feathers and how it was kept for the bravest of warriors; those who had proven themselves in battle with heroic feats of courage and bravery and whose wise ways earned the respect of their tribe. He would take the feathers from this big bird that ruled the skies, and prepare a war bonnet for Ned. In doing that its spirit would find a home and roost contentedly as he had been told in the dream. It all made sense. He carefully plucked the long, elegant feathers from the dead bird placing them in his saddle bag, rode to a high escarpment overlooking the valley and buried the bird in a place that he thought he would have liked. He then rode home.

'Mmmm...mu...mu...mu' he stuttered.

'Get on the wooden horse, son.'

'Mum,' he said as he settled into the saddle, 'I have a dream' and he related to her what was revealed to him. 'I need your help...we have made a lot of things for Roy's Wild West Show which I can use but I need your help to make something very special and sacred. Its an Indian Chief's war bonnet.'

'A what?' she said.

'I have seen from Roy's book that it requires lot of work but I have the eagle's feathers...see here in my bag. Mum, when it's finished, and this may sound silly, I want to take it to Ned. I will ask Gong to help me.'

'Son,' she said, 'have you taken leave of your senses. What have you been drinking or smoking? You haven't been with those celestials and Joe, have you boy?'

'Mum, don't make fun of me...this is serious. More things exist than we can hope to know Mum...its spiritual but nonetheless real.'

The little, grey lady thought for a while and replied,

'I will help you as a Mum always does and for Ned and Val, but do not mention your dream to the others. I don't think they would understand somehow. Now my boy...let's get down to business...I think I am going to enjoy this project...it will make an interesting change from the boring saddlery.'

In the following weeks Tennessee crafted tipi poles and fourteen-foot lances from the sheoak stands. He practiced putting the poles together to form the tipi and made a travois in the Indian manner of two poles dragging either side of the horse which he trained the pack horse to pull. On it he would carry all his belongings. He collected the ceremonial shields made of double thickness rawhide, scalping knives, tomahawks and a pair of beaded moccasins in the traditional flower motif which his mother lovingly made for Gong. It was always towards the silent hour of midnight when the two industrious workers cleared the decks of all the practical items, and set about the religious task of creating the elaborate war bonnet.

'Mum,' said Tennessee sitting on his wooden horse, 'you know what I said about the spirit being temperamental...well, I hope you don't mind but I don't think it will help if you smoke while we work on the bonnet...the tobacco smell may show disrespect to the spirit...get up its nose sort of...don't you think Ma?'

'Bah...,' replied the old woman, 'I bet them Indians smoked while they worked. Didn't they have a peace pipe or something?'

'Yep mum, but that was for special occasions,' said Tennessee hoping to finally persuade her.

'Well if making this bloody bonnet ain't a special occasion son, I don't know what is,' she retorted showing that age hadn't slowed her brain.

In four weeks, they had completed their work. They continually thumbed through Roy's book to follow the design patterns seen in the drawings. Two bull horns were polished and sown into a cap made from wombat hide. The horns represent a potent spiritual power. Across the top of the cap they arranged cropped, pinkish galah feathers. It would represent, he thought, the dare devil sense of fun and larrikinism seen in those birds and the fun-loving character in Ned. Often, he had seen these birds perched on the telegraph line a few hanging upside down and it made him laugh. Tufts of owl feathers were placed either side of the cap to signify the deadly, quiet movement of the owl when it swoops on its prey at night and its wisdom. He was not sure what the wombat represented for it was a round, cuddly animal that dug holes in the earth but its hide had thick fur and was comfortable. Perhaps his mother thought it would signify a connection with the earth, someone with a firm sense of reality and who could go to ground to avoid his enemies much like Ned had to do. Down either side of the cap hung a strip of leather some seventy-four inches long adorned with intricate art work done by Tennessee to which his Mother had sown with red or white colored thread the beautiful long feathers of the wedge tailed eagle. To the ends of the feathers and the tips of the polished horns dangled pendants of red dyed horse tail. When finally done it was a work of high art and a magnificently crafted combination of colored, raw materials that compelled your respect and reverence.

Every night they two collaborators stealthily placed the magnificent headdress into a locked cupboard knowing the spirit of the eagle would soon come alive in the headdress. Once alive and received by Ned the spirit would protect him in battle and from his enemies who were increasing in number every day. Its spirit would imbue him with wisdom, courage and foresight to conceive and carry acts of daring and courage beyond the abilities of ordinary men. These things Tennessee and his wise, tolerant, and industrious Mum knew and believed.

Tennessee was in a hurry to leave for the Ranges as he felt a brooding restlessness from the dusty cupboard where they had imprisoned the brightly colored and spectacular bonnet. Some nights as Tennessee lay in his bed staring out his window at the stars, he swore he could hear the cupboard doors rattle. He sat up and strained his ears to hear. An impatient rattle it was, loud and insistent. In the dead of the night it sent shivers down his spine. He didn't dare leave his bed. He told his mum they would have to make a strong leather bag with several straps to carry the bonnet to Ned.

'No gaps or holes, mum,' he said.

'Ok son- I know. I heard the cupboard rattle too...the spirit is alive and kicking...we must have done a good job.'

'He doesn't like sitting around either, Mum. Me and Gong have to get going into the Ranges soon to find Ned and boys.'

Somewhere out in the scrub, Ned sat alone next to a camp fire...thinking, waiting and wondering how the hell he was going to get himself and his boys out of this mess they had been thrust into. He was their leader, they looked to him for guidance, but he had nothing to offer them.

Lay lady lay, on your big grass bed

Persian observer of Genghis Khan's Army

Their stench was more horrible than their colour. Their heads were set on their bodies as though they had no necks, and their cheeks resembled leather bottles full of wrinkles and knots. Their noses extended from cheekbone to cheekbone. Their nostrils resembled rotting graves...their chests in colour half black, half white were covered with lice which looked like sesame growing on bad soil.

Two make-believe Indians, one Chinese and the other Australian, traveled high into the Ranges camping on a grassy flat by a small stream. Tennessee hobbled the horses and set up the tipi placing the poles together at the apex. With the help of Gong, he wrapped the tanned animal hides around the poles. On the ground they placed the woolly sheep's skin and in the middle Tennessee placed some wood for a small fire for when the chilly mountain air set in at night. The long trip from the flats, hours in the saddle and the heat of the mid-day sun, and their work made them hot and uncomfortable. They undressed and bathed in the clear waters of the nearby stream frolicking, diving, surfacing, tumbling, and swimming.

Isolated in the uninhabited regions of the Ranges, and absent from the confines of their families, their youthful passions stirred. Gong let Tennessee make love to her. Before when they courted, she had steadfastly refused his nervous, hesitating advances but she felt now the time was right. Her youthful body told her so. As his hands roamed over her tightly sprung frame, he felt the smooth roundness of her feminine curves. He saw a milky whiteness about her... no flaws, bruises or sun damaged, freckled skin like the often rough and ready Australian girls. Her sweet, tulip, lips of fire engine red, when touched with his, sent their lotus fragrant flavors and scents spiraling to his fuddled brain, exciting him and releasing his shyness and inhibition. Gong whimpered as he caressed her more private regions, gently stroking her cherry blossom, making her jump, stiffen out like a wooden plank, letting out short, breathless, high pitched, strangled screams and words of awakened passion in her foreign tongue. Words, utterances he had not heard before but tantalizing to his Irish, Celtic ears. With her back to his, her hand franticly searched for his erect organ, gripping the rock hard, turkey neck firmly with her small, fat fingers, squeezing and releasing, working it like a blacksmith's bellows. In their fervent love making and experimentation she rocked rhythmically to and fro, giving little moans and sighs like the plaintiff cry of distressed soul shipwrecked and lost in the vast darkness of the South China Sea. He swiveled her about to face him. She lifted her strong legs to encircle his waist, and clamping on with her tremulous body, and balanced by the buoyancy of the stream. Tennessee drove into her. The short, sharp pain of entry gave way to waves of intense, penetrating pleasure. Pleasure she never imagined existed in the passionless strictures of her closed community. She hung there suspended, one moment smothering him in soft, butterfly kisses; then in another, deftly slipping her wet shirt around his neck like a ribbon, and gripping the ends of the fabric for support, she erotically arched her supple spine as her long, raven black tresses dipped in and out of the immaculate, clear waters of the stream in a holy baptism of first love. Transfixed, she gazed open mouthed into the cloudless, blue sky with her pretty frame pulsating, rocking and shaking like a delicate live fish held on the end of a chopstick.

Tennessee could see her face, strained and contorted, with newly discovered pleasures racing through her lithe body, and her eyes half closed and in an almost pleasure driven hypnotic state; and it made him, in a jealous fit of reversed tenderness, for lost opportunities and denials, to ask...no... to interrogate, to demand of her, in elegant, inspired, educated words that had for most of his muted life evaded him and ran to an embarrassing and humiliating stammer, why she had been so cold, so remote, so indifferent to his desires. Now these words which he knew so well from his tattered dictionary, came from deep inside him in an avalanche of eloquent words...words that were descriptive, powerful, provocative, inquiring, accusatorial and he hoped, a little poetic,

'Ch...Ch...China girl, Asia girl of the Far East, wayward child of vegetable growing, opium smoking, gold seeking Celestials.... with your enticing, almond eyes, your pearly, white skin, your cute, pug nose, your strange customs lost in an alien, bush landscape...what say you now?'

'I sorry, sorry, very much sorry,' she yelled in her stilted English.

From his reading of history, he knew of recent burial discoveries.

'Do columns of your buried armies of terra cotta soldiers and their squat, heavily armored horses rise from their earthly tombs and gallop to your rescue?'

'No, no...I don't want to be rescued,' came her urgent response.

'And do the giant black and white pandas with their patched eyes, feeding in your deepest forests of jungle green, startle, stop gnawing on their fresh, succulent bamboo, turn and strain to hear your cries of long denied pleasure?'

The china girl gave a faint smile, and in resonance with their fornicating rhythm, she cheekily imitated a high-pitched squeak of a baby Panda calling for its mother, 'eek...eek...eeeeek.'

'Or do the Great Wall frontier guards, forever dutiful, wake in their high watchtower apartments, light their signal fires, wave their flags, ignite their cannons, run to their sure footed little ponies, and race five abreast along the narrow, winding, lofty bricked paths to save you from me and the Mongolian hordes, greasy, meat eating barbarians that we are, intent upon scaling your impenetrable stone walls with our crude, wooden ladders and ropes, and drunk with the desire to rape and pillage your white, virginal innocence?'

'Could you repeat that question, Tennessee,' she murmured, and giggled.

Exhausted by their lovemaking, they collapsed drifting apart and floating lifelessly on the water like two stunned fish on the surface of a still pond. Tennessee stirred and saw Gong dreamily floating by, her jet-black tresses fanning the water surface like a peacock's tail. He gently gathered her hair, threaded it through his fingers so he held it tenderly like a silken rope, and waded to the grassy bank, her inert body trailing behind him like a piece of neglected driftwood. He put his arms under her pale, languid frame, raised her from the stream, and placed her gently on the grassy bank. As she opened her sleepy eyes, drugged and hung-over by an excess of pleasure, he lightly kissed her on her cool, damp cheeks and said,

'Lay, china girl, lay...on your big, grass bed.'

'Did you know, Tennessee,' she said dreamily, ' the mortar for the Great Wall was made of rice flour?'

'hmmmm...no.'

'And did you know I have made you some rice cakes?'

He laughed and embraced her kissing as lovers do. The afternoon sun shone gently on their bodies so that they warmed and fell asleep in each other's arms. Tennessee had given her the gift of flight on a winged, piebald pony, and now, after three long years of denial, she gave him the gift of her exotic, porcelain body engraved with her heart on a slow boat from China.

Pinday lickoye das–ay–go, dee–dah tatsun
[white eyes, you will soon be dead]

scalping.

It is said that during the old French war an Indian slew a Frenchman who wore a wig. The warrior stooped down and seized the hair for the purpose of securing the scalp. To his great astonishment it came off leaving the head bare. The endian held it up and examining it with great wonder exclaimed in broken English 'dat one big lie.' History manner and customs of the North American Indians - old Humphrey.

During the evening Tennessee and Gong rejoiced in Indian ways. They painted their near naked bodies in white, black and red paint, and with a drum and rattles they danced and whooped around the camp fire late into the night. Exhausted they collapsed into their tipi, and wrapped themselves in the warm sheep hide. Tennessee told Gong of his plans with the sacred headdress he had in his saddle bag. Gong listened. She accepted what Tennessee said but was a little sceptical. She liked the isolation of the Ranges, and was if nothing else amused by Tennessee's adoption of the Indian culture.

Tennessee woke early in the morning to ride out looking for Ned. Making sure not to disturb Gong, he dressed in his Indian clothes, and took his long lance. He prepared his horse making sure the bag with the war bonnet was securely strapped to his saddle. The spirit he thought was strangely obedient compared to the nightly rattles in the cupboard. Perhaps now that it was entering its home territory it was prepared to be patient. He daubed his pony in war paint, bright red and black, using stripes across the rump, circles around the eyes, hand imprints and signs of the sun on his chest.

He then quietly left as a beautiful dawn was breaking over the mountains. He felt proud and strong in his skins and paint. His horse was moving at a nice pace and the long lance balanced lightly in the palm of his hand. With the lance extended, he imagined he was part of an Indian war party bearing down on their enemy. As he raced his gaudy, painted pony across the plain, he did not know his every movement was being tracked from a nearby high hill.

'I'm sure this Quinn boy and his chink girlfriend will soon bring us to Kelly. Why he's dressed up in that Indian garb God only knows. You should have heard the tun-tun of the drums and whoops last night,' said Sarge looking through his telescope.

'You won't believe it but this time he's damned well given his horse a paint job too. You ought to see it. I think the kid has gone stark, plumb crazy...there's no telling what them Irish loonies get up to. I've never known a people like them given to all sorts of weird beliefs and imaginings.'

Stagger was polishing and oiling his weapon and busily adjusting the telescopic sights. He took out of his pocket a simple distance gauge attached to piece of string and eyed various landmarks about the plain below. The string served to achieve a consistent distance from his eye when measuring different objects. Depending on how the object fitted into the gauge he would know what distance it was away and where to adjust his sights. In a small notebook he noted down the distances. When trained by the Confederate Army, he would regularly have to assess distances in order to improve his accuracy, and now if he had to, he could pretty well make a reliable estimate by just eyeballing the target. He worked methodically and professionally as you would expect from a well-paid professional. When satisfied with his preparations, he adjusted his tripod, carefully placed the barrel onto a small sand bag seated on the apex, and panned the long-barreled rifle around the plain below, and again adjusted his sights.

'No sign of Kelly or his Gang yet Sarge? I'm about ready here for a bit of target practice,' he said with a villainous smile.

'Relax...we have all day and longer if necessary. I reckon he'll bring Kelly back to see that funny looking pyramid thing down there. Remember Stagger, he rides a nice-looking gray mare. What grates me she used to be mine until I sold her to Cobb and Co but bloody Kelly, would you believe, held up the coach and stole her trying to tell them she was his mare and that he bred her.'

'Them Irish are all thieves and liars, Sarge. And that pyramid thing, Sarge, is a Indian tipi - where have you been all your life?' replied Stagger with a hint of disdain.

'I leave them history things to my clerk, Cyril. He knows just about everything there is to know when it comes to books.'

'Four eyes,' said Stagger, 'I'm sure am glad you left him behind. He'd be as useful as a tit on a bull I reckon.'

'He has his uses,' replied Sarge thinking he was the only one allowed to criticize his academic clerk.

'I'm a bit concerned we may lose sight of that Kentucky or Tennessee or whatever he calls himself,' said Sarge to his two troopers. 'You two sneak down the other side of the hill and follow him...be careful he doesn't see you.'

The two troopers, keen to have a bit of action to break the monotony of long day, left winding their way down the through the bush on their horses.

On the way down one said,

'Did you see that crazy guy...he had this long spear in his hand and appeared to be poking it all about at the gallop...damn near the funniest thing I've seen in long while.'

What he saw made him curious, and as he passed a tree with straight, narrow branches, he cut one with his large knife and tapered the point to a sharp edge. He then leant across and pricked his mate in the rear with his new weapon.

'Fucking hell...that hurt...stop it shit head or Sarge will cut loose if he sees us frigging about like this.'

'Stuff Sarge,' he replied swinging his pole this way and that. 'On our miserly wage at least, we can have some fun of our own making. I don't intend to stay long in this dead-end job in any case.'

As they neared the bottom of the hill and hidden by scrub, they could hear Tennessee's horse approaching. One of their mounts let out a loud whinny. Tennessee turned in his saddle, and spotting them in the scrub, pulled his horse off in a different direction.

'That's bloody done it,' said the trooper with the pole.

'I'm going to have some fun with this guy now,' and he took off in hot pursuit. His mate complained saying they did not have orders to pursue him and stayed. The trooper came fast up behind Tennessee. The disgruntled trooper thrust his sharp ended pole both sides of Tennessee yelling,

'How do you like that, Geronimo?'

The rider shoved the sharp end of his pole directly into Tennessee's back piercing and wounding him. Tennessee tried to escape but the trooper was on a good horse and had his measure. As he was readying for his second plunge of his pole, he thought he could hear behind him a rider closing in fast. He turned, and to his amazement saw a colored pony ridden hard by a China girl with a deadly lance aimed right at him. War paint covered her face; one half of which was bright yellow and the other half red; and down the parting in her black hair was a vermillion stripe. He felt the sharp end of Gong's lance pierce his behind. He yelled out in pain,

'Come on China...I was only jokin with your boyfriend...please,' he cried.

'Drop the pole,' she demanded pushing her lance a little harder into his rear end.

He complied instantly.

Sarge and Stagger with their high vantage point could see the whole performance taking place on the plain before them.

Stagger stood there shaking his head in disbelief.

Gong guided the trooper with her lance back to the hill where Sarge and his hired sharpshooter were watching in dumbfounded amazement.

On coming to the top of the hill she pulled Panda to a halt about thirty yards from where they were standing, defiantly stuck her lance into the ground, and stared at the four men. The long-barreled gun on a stand took her attention. It didn't take her long to understand the significance of the little gathering. Before the others could realize her intention, she galloped straight at the deadly contraption kicking it from its stand, and heading down the hill to where she could see Tennessee making his way up.

Stagger went into a mad rage. That rifle was the only thing he truly loved in his life. He picked it up, cradled it in his hands, cursing the China girl.

'I've had enough of this fucking around, Sarge...back home we have our way of dealing with this trash. No chink Sheila's going to make a fool of me - the only good Indian is a dead Indian.'

Stagger reset the tripod, lifted his rifle back onto the sand bags and took aim at the retreating rider.

Sarge yelled 'Don't shoot' but he was too late.

The rifle exploded the bullet on its deadly path.

Gong was about twenty yards from Tennessee when the bullet thudded in her chest knocking her from her pony. Tennessee saw it happen as if in slow motion before him. He leapt from his horse holding the dying Gong in his arms. Stagger's hexagonal bullet had blasted a hole in her chest and she was bleeding profusely. Tennessee tried to stem the bleeding, but it was hopeless.

Through his tears, he kissed her painted cheeks and stroked her hair.

Struggling for breath and her life ebbing from her she managed a half, cheeky grin,

'I'm going fast... tell my mum I'm sorry for the trouble I've given her.

I love you both...hold me tight Tennessee,

Look after Panda for me...we had a good time in the river, didn't we?'

'The best time of my life, Gong,' Tennessee softly said trying to hold back his tears. Her eyes closed over and she was gone; gone from a world that she briefly inhabited on her own terms; and now paying with her life for her stubborn, courageous individuality. Tennessee wiped his tears, stood and let out loud scream that pierced the ears of the four men watching on the hill. He grabbed his lance, mounted his horse and charged towards them. He could make out the tall, thin man with the rifle and saw that he was taking aim a second time. He dived to the side of his horse balancing in the rope plaited in its mane. The bullet whistled over his head. Sarge had had enough of Stagger, and grabbed his gun knocking it into the ground.

'What the hell are you doing...you want to get killed,' cried Stagger but by this time a determined, painted warrior with a sixteen-foot lance was bearing down on him. He realized it was too late to do anything but run for his miserable life. Tennessee flew past Sarge and the two troopers pursuing the fleeing hired executioner. Just as Tennessee was about to reach him Stagger stopped, turned, and fell on his knees pleading for his life.

'I was only doing my job', he yelled as the cold, steel tip of the lance ripped into his chest with such force that it protruded clean out of his back. He staggered in a circle holding onto the lance, and grunting ape-like as he gasped for air. He then fell backwards embedding the sharp point of the lance into the earth, and leveraging himself in a half-suspended state off the ground. The wound let loose a torrent of dark, red blood flooding up through his lungs and bubbling from his mouth and nose. The sudden realization of his imminent demise gripped him with fear. A fear that he may in eternal scheme of things face the same cold-blooded death he had dealt out to all who came into the cross hairs of his expensive rifle. As he hung there heaving, he felt a soft brushing on his face. There flickering in the breeze was a single feather of the wedge tailed eagle attached to the lance - the very feather of the majestic eagle he had so callously shot from the sky. The prophecy of studious clerk, Cyril, had come home.

'Die, you mongrel bastard,' said Tennessee leaping from his horse and taking out his knife. He grasped him by his dreadlocked hair jerking his head back so that he could see the fear in his victim's last moments and deftly ran his blade across his scalp ripping the hairy flap from his skull with a muffled, popping sound. He let out a victorious yelp and looking up to the sky, words he did not know spilled from his mouth as though it were his native tongue,

'pindah lickoyee das-ay-go, dee-dah tatsan

'White eyes... you will soon be dead.'

Perhaps Tennessee should have said green eyes in the Indian language but his intent was clear enough to those watching the grisly scene.

'Jesus, he is scalping him alive,' said Sarge.

Sarge couldn't help but think that Stagger had got his just deserts. He didn't have to shoot the China girl. She was only having a bit of fun. He could have laughed it off but his ego wouldn't allow it. He thought it better to drive a bullet into her adventurous, heart. Now he could taste his own pain and mortality and perhaps understand in his last, agonizing moments that what you give to others will in time come back to you. The others watched in near panic-stricken terror. Sarge refused them permission to shoot.

'Only if he comes for us,' he said hoping he would be satisfied with one victim. Tennessee tied the scalp to his belt, knelt, and broke into an Indian death song. *'Nothing lives long except the earth and mountains.'* He raised himself, looked at the other three about two hundred yards away, got back on his pony, and rode to his death. A shot rang out knocking him and his horse to the ground. He was dazed. He stood and stumbled towards them with his hatchet in his hand. A bullet seared through his left shoulder, and another ripped into his thigh. He buckled over. The third bullet punched into his chest, knocking him backwards. He raised himself on one hand and clasped his chest with the other trying to stem the blood gushing from the gaping hole.

'For God's sake man, give up,' cried Sarge.

Tennessee gave them an anguished look, and fell back dead. His horse, cut from a flesh wound to its shoulder, and spooked by the gun shots, raced away down the hill disappearing into the scrub.

'It was him or us,' said Sarge and he was probably right.

The two troopers strapped the three bodies on the spare horses placing Gong across her little piebald pony, and headed back to town.

'What was he saying, Sarge. It seemed a strange lingo,' asked one of the Police.

'I don't know,' said Sarge, 'it was probably something the China girl taught him...I have to give it to her though...she sure had some guts... what being Chinese and all.'

'And she could ride, too,' said the other Trap rubbing his punctured behind.

The townspeople lined the streets as the small party headed to the Police quarters. They turned their heads in shock and disbelief at the sight of three limp bodies draped and strapped across their horses in single file. One of them commented, 'That girl's hair hanging like that in the dirt, I don't think I'll ever forget it...whatever did she do to deserve a fate like that.' His friend replied matter of fact like, 'She was a bold one, that China girl...maybe it wouldn't have happened if she'd stayed with her lot rather than trying to be one of us. Our mob don't mix with the celestials ...the gold fields have proved that.'

The newspaper headlines read the next day,

'Police and sharpshooter ambushed by Indian war party in the high Ranges, have to shoot their way out, three dead, and Kelly sharpshooter scalped alive.'

Justifiable homicide the authorities called it in relation to Gong and Tennessee and one case of murder of a deputy Marshall of the United States of America. Sarge knew that the China girl was brave. She defended her boyfriend, and for that Stagger slaughtered her with his expensive English rifle. Secretly, recessed in the furthermost regions of his ordinary, mundane, conventional heart, Sarge saw why Tennessee loved and admired the wayward girl from the Chinese mining camp. Despite what others said, he remained silent and would not criticize the China girl. He was co-operative with the parents handing over the bodies for a burial. He had some decent ways about him, Sarge did, and when you least expected it. Nevertheless, he and the wily Four Eyes shared the State money they took from Stagger's saddle bag. He sent a telegram to one of Stagger's friends in America. He did not appear to have any next of kin, at least, that is any who would own up to it. The friend on learning there was no money told Sarge to keep Stagger's fancy buffalo gun. Sarge hacksawed two feet off the barrel and used it to shoot rabbits. It didn't seem to work for him. Perhaps it was made especially for buffaloes he thought, or maybe the china girl or he damaged its delicate balance when it was knocked over. It didn't occur to him that two foot of finely engineered missing barrel may have been the cause. He left it to rust in his storage shed. The memories were not nice to him. Roy read the headlines and gave a sigh of relief. In the recesses of his mind, he knew that America, like the famed Texas Rangers, always got their man.

She wheels her wheelbarrow

Grievances of the Chinese.

'Why this tax on Chinaman? Chinamen pay for what they eat, Chinamen work very hard, but little money earn, and can't afford to pay tax.... we obey the law, we make no noise, we have feelings like other men, we want to be brothers with the Englishmen.... why not let it be so? Argus newspaper 26th May 1859.

A solitary trooper rode into the small Chinese community. He told the Elder in formal tones that Gong was dead and so was her boyfriend Tennessee. He said she posed a threat to the lawful activities of the Police and although the facts were not clear it was justifiable homicide. He added her body was available to be collected from the town morgue and that his Superior passed on his condolences. He then left. The Elder spoke to Gong's mother and father in a hushed voice. Gong's mother wept. Her father shook his head and said,

'I knew that no good would come of her ways.' He then went on gardening. The Elders had a meeting to decide on the burial. One said 'It will do us no good to give her a Chinese burial. The Europeans will see it as our consent to her defiance to their laws. We are already subject to unprovoked attacks by miners and racial hatreds.' The others meekly nodded their approval. Another said, 'she was not one of us. She was contemptuous of our ways. I say we only look after our own. Let her be buried by those she aspired to be.' At that moment an enraged mother burst into the tent disturbing the meeting.

She asked, 'Is that the decision of you all?'

They replied, 'Yes, it is.'

Enraged at their inhumanity, she cried,

'You pathetic old men, you cowards...you have stifled our youth with your silly ancient customs and your pernicious drugs. We have no hope in this country unless we assimilate. My poor daughter has courageously tried to do that. To prepare a path for others to follow so that, like the Europeans, we too can be an active part of the county and its wealth and you, with your mean spirit, dare to disown her. I will not be part of it. I will speak with Tennessee's parents to have them buried together at the Town cemetery. I invite the bold hearts to attend with me. If not, I will walk there on my own and for those who remain, I pity you.'

She then turned her back on the esteemed gathering of wise men and left. The wise men looked sheepishly at each other. During that afternoon she arranged for a message to be passed to the Quinn's that could her daughter be buried with Tennessee and she would attend. The next morning, she rose, tidied herself, put on her black clothes, went to the garden picking the best single stem, red roses she could find, wrapping them in wet hessian, and putting them into her wheelbarrow. She loved that wheelbarrow. It had taken all her possessions across country from the coast after they had landed in this strange country, and she liked its familiar feel and balance. In her spare time, she painted its tray and oiled its wheels. She then pushed her barrow past her community who averted her gaze and pretended to be occupied with their work. The womenfolk in their hearts felt for her but would not openly offer their support for fear of alienating themselves from their community. It was all they had to rely on away from their home. Her husband did not join her. She left with her wheelbarrow and a child, Gong's sister, a little girl aged six years. They put on their coolie hats to shade the mid-morning sun as they walked the distance to the town. The little child shortly wearied of walking and her mother stopped for a while taking a water bottle from the barrow and giving the child a drink. Putting the flowers to one side, she lifted the child into the wheelbarrow and pushed on into the dust and heat.

The child asked, 'are we going to see Gong, mummy? I haven't seen her...why hasn't she been home? I have been missing her.'

Tears welled in the eyes of the mother at the innocence of the child's question.

'I will miss her too little one. She was a special child and dear to us, wasn't she, and we will not forget her, will we?'

The child was puzzled at her mother's response and looked into the distance seeing the outline of the timber shacks and homes that made up the small country town.

'Gong will be asleep when we see her darling and you can put one of these pretty roses on her bed.'

'But isn't she coming home with us Mummy?' asked the child.

'That's not possible my love but there will come a time when we shall all be together again,' replied the Mother wiping her tear stained face.

'Don't cry mummy...you'll make me sad. She will come home with us, mummy...I know that,' replied the child with a concerned expression.

The child looked ahead saying, 'Look at all those tents.'

'They are houses little one. One day I hope you can live in one and get to know all the different people who live in them like Gong tried to do.'

The main street was wide, dusty and went through the middle of the Town. At the end of the street they could see a crowd massing around a cart hearse with two boxes on it. As they got closer, the crowd noticed them and began to chatter and point in their direction. They all looked to the end of the street seeing a diminutive woman in black pushing her wheelbarrow with a child.

The child said, 'Mummy I'm frightened.' She remembered the angry European miners who gathered outside their camp. Gong's mother stopped for a moment, lifted her child from the wheelbarrow, and took her trembling hand.

'Don't be afraid little one,' she said as she comforted the child frightened by the stares of the people. 'We must be brave like our Gong. Look here's a flower you can put on her bed and one for Tennessee.'

She collected the remaining roses with her other hand and they walked together to the gathered crowd who parted in silent respect allowing the two-clear passage to the coffins. She lifted her child onto the cart to put her flower on Gong's and Tennessee's open coffin which she obediently did, but before her mother could lift her off, the child looked sternly at her sister and demanded,

'Gong...wake up and get out of the box...you have to come home with Mum and me...Mum said so.'

Her mother lifted her off and placed a flower each on both coffins pausing for a while to study the peaceful features of her daughter. She then lent over and kissed her pale cheeks and stroked lightly her joined hands. She then gave a rose to Tennessee's mother Mrs. Quinn. She accepted the gift, giving her an embrace. The onlookers, moved by the quiet dignity of the scene, gave a spontaneous and respectful applause. Gong's little sister, startled by the noise, began to cry. Paddy Quinn gathered her up, and the child comforted in his large, protective arms and friendly face. Together they merged with the mourners in their grief, and the gathering became as one. Paddy placed Gong's mother and her child into his four wheeled buggy saying,

'I hope you find this more comfortable than the wheelbarrow, little one.'

'I like my wheelbarrow,' she responded in an indignant, little voice.

He smiled, and joined the local priest on the cart carrying the coffins and they led the others out of the town and up the long and winding road to the cemetery on the hill.

During the ceremony a very strange thing happened. On a ridge in the distance they could make out four horsemen- one in front and three behind him. The one in front seemed to be wearing a long headdress that draped down the sides of his horse. Ma Quinn recognized her magnificent, flowing war bonnet and in an excited voice cried,

'It's Ned and the boys, and he is wearing it.'

The others were puzzled by what Ned appeared to be wearing and thought maybe it was some subterfuge. Ma Quinn was careful not to explain. You do not lightly speak about sacred matters. The four rose in their stirrups brandishing their rifles in the air, and then firing off a volley of shots that echoed into the hills. The mourners broke into cheers and excited waving. The horsemen swung their horses about and galloped off with Ned's long, spectacular bonnet streaming out behind him.

The two bodies were lowered into their graves next to each other, flowers were spread about and the people went home. Not long after, Paddy's neat, black buggy sped into the Chinese encampment returning a mother, her sleepy child and their wheelbarrow. They resumed their place in their community and nothing was said about their solitary journey to the outside world or the wayward teenager who died a violent death. The Elders knew her rebelliousness would come to no good and hoped it would be a lesson to the others to stay cloistered in their community. In the hearts of at least one mother and a child of that closed community, the China girl died a courageous heroine forging her life in a strange country on her terms, and up against the time-honored customs of her kin folk built up over a thousand years or more.

The night has a thousand eyes

Wintu speaks of the spirits about us.
*Spirits are all about us – in a gust of wind, or a light wind whirling
around our door, that is a family spirit of our loved ones, wanting to know
that we are safe.* 'From the heart' - by Lee Miller.

The night Sarge and his small party took the three bodies back to town, Ned tossed and turned in his makeshift swag. The wind buffeted and whipped around his canvas tent tearing at the flap keeping him awake so that he slept only in fitful starts. His camp was about twelve miles away from the fateful hill where the shootout took place. They would pass the same hill on their way to the low country. Sarge's information was accurate.

Tennessee's rider less horse wandered about the scrub, sniffing the light breezes which told him things humans can never know. It told there were horses that he knew not far away. He put his head to ground to confirm what his senses told him and trotted off. He followed the trail like a blood hound. Through the dense bush, along the barely discernible tracks, sometimes lifting his head to sniff the breezes again and finally up the Mountain it went to where he found the Gang's horses.

Ned thought he heard the horses' nicker and whinny during the night, but he relaxed when they settled and tried to go back to sleep. Before dawn came, he gave up the struggle and left his tent to warm himself by the camp fire. He put a few sticks and a stump on the dying coals, sat on a log, and put his cold hands close to the warming embers. The embers soon glowed red and flames danced from the dry timber throwing shadows about the camp that darted and flitted like nervous ghosts in the night. Suddenly Ned was overcome by a tingling starting from the tip of his head and trembling down his spine. It made him shiver. He could not understand it. He looked up from the campfire, and there directly in front of him in the half-light was a horse, saddle hanging to the side and reins dangling, but no rider at least as far as he could see. It stood there stock still as though the four-legged messenger had come from the heavens to deliver a sacred message.

Ned stood and walked towards the horse.

'There boy, there boy,' he said not wishing to spook it away. He could see a flesh wound across its chest and that it was painted in a bright war paint with symbols. It had a face mask of black with intricate art work and gold lightening markings. The saddle had fresh blood stains on it. He recognized it as Tennessee's horse, and he feared the worst. He called out in the dark for Tennessee but there was no answer. He saw a long, leather pouch hanging from the saddle and on it he saw his name in clear black letters. He hesitated to open the pouch for what reason he could not say. He took a deep breath and opened the large pouch. Inside was the most magnificent Indian battle war bonnet he had ever set eyes on. He carefully took it from the pouch and saw unfold before him two trailers of beautiful, majestic eagle feathers, sown with porcupine quills, and featuring fine embroidery and leather work. Two finely polished, curved bull horns were stitched to soft head covering of warm wombat fur and fringed with close cropped pink and gray galah feathers. His hands trembled as he held it. Instinctively he placed it on his head.

Immediately his head began to spin. One moment he felt he was soaring high in the heavens and the next he was diving and plummeting towards the earth. He heard the flapping sounds of a large bird as it comes in to roost. The moon suddenly burst through dense, racing clouds and struck a single beam of light like a torch directly onto his camp. His war bonnet shone luminous and everything about him came alive. He heard birds singing and chirping above him, and saw the shapes of horses dancing in the sky. He saw flocks of wild pigeons in formation swooping down the moon beam and circling his camp. All around him a thousand eyes burned bright in the dark. It seemed that the forces of nature and all the wild, untamed animals of the bush had come together for the anointing of man into the animal spirit.

The restless eagle spirit had left its temporary abode and roosted in him like a hen finding her nest in a chook yard. And as the Indians culture and Tennessee knew, it would give him wisdom and guidance in the important decisions he would soon have to make. The clouds closed over and complete darkness returned. A warm wind sprung up and blew the long trailer of feathers out behind him as he stood there stunned and unable to make sense of what he saw or felt. He neither spoke nor reasoned about what had occurred but he felt his body being inhabited by a force that he was powerless to resist. A force that started in his head and seeped into every pore of his skin and limb of his body heating his core like a raging fever, and making him sweat profusely so that his clothes were soaked wet. If he attempted to speak only a birdlike chirp emanated from his lips as though he were possessed by a demonic spirit. He lay down flat on the ground with the long bonnet embracing him like a warm bed and slept.

With the coming of the dawn, he felt different. It was the best he had ever felt. He was reinvigorated and renewed, bold and unassailable as though his previous fears and anxieties had all fled into the dark of the night. He put the war bonnet away, and woke the boys. He did not want to tell them about all that happened that night – only about the horse. They might doubt his sanity. They went looking for Tennessee riding past the hill and seeing the deserted tipi by the river. Unable to find Tennessee they rode to their friend's farm and heard the terrible news. Silently they returned to their hideout determined to avenge the deaths of their two friends. Ned called the other three to him. He said it was now time for a radical rethink of their tactics, and what they could achieve. He said they could continue to hold up the isolated squatters and stagecoaches but that was hardly different from what others had done before them. It was his opinion that they needed to take the initiative and increase the stakes. He said they take over towns, raid their banks where there was likely to be large amounts of money and use the funds for a political purpose. They should speak and explain to the townsfolk what they were about, that they were not mere criminals intent on violence and theft for their own personal greed. For the first time in many months Ned was thinking clearly, radically and strategically. He said it would take daring and consummate planning which they were capable of. With the large sums of money, they could buy arms and galvanize the people's dissatisfaction into a political movement. They would train an army of sympathizers

'What's the objective?' asked Steve.

'The Republic of north east Victoria,' said Ned. 'Joe and I will draw up a Constitution. I've given this a lot of thought and I owe it all to Valerie. We'll have meetings with our supporters, and get a good feeling for what they would like changed. I'm sure it will succeed. America proves that it can be done. When people see that we can challenge the State by taking over towns and not just a few coaches they will understand that we can become a dominant and effective force, able to protect them. We refuse to be labeled as criminals, and we will treat the people with respect.'

The others sensed an air of authority and statesmanship in their leader not seen in that intensity or clarity before and liked what he said. They didn't want to be continually on the run, cowering in the face of a larger force and looking behind. Hunted down like a pack of wild dogs.

'Where the hell did you think this up?' asked Joe, 'I like it.'

'Since last night,' said Ned. The others laughed thinking he was joking.

Later they heard there was going to be a joint funeral the following day at the town cemetery. 'We will be there,' said Ned. As they prepared their horses to leave for the funeral, Joe observed Ned to attach a pouch to his saddle. He asked what was in the pouch.

'You will find out soon enough,' said Ned.

Bang...bang...

A young, good looking Yankee is shot

'I remained perfectly still, and in a few minutes, I saw a young Yankee lieutenant peering through the bushes. I would rather not have killed him, but I was afraid to fire and afraid to run, and yet I did not wish to kill him. He was as pretty as a woman, and somehow, I thought I had met him before. Our eyes met. He stood like a statue. He gazed at me with a kind of scared expression. I still did not want to kill him, and am sorry today that I did, for I believe I could have captured him, but I fired, and saw the blood spurt all over his face. He was the prettiest youth I ever saw. When I fired, the Yankees broke and run, and I went up to the boy I had killed, and the blood was gushing out of his mouth. I was sorry I shot him.' 'Co. Aytch' - Maury Grays.

No longer did the Gang hide away in the bush. They swept down from the Ranges into the small towns bailing up the constabulary and emptying the vaults of the banks taking only the deposits of the wealthy squatters and destroying the mortgages of those who they knew to be struggling. At Euroa they netted several thousand pounds, a small fortune. Plans were conceived that were brilliant in their originality and execution. Their spies checked the layout for weeks before. The movements of the Police were carefully noted. Escape routes were planned. They practiced with their horses travelling long distances, using streams or rocky ground to hide their tracks. They made leather slippers for their horses to further confound the Traps. If pursued they would divide and meet later at arranged places. They honed their fitness and saved their horses by running beside them and getting off their backs when climbing the steep mountains. This way they could outrun their pursuers by going the distance whereas the Traps unfit and with horses too fat and unconditioned soon fell behind. If cornered they trained their horses to stand still in the bush, in the lakes and streams, and in the dense reeds as their pursuers raced by oblivious of their presence. They used daring imagination hiding in the rear of a wagon and travelling right up to the steps of the police quarters and disarming them before robbing the bank

'As game as Ned Kelly,' the people would say.

They took over whole towns and bought the townsfolk drinks at the local hotel and took the time to explain what made them do the things they did so that those with an open mind could understand. They wanted equal opportunity for ordinary folk to acquire land and above all independence and fairness in the justice system. To lighten their message, they entertained the townsfolk with daring feats of horsemanship galloping up and down the main streets vaulting and hanging precariously from their saddles.

Steve dressed as a woman entered his horse in a picnic race wining by a more than comfortable margin. They attended local dances and cavorted to the late hours of the morning. Although death stalked them from every tree, bush, suspect farm house, and informer they did not falter in their plans and execution. They would remain part of the community from where they came and challenge those powerful interests that oppressed and bullied them in the form of the squatters, the Police and Judiciary.

The Authorities were dismayed at the Gang's daring, popularity and success. What worried them was the tide of public opinion was turning against them. They fought a rear-guard battle, imprisoning suspected sympathizers and directing the Judiciary in closed meetings at the Melbourne Club to hold them in custody indefinitely without trial. Ned financed a Supreme Court application for habeas corpus but Judge Barrington refused it on a technicality. The supporting affidavit was not witnessed correctly he said with all his pompous adherence to formality.

Ned was now ready to take the stakes up a notch. He wanted to politicize the struggle, to get away from the image of a bushranger. He wanted a Republic for north-east Victoria and if that were successful it could take on a momentum of its own. He had read in Valerie's books that the World abounded in examples of political self-determination. America led the way. Later their Civil war showed that a ragbag army of individuals in the South could give it a good go. And had they not heard from Roy how the Indians with their small bands, horsemanship and lightening raids clearly gained the upper hand against the Army in their struggles on the American plains.

Ned hated trains bringing the City into the countryside, with their truck loads of uniformed Police and sycophantic bureaucrats filling out interminable forms. He resented the telegraph poles and lines that snaked into the townships and betrayed their secrets to the City. He reasoned a decisive victory against the Police would be a precipitating event in their struggles. He planned to engage the enemy in a head to head combat. His sympathizers would then see the vulnerability of the Government and take heart from his success.

Virgil and Roy met the Gang in their hideaway and together they planned the rebellion. Roy as could be expected was secretly calculating what money he could make or steal. Sympathizers were brought together for training by Virgil. He taught them how to whoop and yell as they raced their horses at the imaginary enemy; how to wheel about in formation, to form wings and to leave gaps for the enemy to run into and then be hopelessly surrounded. Surprise, speed and daring instilled fear into the other side who panicked, dropped their weapons and fled. He had seen this happen time and time again when the Johnny Reb had the Yankee on the run, but their mistake was to hold back when the momentum was on their side and allow the Union forces time to reform and with superior numbers and equipment eventually winning the war. Here he had planned for one attack and victory to quickly follow upon the last so that the momentum would not be lost. They would start out small and as the people realized the Government forces could be beaten, their numbers and support would swell.

The greater fire power of the Police was a problem. Ned returned to his oriental friends and made sketches of the suit of armor. He would need steel plates for breast and back plates, an apron, shoulder and upper arm coverings. As the two rode back, Ned noticed the ploughs in the paddock of a local squatter, and the idea came to him to take the plough discs and shape them into the body plates they needed. Under the cover of night, they unbolted the plough parts and took them to their camp for shaping. In the high reaches of the Ranges, a blacksmith hammered out four protective suits from steel plates heated bright red. A tree trunk was dropped across a creek and used as a template upon which they fashioned and bolted the plates into cumbersome coats of armor. Leather straps joined the parts into a moveable whole.

'Are you sure bullets will not go through this steel?' asked Joe who was not convinced of their usefulness.

'Only one way to find out,' replied Ned. He placed the breast plate against a tree. At ten yards he fired. The bullet left a dent but no hole. Three times he fired from different distances, and three dents followed. A cylindrical piece was made for the helmet leaving a rectangular slit for the eyes. Ned peered out on his narrow view of the world, and felt protected. His sisters made a skull cap quilted with cotton wool to cushion the hard metal. Ned was now ready to put his plans into action, but Joe had one score to settle which would neatly dovetail into the plan.

Joe heard his mate, Declan Cassidy, was scheming with the Police for the Gang's capture. Joe wanted him dead.

'What have we to lose? They are going to string us up after Stringybark. I mean this bastard has been one of us. For God's sake we grew up together like blood bothers and now he intends to betray us for thirty pieces of silver. To make matter even worse he stood up my sister for the that flash little piece Angel. It hurt her bad and she will be years getting over it.'

'I don't mean to be rude,' said Dan 'but just about every guy wants a piece of that girl's arse. She sure is pretty.

'You saying my sister is not pretty,' said Joe looking a little annoyed.

'No but if it comes to a choice, I know who I would have.'

'Cut out that crap you two,' said Ned 'Joe, I don't agree with you about Declan...just give him something to think about...get the Traps looking for us.'

Ned knew the authorities would send a train with Police and black trackers from Melbourne when they heard that Declan had been dusted up and threatened to keep his mouth shut. He conceived a plan to derail the train at Glenrowan, take the Police hostage, and use them to bargain for his mother's release and political concessions. There were no civilian trains on Sunday and they would lift the tracks a short distance from Glenrowan. After securing the hostages, they along with a small army of sympathizers would ride to Benalla, raid the Bank and blow up the Police Quarters. It would be difficult. He along with Joe Dan and Steve would have to take the brunt of the attack and then call in his small rag tag army hidden in the scrub and waiting for their signal to come, a rocket piercing the night sky

On Saturday night, Joe and Dan spent the day camped in the hills near Declan's hut. They had other plans for Declan. That evening they quietly rode to his home holding up a local on the way.

He was told knock on the door and call out for Declan saying he was lost. The nervous local did as he was told. Declan recognizing the voice appeared at the door not expecting trouble

Joe's finger was on the trigger.

Are you old enough

An antidote to wide and weary world and dumb little gods
*It was good to lie between the soft thighs of a woman. To feel the softness
of her coming to you on a trembling wave, drowning you, breaking
warmly over you. Nothing is better in this wide and weary world. Take
that away, and what have you left but dumb little gods and lonely little
deaths every hour you draw breath* - Down all the days – Christy
Brown.

Declan answered the knock on the door. It was a foolish thing to do but he had spent
the day at the pub and thought himself invincible. It was dark and he couldn't see. The
blast of a shotgun lit up the dark doorway and spun the double-dealing Declan to the
floor with a ragged hole in his chest. He was an imbedded spy for the Victorian Police.
The Constabulary wanted to catch and hang the Outlaw Gang hiding in the vast
Wombat Ranges. Declan's crime was that he was a trusted friend of the Outlaws. It
was the act of a traitor, and it spelt death.

His teenage bride, Angel, ran to him and cradled his head in her arms. She had
tried to dissuade her husband but he was a headstrong lad, and his mind was fixed on
the reward, and an easy life free from the boredom of regular work. His loyalty went
to the highest bidder and at the back of her mind Angel knew that one day she too
would be outbid for his affections. Now he was dying with his blood pooling on the
bare boards of their rudely built, bush timber shanty on the outskirts of a one-horse
town. In his last words he said drawing deep breaths,

'Joe has shot me down Angel.'

He lifted his finger and pointed towards Joe standing in the dark of the porch way,
'Bang bang ...why me you old china cunt.'

Angel didn't know even at this shocking time if Declan was not trying to be funny
one last tragic occasion for his teenage wife.

'Let that be a warning to you Angel and others who would have us swing. Treachery
has a price. Who else is with you Angel?' asked Joe. Joe felt bad for her but not Declan.
He had it coming. She did not tell Joe that Declan expected he would soon be coming
into a big sum of money delivered by the Authorities under cover of night by the nearby
waterfall. Now after a few months of marriage, she had no husband, no money and no
reward. She could expect no help from Declan's parents. Declan was a Protestant, and
she was a Catholic. His parents refused to attend their wedding. She was slip of a girl,
barely seventeen years old, but it was not unusual for girls to marry young in the
Australian Bush. Her name was Angelica Sullivan before she married Declan, but
everyone called her Angel, and unlike many others blessed or burdened with that
name, it suited her. She had a head jerking beauty with a character that did not run
with the herd. She flew above the lamb-boys grazing and frolicking on the vast

Australian Plains with the huge wings of a wedge tail eagle spiraling high in the thermals of an iridescent blue sky, eyeing the movement below, and swooping every so often to pick one off for a meal so to speak. One such meal or perhaps better described as a smorgasbord was the madly popular boy-wonder, Declan Cassidy.

Further scuffling was heard in the house.

'I know there are Traps living in your hovel Angel to spy on my folk's farm, and to protect that dog, Declan. A great lot of good it did him to sell us out, didn't it Angel...do what I say and get them Traps to come out with their hands high.'

Four ashen faced Police scrambled to get under the bed. When Angel and her mum went into the room, they held them under the bed they said for their own protection. More likely they were held as hostages. The Police remained there for what seemed an eternity not daring to venture outside. They had weapons but it was dark and they thought they would be shot down without even being able to see the Outlaws. Perhaps they were cowards but that is too easy a word to throw about. Maybe a longing to live and a cautious discretion are better words to describe their behavior that night. If they did have courage, it had rapidly dissipated on hearing the blast from the shotgun and Declan slump to floor. They were moments before happily seated around the kitchen table discussing the day's events with Angel and her mum busily cooking some tucker. Now as they huddled under the bed, they knew their lives were in the balance.

Yet oddly enough a stronger deeper passion took hold of one of the Policemen that fearful night. He held the dead man's young bride in places where he should not have. He was excited by the pretty girl he held close to him. He knew there were armed criminals outside waiting to shoot them down. They might even come inside or set the hut on fire. Only a few months ago three Police bodies at Stringybark in the far reaches of the Ranges, and now he thought four more in Declan's hut. He would be one of the four. In the two weeks he had been at the home, he got to detest the boasting, self-centered, little shit, Declan, and his lazy, indolent ways. His sweet, fresh-faced bride...now that was a different matter. He and his three mates were acting as bodyguards, and as Joe's parents had their farm next door, they were expected to keep a close eye on the comings and goings in the District. Leon unlike the other three Traps who wandered off during the day looked to do repairs and improvements to the run-down premises and to assist the young couple. Declan was no help at all. He left early, spent a good deal of time at the pub, and returned home late at night demanding his tea. Some nights he didn't come home at all. Leon got to spend most of his day with Angel. He would help her in the garden, cleaning the house, doing repairs and preparing meals. Every couple of days Angel would do the laundry, and then have a bath. After the clothes were washed and hung out Leon would heat extra water in buckets on the outside fire, bring them into the hut, and pour the steaming hot water into the old tub. Angel seated herself patiently by the bath in her dressing gown grooming her hair and smiling kindly at Leon each time he entered the room with a steaming hot water bucket. She had in her hand a pair of small scissors and placed her legs onto the bath lip to trim her toe nails.

'I can do that for you,' he jokingly said. 'The Police Department taught me how to shoe a horse, and that can't be much different.'

She tossed back her luxuriant, blond mane, and laughed.

'You calling me a horse, Leon?' Leon blushed like the modest, polite man he was, and did not answer.

'Ok trim away.' She handed him the scissors.

He pulled up a chair, placed one of her shapely legs onto his lap and nervously began to trim her toe nails. The feel of her smooth, pretty leg resting lightly on his lap stirred something inside him that he had not felt for a long time. He had only a few days before seen what a magical spell those legs could weave on his guileless mind. Angel told him in her early formative years she received elementary ballet lessons from a cultivated Russian Emigre, and found she had a natural talent for the discipline. Her ballet teacher had explained to Angel in broken English that she had unusual ability for a child; a perfect sense of rhythm and balance coupled with a inventiveness, poise and flexibility that would have marked her for stardom in Europe or Russia, but that it would come to nothing in Australia.

'Why?' asked Angel.

'The answer is obvious - Australia has no culture,' she replied matter of fact.

'It is a land for those seeking instant wealth or those too crude to live in a normal society- people like gold diggers, convicts, bog Irish and English land grabbers like the Squatters. They do not appreciate high art or to work hard to achieve perfection in anything other than making money; they dig, uproot, drink, ride and fornicate like peasants and devil worshippers. There is no hope for your talent here, child ...sadly you and I live in a brutish land without culture or sophistication.'

'What does fornicate mean?' asked Angel.

'I cannot tell you my talented and beautiful child but you may find out soon enough.'

'Ok ...I will be good at that then... whatever it means if I cannot be good at ballet.'

They were prophetic words from one so young.

Despite stopping her lessons on leaving school Angel could sometimes be seen practicing her ballet steps and going through her exercises using the well-worn horse rail at the front of the hut as a practice bar. After placing on her old ballet shoes, she proudly demonstrated her art to the interested Leon. On the bare, hardwood floor, she rose on the tips of her feet, extended her arms in graceful circle above her head, and then ran and leapt with her legs high in the air and her back arched like a bow as though defying gravity; immediately on landing she balanced for a second then pirouetted like a spinning top moving gracefully around the circumference of the room so that he got dizzy watching her; and finally, as though delivering him a coup de grace, she went up en pointe with a fully extended, vertical foot and the other balanced delicately behind her. She smiled kindly at him, and dropped to the floor a little exhausted by her magical display.

'That's my performance for today, Leon– what do you think?'

Leon was an enthusiastic and rapt audience. He generously applauded her spectacular routine, yelling bravo and begging for an encore. It pleased Angel immensely for Declan ridiculed her efforts to be a dancer.

When Leon finished trimming Angel's nails, she unexpectedly demanded,

'Kiss my foot, Mr. Hoof Trimmer.'

He was taken aback, and looked at her a little shocked by her demand. She cocked her head, smiled, and as though daring him, raised her eyebrows waiting for his response. She was whimsical, unabashed and carefree unlike anyone he had ever known. And he was entranced. He lifted her pretty foot with a high arch and kissed it.

'Bellissima Angelina prima donna ballerina,' he said with a dramatic flourish of his hand accepting her dare. He held his lips lightly on her foot while he glanced to observe her reaction. The brush of his moist lips and the slight bristle of his cheeks against her skin had a drug like effect on her. She sighed and her eyes half closed. He did not know what came over him, but he smothered her foot in gentle kisses. Her sighs, the sweet taste and aroma of her youthful body flooded his senses and excited him. He felt dizzy and out of control.

He stopped.

He was embarrassed.

'Go higher,' she protested, and stretched out her leg in a provocative gesture.

'No,' he said.

'Kiss me on my sweet tasting, cherry lips, then... or are you just a one trick pony, Leon?'

'This is going too far. You are not old enough, you are married, you should know better, and I represent the Victorian Police Force, and in case you are not aware, I have duties and responsibilities to carry out,' he said, and stood up.

'Yes sir...Sergeant...Major General... or just private,' she shot back showing all the signs of going into spoilt tantrum. She raised herself and casually let her flimsy gown slip from her shoulders to the floor revealing herself to him in all her breathtaking beauty. It stunned him like a bolt from the sky. He went faint unable to interpret or comprehend the spellbinding vision of paralyzing beauty in front of him such that it caused him to shade his eyes. Between his fingers he spied such extraordinary symmetry, natural grace and harmony that he struggled to get his breath. Tall of stature with willowy looks, corn blond hair falling to nicely rounded shoulders, a slim waist, narrow hips, and a tantalizingly shaped bottom tapering to her fit, slender legs. All this with a smooth ivory skin lightly blended by the hot Australian sun, a bewitching smile and playful disposition, a simple, clear sighted understanding of life for one so young, and a fondness to what she found logical and enjoyable. He made a feeble excuse, and retreated out the door, walking backwards, and bowing as he went. She giggled and splashed him with her bath water.

Another time she put on her snow-white bridal gown, the only garment she kept in her battered trunk, and appeared in front of him while he was sleeping in the shade of a spreading peppercorn tree. He awoke blinded by an angelic figure transfigured in a brilliant sunshine against the shady, green speckle of the giant, overhanging tree and the washing flapping on rope line. He squinted, and saw in a blur the heavenly figure had feathered angel wings, wings that someone had given her for a joke, and he thought for a moment he was in Paradise. She brushed him lightly with one of her wings like a butterfly and flew back to the hut, dodging the hanging clothes and laughing all the way. She entertained him endlessly with her joyous, childish pranks.

At night he and another Constable had to sleep on the young couple's bedroom floor. 'Do not let Declan out of your sight,' ordered their Supervisor. 'There will be hell to pay if the Kelly Gang get him like the others.' Leon could hear and sneak furtive glances of the young couple making love. It excited him and gave him a hard on. Declan would, in the heat of a vigorous, enthusiastic lovemaking, fling off their bed clothes and go for it like a demented, crazy Irish Hurley player, slapping, twisting and bending his young, submissive wife into every unimaginable position that sex could be had or dreamed of. She was a willing and complicit partner, and responded like a travelling show contortionist from far away India. She was as tantalizing and beautiful on the bed as she was practicing her ballet. It was all there - every tender caress, every demeaning assault and slap, every loving mercy, every uttered protest, every passionate kiss and embrace; limbs and body parts twisted, stretched, choked and contorted into a jigsaw of every carnal desire, stimulation, perversion that existed on God's Christian and heathen earth until Angel, too tired to continue, said 'back off, Dekkers- I'm about done in for the night,' and fell asleep.

Leon knew Angel to be a most unusual sensual and evocative girl. He could have watched her all night long. The spy had turned his preying eyes from the farm next door and the covert reporting of the arrival and departure of Kelly sympathizers to this amazing country girl, unaffected and contemptuous of the commonly accepted morals and standards of the Society in which she lived and which constrained his existence. She was truly in the full bloom of her life. The serious policeman, with an impressive record in the Constabulary and marked for advancement, was now a fully-fledged voyeur, addicted to watching every intimate, private and public detail, every seemingly insignificant, and humdrum happening in her ordinary life. He so badly wanted to say to her 'be my baby' but such unrestrained words would sound silly even before they left his mouth. She would mock him and ask if he was speaking a foreign language. Declan could say it a hundred times a day to the same girl and each time it would sound better than the last time. He could not with all his imaginings bridge this impossible gap. It seemed a mile wide. His sheltered upbringing with its high morals and strict discipline clouded and confused his thinking to the extent that he almost forgot what he was paid to do... to see that the young married couple were safe from revengeful Outlaws lurking in the wild Ranges surrounding them. In their disguise and their desire to do away with the traitor these dangerous men may have ridden along the bush track, hidden behind a tree and spied him ogling Angel; seen what a dirty bastard he was; and casually remarked that his offending eyes could soon look down the gleaming, silver barrel of colt revolver, stolen from his dead compatriots at Stringybark.

Leon could not sleep. All night he stayed awake obsessively thinking about the seductively relaxed and accepting teenage bride. She drove him insane such that he wondered what he and his strict, church going, unimaginative wife had been doing for the last fifteen years. Or perhaps he had been the unimaginative one. He now understood why this brash, swaggering boy was so popular with the girls, and it was not only because he was funny. He was crazy. He took them places they never knew existed; he awakened their hidden and undiscovered passions; he was reckless and uninhibited; he made them laugh, and they wanted more of him. Declan knew this, and to have sex in the public way that he did, only bolstered his ego for he had no shame or modesty. He hoped that his sporting prowess in the bed would be the topic of conversation at the local pub, as it invariably was, and he could swagger through the swing doors to their knowing smiles and congratulatory slaps on the back.

But to the conscientious Leon, it made him mad that he was good, and that his goodness made his daily existence boring and dull. At the end of the day, all he had to show for his goodness were smug approving parents, an ordinary pay packet, and a fat, unimaginative wife spending that hard-earned cash on confectionary, cream cakes and ridiculous religious memorabilia and pictures which she hung all over their home. Now with two members of the Kelly Gang outside, a body in the passageway, and Joe issuing deadly threats, this respectable and ambitious lawman had every reason to believe it might be the last time he could feel a young girl's freshness and budding womanhood. He could smell those intoxicating perfumes and soaps that he had so carefully prepared for her bath like she was a Roman Princess to be feted and waited upon. She did not resist when his exploratory hand cupped her small but firm breasts. Encouraged he hiked her skirt up fingering and pulling down her cheap, cotton underwear. She yielded to his advances. Six of them – three police, her and her mum, all crammed together under an old, rusty bed was not going to stop him. They could not hope to understand the temptation this disarming girl exuded. No man could resist her. And there might not be another opportunity if Joe's threats were carried out. Lately he had come to thinking there was something that did not ring true about his commitment to hard work, respectability, and fidelity. When a small child his parents doted on him. They dressed him in little tweed, long pant suits and hat to show off to their friends and instilled into him all those worthy and respectable Protestant values and habits of going to Church each Sunday, doing his homework and achieving good grades, hard work and being exceedingly polite to everyone.

'What the hell's going on with you two?' asked one of his policeman friends

'Can't help it, mate...she's trying to get away...I have to hold her down but she is resisting and bucking against me.'

'It doesn't look like that to me,' he replied.

He poked his mate in the back, and pointed towards the two where the secretive business of opportunistic sex was running its natural course.

'I didn't know that was on our 'to do list,' he whispered.

'I didn't either, but I have just added it to mine,' he replied.

Angel climaxed. It was overpowering, deep, forceful, and her delicate frame stretched, quivered and shook. At the same time as she came, she screamed 'Jeeeeeeeeesus' seeking release from the intense pleasure that swept over her. It startled her companions under the bed. In a less than ingenious attempt to hide her illicit coupling she again yelled, 'Jeeeeeeeeesus will make you pay for shooting Declan, Joe.'

Joe calmly seated on his horse in the half dark glanced at his coconspirator Dan and laughed.

'That's Angel for you,' he said, 'invoking the Lord again. Here's my message to Jesus, Angel...duck your heads my darlings,' he yelled, and fired a shotgun blast into the bedroom shattering the glass window. Joe's death threats and challenges to the Police bounced off the thin, hut walls and muffled into the cheap, calico ceilings while the gunned down Declan, the town clown who made all the girls laugh and excited them to a fever pitch, went cold and stiff ten paces away from where the not so clandestine adultery had taken place. Angel pulled Leon closer. What they did was sinful in the eyes of the Church but it was not done out of any disrespect for Declan. He had laid down the rules. She did it because she had a sort of love for the prim and kind policeman who did everything for her. She did it because it may have been the last loving, joyful act she could do before going up in fireball. And she did it because it thrilled and excited her more than anything on this dull, tiresome, ordained Earth. Maybe it was the only reason she did it.

If given the opportunity she would have said to Declan,

'I have died a thousand deaths for you, Dekkers.'

He would have replied 'oh yeah... Angel baby...when?... you two timing bitch.'

She would reply calmly,

'Each time you lied, each time you cheated on me with my girlfriends, each time you came home rolling drunk, and smelling of cheap perfume, I mean all hours of the night and morning and sometimes the next day. And if that was not enough, each time you betrayed our innermost secrets to that swill you call your mates at the pub, each time you mocked my ballet efforts, each time you did those things, Declan, I died a little. And not to forget the hovel you made me live in, and the contempt of your Parents... but that is alright with me, Declan. I have no recriminations or regrets. I bear no grudges. I can give as good as I get. I have learned in my short life to live with my disappointments, and live each day as though it is my last. We do what we do, and live with the consequences. You must have known that if you betray your friends for money and fame, there would be a price to pay. If you had got the reward for betraying your mates to the Traps, you would have left me and spent the money on some trashy sheila. Did you ever have a quiet moment and think about that, Declan? Did you ever think about anything except yourself, Declan? Leon just got caught up in our twisted lives, that is all. There is nothing more to it than that.'

Declan was nobody's fool. He would have replied,

'Fine fucking words, Angel. You are nothing but a two faced, cheating bitch and what with your high and mighty airs about what you could have been if things were different. But you know what...they are not different. We live in this crappy world and your fine imaginings, your airs and graces, your arty farty pretensions will not change it one bit. It is not safe to have a man in the same house with you. And I had three of the bastards, and they did nothing to protect me except hide under our bed and snigger while one stuck it up you. And did you stop him? no... no...no... for fuck sake, Angel... right there in front of your Mum...and under our bed...and you kept on whoring. What you are, Angel, if anything is a shag artist...a shag artist par excellence...you see I can be arty too. Every spiv, every drunk, every pervert in the pub knows it, and they are dying to fuck your impossibly beautiful arse. They won't let me stop telling them all about how I fuck you inside out and upside down all night, how you howl and scream the place down, and do your acrobatics. You should join a fucking circus Angel- you... you...you could do it on a tight rope, with some greasy Italian in his tight pants and moustache, up high, for all the wankers to line up, pay and take their seats...roll up, roll up, roll up ladies and gentlemens, and wankers...get your tickets here to see the greatest show on earth...Angel fucking on the tight rope...and without a net...how about that Ladies and gentlemens...one slip in her shag act, and she will drop from the sky to her death.'

Angel laughed almost hysterically when she conjured up the image in her head. Declan's ability to make her laugh, even when he didn't mean to, made her love him.

'You are letting your vivid imagination and dirty mouth run away with you now, Declan, but go on ...I am enjoying it.'

'Is that so, Angel...only you would laugh...most decent girls would be ashamed. Save your pathetic excuses for someone more gullible than me - someone like your trap lover, a damned queer old enough to be your father, Angel. It's disgusting what you do when I am not here. I risked and lost my life to get you a better world, Angel, and all I got was a duck shot blast into my guts when I answered a knock on the door.

And my life is over before it even began. There's another word for you. I should have listened to what my Parents said about you bog Irish, spud eating Catholics, pretending to all goodness and light, whereas the truth is, Angel, you are the bastard child of the devil himself. You are a shameless fornicator, Angel.'

Angel's prophetic promise to her ballet teacher, a promise made when she had no knowledge of the word her foreign teacher would not explain, had come home to roost.

'You are right, Dekkers,' she said to herself. Tears rolled down her pale face, tears of guilt, and she went silent. But was her admission out of her sympathy for Declan's tragic end? Was she guilty by her own confession so innocently given several years before? Was Declan's impassioned plea that he was cheated on and hard done by to be believed? Or was she more devious and a better liar than him? Or were they both fooling each other? Who was right and who was wrong? Or do these words so often used to justify or accuse one of infidelity, hurt and disappointment mean nothing at all - just hot air and a bit of empty posturing?

Joe and Dan reckless with a traitor's blood on their hands, raced wildly through the night to rendezvous at Glenrowan where the Gang planned to derail a police train.

After her husband's burial, Angel went to her parent's home, and in time, the suitors returned like migrating geese, first riding past and looking, then building up enough courage to knock on her door. She never wanted to answer a door knock again. The bashful suitors stood there with flowers, and impure expectations. The memory of the bawdy jokes and men's talk about Declan and his pretty child wife at the pub lingered with them and inflamed their basic instincts.

'Go see who it is, Dad,' she said while she sat in her room combing her long hair with slow deliberate brushes. Shortly, after an exchange of pleasantries, she and her visitor would go walking, and talk in hushed tones about her tragedy. He would respectfully enquire about her health.

'I have troubles getting over my grief...some days are good, and some bad,' she would reply dreamily in an indifferent, matter of fact tone while staring right through him with her pretty blue, doleful eyes, and across the empty paddocks to the distant Ranges. Before long the two would be enmeshed in a hurried knee trembler with the teenage widow pinioned against the solid trunk of a big, gum tree, and she thinking lewd thoughts of not what happens in but under the marriage bed, and where threats of impending death and lust are the strange bedfellows. It was a good day for the young widow, and for her visitor.

'Dear Declan had such good friends, didn't he dear? I mean all concerned about your welfare,' remarked her Mother when the visitors left.

'Yeah – whatever, Mum,' she replied and retired to her bedroom.

Leon left the Victorian Police. Some said he was pushed. He left his wife, and he was not pushed. His Parents could not understand what happened to their obedient boy in which they had placed much pride. He broke off all contact with them. When his Parents read in the local paper their son had been charged for peeping tom offences in the township, they burnt his little tweed suits which they had faithfully kept in the wardrobe for years along with the carefully preserved birthday invitation cards.

'After all we did for him,' they said.

When Leon heard about the suits from his sister, he said,

'They were too bloody hot for a kid to wear in the middle of summer, anyway.'

He hesitated for few seconds, and then added,

'Like them starchy, police uniforms.'

'Well, what are you doing for crust now, Leon?' his sister asked a little upset with the way her brother's life was turning out.

'Nothing at the moment,' he replied rather blandly.

Then he thought again for a moment and said,

'Just a bit of bird watching, Sis. It's a habit I find hard to give up.'

Ground control to Major Tom

To imagine the Universe

Aurelius writes: 'Many of the anxieties that harass you are superfluous: being but creatures of your own fancy, you can rid yourself of them and expand into an ampler region, letting your thought sweep over the entire universe, contemplating the illimitable tracts of eternity.'

Edwin Hubble gazed out of his telescope and discovered, to his shock, that the universe was far bigger than we imagined, and getting bigger all the time. Today, astronomy suggests Heraclitus was right that the universe is an incessant flux of creation and destruction, with black holes consuming galaxies, and then vomiting them out again as new stars. 'We must know that war is common to all,' Heraclitus said, 'and all things come into being through strife.'
'Philosophy for Life: And other dangerous situations by Jules Evans

Ned had a small army of loyal men waiting on the steep hill overlooking Glenrowan –a rag tag army of sorts molded together by blood relatives and those of, Irish origins, and a brooding discontent with the ruling classes. And present were Roy and Virgil – two Americans who came to these shores for a new life. The peril to their families of these committed men weighed heavily on Ned. They were taking a big risk. If they lost the struggle, their land and possessions would be confiscated and they would probably hang for treason. Families, children would be left without financial support. He knew firsthand how difficult it was for his sisters to manage without his mum and him around to help. He had planned for him and his Gang with their armor to do the dangerous work and the identity of his supporters kept hidden for as long as possible. A substantial victory against the Police and State would dramatically change the odds in their favor. The vulnerability of the State Institutions would be exposed, and people would come to see that well planned armed rebellion had every chance of succeeding and improving their lot.

Virgil knew the mistakes he and his Southerners made and he was keen to get back into the fray. He had a mutual dislike for the British, and the struggling Irish here had the same rough and ready ways that endeared him to his Southern men during the Civil War. Despite being heavily outnumbered, they took the advantage in the early stages of the war with lightening raids, unorthodox planning and raw courage. No uniforms, no parade drilling, no clear order of command, poor weaponry, they swept through and behind the enemy lines routing them and scoring a formidable list of victories. They could all ride and shoot and their horses were resilient. Surprise instilled fear, and fear made the opposition run. Virgil despised that craven fear, but he knew if it could be instilled into the enemy it meant certain victory.

Roy on the other hand knew the value of running, or to be more direct desertion. It gave him his life when all his regiment were slaughtered to a man. He lived to become successful and rich, to enjoy the better things of life. He didn't believe in a divine justice or retribution - the rain falls on the just and the unjust and he was living proof of its truth. He ran from the Little Bighorn and fortune shone brightly on him. Ned, his sympathizers and Virgil could rabbit on about their plans but Roy, this Yankee doodle dandy, this survivor, this self-made man had other matters on his mind than risking his life in a one sided battle. He was thinking of doing another runner if things didn't turn out as planned, but he would hedge his bets in the beginning and see where the strength lay. If Ned succeeded then he may profit by staying with it he thought. There was a Bank at Benalla to be blown up with the explosives and loot to be divided. He would grab all he could in the confusion and then do his runner... this time back to States. Life was getting dull and he was looking for a way out. He had a lucky escape with the death of Stagger and things were getting a little too hot for him. He wanted to go back to his family in the States. He had the help of Elly's girls to look after their child. Elly was in jail, and it had aged her. He had lost interest in their marriage. He did not need her. He wanted to leave this backward place where there was little commerce or imagination, and a class ridden Government holding on to old, colonial values of a distant Mother Country.

Ned, Steve and two men took four spare horses, two pack horses and a buggy and set out for Glenrowan. On the buggy they packed four suits of armor, ammunition and a drum of dynamite to blow up the Police quarters and the Bank vaults at Benalla. They rode quietly and purposely through the moonlit night hoping to arrive at the small town of Glenrowan near midnight. Ned and Steve wore warm, long coats under which they would later put their armor plates. White mists and fogs came in waves as they trotted up the hills and cantered easily along the dirt roads. They hit pockets of cold air trapped in the low valley's that numbed their faces and hands, but relief came as they ascended into the warmer air of the rises.

When almost every living creature is wrapped in slumber, hidden in their nests, lairs, and farm houses, the night belonged to them alone. Ned spotted the outline of a barn owl sitting solemnly on a fence post. It remained stock still as he passed closely by. It showed no fear. That night the bird would wait, watch and then swoop with deadly accuracy on its prey. Ned thought, he too, was about to wait, and when the moment came, swiftly strike his enemy when they were least expecting it. He and the hooded owl were friends, inhabitants of the night, coursing their territory and doing what they had to do to survive. When the train tumbled from its iron tracks, and spilled down the cutting like fleeing, field mice, he and his men would swoop protected in their steel, owl gray, body plates on their frightened prey.

Ned turned his attention to the clear, night sky. The stars shone brilliantly. They seemed so close that at times he was tempted to duck for fear of striking his head. For a brief moment, this imaginative bushranger thought he was floating in space between the stars on an inter-stellar journey. He was about to call out to Steve, 'mate, I'm going to drift over to Venus for a while and then, if the mood takes me, I might meander back along the Milky Way.' His mare, Music, was relaxed, gliding through the dark and now and then dropping down to a trot to climb the incline of the hills, and seamlessly back into an easy canter on the flats with no more than a loose rein. Ned could have gone on for ever in this dreamlike state. He was in a state of euphoria and had no fear about the oncoming battle where lives may be lost. He was tired of running and hiding; where every sound, every sudden movement, every stir of the wind and even every suspicious look of a friend made him anxious and hyper alert. It was not the way he wanted to live his life and his boys felt the same; waiting to be shot out of the saddle from someone hiding in the bush and expecting a large reward as Stagger had intended. He had made plans for a showdown and his mind was at peace whatever the result. They were going to lose their lives anyway after Stringybark. As they travelled down the soft dirt road in the near silence of the night under a star studded canopy and full moon, Ned experienced a moment ecstacy, of complete understanding of the World and love for those who struggled to make the best of their lives no matter what the odds and no matter on whose side they were. He did not want to sacrifice their lives and impoverish their families. Even if only the four of them died in the coming conflict, if they went with courage maybe the tide of public opinion would turn and the grievances of his people would be lightened. He saw above him the path of the Milky Way stretching across the firmament in all its ashen splendor and he hoped that Val would be looking down kindly and reminding him of her insights into the American Civil war and her thoughtful analysis of right and wrong. If he could achieve a resolution with the Authorities by showing that he and his followers were a contest for their Police, if he could be given a public voice to air his protests and if his success brought many to a fair minded understanding, then possibly he had a chance but it was slim. The plated armor he had in the cart would he hoped even the odds; and with it he hoped he and his boys could take big risks against the fire power of the State. And in doing so maybe avoid the prospect of other's lives and families being lost. A voice from the buggy broke the silence.

'We'll put the horses in the stables at McDonald's hotel and some at Mrs. Jones's pub across the line. McDonald's one of us but I need to see Mrs. Jones...I'm not sure about her...she can be a bit of a tyrant,' said Ned.

The others stabled the horses while Ned knocked on the door of the rough bush pub. He heard some movement inside.

Me and Mrs. Jones

Mrs Jones describes Ned in a letter
Ned could not go through the waltzes- he was laughing and amused all around him... he said he would have to nock off as he was no dancer. David Mortimer said he would be the M.C. and put them through it... the people did not think about the special train. It took up their attention watching the Gang as they were noble looking men...the divel was in us...we had to be looking at the darling men but to be sure Ned was a darlin man.

'Piss off...the pub is closed,' came an irritable voice from within.

'It's Ned here, open up,' replied Ned in serious monotone.

'Yeah and I'm bloody Father Christmas, now clear out...I've had enough jokes for the day...go to the pub across the line if you want some grog.'

'If you don't open up, I'll push your flimsy door in Mrs. Jones - now do as I say and open up.'

The door half opened and a pair of eyes peered through the space.

Ned pushed it further and heard a thud. He looked inside to see Mrs. Jones up ended with her nightdress up around her head and a not too unattractive pair of legs exposed.

She let out a mouthful of vehement abuse. Ned laughed, apologizing for his rudeness, and assisted her off the floor. As she righted herself, he couldn't help but notice that although the creep of middle age and adversity was there, she had an open, pleasant face that exhibited character.

'Well bugger me if it isn't the man himself,' she said as she surveyed the flash youth holding her arm. She recognized him from one or two previous visits to her Hotel.

'What did I do to deserve this pleasure,' she said.

'Can you and your daughter get dressed and come with me Mrs. Jones. Your young lad can stay in his room. I need to get the plate layers to lift the line and I don't want anyone running to Bracken, the local trap ...if you don't mind, we need your horse yards and your hotel for a short time but we will pay you well for your services.'

'Be my guest. I don't suppose I have any choice being who you are and all that.'

Mrs. Jones awoke her teenage daughter Gloria. They both dressed and went with Ned to the Station Master's house.

'Why do you want to lift the line?' Mrs. Jones asked.

'The Traps will be coming with black trackers from Benalla ...we would like to give them a bit of a welcoming party.'

'You and who else,' she said in disbelief.

Ned smiled, 'I cannot give you military secrets.'

He got the Stationmaster to rouse the plate layers from their tents nearby, collect their tools, lamps and march under gunpoint down the line about a mile to steep cutting where they were ordered to remove a section of line.

When they got back, they saw Joe and Dan weary from their visit to Declan's house and cross-country ride to Glenrowan.

'What happened? 'asked Ned.

'Declan won't be lagging to the Traps anymore,' said Joe. 'You can count on that - I should expect the train anytime Sunday. Are the others about?'

Ned didn't reply. He was upset that Joe and Dan had ignored his orders and shot Declan.

'It makes no difference,' said Joe. We are in it up to our necks after Stringybark. And he was lookin for it with that big mouth of his.'

Ned wanted to say as little as possible with strangers about. Ned ordered them all back to the Jones hotel where they lit the fires and waited. His men took it in turn to keep a look out for the Police train. To pass the time they drank, danced, and sang. Mrs. Jones's thirteen-year-old lad gave a stirring rendition of the Wild Colonial boy and Ned and his boys rewarded the lad with a handsome sum of money.

After midnight Ned left the party and went for a walk to the Station to listen out for the train. Mrs. Jones took the opportunity to accompany him, to get a bit of fresh air she said. She had been watching the lean, good-looking bushranger for some time out of the corner of her eye. She liked what she saw. He talked honestly with the people, and he treated them well, even the policeman. He bore no grudge and respected views different from his. He had a keen sense of humor. From what she had heard, and that was quite a bit, he led by example and people admired that.

She had known many men in her life as a publican and it was not exaggerating to say many were loudmouths, boasters, shallow-witted men, and what she despised more than anything, they lacked guts. A man without courage was not a man to her way of thinking. When things got tough, they would pack it in and leave, swagger off down the road, to bore and harass another guileless victim, and drink her hard-earned savings. Her husband left six months ago when the hotel was struggling with debt and the young boy suffocating every night with rasping asthma as the cold, moist air choked his phlegm ridden lungs. She could have done with a good man's strength then. Someone to heat the kettles and pipe the steam into a makeshift canopy over his bed while she tried to pacify a terrified child going blue in the face through lack of breath. But no...he just turned over and pulled the bed clothes over his head. He said he couldn't stand the sound of the boy choking...it kept him awake and he had to get away. She'd even put up with the odd drunken abuse she got if he could just show some spirit, but the gutless wonder couldn't even give her a decent belting when she abused him in front of his mates.

'You wouldn't think a man would bugger off from his family like that...would you Ned...in a time of need. I'm sick of these fickle men. If things get too tough they piss off leaving me to look after the kids and pay their debts. He went bankrupt and I bought this block for six pound and had a few friends knock up the pub. It's not much but what can you do when I am left with nothing after fifteen years of marriage.'

Ned knew she was right. He remembered his mother languishing in jail, his sisters caring for the children, the Police raiding their home threatening the girls and tipping their flour and food on the floor. There was little doubt in his mind that women were the strongest when things got tough. He admired their courage and inner strength. He knew what this middle-aged woman was saying. He put his arm around her shoulders and drew her close as they walked to the platform to show that he understood what she was saying. The physical closeness of Ned's arm around her made her feel better than she had for years.

She changed the conversation to more intimate matters.

'I like you a lot, Ned,' she said, 'You're a grand boy and everything they say about you is true. I wish I had my time again and I wouldn't waste my time looking for love in all the wrong places...bars, braggarts and bastards, men with hearts the size of a button. Why, next to you like this, I can feel your big, bold heart thumping. Those bragging Traps don't know what they're up against. I've heard them boasting in my bar about what they'll do to you and your young boys, but when the time comes, I'll warrant they'll ride the other way, jumping over each other in their hurry to get away, like that no-good husband of mine. You Ned, you go out to meet your danger head on....no pussy footing about. I like that in a man but it has taken me years to recognize it. I'm a slow learner but I know why you and the boys are out there in them mountains, wondering where your next feed or root is coming from. It's because you don't take the shit coming from the Traps, the courts and all them authority, and you fight back for a better life. Them Traps and the Squatters have done it to you and your family. Put your mum in jail, orphaned your little brother and sisters and the Judges are just as bad. They all want you out of the way, Ned, because they know you can give it back to them...tenfold...and that worries them. People haven't stopped talking about those towns and banks you and the boys have done over and I should know...I hear it every day in the bar talk. And I see them high and mighty squatters go by in their expensive buggies and hangers on...too damned snooty to come and have a drink in my place like that school teacher Kershaw. I've seen how they get the best land and plenty of it, too, from their friends in Government and the fucking Judges for what they worth. All in it together they are...snouts in the trough and feeding off each other. Its only you and your boys they're frightened of Ned. I hope you give them a pasting when the time comes. God knows the bastards deserve it. The ordinary folk like you Ned... there's a lot of good country people loving you out there Ned...and I want you to know, if you don't know it already, none more than this girl here.'

Mrs. Jones sure could talk... a talent she said came with the job. This confident, middle aged mother ran her hand lightly across the front of Ned's trousers in a not too subtle indication that she was up for more than a conversation.

'I should have worn my armor, Mrs. Jones.'

'I can burn a hole through steel, Ned,' she said as her eyes fixed resolutely on him and she began unashamedly to seduce him. Although some sixteen years his senior, Ned was not indifferent to this mature, forthright but disillusioned publican's wife doing it on her own terms against the world. They strolled kissing like lovers about to depart on a long train journey, danced a lazy waltz on the narrow, railway platform in the half light of the kerosene lamps to the music drifting across the frost tipped paddock, and stumbled through a creaky screen door into the Stationmaster's drab, little office. She leaned provocatively against the big desk belonging to the Stationmaster. Ned was going to have his fun too. He plucked her from the desk gripping her by the leg and arm like a child, and swung her on a low trajectory, a dizzily exciting merry-go-round, then flinging her up, up into the air, and catching her as she floated back to earth entwining and anchoring herself about his solid and tightly sprung frame. It both frightened and thrilled her. She slipped slowly, limb by limb, to the floor. There, on her knees in the stationmaster's wood paneled office, she genuflected before the Cuban heeled, demi God of the Australian bush arrayed in his patented, black leather, full length riding boots, the once proud property of a Victorian mounted Police. For a brief moment, she thought she could see her reflection in the brilliant shine of the patented leather...an image of her in her youth, joyful and full of hope and ambition.

Her gaze moved to the fancy set of spurs strapped to Ned's boot heel so that when he walked, they jangled, almost like wind chimes in the light breeze. Her eyes were riveted on the silver-plated rowel at the tip of the spur with blunt little half-moons around its circumference, all of different colors, and impregnated with exquisite emeralds and rubies; a gift from the mercurial Roy and his penchant for flamboyance. She imagined this booted jewelry, stained and encrusted with the honest sweat of his mare, being raked up and down her soft, white flanks, spurring her aging and weary limbs on towards that peak that had always stayed just out of reach, and which she knew held a promise nay a lick of what she knew so well when young and spirited. She ran her hands behind the raised heels to the spurs, her fore-finger lightly touching on the silver rowel and flicking it so that it hummed like a bee ready to sting.

She cocked her head to one side and looked up.

The demi god looked down.

Their eyes met.

She traded a benign smile, but it was disguised and born of bar room knock-em down, drag-em out cunning. She made to kiss the tip of his boots but as quick as a viper, she pulled Ned's legs out from under him landing him on his back with a resounding thud. He winced and groaned as they fought and wrestled like two kids. Ned lifted her from the floor, and put her down firmly on the desk. There, on the polished, mahogany table, with her legs spread-eagled over Ned's strong shoulders, and her comely arse pushing aside train schedules, quill pens, and knocking an ink bottle over an embossed letter from the Director-General of Her Majesty's Railways commending their obedient station master for his dull attention to duty, Ned shunted into his older partner with the all the vigor, strength and courage she longed for and failed to get in her dismal collection of fake, drunk, feeble lovers and decamping husbands. This near worn out publican's wife liked the spectacular, the rough and tumble, the hard and soft, the come and go, the push and shove, the embrace and release, the whole fucking contest. She wanted it all before it was too late. When the midnight Special, carrying its diminishing cargo of life's time and opportunity, was rattling on down the track towards her, she longed for another chance rather than the lackluster, missionary pump by a dead pan lover. My God, how many times had she stared at the droopy calico ceiling in her pub bedroom wondering if life would grant her just one decent fuck to remember before her looks packed it in and she was reduced to domestic chores and became invisible to men.

It was minutes after midnight, and yet the train full of Traps and six black trackers from Queensland had not come to the lonely siding. Ned jumped off the platform somewhat stiffly and put his ear to the railway line.

'They say you can hear it coming from miles away but I can't hear a damned thing.'

'I hope it doesn't come, Neddy...I hope it doesn't come for all our sakes,' she said reflectively, 'anyway I couldn't hear it...my ears are still ringing.'

'My back feels as if it's broken,' he complained.

'Never trust a bar maid not to bring you down, Ned,' said the middle-aged publican as she threw back her hair, and gave a delightful laugh.

The two contenders joined hands in an amicable if not admiring truce.

Together, they walked slowly back to the noisy hotel, the drunks, the braggarts and soon a scheming, dissembling schoolteacher, the worst of all do-gooders in this world of well-meaning citizens.

Do the locomotion

parson lectures, then runs when the guns boom.

This same brave chaplain rode along with our brigade, on an old string-haltered horse, as we advanced to the attack at Chickamauga, exhorting the boys to be brave, to aim low, and to kill the Yankees as if they were wild beasts. He was eloquent and patriotic. He stated that if he only had a gun he too would go along as a private soldier. You could hear his voice echo and re-echo over the hills. He had worked up his patriotism to a pitch of genuine bravery and daring that I had never seen exhibited, when fluff, fluff, fluff, - a whir, a boom! and a shell screams through the air. The reverend stops to listen, like an old sow when she hears the wind, and says, 'Remember, boys, that he who is killed will sup tonight in Paradise.' Some soldier hallooed at the top of his voice, 'Well, parson, you come along and take supper with us.' Boom! whir! a bomb burst, and the parson at that moment put spurs to his horse and was seen to limber to the rear, and almost every soldier yelled out, 'The parson isn't hungry, and never eats supper.' I remember this incident, and so does every member of the First Tennessee Regiment - 'Co. Aytch' - Maury Grays, First Tennessee Regiment.

That morning Ned saw a buggy approaching the hotel.

'It's that stuck up prick, Kershaw,' said Mrs. Jones, 'going to Church I expect.'

Ned fearing he may have seen more than he was supposed to left the pub and approached the buggy, taking hold of the horse,

'I'd be obliged if you would alight and come to the hotel,' said Ned. 'Why,' he demanded in a pompous tone as though he was talking to a bunch of school children in his classroom.

Ned pointed his colt at him and said, 'this is why...want to argue the point Mr. School teacher...I am Ned Kelly.'

'Of course, Mr. Kelly...I will not cause any trouble. I have my family to think of.'

Over the morning, Ned collected more customers for the hotel including traveller and local residents. By the afternoon there was a small crowd at the pub chatting away and enjoying a picnic atmosphere. Ned and his gang were used to organising people. They had done it at Euroa and Jerilderie. No-one was allowed to leave. Kershaw made a special effort to endear himself to the outlaws and gain their confidence. He spoke to Ned letting him know who he could trust and where the local trap kept his guns. As he was used to such things like organising the playground, Ned placed him in charge of all outdoor activities, dances and amusements. Surprisingly, Kershaw found he was having a good time. He had a captive audience. He spoke in moral tones about democracy and right of every citizen to partake of the riches of this new, exciting land. He said that this democracy would only come about by through fearless opposition to oppressive behavior whether it be by the police or Government, and he had a duty to educate and instruct the youth in these admirable qualities. They were heartening words to the Kelly Gang and they warmed to the teacher who had in the past, by his idiosyncratic mannerisms, unintentionally isolated himself from the community. Towards the evening Ned allowed the teacher, in whom he had confidence, to return to his house to check on his wife who was not well. When he arrived home, he immediately told his wife of his activities at the hotel.

'Ned and I got on like a house on fire, Ethel...you should have seen us...you know he's not such a bad fellow that Kelly...everyone is having a ball ...drinking dancing and running races...you want to come back this evening and have some fun?'

'Come to your senses, Martin,' she said. What are they there for?'

'We had much more fun than going to Church, Ethel. They are waiting to derail the train and discuss matters with the Police I think, although I am not sure.'

'My God ...discuss matters with the Police...be sensible Martin. You mean discuss things with the Police like Stringybark. You know what happened to them Martin? The place will be a blood bath, and you are asking me and the children to go there tonight and carry on with all that disgusting dancing and drinking. I have warned you about the Irish before Martin ...now come to your senses.'

'Look Ethel,' he said 'you might not understand this but men don't really respect me. I'm seen as a pen pusher...someone to say hello to and how is little Johnny progressing with his lessons. I am not one of the mates. I'm not invited to the pub. The couple of times I have made the effort, they all looked at me and went silent. I had a lemonade and left. As soon as I got out the door the conversation starts up again. It's humiliating, Ethel. And as for the church guild, tea and scones, rude and grubby faced kids Monday to Friday and then again for Sunday school. Is that all there is for me, Ethel? Kelly made me feel good and important for once in my life and I want to go back. He needs me he said and I don't want to let him down. He's a decent man and he sounds educated too. You should have seen how the townsfolk looked up to Kelly and you know I heard the publican, what's her name, Mrs. Jones was having it on with him in the Stationmasters office... he sure is a larrikin, that Kelly.'

'What do you precisely mean Martin? Am I, the children, your important work at the school and Church...do you mean to say these things mean nothing to you? And the publican ...fancy her at her age doing something immoral like that...cavorting with bushrangers like a common prostitute. What is the world coming too Martin? And what are you coming to?'

Martin went silent. Then animated again he said,

'Ethel... we all danced, sang and had a good time back there...it was great. We all joined up in long line, like train carriages joined together, and hooted just like a train whistle...they called it the locomotion, I think.' And he imitated the dance steps for his serious wife, hooted like a train whistle and laughed.

'Martin...locomotion...are you plumb loco? have you been drinking Martin? Get a hold of yourself, Martin...you can be a hero. Here take this red handkerchief... go and stop the train and warn the police what is in wait for them. Be a man and not a silly kid.'

Martin took the handkerchief and waved it disinterestedly. The excitement had left him. There was no escape. He would have to do the proper and correct thing. He would have to be the do gooder again. But try as he may he couldn't get his head around betraying his new mate or mates if you included the rest of the Gang. She reasoned with her conflicted husband. She said a heroic act in alerting the oncoming train would change his place in the community. The publicity she said would thrust him into the upper echelons of the Education Department after fifteen years of going nowhere except headmaster of a one roomed school in a forgotten country town. How could, she thought, the Education Inspector when he saw the long list of names seeking promotion not remember Kershaw, the brave man who saved the Police from the Kelly Gang.

'What if Kelly wins...beats the Police...will he then come looking for me, Ethel?'

'We'll worry about that if and when it happens,' she replied pertly knowing she was safe.

'You know, Ethel, he trusted me. No one else was allowed to leave the hotel.'

'What is the trust of a common criminal worth,' she said.

'Maybe my life, Ethel...maybe my life...although the way that has gone, it is hardly worth saving.'

'Martin, I never knew you felt this way about us and children. It's quite a shock you know to hear that you value us so poorly.'

Martin sank down into his chair and thought.

Ethel went to the kitchen and rummaged in the paper bin. She pulled out last week's news, straightened a page and brought it to her husband.

'Here read this, Martin...the headline...see what it says about the reward leading to the capture of Kelly's...one thousand pounds. Martin. We have never seen such money...think what it could do for us and the children. We could leave this barren outpost and live in luxury in Melbourne. You could be a headmaster of one of those posh, Protestant schools like Geelong Grammar where the doctors and judges' kids go. I tell you straight Martin...if you don't take this rag and lamp and go and stop the train, me and the kids are going to leave you...leave you to your new mates...see how you get on then. You can do that silly dance...what do you call it... the locomotion, that's it... all your damned life for all I and the children care. They will probably put you in jail, too. Not much room to carry on in those small, cold cells, Martin but you would be with your new-found mates of that I can vouch.'

'I have been in jail, Ethel...for thirty years.'

'Well I never,' she said and stormed out of the room

Later that evening after he had done the sums, a Judas school teacher left for the railway line with a red rag and kerosene lamp in his hands. He waved down the train and told them the Kelly Gang were waiting for them at the Glenrowan pub and that the line had been lifted near the cutting. They thanked him and handed him a revolver. He said, 'what am I to do with this?' Steele replied 'you might need it before the night is out.' Kershaw asked, 'can't you lot protect me?'. He replied 'no mate... it's every man for himself. I cannot afford to allocate any men to guard you because we are short enough as it is.. I suggest you go back to your house and wife, and keep a good lookout.' Although he was no business man, the conflicted school teacher felt he was short changed, and regretted his duplicity to Ned, and that he had betrayed his trust.

He was now a target, and on his own. On his lonely way back home, he was twitchy. He thought he heard a sound in the bush. He called out, 'is that you Ned? I didn't tell them anything... promise... on my heart...over my dead body.' There was no response. He fired his gun. The recoil and the loud bang frightened him such that he dropped the revolver and on hitting the ground it fired again just missing his foot. A goat rushed out of the bush, bleated at him, and ran off. When he got home, Ethel told him he'd better leave the house and sleep in the scrub that night in case Kelly came for him. She could hear the guns going off and the shouting. 'Me and the children might get harmed if you are here, Martin,' she said. Martin was now truly alone. His heroism had come at a price. He took a blanket and found a bush in the scrub to snuggle up and hide under. All night he could hear the gunfire and screams of the women and kids. He thought to himself what have I done. He saw the sympathizers ride by on their horses and talking in hushed tones. Two dismounted to relieve themselves on the bush next to him. He could hear one say, 'Kelly says he was betrayed by the fucking schoolteacher and for us to stay out of the fight.' His mate replied 'What a fool...nobody trusts that weirdo pen pusher...I wouldn't like to be him when Ned gets out of this pickle. You heard what happened to Dekkers, didn't you?'

Back at the Hotel Ned had fallen into discussion with the local policeman Bracken.

'I don't know why they bother about me and the North East ... this is our country Bracken.'

'How do you think you would get on without a policeman if you were a law-abiding citizen?' asked Brackan trying to justify his position and with a wry grin.

'Do you think I am a blackguard, Brackan?' said Ned looking him in the eye.

'I'll be damned if you not,' replied Bracken, and they all laughed none more than Ned.

Ned took his prisoners to the paddock at the back of the hotel and he and his boys organized a sports day; running races, hop step and jump and whatever games they wanted to play. It was a carnival atmosphere. During the three-legged race Dan teamed up with Gloria, the fifteen-year-old daughter of Mrs. Jones. She was a wiry, coppery skinned girl with a shock of thick, wavy auburn hair and lustrous brown eyes. After her alcoholic dad had left for the last time, she spent her time helping her mother about the bar, riding her horse in the bush, and quickly became a favorite amongst the regular drinkers. Later that afternoon, the two youngsters could be seen talking together. Dan's natural reticence seemed to dissipate in her company and his often too serious presentation gave way to exuberant smiles and spontaneous laughter. When his back was turned, she got game and pulled his revolver from his belt. He went to grab it back but seeing her smile, hesitated, and allowed her to hold the gun. While Ned, Joe and Mrs. Jones played cards, she helped Dan watch over those in the hotel. She added up their numbers, pointing Dan's gun at each as she counted them off, and if she suspected they were planning escape, she warned them in very clear terms that they had better think again. She held her heavy pistol pointed in Bracken's direction for a little longer knowing he of all the captives was perhaps the one to break up the happy gathering.

'How does it feel Mr. Policeman to be looking down the barrel of colt 45?'

'I feel I am about to poop my pants, Gloria.'

The crowd burst into laughter. Bracken had a sense of humor and the townspeople liked him.

'Give me the gun,' said Dan.

'Come and get it,' she said.

He grabbed her and they wrestled with her gun holding hand flaying about her head and sending the customers scurrying for cover.

'Jesus Gloria...you will get me into strife with Ned with your mucking about.'

'I was only having some fun,' she said as she handed back the gun.

She was curious about his existence in the Ranges and asked,

'Can I come and join you Dan? I can cook and ride...serve beer too- done a lot of that.'

'It's too risky for a girl but I'll come and visit you if you like.'

'It's the risky part I'd like,' she replied.

'Come on, I can hear music starting up...let's dance.'

They followed the music to see people in a long line like rail carriages snaking around the room and kicking their heels and hooting as they went.

'Come do the locomotion,' they yelled.

Dan took hold of her slim waist and held on as she weaved and kicked out her legs to the rhythm of the squeeze box.

Late that night, Ned had come to the realization that the train would not be arriving. Near midnight, with he and his men tired from drink and lack of sleep, he summonsed the audience for a final short speech before they were to be released to go home. They gathered in the room, their good humor and high spirits dulled to a hush as Ned elevated himself to sit on the bar. Before he could utter a single word, the silence was broken by the clear and unmistakable high-pitched whistles of an approaching train. The revelers froze knowing lethal danger was coming to them, rattling up the cutting towards the small, deserted platform and with a cargo of guns, men and horses; and forewarned by a do gooder who harbored in his orderly heart an impossible dream to be one of the mates who drank at the Pub.

runaway

Federal retreat at the First Bull Run

a veteran war correspondent, Russell had never seen anything like this 'cowardly rout- a miserable, causeless panic...negro servants on led horses dashed frantically past; men in uniform, whom it were a disgrace to the profession of the arms to call 'soldiers' swarmed by on mules, chargers, and even draft horses, which had been cut out of carts and wagons, and went on with harness clinging to their heels, as frightened as their riders. Men literally screamed with rage and fright when their way was blocked.' Best little stories from the Civil War by C Brian Kelly with Ingrid Smyer.

Genghis Khan and deserters

Armed units were divided into units of multiple of ten. When the army is at war if one two or three or even many of the ten men flee, then all ten are executed. And if all ten flee, then all the men in the hundred to which they belong are executed unless all have fled. Genghis Kahn – M Hoang.

Ned left the pub, went to his mare and rode down the track. He could hear the train straining up the hill and see the dull lights of the lead engine. He and his men were tired from lack of sleep and their drinking and partying did not help. When he returned the merry makers now huddled in frightened groups knowing their lives were now in grave danger. In the backroom the outlaws lifted on the heavy armour, prepared their ammunition, and checked their guns.

A rag tag army of men were mounted, armed and waiting in the bush not far away. Some were mounted on Paddy's best horses. There waiting with the men were Virgil and Roy. Virgil, now a successful cotton grower, knew a thing or two about war. Roy was a reluctant conscript. Politics held little interest for him. Although the boys had courage and he and Elly had been beneficiaries of their daring bank exploits, he thought the plans of a Republic half-baked and impossible to achieve with the size and backing of the Government forces and Police.

As Ned placed the heavy metal armour on the two youngest boys, he remembered how the blacksmith had heated, cut, hammered and sculptured these grey, cold metal suits stolen from paddock ploughs.

'These suits will keep you safe, lads,' said Ned.

'We have to confront them, we will be outnumbered, and they will be well armed. This armour is heavy, it will restrict our ability to move but this time we are standing our ground. Without this protection we will be shot to pieces. With this armour we will be impenetrable.'

The train hissed to a shuddering halt at the Station, and shadowy figures could be seen scurrying across the platform like mice across a kitchen table. The boys could hear a voice like Bracken's telling them the Gang was at the Pub with the hostages including women and children.

'It's your mate, Kershaw,' said Joe to Ned, 'he's alerted the Traps and now we have a real fight on our hands.'

The Gang lined up along the Pub veranda and steadied themselves raising and lowering their guns in the direction of the Station. The sound of horses, rearing and pulling as they disembarked, could be heard.

'Leave the horses and follow me,' one yelled.

The net was closing in.

Ned fired hitting their leader Hare in the wrist.

'My God,' he cried 'I've been hit.'

The volley of gun fire lit up the four figures lined along the veranda of the hotel like flashes of lightening in a storm. The police returned fire using repeater rifles and spray buckshot. Lead split the timber walls of the Pub and rang off the metal armour of the four men. In the initial exchange, Ned was hit in the arm in two places, and a bullet seared through the front of his right foot coming out the heel. Joe was hit in the leg. Their steel armour could not protect them from the sheer mass of firepower raining down on them.

In a matter of seconds, the stakes reversed dramatically.

Two were now wounded; they were outnumbered, outgunned and fighting for their lives. Plans of taking hostages and leading his men to the Benalla Banks were gone; lost in the alcohol haze, the boozing, and the entertainment over the last two days. Their daredevil ways, their predilection for carousal and drink, and a misplaced trust in a dissembling schoolteacher were going to demand a heavy toll before the night was through.

'Come on you cocktails,' yelled Ned 'you can't hurt us,' as he thumped his pistol on his chest plate but he and Joe were hurt. The pain although numbing when first hit was now a throbbing pain, and the bleeding did not stop. Mrs Jones's boy was hit in the side of his chest. The poor child screamed like hair caught in a trap...loud, high pitched screams that interrupted the crack of gunfire. Joe called out to release women and children who, huddled together, ventured only a few yards from the hotel before they were fired upon by the Police, and forced to rush back.

Two rockets soared into the night sky momentarily lighting up the battle scene. They came from the hotel across the line and Ned had not wanted it. It was the signal for the men waiting at Morgan's bluff to come down expecting the train had derailed. Ned knew he must stop his supporters from joining a struggle that had turned into a disaster. He knew it was his fault. He should have been stricter with his men. He should have run for the hills when the train arrived. Their pride and the drink stopped them. He hobbled to the rear of the hotel to get his mare. He could feel a warm, sticky blood soaking his shirt and filling his boot. Hidden by the trees and the dark, he dropped to the ground discarding his heavy plates as best he could. He found his mare in the yard, crawled on, and headed up to the bluff. He balanced as best he could with his one good foot. He was getting dizzy from loss of blood. About half way there he came across the others coming down the bluff with their arms at the ready. He recognized his brother in law Tom, and Virgil out the front. Virgil had on his faded, grey uniform which he had carefully folded in his locked chest kept over the years. He told them the bad news and that he and his boys would see it out. They were to disband. The men were unwilling to leave and were planning to intervene against Ned's orders. Roy knew it was time to go before he was implicated in their hopeless plan.

He spurred his horse, Blue Doggy out of there for all he was worth.

'Where you going Roy?' yelled Virgil but there was no reply except the distant sound of a galloping horse.

'Come on little doggy,' Roy yelled into his flattened ears as they sped down the dirt tracks heading home. 'We have done this before so we can do it again.'

Old memories flooded back as he galloped down the soft, dirt track in the moonlight. His old familiar cowardice excited him so that he felt young and fit again, like when he was in the Custer's Cavalry.

'Go blue doggy,' yelled Roy. The faithful Appy didn't have the speed like when he ran from the Indians but it was enough to get him and Roy out of the unfolding disaster. He had only to go back to his home where Kate was looking after the brood including his two kids. Roy intended to get the buried savings, ride to coast, and sail back home; go back to the States where he always wanted to be. He had enough of Australia, the bush, the heat, the flies, and the lack of enterprise of its dull, convict inhabitants. The Kelly problems were not his problems. His partner Elly was in jail for her part in the Fitzpatrick affair leaving him and her eldest girls to look after the kids. The gloss on their affair had dulled, and he wanted out. The nosey lawman, his waning relationship, his disinterest in things Australian, his loyalty and devotion to America, and now Ned's failed plans told him the time was right. Roy was homesick for America.

Back at the Bluff overlooking Glenrowan, Tom attended to Ned's wounds, bandaging and trying to stem the loss of blood. Tom and Virgil accompanied Ned back to the trees at the rear of the hotel where Ned had left his steel plates and guns. It was still dark and intermittent gunfire could be heard. They didn't want him to go but there was no changing his mind. He must join the others and help them escape. Dawn was about to break. He staggered off in the dark to the hotel.

While Ned was away, Gloria spoke to Dan,

'I have to see if I can get the women and kids out of this. Can you hold your fire for a while and I'll call out to the police that we're coming? I don't want to leave but if someone doesn't make a move soon, we'll all be shot up. Already my little brother is wounded and mum is going mental.'

'I'll speak to Joe...you get them ready.'

'Look why don't you put on a dress and come with us...I'll take you to my pony and you can escape.'

'I can't leave the others.'

'Dan, you'll die here if you stay...you're outnumbered and they will have more police here soon...there is no hope if you stay...come on... promise me you'll come.'

He knew what she said was true, but for him there was no choice.

She kissed him 'I love you, Dan Kelly,' she said.

He hugged her and she left, taking the women and children with her. This time the hostages made it to safety but it was not without the Police shooting at them.

Mrs Jones had a bullet hole shot clean through her shawl as she and Gloria carried their badly hurt boy who only hours before had sung the 'wild, colonial boy' to the loud applause of the Gang's captive audience. The Gang had given up their last chance of escape by freeing the hostages. Dan, Steve and Joe were now alone in the shot-up Pub, and kept up a sporadic fire. They called for Ned but did not get a response. There was only the dark to assist them now and that was rapidly giving way to the dawn.

There's nothing quite as pretty as Music in the morning

Devoted horse in Civil war

For a few minutes the situation seemed most critical, and just then a piece of shell struck General Gregg's horse in the stomach behind the saddle girth, grazing the General's leg. The horse sank under him and in an instant one of his orderlies dismounted, gave the General his horse, and took the saddle from the wounded animal. At this moment General Gregg ordered a cavalry regiment, I think the Sixth Regulars, who were nearby in a field, to make a counter charge, which, after a little delay caused by the presence of a stone wall, they did. This charge, with our men, who rallied, co-operating, resulted in driving the enemy back into and through the town. To our surprise, the General's wounded horse had struggled to his feet and was running beside him with his nose against his leg, his entrails dragging on the ground. Noticing this, he exclaimed, 'For God's sake, somebody shoot him!' Whereupon I discharged my pistol in the horse's ear, which killed him. - Civil War Experiences under Bayard, Gregg, Kilpatrick, Custer, - Henry Coddington Meyer.

As Ned entered the rear of the hotel, he could see the dark outline of Joe inside the bar swigging from a whisky bottle. Now and then he would shoot indiscriminately out of the windows and doorway. He was shot in the knee and dragging his leg as he lurched from bar to window. Each time the inebriated bushranger fired a shot, a volley of return fire peppered the Pub. Indifferent to his life, he neither ducked, hid, nor sheltered from the bullets splintering the rough timber frame and smashing the bottles. Amidst all this destruction and danger, he just carried on drinking, and muttering to himself.

Ned appeared in the doorway.

'Where have you been mate...the boys have been calling for you?'

'I went to stop the others, Joe .... come on...we clearing out of here. I'll get the boys. It still dark outside and they haven't closed off the bush at the rear. You can see Traps creeping about but it's too dark to recognise anyone...we still have a chance to get out of this mess.'

'Whatever you say Ned...I think I have just about drunk the place dry anyway,' he said putting away the dregs of his whisky bottle.

'The women and kids have cleared out ...thank Christ for that...I couldn't stand their screaming. That young kid Gloria led them out ...she got some guts that girl ...you would have been proud of her.'

'Come on Joe,' said Ned as he grabbed his arm, 'where are the other two?'

Joe pulled away.

'One for the road, hey Ned, here's to the Kelly Gang,' as he hobbled back to the bar grabbing another whisky bottle. With an unsteady hand he filled the glass, but before the strong, anaesthetising liquor scorched his lips, a stray bullet smacked into his groin slicing his femoral artery, and spinning him to the floor with a heavy thud.

Another one struck the grandfather clock in the bar setting it off into a series of loud, resounding gongs while Joe's life blood pumped from his fatal wound, and pooled beside him.

He laid moaning and writhing on the floor, shortly to be gone from the world.

Dying in a dingy, bush pub with no sweetheart to lovingly hold his hand or whisper tender words of everlasting love in his ear; no devoted parents to fuss and grieve over him; no family to say his last goodbyes to; just face down on a dirty floor littered with stubbed cigarette butts, beer and whisky slops like some stinking, pig pen.

Ned knelt beside Joe and cradled him in his last moments.

He mumbled. Ned put his ear close.

'It was an expensive drink, hey Ned. It's better this way then being strung up.'

His eyes glazed over and he was gone.

Ned went outside challenging the Traps surrounding the pub. They took cover behind the trees and logs. He called for the boys. There was no response. He stumbled off into the dark hoping they had left the hotel. He got to where he had left Tom and Virgil. The boys were not there.

'They are still back at the hotel,' said Tom.

'Joes gone...dead,' said Ned.

Ned fell to the ground exhausted and lapsing into and out of unconsciousness from loss of blood. The two men revived him and again tended to his wounds. They wanted to take him away. With what little strength he had left, he resisted. He saw his place was with the two boys, and he was going back.

'They have little chance now.... I heard the train...I think reinforcements have arrived and the hotel will be completely surrounded before long. It would be crazy to try and a death sentence for sure,' said Tom trying to dissuade him.

'I could not live with myself knowing that I had left the others. Maybe I can still get them out.'

'There's no hope,' said Tom.

'It doesn't matter. I'll die with them. Joe has gone.'

'Ned, I don't want to see you die but we will not stop you from going back.'

Ned sighed, and sank back to the ground to rest.

'Stay with me a while...I'll leave shortly.'

The men sat together in silence listening to the intermittent crack of gunfire about the hotel and scrub. Figures flitted by. Tom placed his hand on Ned's wounded arm. No words passed between them. Tom knew Ned would not go with him. If he did not die there in the scrub trying to extricate the two boys, English justice would in the end do the job. He sensed Ned knew it too but he would not leave his boys no matter what the consequences.

With an arm shot and useless, a boot full of blood, and hobbling on one leg, Ned's energy reserves had run dangerously low. Somehow the reassurance of Tom's hand on his arm just resting there in the dark without words lessened his pain, and gave him the strength to go on. He intended for the Police to know they had a battle on their hands. He would give them a Waterloo they'd not easily forget.

Just as the darkness was beginning to lift, Tom helped Ned put on his heavy, steel plates, clean his revolvers and load them. He would emerge out the mists and scrub and do what he had to do. He would draw the attention of Police away from the Pub and give his boys a chance to escape.

The men briefly embraced.

'Farewell brother,' said Ned.

He left as the morning light peeped through the tall, slender gums.

He walked by his grey mare standing silently in the yard, her big, expressive eyes showing her unease. There was some effort by one or two Police to shoot the horses and he could see the mare had been cut across her chest as though glancing bullet slit her skin like a knife. Ned stopped. He took off his helmet. She was tender near her wound, and flinched. Is it possible she understands all this he thought... he didn't doubt that she did. He put his revolver in his belt. He ran his hand gently over her soft ears and rubbed her broad, intelligent forehead. He held his bruised head against her jowls, inhaling the familiar horse scents...more sweet and dearer to him than anything else in this big, wonderful country they had roamed together; the human breath she knew intimately from the very time she came into the world at Ole Man's Quinn's stable. He knew he would not see his mare again, and he wanted to share with her the little time he had left. He remembered his promise to Kev. He took her out of the yard and led her back to Tom.

'Look after this mare, Tom. She means a lot to me. Take her with you, and if there's a slim chance me and the boys get out, I'll take one of the three left in the yard. I don't want to risk her getting shot up...she already has a flesh wound from those bastards trying to crucify her. If the worst happens to me as I expect it will, I would like her to go back to Kev Kavanagh. He's a driver with Cobb and Co in Melbourne. He knows about it. I know he will look after her well...I know that for certain...he's a good man and you can trust him to do right by us and the mare.'

'I will Ned ...I'll put my life on it.'

With this final request he put on his heavy, steel helmet, and slowly disappeared amongst the pale gums beginning to weep droplets of cool, morning dew on the damp, spongy earth. The small, wet beads glistened like diamonds as they streaked down his steel helmet, hung there for a moment, and then dropped across his slit view of the bush and Pub ahead of him.

'We'll wait a few moments,' Tom said to Virgil.

Shortly they heard gunshots starting up again, men yelling at the tops of their voices, and the ringing of bullets against steel. They mounted and left with heavy hearts. Tom led Ned's mare from his horse. Half way up the hill he felt reluctance in the mare to follow. She baulked, pulling the reins from his hands, and galloped off back to the hotel.

'Damn...I'll have to let her go otherwise they will see us,' Tom said.

Ned appeared like an apparition out of the cottony mists that hung low to the ground. He banged the pistol butt on his breast plate, and the hollow, metal ring startled the Traps standing behind trees and logs and lying in ditches with their guns ready.

When they looked, their eyes bugged out of their heads at the terrifying, alien form lumbering towards them out of the white mist. They yelled to each other.

'Is it ghost?'

'No... it's the bunyip,' yelled others as they gaped in disbelief and fear. Two or three dropped their guns, and fled to the safety of the Railway Station.

A hollow voice from within the armour laughed, and bellowed its defiance,

The aboriginal trackers bolted back to the bush.

Dan and Steve appeared at the back of the hotel firing at the Police now beginning to direct their fire power at the advancing alien form.

'Come on you buggers...I'll pink you all yet,' the wounded bushranger yelled.

Their bullets ricocheted and rang off his heavy, steel plates knocking him this way and that so that it was difficult to balance on his feet. Dan and Steve emerged onto the veranda firing to try and direct their bullets away from Ned.

A voice from within the helmet gave a loud, muffled laugh, deriding their desperate efforts to bring him down. One or two police scampered closer to see if they could shoot the figure in the legs.

In the confusion Ned heard a sound of something crashing through the undergrowth behind him. He swung around to see his mare coming to him at a pace.

He blinked and looked again, doubting what he saw.

It was his mare, Music, saddled, and her reins swinging loose. She had come when death was stalking him from behind every gum tree, fallen log, and ditch, and when every gun barrel had him firmly in their sights. Had an instinct, honed over generation of years of protecting their own, alerted this remarkable mare to her rider's terrible plight?

What messages sped through the darkness and bush to this sentient mare on that sorrowful and tragic night to make her abruptly pull away from Tom's hold, and instinctively run to Ned as a mare will do to protect its young and defenceless against the wild dogs, dingo's and predators?

Living together as they did in the beginning and now in the Ranges, the mare came to know his every emotion, movement and heartbeat; like a mother to her child, a lover to her beloved, and a man to his horse, the two became one like the fabled centaur, half horse, half man. A man just doesn't sit on a horse and a horse just does not carry a man like an inanimate object– at least these two didn't. She felt every movement and lift in his lithe, fit body; every gentle pull of the rein; every squeeze of his leg or touch of his boot; every word of encouragement that passed his lips; every pet or caress of his sensitive hands over her finely, muscled frame; and she felt the electricity of his excitement, his sorrow, disappointment and despair.

She knew all his moods.

And as she carried him day and night, he looked after her like a daughter. He took her to where the grasses were sweet and let her graze. He bathed her in the cleansing, cooling waters of the mountain streams washing out the dry, hard sweat and grime. He groomed her coat until it shone like the sun, and felt like silk. He oiled and cleaned her saddlery so that it did not rub or injure her, and saw that it fitted like a glove. He rugged her if the days and nights were cold and cooled her in the shade and light breezes if she were hot. He tendered to her cuts and swellings using soothing ointments and clean bandages. He trimmed and fitted the steel plates to her hooves, and groomed her ears, mane and tail like a loving parent. All these things he did for her and it gave him joy.

She broke free from Tom raced down the steep hill, crashed through the scrub to where he stood alone against a phalanx of armed, revengeful men with their guns aimed directly at him. Ned could not believe what he saw through his small rectangular slit in his heavy helmet; his mare was beckoning him to ride away with his life. His whole attention was directed to her - he didn't care about the bullets, shrapnel and grapeshot that hit and bounced off his armour, and punched him about so that he looked like a lurching drunk. In his dazed and weakened condition, oblivious and careless to his fate, the bullets hitting his armour sounded to him like the distant tolling of church bells. In moments of near death, it is said events dear to the heart flash before you...Ned's mind drifted, and fanciful thoughts and imaginings came and went in what seemed like a lifetime but were in truth only a few precious seconds.

A bullet slapped into Ned's helmet, startling him back to reality.

He wanted to throw off his armour and leap onto his mare's back to be carried to the safety of the Ranges. Then he heard the boys calling out to him,

'Ned - over here -they are closing in on you.'

He knew his duty was to stay.

His thoughts again went back to his courageous mare waiting for him in a hail of bullets. If fate said he was to die on this cold dawn with the Traps closing in on him and baying for his blood, he would at least die knowing that he had bred, owned and ridden a mare that was all you could hope her to be, and more; and that the mere thought of her sustained him and made him believe, in his terrible predicament and anguish, that life was worth living after all.

He remembered that it was she that watched over him as he slept restless and cold in his makeshift bed in the bush; it was she who carried him safely and surely down deep ravines, scaled steep mountains and hid in lakes and swamps, when the Traps were hot on their tails; it was she who carried him long distances away from the towns after daring raids on the Establishment; it was she who entertained the townsfolk in their main streets with her amazing feats of speed and agility as Ned swung, stood and vaulted about her like a circus rider; it was she who carried him to his sisters and friends in the middle of the night to rendezvous without the preying eyes of accomplices and spies seeking the wealthy rewards offered by the Government for their capture, dead or alive; and it was she who under the guidance and tutelage of Kev became the best of all the Cobb and Co horses.

He would turn his back on his enemies closing in on him, and before a bullet pierced through the gaps in his armour and seared into his flesh, pay homage to a mare dearer to him than anything that walked and lived on this earth.

Standing obediently there, her dark, wise, all seeing eyes begging him to go; her refined, feminine features silhouetted in the breaking dawn, with the morning light peeping through the tall, ghost gums surrounding the hotel, and colouring her in vivid, heavenly hues; there amidst the crack of the rifles, the shouting, yelling and flying lead, the vehement abuse, the image of this kind, brilliant mare burnt itself into his consciousness and comforted him, took away the weight of his armour, the pain and hurt of his many wounds, and eased the utter hopelessness of his endeavour so that he no longer cared what happened to him.

But he wanted his mare out of danger. Another bullet ripped into his right leg causing him to buckle at the knees. As he fell, he slapped his mare hard on the rump, sending her running into the scrub, and out of danger. Three of the Traps rushed upon the fallen bushranger. They pulled his heavy, steel helmet off. Constable Steele lifted his rifle accusing him of murder, and was about to shoot when his gun was pulled aside. It was Sarge. He had come when he heard the news of the siege. He wanted to be there at the end. He was no longer driven to hunt the Kelly's; he'd seen enough violence and death; his tired heart wanted to play the role of a peacemaker. Out of this change of heart grew a grudging respect for the man who now lay helpless before him.

'If anyone harms this man, then God help me, I will shoot that man myself. He has to be taken alive.'

Another said 'I don't think he has long to live by the way he is bleeding.'

As the Police gathered around, they were incredulous about what they had just seen.

'Did you see his grey mare come to him?'

'I've never seen anything like it before...have you?'

'I thought he would take the chance she gave him to escape. I was about to shoot the mare but I couldn't bring myself to do it...it seemed such a grand and heroic act for a horse.'

'Naaah...don't get carried away...probably spooked by the gun shots,' replied Steele,

'Bloody, mongrel horses don't do things like that.' He thought for a second and in moment of levity added, 'maybe one of our thoroughbreds would.'

The others laughed.

But it was an uneasy laugh. Something they couldn't quite explain or comprehend had come upon them and it left them puzzled and uncomfortable. A scared bewilderment roosted in their excited, fast beating breasts so that when they carried the prisoner back to the Railway Station, their spines tingled and they couldn't feel their feet touching the ground.

Something had spooked them all.

Only the wide-eyed blacktrackers hiding in the bush, too frightened to venture back, knew and sensed its unmistakable presence, but they would not say or speak of it. It's a secret they held close to their primitive hearts for the last fifty thousand years while the white trespassers blundered on oblivious in their country, trampling on their sacred sites and beliefs. That secret is that spirits, souls, screams, and ghosts move and flit about in the darkness of the night, and you had better believe it, for it surely happened this conflicted night between a desperate, courageous man and his mare.

They carried him to the Stationmaster's office and laid him on the floor. His wounds were bandaged to stem the bleeding. A rug was placed over him and a pillow under his head. They thought he might not live. He was deathly pale from loss of blood and lapsing into unconsciousness. A Priest was called to administer the last rites while others stood guard outside. His capture, the death of Joe, the inability to rescue his two boys, the loss of his mare and his wounds had drained him of his life force and will to live. Having fought his battle and lost, he wanted to die. The doctor arrived, cleaned and attended his wounds of which there were many. The doctor gave him brandy and water and hoped his efforts would bring back some signs that he would live. He woke once or twice. The doctor listened. He said little except to praise his mare. He told them he had had enough of running, hiding, listening to every twig snap or break in the night, and wondering if he would be shot from his horse without even knowing where or who the assassin was. He had come to have it out. Ned could have shot men who passed close by him that night as he lay in the bush. He could have ordered his men waiting on the bluff into the battle with a large loss of life, and given him and his boys a good chance of escape but he chose not to. They could have surrounded themselves with hostages, and made their escape that way but they let the townsfolk go. He could have mounted his mare and rode off. But he chose to stay. Heavily outnumbered Ned and his three boys took on the Police by themselves. It was foolish, brave, and the odds impossible. And it would cost them their lives.

Ned's sisters arrived and were allowed to see their brother. They held and kissed him. They wanted him to live. His mare, Music, wandered aimlessly in the bush lost, wounded and alone.

the boys lite up

The news of the shootout at Glenrowan spread over the countryside and into the big Cities. Police reinforcements had arrived during the night and the sporadic shooting had ceased. Photographers arrived and people posed on the railway platform with the hotel in the background. It was taking on a carnival atmosphere. Sympathisers mingled with the crowd of spectators and an air of excitement hung in the air. Two young boys were still holding out in the ramshackle Pub. What would happen next?

The Police couldn't stop talking about the capture of Ned in his steel armour and what his mare had done. Dan and Steve's chances of escape were near impossible due to the daylight and the extra police surrounding the hotel. Their horses had been shot. There was talk of setting the building on fire before night set in. Telegrams ran hot between Melbourne and the Police. They were intending to rail up big generators to light up the Pub, and a cannon to blow it and two remaining bushrangers into oblivion.

Tom with ten of his men came galloping down from the bluff wheeling around in a tight knit group and coming to sudden halt. The Traps became nervous as the group sat silently on their horses with grim expressions on their faces and staring at the hotel and the Railway Station where Ned was being held. The police wanted to remove Ned to a prison before nightfall to prevent any attempt by the sympathisers to rescue him. They heard from one of the hostages that Ned had a script of the Republic in his saddle bag and there may be names in it that would be of interest to them. They had sent three men scanning the scrub for his grey mare.

Gloria overheard their plan to catch the mare, saddled her pony and left when no one was watching. She wanted to do it for Dan and the Gang. She knew the countryside near her town and thought she might know where the mare was. Her pony often escaped from his small yard next to the hotel and he always headed for a plain nearby where the pasture was fresh and sweet. It was her intent to get to the mare before the Police did.

The boys retreated to the back room. 'We cannot give ourselves up,' Dan said to Steve, 'if we do, we will be hung like dogs. It's over...it's only a matter of time.'

He sauntered across the floor casually kicking the bits of rubbish and picked up the squeeze box abandoned from the weekend's festivities. Steve looked about. There on a bullet holed piano angled awkwardly to the floor, with its leg shot off and its wires broken was a big drum and a stick. He lifted the drum up, and inspected it. The skin was tight. They looked at each other and remembered the times back at the bar where they played and jammed for hours. In that broken down and wrecked pub without a hope of salvation and knowing their time was drawing near, they threw caution to the wind and made music; joyful music that swept their cares away and made them smile though staring death in the face.

'I am doing it for that grey mare of Ned's, Steve - Music, did you see what she did to save him?'

'Let's play '*Danny Boy*' said Dan as he strolled nonchalantly out the open door and down along the building pumping the squeeze box, and ignoring rows of bristling guns pointing in his direction. The Police nervously fingered their triggers. Steve followed with his big drum attached by way of shoulder straps. Spontaneous clapping and cheering erupted from the public observing their daring. Some of the sympathisers picked up on the tune and began to sing along. Sarge who was now in charge told his men not to shoot unless they were threatened or it was absolutely necessary. He didn't want any more killing. They had released the hostages exposing themselves and he would allow them time to surrender. He was directed to take them alive if at all possible. The State desperately wanted to make public examples of them in their court system. He was also familiar with their ways; reckless, bizarre behaviour in the face of death.

'Don't worry men...they're Irish ...it's just their way,' he said. 'If it gets out of hand, I'll soon put a stop to it.'

One of his men got a bit eager, and made a dash towards them. Steve saw him coming and without losing a beat, pulled his revolver and sent a bullet digging up the dirt in front of him. The would-be hero skidded to a stop and hot footed it back to the safety of the Police ranks like a scalded cat much to the amusement of the crowd who hissed and booed him. The two Kelly sisters, Margaret and Kate, broke through the cordon and sprinted holding up their skirts towards the boys but were intercepted and carried back screaming and kicking. The crowd loved it, cheering and clapping as one crazy event followed another, and the rolling rhythms of the classic folk song filled their hearts.

Sarge thought it was getting out of hand and decided to put a stop the entertainment. He took a rifle, aimed and fired putting a neat hole through Steve's big drum. It gave out a wheezy, asthmatic gasp, and went limp. The music and cheers of the sympathisers abruptly stopped. This time the Police cheered and clapped Sarge, and the sympathisers went quiet. Sarge acknowledged his men's cheers and taking off his cap bowed gracefully to the crowds. The sympathisers weren't the only ones who could enjoy a bit of humour during a deadly event.

'What are we going to do now?' asked Steve as they sat down on the floor in the back room. The morning breeze sprung up and blew small snow-white petals of a nearby walnut tree in bloom through the window. They landed on and about them like confetti. Dan picked up one and studied it closely. They were heart shaped with a small blood red tip. He said,

'I think our time has come. Ned is probably dead. Poor Joe...well there is no doubt he is dead. I cannot bear going into the bar seeing him lying there stiff and cold...lets go out together.'

He took out a small brown packet of poison powder.

He waved it about so that Steve knew what he was on about. Steve took out his. They, Joe and Ned had discussed it before and rather than be taken alive and wait to be strung up, they would take their own lives. Dan grabbed a bottle of half empty whisky lying on the floor, emptied the powder into his mouth and washed it down. He hugged Steve,

'see you on the other side, mate, for a better life.'

'I don't know,' said Steve as he took his dose, 'this life sure was exciting.'

They both lay down.

Their eyes slowly closed over, and they both went simply and quietly into another world where they would not be hunted and shot at.

Later that afternoon Sarge felt something had to done to get them out before nightfall. A volunteer crept to the building and lit a small fire by the wall. The dry timber crackled, the flames flickered and then took hold. The crowd yelled their disapproval while the Police pointed their rifles at the exits, nervously awaiting a hurried exit. It did not come. Murmurs of discontent rumbled from the gathering as their attention was riveted on the flames enveloping the slab walls and taking hold in the roof. It would soon burn like a bonfire on Guy Fawkes day.

A priest ran to the inferno. The smoke blinded him but he saw in the back room two young boys lying peacefully on their swags. He looked closer into the smoky haze and saw they were dead. Another person followed him and dragged Joe's corpse from the barroom floor before it was consumed in a fireball. The crowd ran to the burning Pub yelling for the boys to get out. The heat forced them back, and the flames, sensing their victims might be stolen from its fiery clasp, sprinted rapidly along the floor boards licking at and then engulfing the two sleeping corpses. The walls collapsed so that the crowd milling around could see the fire consuming its victims. In the intense heat, the bodies of Dan and Steve came alive, sitting up and laying back, and contorting their arms and legs so that their limbs moved eerily in a slow motion, gruesome display. The boys had lit up. The crowd gasped in horror at the scene taking place before them. Only Joe's body was saved.

The dilapidated bush hotel shot to pieces and soaked in alcohol roared its protest as the fire took hold and engulfed it in glorious plumes of red flame fringed with angry cobalt blue tinges and exploding bottles. This crudely built, timber, slab Pub that harboured all the sad stories, the hopes, the crazy impossible ambitions, the heartaches, the laughter, all the bitter disappointments that life brings to the ordinary man, paid its last respects to the Gang and held the bodies of the two youngest from the clutches of their pro English rulers.

Gloria in excelsis

Gloria kept her eyes and ears open as she rode through the scrub. She was already in trouble due to her open allegiance to the outlaws. Some of the hostages wanted her arrested. Others saw her courage in leading the women and children to safety and wanted her left alone. Taking this mare before the police may tilt the balance against her. She didn't care. Her mind was made up. To hell with what they could do.

When she came to the grassy plain, she saw her hunch was right. There in the distance was the mare grazing by herself. As she put her pony into a brisk trot, she saw in the opposite direction coming out of the scrub three mounted Police. They both saw each other. She pulled her beanie over her head still seeing through the broad weave and went for it. The other three accelerated their horses. The troopers whipped their horses while Gloria just dug in her heels and went for it. They both reached the mare at about the same time but the girl was quicker, and scooped the reins of the startled mare up and they both disappeared into the thick scrub. The three Police wheeled around, but she was gone as quickly as she came.

'What the hell was that?' one said.

'I don't know ...I couldn't tell whether it was a man or a woman,' another said puzzled,

'We'll have to see if we can track them.'

'I don't know why they want the flea-bitten mare. Let's just say we couldn't find it... it'll take all day to find them. Anyway, we can't be sure that was Kelly's horse.'

'Yeah, we missing out on the fun and photos back at Glenrowan...let's forget it and go...I wanna be in one of them photos to show my kids.'

Having agreed, they left.

Gloria hid in the scrub, excited by her success in getting to the mare first. She saw a deep cut to the mare's chest which she cleaned as best she could in a nearby creek. It worried her that the bullet may still be embedded in the mare. Later that evening she watched the road waiting for Tom and his men. Her curiosity got the better of her.

'You are a lovely girl,' she said as she patted and stroked the mare's neck, 'and very brave too...you were lucky not to be killed like your friends. Let's have a look what is in your saddle bag.'

She undid the two leather straps and took out some papers rolled up in a rubber band. Ten pages were headed the Republic of North-East Victoria, and at the end of the document there were some twenty signatures. It was political stuff and it didn't interest her. She put it back. She dug further and felt something feathery. She took it out and found it to be a ornate, Indian headdress. She put it on her head and danced in a circle imitating an Indian dance and patting her mouth in a whooping sound. Young Gloria was a card. She heard the sound of several horsemen approaching. She quickly put back the items and peered out from the thick scrub. It was Tom, his men and a cart carrying two coffins. She got on her pony, grabbed the mare's reins and galloped after them.

The group stopped when they saw her approaching.

'I think I've got something you are looking for,' indicating the mare next to her.

The men were ecstatic, embracing and patting the girl affectionately on the back. The mare meant a lot to them. They had heard of her going to Ned offering him an escape and it moved them. They had been searching for her everywhere. Gloria ran her hand down Dan's coffin,

'not good,' she said.

'They went bravely,' replied Tom, 'the Traps set the hotel on fire.'

'My home,' she said, 'how is mum and my brother?'

'They have been taken to hospital...we'll pray for your brother the same as the others...it must have been a terrible ordeal for you.'

'I hope Ned recovers,' she said, 'he and the boys really put it up those Traps.'

'You're the publican's daughter?' asked Tom.

She looked at him with her lovely, brown eyes.

'Yes...Gloria,' and she spelt it aloud for them aloud - g-l-o-r-i-a'

'Gloria,' they all chorused, and politely laughed.

One inspired by a moment of fond admiration for what she had done said simply 'Gloria in excelsis'.

Tom added, 'we will not forget you or your family, Gloria...come with us until your mum is able to cope...we will look after you...of that you can be sure. Bringing this mare to us before the Traps got her is the best thing that has come out of this terrible tragedy...she means a lot to Ned and us. They would have taken the bodies of Dan and Steve as well if we had not moved quickly, and getting this mare is a bonus.'

'No, I will go home, or to what's left of it. I have done what I came for. I owed it to them Kelly's. I only regret I could not have ridden with them. Dan and me had a good thing going. Pity it had to come to this.'

By the way she added, 'that mare's a beauty, isn't she?

'You probably didn't see what she did back there...I still don't believe it myself. And you'll get surprise when you see what's in her saddle bag.'

'Too true, Gloria,' replied Tom as he and his men watched her leave on her pony. The plucky teenager could see the men waving and calling 'Gloria' as she disappeared into the scrub. I like my name she thought to herself. It was the one thing her mum got right in that little, shanty Pub at Glenrowan.

Baby, don't hurt me

Sam Bass dies with the world bobbing around him.
Sam Bass, 27, dies after the botched robbery at Round Rock, Texas. although the Texas Rangers had filled him with lead, he held on for a couple of days so that he could die on his 27th birthday. his last words are 'the world is bobbing around me.' The Old West - Mike Flanagan.

Cynthia Parker, a white girl captive adopted by the Indians
From the corner of her eye Cynthia studied the girl's delicate profile as they rode along, and watched how she handled her pony. Her long, bare legs gripped the mare's sides, lifting her body slightly in time with the stride. Her thin suede dress was hiked up past her knees, and the fringe at the hem had fallen away to show her strong, smooth thighs. She sat lightly and swayed from side to side, as gracefully as tall grass rippling in the wind. Long curtains of fringe swung from the high curved pommel and cantle on her saddle, and from the V-shaped yoke on her dress. The reins lay loosely in her right hand as it rested on her thigh. Her left arm was bent, her hand riding at the crease where her leg met her body. She sat straight and supple, moving in perfect time with her pony. Her hair was tied into two thick braids wrapped with thongs, but wisps of it blew around her face in the wind. The bells and dewclaws dangling from the side boards of the saddle made a lilting castanet clatter. Something Good was the wife of Pahayuca, who was Medicine Woman's brother and Sunrise's uncle. Ride the Wind (Lucia St Clair Robson)

Roy galloped Blue Doggy to a hut, waited a day or two and when he thought the it was safe, he went the back way to the Kelly home. It was time to leave Australia and return to his real home. The very thought of returning to the land of opportunity and the free thrilled him. It was where he was born and where he belonged. The country had moved on from the Indian wars and he hoped there would be a reconciliation of sorts about previous misdeeds.

Kate rushed out. She asked Roy where he had been and that some were looking for him. She told Roy what had happened at Glenrowan. Roy already knew.

'Kate,' he said 'things are getting bad...I have to run...leave the country before they arrest me...and I will swing with the rest of them for sure.'

Kate was suspicious. She was old enough at sixteen to know how devious Roy could be. She had heard Roy was sighted near the river when Valerie went missing. Valerie was a close and affectionate friend to her.

'No time to talk now sweetie,' as he grabbed a few clothes and stuffed them into a saddle bag.

He leapt on Blue Doggy, and took off towards the scrubby back paddock. Before he left, he tied to his horse two large saddle bags on either flank behind his saddle. Kate thought it strange that he put nothing in his two bags. Then she remembered when a child, she had followed Roy there. He spied her, and gave her a thrashing with his whip. It hurt her.

'This is my special, private area, Kate,' he said 'and you and kids, or anyone are never to come here.' It was about two miles away hidden in the bush. Kate grabbed her pistol, a small derringer which Ned had given her to use for her own protection saying,

'It's small but if your aim is good and target close, it will do the job. Best of all it is easy to hide.'

She looked to see it was loaded, bedded the kids down and ran after Roy holding it in her hand. She knew Roy had made a lot of money from the Pub, circus and from Ned's bank robberies. Her mum said the money was for the family in a time of need. She had recently asked Roy about it because things were tight with her mum in jail and Roy said,

'all in good time Kate... all in good time.'

She needed that money now more than ever. She was a teenager looking after a brood of very young, hungry children including two of Roy's. She had no income. Before she had survived on what Ned had given her, but if he were not around, she and her siblings would struggle and perhaps not survive as a family. The Traps would at all hours of day and night storm into their home, spill the milk, throw food onto the floor, turn the house and their few belongings upside down, terrify the children and abuse the girls demanding to know where Ned was. She needed help, and not just kind words. Roy was away more than he was there. She suspected Roy was going to load up with the family's savings and decamp. She also knew that money would be needed for Ned's defence and to pay the city lawyers. She had to do something and quick.

She ran as fast as her legs would take her through the scrub following Blue Doggy's fresh tracks, jumping logs and bushes as she went, stumbling, falling over but all the time firmly holding the derringer in her hand so it didn't accidentally discharge the one bullet she had carefully placed in its chamber. Exhausted and out of breath, she could see Roy through the saplings and on his hands and knees trying to extract something from a hole he had dug.

'Watcha doing Roy?' she asked hiding the small pistol in her dress pocket and trying to regain her breath.

'Damn it, Kate...you gave me a heck of fright, sneaking up on me like that.'

'What are you doing?'

'I thought I told you and the others never to come here. Don't you have kids to look after?'

'That's why I am here, Roy...for the kids. What are you doing?'

Roy pulled a metal box out of the ground and opened it. It was full of notes all neatly stacked in packets. Kate's eyes widened.

'There must be thousands there, Roy.'

'Yes, and I need it all, Kate. I am going to have to bribe me and Blue Doggy's way back into the States and that is going to be expensive-you know, big trip across the wide Pacific with horse to pay for and he will cost more than me.'

There was canvas bag on the ground.

'What's in that one, Roy?'

'Questions, questions questions...haven't I taught you girls to mind your own business?'

'I need answers, answers, answers, Roy. I am no longer a child. I have the responsibilities of a mother, and in case you haven't noticed no bloody money to carry them out.'

'I'll show you, Kate.' He carefully undid the bag and there was the calcified head of an aboriginal like a marble bust.

'My God, Roy - how did you come by that?'

'I rode to the South Australian border... to a little town called Naracoorte to see their limestone caves I'd heard about...you know Kate I am a promoter and these things are like underground cathedrals. And behind some bars was this black fella all petrified from the water dripping on him. It appears the settlers shot him and he hid in the caves and died. I tried to buy him but they wouldn't have a bar of it. Can you believe all these people coming to see him and the Government not charging anyone? You can imagine the fortune I would make putting this black fella on display back in the States so I took him. It was like taking candy from a child...a big empty cave with no one around late at night.'

'Roy... what you did is a criminal act, a sacrilege.'

'Bullshit Kate - it's only criminal if you get caught. Where it was and what they were doing with him - well, I would call that criminal and a shameful waste, and I have rescued him. Look at it that way. And you of all people...you and your family accusing me of being a criminal. You lot have made criminal into a fine art with the things you lot do.'

'What about mum?'

'What about her...she is being looked after by the State the last I heard...she is as good as petrified as this poor black fella.'

'That's offensive, Roy...so what about us and your kids?'

'So, what about it...want me to give you lot a hand out again. I don't belong here - the locals don't respect me and my two kids are part of your family. I can't separate them, can I? I didn't want the kids ...your mum did and where is she now? In iron bar hotel and not likely to see daylight for couple of years.'

'What about Ned?'

'Ned has no hope...he is going to swing for sure. And I will get the same when the full story comes out. Even if I wanted to stay, it is out of the question.'

'I heard you did a runner...from Ned and now your family. The ones you are supposed to love and support. You are a two-timing snake Roy and coward to boot.'

Roy stopped packing the notes into his saddle bags, let out an exasperated sigh, stretched his hands out onto the saddle and looked at ground with his back to Kate. He stood there like that for a while thinking.

'Fuck the family, girl. I got a real family back in the States where I am goin...I have been away too long in this shit hole full of convicts and forelock pullers And I have never been accused of cowardice, Kate. Ned told us to clear out because his situation was hopeless. What did he and his gang expect after boozing for two days and carrying on with the hostages...with the right planning, training and expertise I could have taken over this tin pot country but they didn't want to hear from me.'

'I heard you left before Ned came, Roy.'

'Listen I am not going to argue with you Kate... now git back to them kids and forget you ever knew me.'

'Give me half of that money, and I will go gladly.'

'What don't you understand about the word nothing you feral brat? I'll give you half of nothing...now work out how much that is, smart arse.'

'I'll just pull out my bean counter, Roy, and see what it comes to.'

Kate snapped out her small derringer, and held it to Roy's head, squarely on his temple.

'Now I count to five, Roy, and I want you to throw out half that bundle from your saddle bag...understand.'

Roy gave a contemptuous laugh.

'What are you going to do with that tiny pea shooter, Kate...part my hair?'

'No...I am going to part your thievin brain.'

'Ohhh... baby, don't hurt me. Don't make me laugh. It's a toy and it's probably not even loaded. And it's not thievin to take what you have earned.'

Roy, we have all earned that money. It is not yours to take. I don't want to do this but I am a kid looking after kids...I'm desperate...it belongs to mum and the family and if Ned is in deep trouble, we will need it even more. I am not asking but telling you, Roy...you have enough to give me half at least.'

'Half be buggered you little, black haired bitch.'

'And I want to know if you had anything to do with Valerie's drowning. You were seen near the river that day. She was my dear friend, Roy.'

'Look, all I'm saying is I did nothin to that girl, but she knew too much. That should be a warning to you. I'm going to call your bluff, Kate, if the pistol is a dud or you don't have the guts to pull the trigger, then you are going to look down the barrel of my colt...and I assure you it works. Which is it pretty one? you say ole step daddy Roy lacks the ticker...let's see who is the one to blink...put your cards on the table, girl.'

'Don't do it, Roy.'

With a cunning smirk, Roy reached for his colt and pointed the silver barrel directly at Kate. Kate, sensing he was about to shoot, quickly shoved his hand away and deflected a bullet meant for her. The bullet smacked into the black boy shattering him into a thousand pieces of dark marble.

Roy ran to his stolen treasure. He went down on his knees and tried to piece the bits and fragments together but it was a hopeless and desperate act. Tears and look of hate and revenge coloured his face.

'God dammit...that's done it Kate...my financial security gone...the only thing you are getting now is one-way ticket to see your dear friend Valerie, and both of you can do all the snooping you want up there.'

Kate knew he wouldn't miss her the second time, and as Roy braced himself for second attempt, she aimed and fired her pea shooter putting the neatest, little hole you ever saw into Roy's scheming brain, about the size of pea. He staggered backwards then seemed to regain his balance, took two unsteady steps towards her, raised his colt revolver known as the 'peacemaker' which he had imported from USA, aimed it's gleaming, silver barrel directly at Kate's head, and said,

'I told you it as a pea shooter Kate me darlin... now I will show you what a fine piece of American engineering will do...any last words my lovely'.

'Shoot me Roy...I deserve to die for what I have done.'

Roy and dropped his colt as he fell to the ground. 'you are good kid Kate... say goodbye to my babies, and bury me with my flag...I would like that...and there is letter in my bag to my family in America ...can you see that my wife gets it.'

Kate ran to him cradling him in her arms, and said,

'I will do all those things Roy...I'm so sorry this has happened.'

And with last loving look at his faithful horse, Roy said in faltering voice,

'I am going to miss you, buddy... look after him, Kate.'

Roy knew it was the end and it saddened him. He liked life, scheming and making a dollar. This profiteering, inventive, risk taking, double dealing Yankee was blessed with an intimate association with lady luck. A luck which saved his life at the Bighorn, made him a fortune on the Californian goldfields, and another stash in Australia, but had run empty at the end of a teenager's pea shooter in the dry, desolate Australian scrub. It was one gamble, one risk too many, and his luck had abandoned him.

'I wish Virgil was here to sing me one of his slow songs ease my mind a bit...me and him were good buddies Kate. Bury me in that hole I dug, Kate...save you digging another and let my end be a mystery... let them think I have done another runner.'

He gave a little laugh, coughed and went still. Kate held him in her arms for some time weeping and remembering that Roy had made her mum happy, and no matter his obsession for money, he did make life interesting and exciting. She then stood and tried to carry him to his freshly dug hole in the ground but he was a dead weight.

'You can help me bury Roy,' she said to Blue Doggy. He stood their silently but his eyes showed he understood. She undid his lasso and tied one end to Roy's legs and the other to the horn on his western saddle. Together they dragged Roy to his dusty grave. His limp body fell into the hole with a hollow thud. The thump startled Blue Doggy and he looked back. Kate thought he too looked sad. Blue Doggy had carried Roy from the marauding Indians, saved him from the tribe of boomerang and spear throwing aborigines, sped him from the impending disaster at Glenrowan, and was now towing him in a rather undignified way to ending. Kate said 'don't worry Blue Doggy- I will look after you along with Roys kids.' She took the rope off the saddle horn and released the loop from Roy's legs. She coiled the rope and felt its weight. For some unexplained reason she felt the urge to swing some lazy loops above her head like some weird funeral rite and then dropped it in the grave with Roy. She picked up his wide brimmed western hat, dusted it off, and placed it into the grave as well. It would she thought bring some solace to Roy to have his two much loved items of Americana with him. She carefully gathered all the pieces of the petrified aborigine and placed him in the grave with Roy.

'Some company for you, Roy.'

Poor Roy, forced to look over his shoulder for most of his life, running scared and not knowing if someone like the suspicious Valerie might expose him; and finally coming to an inglorious end in a dusty patch of Australian scrub where only slow moving lizards, tunnelling wombats, screeching galahs, sparring kangaroos and perhaps the odd inquisitive, lone dingo scratched and defecated in the dry stick undergrowth of a colourless bush and under a hot, relentless baking sun. They didn't find his body at the Little Big Horn. And if Kate had any part in it, they would not find his body in the Australian scrub. She rummaged through his other saddle bag. There she saw a neatly folded American flag and the letter. She unfurled flag admiring the brightly coloured star-spangled banner, a flag that Roy had specially imported for his Wild West Circus. Ned had a war bonnet in his saddle bag and a draft constitution of the Republic of North- West Victoria and Roy had the stars and banners in his along with letter to his wife and kids in America. Out of deep respect for Roy she did not open the letter but would see it posted to the given address as he had asked in his dying wish.

Roy, this maverick, this can do, risk taking, scheming, money making American was to his very end a true and faithful patriot of United States of America. Kate carefully laid the colourful flag over his crumpled body, grabbed his small spade and covered Roy and the shattered, stone aborigine with gravelly earth, clay and rocks. She then broke a leafy branch off a sapling, swept the footprints away, and threw dead leaves and twigs about so that it looked like pristine scrub. For a sixteen-year-old, Kate was not without sufficient guile to cover her tracks. She had stood by helpless as the Traps dismantled her home, chucked her and the kid's food on the floor, and searched for signs of the Gang, and it made her vigilant and cautious about small things.

Having completed her work, Kate and Blue Doggy stood respectfully by the makeshift grave to pay their respects in a moment of reverence and silence. For comfort she put her arms around Blue Doggy who stood respectful by her side and there they remained together in their grief. It consoled her to have Blue Doggy by her side standing solid as a rock and the warm feel of this grand, coloured pony born on the vast American Plains gave her encouragement to go on. Kate wiped her tears, attached the money bag behind the saddle, mounted, and with her dress hiked up she rode home. She rode home to screaming babies and hungry kids running amuck in a timber shack looking for food, and to her role as a mother well before her time. She didn't tell anyone about what happened. She said Roy came back in mad rush, yelled he had to go away quick, and left me, Blue Doggy and a stash of cash for the family. How he left the town she said she did not know...maybe the fast Cobb and Co which he always used when going to Melbourne.

Roy really was a good man his friends and associates said when they heard of his generosity. 'We had him figured wrong after all,' and they made lame excuses for his running out on the small army at Glenrowan. 'That man deserves a medal for what he done for those kids,' said the old Southern General. He added, 'mind you he helped me too...brought me here and gave me a start in this great land, a land much like the Old South before the war, and I love him for it. God bless Roy, and Ole Dixie and Kate... here is some money from me for Ned and Roy's kids and his hoss.'

'He was a fine man,' said Kate 'and I will miss him. I hope he'll come back sometime when things are better.'

'Amen to that.' replied the old Southern General and took off his dusty Stetson and held it respectfully low in front of him with his head bowed.

I would like to sing him a song Kate...one that comes to mind is 'Amazing Grace how sweet the sound'.

get ready

Frank James is not convicted by Missouri jury and retires.
*six months after Jesse James death, his older brother Frank turned
himself in. 'I have known no home, he said. I have slept in all sorts of
places- here today- there tomorrow...I am tired of this life of taut nerves,
of night riding and day hiding, of constant listening for footfalls, cracking
twigs and rustling leaves and creaking doors; tired of seeing Judas on the
face of every friend I know- and God knows I have none to spare - tired
of the saddle, the revolver and the cartridge belt...I want to see some way
out of it.' A sympathetic Missouri Jury refused to convict him. The West
- G C Ward.*

The train was on its way to Benalla. It was taking Ned to the police prisons away
from his supporters. Joe's lifeless body was dumped in the adjoining van like a piece
of meat. Early that morning Ned could hear voices outside the prison.

'Sling him up here,' one called out.

'He'll fall over,' said another.

'Tie him across the chest to the prison wall...in front of the door.'

The warder was getting annoyed at their requests.

'Look you lot...I don't like doing this. It's not right doing this to dead man whatever
wrong he did.'

'We've spoken to the Superintendent, and he has given permission for us to
photograph him. It's an important historical event. This is going to make great news.'

They slung Joe up against the door, and there he stood, precariously perched on
his Cuban heels and leaning to one side held only by two thin ropes across his chest.
Under a black hood, they went to work flashing their bulky cameras positioned on
tripods. Dried blood was caked on Joe's clenched fists, and his clothes. His eyes were
cast downwards as though embarrassed by the ghoulish spectacle taking place in front
of him and the crass commercialism of the press. But the siege at Glenrowan was big
news and with photographs the sales of their newspapers would race to record
numbers. There was no greater news than the Kelly Gang, and their daring exploits
had held them spellbound.

Back at Greta a wake was held for the two boys. Nearly two hundred people came.
They arrived on their horses and buggies in their Sunday best suits for the funeral.
The body remains, no more than charcoaled stumps, were placed on a table in a room.
At one stage it looked as though the mourners excited by revenge and alcohol would
rush the room until Ned's sister Margaret brandished her rifle to restore calm and
order. All through the day and night there was a steady stream of men going across to
the local hotel to purchase booze to drown their sorrows, and fuel their hate of the
Police. Tom showed Margaret the papers he had taken from the saddle bag and told

her that he intended to return the mare to Kev when the time was right. It was Ned's wish that his mare be returned to Kev, and he would see it done.

'You wouldn't believe what that mare did Margaret... going to him like that. I mean how she knew he was there, and the bullets and noise...you'd think it would have scared her off. They reckon if he had got on, he could have got away.'

'It's a damned pity he didn't,' said Margaret, 'but Ned doesn't run from a fight and he wouldn't leave the others there to save his own skin. He went back to get them. He's a God that brother of mine, Tom.'

'He surely is Margaret...he surely is.'

Tom rode to Benalla to see if he could get Joe's body. They refused. They asked him where Ned's mare was. The Police buried Joe in the Benalla cemetery after the coronial enquiry. Back at Greta, the sympathisers buried the remains of the two boys in a secluded paddock.

Rumors ran wild. It was said that Kate Kelly had shot Constable Steele, and those who knew her to be a high-spirited girl thought it true. Margaret, Kate and Tom and others waited at the Benalla Station to see Ned before he was taken to Melbourne. He had to be taken to the train in a spring cart. He saw them, and lifted his right arm in recognition. His left arm was disabled by a bullet having tunneled its length and embedded itself between his elbow and shoulder joint. A doctor, Steele and a special contingent of six guards accompanied him on the trip to the City. They wanted him alive to face trial and to be made an example to others. Crowds queued at the Railway Stations to see him as the train passed through. A larger crowd was waiting at Melbourne. The Nation's newspaper blazoned headlines of their gallant stand at Glenrowan capturing the public's imagination, even more than their previous feats of daring. The Kelly's sold newspapers like never before.

The public was moved by the reporting of the sudden appearance of his grey mare just prior to his capture. The State wanted that mare. She was taking on hero status amongst the rebellious Irish and they didn't like it. They knew that the contents of her saddle bag would bring them the information they needed to put his supporters behind bars, and if it were treason, they would face a similar fate to Kelly.

Ned was allowed to see his mum. She worked in the laundry jail and was nearing the end of her sentence. The two were overcome to see each other but not demonstrative. They would see their troubles through with a stoical resolve. They were allowed only a brief meeting. Ned told her of the siege and his grey mare. In the loneliness of her cell, the mother wept for her family, and the loss of life. She could read the words in Ned's heart without him speaking them. He wanted to tell her that he and the boys did not shoot the three police at Stringybark until they were forced to defend themselves. That they had tried to negotiate her release, and if things had gone better at Glenrowan, they might have been successful in getting her out. She was told her partner Roy had left for the States and had left the money for the kids.

'I loved Roy,' she said to Ned. 'He did have a good side to him, and you can see that in the unselfish way he has given his money to the kids.'

'It was your money too, mum,' said Ned.

'No Ned... it was his push and money-making ways that got it for us. I just went along for the ride.'

Both her and Ned knew they would get little respite from the pending court case. The law was an alien and remote world to her, her family and country folk. They talked in a strange, antiquated language and things that you wanted to say, things you wanted to explain as one person to another were denied to them under the guise of the pedantic laws of evidence. It seemed as though only wanted to hear the things that were not important. She even guessed that they would usher in the hanging judge for the job, Judge Barrington, the one who had sent her to jail and made threats about what he would do to Ned if he were before him. There was nothing more they could do but brace themselves and see it through. Visitors were kept from Ned for fear of giving him poison.

Ned wanted to give evidence at the preliminary hearing but his Counsel advised him not to make a statement.

'Wait till the jury trial,' he said, 'do not show your hand.'

Ned was charged with the murder of Thomas Lonigan. A heavily guarded train took him to Beechworth for the committal hearing. As he left the jail to be taken to the court, he saw Tom, his sisters and supporters in the street waiting for the hearing to commence. They greeted him from across the street. He lifted his handcuffed wrists to acknowledge them but was pushed on by the several armed warders.

McIntyre gave evidence about the events at Stringybark but omitted any description of the three plain clothed police going for their guns. He did not say anything about the boxes of ammunition and the body bags they took with them. He had carefully rehearsed his evidence, having being schooled by the Prosecution. To some he had left the others to their fate having grabbed Scanlon's horse and galloped for his life. The insinuating questions of Ned's Counsel made him nervous, and he responded in high pitched and excited tones. Several witnesses gave evidence of what Ned said on other occasions about the shootings. The Prosecution claimed these conversations constituted admissions to unlawful killings.

The Press was there to print what they heard. They would only be hearing one side of the story. It was poor legal advice for the public wanted to hear from Ned. He was capable of explaining that he acted in self-defense when the others went for their guns, but his lawyer didn't want to take the risk that he might incriminate himself. He wanted to play it safe. He should have known in this case the onus of proof was reversed. Ned was guilty until proven innocent. It was not a time to be silent. The whole country was waiting to hear from him.

On the train trip back to Melbourne Ned saw the ashes of the Glenrowan hotel.

'Three good men died there,' he said.

He looked wistfully at the Strathbogie Ranges. At the Station children ran excitedly after his cab. Ned lent out and pointed his finger at them like a pistol.

'Shoot me, Mr. Kelly,' they shouted.

Ned was amused by their childish spontaneity and fun.

He would have liked to have a family and a child; to teach him or her about the simple things that he loved; the bush, good companionship and horses; to live in peace, free of interference from the Police, with his friends. He'd just about achieved it with Valerie until Fitzpatrick came along to arrest Dan. He lay back on his prison bunk, reminisced, and sang a song that came to him, the 'the sweet bye and bye'. The sad words echoed off the cold, stone walls and down the clean, scrubbed corridors of the notorious jail to the ears of hardened criminals.

The warder with whom he had made friends brought his young son in to meet Ned.

He said 'I'd like you to meet a friend of mine son...this is Mr. Kelly the famous bushranger.'

'Pleased to meet you, Mr. Kelly,' the boy said politely.

'It's a pleasure to meet you also my fine, little fellow,' said Ned shaking his small hand 'I hope you grow up one day to be a decent man like your Dad here.'

Ned didn't expect that he would get a fair trial but he wanted to have his say. The Prosecution made an application to have the trial heard in Melbourne away from the place where the offences were alleged to have occurred.

'Your Honor,' said the Prosecutor to Judge Barrington, 'the accused has a strong following in the country from whence he comes, for what reasons I am unable to fathom, but be that as it may such sympathies are not conducive to the proper conduct of a trial as I am sure Your Honor will agree and in the interests of justice we seek that the trial be conducted here in the City.'

'Quite so,' replied Barrington seeking no further explanation. He had been waiting for this opportunity for a long time to lock horns with this notorious youth who thumbed his nose at the law and bore the reputation of a local hero.

Barely acknowledging defense counsel, he added,

'Any objection, Mr.Gauldron?... it seems a sensible application in the circumstances.'

'With respect, Your Honor, the interests of the State rather than the interest of justice would be better served by granting the application.'

'That's a most improper and impertinent comment,' cried the indignant Prosecutor 'they are the one and the same thing.'

'I agree,' said the Judge 'and I remind defense Counsel to temper his remarks with the good sense and discretion that is to be expected of Counsel. The application will be granted and I will direct the case to be heard before me in two months' time.'

Back at the jail the warder said,

'That bastard Barrington is a hanging judge and he is after you, Ned, Get ready for the judgement day.'

Ned's lawyer suffered the common curse of much opinionated Counsel thinking they are the font of all wisdom. He was also inexperienced. They assume they know how the common man thinks, but in reality, they know nothing of how they live or what motivates them. Their overweening pride makes them think their words and tactics are the only ones to sway or persuade the Jury. Their learned wisdom is unintelligible to the ordinary man. In this case the client with his plain-speaking ways was more eloquent than his hired mouthpiece. His Counsel needed only to listen to his client to understand he wanted to tell his story his way without his imagined clever, legal maneuverings. He wanted to face this trial the same he had done with most threats in his life ... up front and out in the open.

The trial came. Crowds assembled including Ned's sisters and friends. Judge Barrington, who left Ireland because he could not get enough work was dressed regally in his long wig and blood red robes, motioned to the Prosecutor to begin the case. MacIntyre was called to give evidence. Of the six persons present at Stringybark only two were left...MacIntyre and Ned. He was the Crown's prime witness. He said that first Lonigan and later Scanlon were shot by Ned when complying with his request to surrender. He made it appear that he would have no hope if he stayed in view of such cold-blooded killings. Ned's Counsel asked a few harmless questions, and let him go almost unchallenged in his evidence. He had not prepared his case, and was nervous and inexperienced before a Judge determined to have his victim in the defendant. MacIntyre had given differing versions both immediately after the event and at the committal hearing about the deceased having hold of their guns. There was no close examination of conflicting statements, and no examination of the medical evidence relating to the wounds and direction of travel of the bullets.

And what about the apparent purpose of the four Police. Why had they gone in plain clothes if the wished only to carry out the warrant of arrest and why had they carried more than double the ammunition they needed and why didn't they have the warrant with them. They were heard to boast of what they would do with Kelly when they found him and had carried with them body bags. Did not the reward say dead or alive. If it was the Gang's intention to shoot without warning, why did they bother coming out of the spear grass and not shoot them from a position of shelter. His Counsel opposed the admission of statement prepared by Ned which he wanted telegraphed to the Press at one of the Bank holdups because it wasn't proved to be signed by him. The statement would have explained to the Jury why the Gang had to seek refuge in the Ranges, the political background to the troubles with the Police and a full explanation of the Stringybark killings.

Everything went wrong. He may as well have gone to the gallows without a trial. All Ned could do was stand mute and listen. Finally, his lawyer persuaded him not to give an unsworn statement for fear that he may appear too smart to the Jury. The one possible persuasive voice for the defense was silenced, and his words of explanation denied to the Jury.

After Judge Barrington gave his summing up the result was inevitable. He said what right did Kelly have to hold up four men going about their lawful business of apprehending him. They were Police on duty, no matter in civilian clothes, and had seen warrants for their arrest for attempted murder of Fitzpatrick. There was no mention that Fitzpatrick had since been subject to dismissal from the Police force due to dishonesty. He reiterated what happened after the shootings with the killing of Kennedy. The defense had objected to this evidence without success. His Honor said it would give color to what happened before and was admissible. The Judge did not outline for the jury that they had to consider whether the police were acting lawfully if their intention was not to apprehend Kelly but to kill him, and that Ned when threatened with his life, after having given them the opportunity to surrender, could be said to be acting in lawful self-defense. This biased and pompous Judge eagerly wanted the rope for this accused, and now that it was so near, a few well-chosen directions to a Jury would see the job done. This crooked Judge, unfettered and unchallenged by the accused's inexperienced Counsel, and spurred on by his wealthy, squatter friends, was about to achieve his not so secret ambition to rid the country of the Kelly's.

The Jury returned with the inevitable verdicts of guilty. Ned did not blame them for their decision. The way the court case had gone, they could have come to no other decision, but if given the opportunity he would take on the beak, and let him know, in his own words, some of the things that should have been said in the trial. After the guilty verdict, the Judge asked Ned if he wanted to make a statement.

Transcripts from trial
'Well it is rather too late for me to speak now. I thought of speaking this morning and all day but there was little use and there is little use blaming anyone now.

Nobody knew about my case except myself. I wish I had insisted on being allowed to examine the witnesses myself. If I had examined them, I am confident I would have thrown a different light on the case. It is not that I fear death; I fear it as little as to drink a cup of tea.

On the evidence that has been given, no juryman could have given any other verdict. That is my opinion. but as I say, if I had examined the witnesses, I would have shown matters in a different light because no man understands my case I do myself.

I do not blame anybody − neither Mr Bindon nor Mr Gaunson; but Mr Bindon knew nothing about my case. I lay the blame on myself that I did not get up yesterday and examine the witnesses but I thought that if I did so it would look like bravado and flashness.'

Ned spoke simply and eloquently as Valerie had instructed him. The Judge egged him on,

'Edward Kelly, the verdict pronounced by the Jury is one which you must have expected?'

'Yes, under the circumstances,' replied Ned.

No circumstances I can conceive could have altered the result of your trial.'

'Perhaps not from what you can now conceive but if you had heard me examine the witnesses it would have been different.'

'I will give you credit for all the skill you appear to desire to assume.'

'no, I don't wish to assume anything. There is no flashness or bravado about me. It is not that I want to save my life, because I know I would have been capable of clearing myself of the charge, and I could have saved my life in spite of all against me.'

His Honor - 'the facts are so numerous and so convincing, not only as regards the original offence with which you are originally charged but with respect to a long series of transactions covering a period of eighteen months, that no rational person would hesitate to arrive at any other conclusion but that the verdict of the Jury is irresistible, and that it is right. I have no desire whatever to inflict upon you any personal remarks. It is not becoming that I should endeavor to aggravate the sufferings with which your mind must be sincerely agitated.'

The prisoner - 'no I don't think that. My mind is as easy as the mind of any man in this world as I am prepared to show before God and man.'

His honor - 'it is blasphemous for you to say that. You appear to revel in the idea of having put men to death.'

The prisoner - 'more men than me have put men to death but I am the last man in the world to take a man's life. Two years ago, even if my own life was at stake and I am confident if I thought a man would shoot me, I would give him a chance of keeping his life and would rather part with my own. But if I knew that through him innocent lives were at stake, I would certainly have to shoot him if he forced me to do so but I would want to know that he was going to take innocent life.'

His honor - 'your statement involves a cruelly wicked charge of perjury against a phalanx of witnesses.'

The prisoner - 'I daresay, but a day will come at a bigger court than this when we shall see which is right and which is wrong. No matter how long a man lives he is bound to come to judgment somewhere and as well here as anywhere. It will be different the next time they have a Kelly trial, for they are not all killed.'

The Judge - I desire to spare you any more pain and I absolve myself from anything said willingly in any of my utterances that may have unnecessarily increased the agitation of your mind. I have now to pronounce your sentence.'

He pronounced the sentence of death.

The prisoner - 'I will go a little further than that and say I will see you there where I go.

The show trial had ended. The State was well pleased with the result. Too bad the prisoner was given no rein by his Lawyers to put his explanation for what happened in his life. Barrington was clean and efficient in his work. Ned's advisors had failed him. He would go to the gallows without his story been put. After the prisoner was led from the court, the barrister and solicitor walked back to their Chambers.

'Well, he never had much chance anyway,' said the Barrister trying to excuse his poor showing. 'Why do I always get the hopeless cases. You got Kelly's money in trust, haven't you?'

The solicitor responded,

'Ned really wanted to have his say. Perhaps we should have advised him differently. He did serve it up to the beak at the end. He had some spirit that boy I'll give him that.'

The Counsel protested,

'You know as well as I do, he would have made a mess of things if we did that, and the Judge would have held us responsible. We gave him a competent representation.'

'I'm sure he wanted to tell his story.'

'Aaah...they're all the same these felons...all the excuses in the world. If the sad truth be known, they cannot control their mad, excitable, Irish temperaments. No self-discipline, bad breeding, you know... it all goes together. What did he want to say anyway?'

'Here's his statement...I thought you had read it.'

'No my boy.... we gave him the only chance he had...to shut up and let us do the talking for him. After all, that's what we are trained for... isn't it?'

There was an embarrassing pause.

'I suppose so but I don't feel good about what happened.'

'Gimme a look at that statement then.'

The solicitor handed him the paper. It read,

> All I want is a full and fair trial, and a chance to make my side heard. Until now the police have had all the say, and have had it all their own way. if I get a full and fair trial, I don't care how it goes; but I know this − the public will see that I was hunted and hounded on from step to step; they will see that I'm not the monster I am made out.
>
> What I have done has been done under strong provocation...I do not pretend that I have led a blameless life, or that one fault justifies another, but the public in judging a case like mine should remember that the darkest life may have a bright side, and that after the worst has been said against a man, he may, if he is heard, tell a story in his own rough way that will perhaps lead them to intimate the harshness of their thought against him, and find as many excuses for him as he would plead for himself.
>
> For my own part I do not care one straw about my life now or for the result of the trial. I know very well from the stories I have been told of how I am spoken of, that the public at large execrate my name; the newspapers cannot speak of me with that patient tolerance generally extended to men awaiting trial, and who are assumed according to the boast of British justice to be innocent until they are proved to be guilty; but I do not mind, for I have outlived that care that curries public favor or dreads the public frown.
>
> Let the hand of the law strike me down if it will but I ask my story be heard and considered; not that I wish to avert any decree the law may deem necessary to vindicate justice, or win a word of pity from anyone. If my life teaches the public that men are made mad by bad treatment, and if the police are taught that they may not exasperate to madness men they persecute and ill-treat, my life will not entirely be thrown away.'

He handed back the piece of paper.

'The boy had the gift of the gab...good turn of phrase too...for a bushranger. You sure you didn't write it?'

'Not a single word is mine.'

The Counsel just shook his head and said,

'Now the Judge... he didn't like Kelly and that was a big hurdle; I mean Chief Justice, Chancellor of the University, kind and generous benefactor to the State and Church of England, man of letters and culture and all that...it was difficult to oppose him but I took it up to him...didn't you think?'

The solicitor remained silent for minute.

He repeated 'we failed him.'

There on the second floor, not far from the street where Ned's barrister and solicitor were discussing the plight of their hapless client, Judge Barrington's mistress had her 'Chambers'. As soon as the portly Learned Judge signed off the execution order, he would hurry off to his mistress to boast how he had done away with Australia's most notorious Bushranger.

'Cheeky bugger he was too,' he said wiping the sweat from his brow.

'I'm not feeling too well, my dear... can you get me an appointment with the doctor tomorrow?'

Bury my mare at Glenrowan

Ned was taken to his cell to await his hanging.

Sixty thousand signatures to have the sentence commuted to life imprisonment was given to the Government.

It was all in vain. They were unmoved.

The prisoner had challenged them in ways they were not disposed to forgive. They were determined that he should hang to deter what they feared were incipient rebellions from the Irish communities in the North West of the State.

Ned was placed in a cell away from the other prisoners, and watched continuously by two prison officers on eight-hour shifts. He was allowed visitors but separated by bars. This is what the regulations provided for until his execution in two weeks. His sisters and friends worked for a reprieve.

Kev visited the jail and they spoke in low tones.

'You probably know why I asked you to come, Kev...can I trust you to do the right thing by my mare?'

'No need to ask, Ned. I have lived for the day when I would see her again. I even took off to Glenrowan when I heard about it, but I got there too late. I searched the bush for a couple of days. Their intentions were I heard to do away with her, but not over my dead body. How are things with you Ned? A lot of people were upset with the way the trial was conducted by that bastard Barrington...I know what the man's like...I've had to take him on the Country Circuit a few times. Arrogant son-of-bitch if ever there was one.'

'No mind me, Kev...my fate was always on the cards but I would like to see that mare safe.'

'She is bloody well near thinks like a human that mare, Ned,' said Kev. 'I hardly did much with her at all...just didn't get in her way because she learnt real quick. I've thought about this a lot in my time with horses Ned. I believe it happens to one in a thousand horses...don't ask me how it happens, a freak of nature or something, more like a dolphin in her intelligence than a horse but it's a heightened awareness for human contact...it's hard to put into words, but you know what I mean.'

'I do Kev... but don't be modest...you are a fine horseman otherwise the mare would not be going back to you. A lot of what she is due to you, Kev, and the way you looked after her.'

'She looked after me, Ned. I was pretty low there at one stage until she came along.'

'The mare will be put in your paddock one night soon, Kev. You'll wake up and she'll be there...you can just say she is another horse you bought. No need for any questions...but promise me one thing...if anything happens to her, God forbid, I would like for her to be buried at Glenrowan. A paddock has been purchased behind the hotel so that it can be done. That place is sacred land for us, Kev, and I will go a contented man if you would just promise me that. The others, Joe Dan and Steve died there and they have been secretly buried in that Glen. I'd like Music to be there with them. As for me I have asked for my body to be returned to my relatives for decent burial but they will not even allow that...pit of lime he in the Goal they said... so Music can take my place and I'm relying on you to do it.'

'I give you my word, Ned ...upon my life, and as any decent man from Casterton would say...it's as good as done. I make that promise to you, Ned, and let me die in Hell if I don't carry it out.'

save the last dance for me

The hanging of Multia, a young Australian Aborigine
*Multia, the native murderer, was executed on the 7th instant in front of
Mr Riddles house about twenty miles from Pt Lincoln. When his body was
demanded in the usual form, Multia was much affected; the tears ran
down his face, and, pointing to the bush, he cried, 'why kill me for this,
who am a boy, - when there are plenty of big men over there who were
at the murder.'* - South Australian Register 19th April 1843 The
Hempen Collar - executions in S.A. 1838-1964 - D Towler T Porter

Updike was a petty thief who spent his time in and out of prison. He was as they
say institutionalized. Prison had become his home. Although it provided him with
three meals a day it did not mean he had to like those he resided with. He had heard
their pathetic stories of who was to blame for their sorry plight, how justice had done
them wrong. Their dull, regressive minds were incapable of thinking other than in
terms of their own self-interest. They thought nothing about their hapless victims
and would do the same again if they knew they could get away with it. They sniggered
when Judges said they would have to live with the burden of their crime on their
conscience for the rest of their lives as though that were a heavy penalty. The truth
was they had forgotten their victims the very day they had committed their crime.

He had been one of them, except he admitted his guilt.

'I plead guilty, your Honor.'

He was that upfront and honest about it some of the Judges did not want to send
him to jail. At fifty-four years of age, he had his eyes on a job, a job he thought he
could do well. He did weights and muscled up. If you were weak in the jail, you went
to the bottom of the heap. He cropped his graying hair so that it exposed his bony
ridges of his skull. He developed friendships with the screws, and warned them of
pending attempts to escape and rogue prisoners' intent upon upsetting the prison
regime. When he was near release, he spoke to the Superintendent. The
Superintendent listened.

Updike said, 'Sir, I want to apply for the position of apprentice Executioner. I know
I can do the job. I think I have a feel for it.'

That was a strange thing to say. The Superintendent acceded to his request mainly
because he had no applications for the position. He was to be apprenticed to the
retiring Executioner for six months. Updike obtained a small, one roomed flat near the
Pentridge jail, and went to work each day. It was not as though there was a hanging
each day but there were accepted ways to practice his trade. He began by man-
handling the reluctant prisoners from their small cells to the trap door, strapping their
legs together, adjusting the hemp rope and pulling the black cap over their fear-
stricken faces.

'May the Lord have mercy on your soul,' said a Priest holding the crucifix in one hand and the black rosary beads in the other. The trap slammed open and the prisoner dropped.

'It has to be clean, efficient and above all quick,' his boss said.

'Make sure you get his feet exactly on the middle of the trap door, where the chalk mark is, because if you don't, he will swing like a pendulum. When I tap you on the shoulder get off quick otherwise you will go down with him.'

The reformed criminal Updike was disappointed when his victims went quietly, resigned to their fate and under the influence of the meddling Priests and queues of do-gooders that flocked to the jails with their predictable diatribe on salvation and the forgiveness of the Lord. They would get no forgiveness from him. He knew them too well being amongst them for most of his life. They were unredeemable, sniveling curs, rapists, murderers and recidivists who deserved their miserable fate without mercy. He gladly pulled them from of their cold stone and cement cells, and marched them blubbering, begging for reprieve to the scaffold. They struggled and fought such that the large entrance room before the gallows came to be known as the 'dance floor'. He wanted to see the stark terror in their bulging eyes, the squeal and anguish of their high-pitched pleas for forgiveness, and it took all his will power not to laugh in their terrified faces. He had little doubt they had laughed at their unfortunate victims as they took their last dying breath. An eye for an eye and a tooth for a tooth, that's what the bible says. He had heard them boast of their sickening crimes; how they choked this one with their bare hands; how they knifed another until the blade broke; how they pummeled some poor drunk's head into a pulp or raped some friend's frightened wife or daughter. They were proud of their violent crimes. What you do will come back to you he thought. When they resisted, he liked to wrestle them down in their cells, have them whimpering like a whipped dog, while the shocked man of God politely extricated himself from the life and death struggle, and the accompanying do-gooders ran for safety. If one or two got the better of him for imminent death brings super strength, he would have reinforcements waiting in the wings. He would forcibly bind their hands behind their back, and roughly frog march them along the corridor, across the exercise yard, up the stairs and through the doors to the scaffold. On opening the first-floor door, the prisoners could see the rope and noose hanging from a large, timber beam and the executioner in a black hood, waiting. The grim scene would set them off like a cracker into the circular dance of death as Updike liked to call it. He struggled with the prisoner, lurching this way and that, until his victim was overpowered and positioned onto the trap door. Updike became methodical, efficient and heartless.

He studied and knew well the technical requirements of the noose. Some people think a rope is an ordinary thing. But the hanging noose is a piece of hempen rope intricately designed and worked to efficiently part the second and third vertebra of the neck. There is a formula to assess the required length of the drop by taking the weight of the prisoner in pounds, dividing it into one thousand to get the answer in feet and inches. A ten stone man equals one hundred and forty pounds, and into one thousand comes to seven feet one- and three-quarter inches. You then have to allow for the noose. Once the correct drop is arrived at, the rope is coiled and held with a packing string which breaks with the weight of the prisoner. If the wrong calculation is made and the drop too much, it might make for a messy job with the head being separated the body. Updike practiced his sums until he could guess the right combinations by simply studying the prisoner. His tutor told him of the importance of placing the knot under the left lower jaw.

'This way it throws the chin back and causes instant death,' he said, 'but if the knot is on the right-hand side, it ends up behind the neck and strangles the prisoner taking some fifteen minutes and a lot of twitching of the body.'

Updike practiced his trade using a sack of sand, pulling the lever and oiling the trap door springs, bolts and hinges. He knew his equipment intimately and lovingly maintained it with a combination of tools and oils. He gave thanks for the regular supply of customers sent to him by Judge Barrington. Only Barrington he reasoned, knew the devious mind of the hardened criminal and was not fooled by the double speak and honeyed words of their lawyers, or their sudden and unconvincing remorse when the game was up. Only Barrington represented the ignored concerns of their damaged and dead victims while the other Judges, described as enlightened and progressive, rabbited on about rehabilitation. In his mind only, he and the Judge stood against the legions of do gooders and bleeding hearts to see that proper justice was done. The jail Superintendent was impressed with his work and gave him fulsome praise for his dedication to his work.

'We are soon going to have a very famous prisoner for you, Updike.'

'I know,' he said, 'I have read it in the papers and been doing my calculations already. About five foot eleven inches and twelve stone, I reckon.'

Updike resented the adulation of the public for this flash youth and his impudence to the Judge. He obtained a copy of the court transcript and was shocked to read the disrespectful language used by the brash accused to the highly, respected Judge. This bold upstart would wish he had died with the others by the time he had finished with him. He secretly observed him in the exercise yard. He had heard that he was handy with his fists. He did his calculations and rechecked them. He filled the sack to the exact weight, carried out a trial run, and tested the rope noting if it stretched and making the appropriate allowances.

The local Priest came from the country to be with Ned in his last moments. They talked about home, the discontent in his community and the possibility of an investigation Commission into his and the selector's complaints.

'Too bad I won't be around to give evidence,' said Ned.

'The lads have delivered the mare to Kev,' the Priest whispered.

'That's a relief,' said Ned.

'Ahhh the mare Ned – she is the talk of the town. Everyone wants to see her but now she is back with Kev, we will have to keep it confidential.'

'Too right,' said Ned, 'them Traps would crucify her if they had half a chance Father. They tried to shoot her at Glenrowan, you know.'

'Shooting a dumb animal... that's a cruel thing,' said the Priest shaking his head in disbelief.

'She ain't no dumb animal, Father.'

'Ned, I want to say that you and your boys have inspired a lot of oppressed people with your bravery, your words and daring.'

'I only did what any man would do in the same circumstances, Father.'

'Ned let me say this to you. I am no philosopher...just a simple man who observes. Jesus was an illegitimate child. He was born of an unmarried mother. He struggled and his life was often one of pain. Your life has not been an easy one with the loss of your father, poverty, imprisonment of your mother, and conflict with the Traps. On the cross Jesus cried out 'my god, my god, why hast thou forsaken me'. There was tremendous disappointment in those words, as there is now in your life facing the gallows. But Jesus was resurrected. The way you have lived your life, Ned, sometimes breaking the law but the law is not always right or just, I can see that you have done your best to deal with it honestly and courageously. And we can ask of you no more than that. If you avoid conflict and error you do not live... that is the true way of life Ned so do not have regret. The great mass of people understands this, although they may not openly express it. You will live in the hearts of all those who are helpless in the face of intolerant and cruel persecution and authority. It is the work the Church should be doing, and I for one am grateful to you. Your life has not been a wasted life, Ned, and I am ashamed the Church has not put its weight behind you. In Ireland your dad may have told you there were the penal laws imposed by the English invaders. The priests fought with the people to overcome the tyranny and wholesale theft of their lands...you have probably heard of the hedge schools...and the priests were pursued, imprisoned and executed. Now, I am sad to say we priests have become too civilized, too timid to move outside the safety of our churches. If I were worth my salt, I should have been on my horse with your men at Glenrowan, Ned.'

'Then you would be swinging with me Father. You are too kind with your words... I am not the hero you make me out to be. I have done wrong, and I seek forgiveness from those I have wronged. I have always felt bad about Kennedy. He was a good man.'

'The time is approaching - shall we pray? said the Priest.

'No Father...let us fall into error one more time and sing...did you bring that old harmonica with you? It will brighten us both up a bit.'

'To be sure, my son. I knew you'd be asking. I like a song myself at times like this. Better than a prayer I agree.'

He pulled out his mouth organ from his coat pocket, and they struck up a duet not hearing the Executioner's footsteps to the cell door. Updike told his assistants to wait outside. Without knocking he burst through the cell door.

'That's enough of that behavior, lad. It's not right to be singing at a time like this,' he said as he impatiently knocked the organ out of the Priest's mouth, and grabbed Ned by his damaged arm.

Ned hit him with a straight right that sent him reeling back against the door where he slid to the floor dazed. Father Murphy, apologetic, helped him up. Assistants pushed at the door. Updike told them to stay out and he would handle it by himself.

'Are you going to come quietly, or will I have to call in reinforcements?' he said holding his jaw.

'We'll only be a short moment,' said Ned.

'Ok... so long as it's no more,' replied Updike as he took a seat offered by the Priest. He sat down at the small table, and keenly eyed the two men for any signs of panic or fear. The boy would die slowly on the end of his rope for that punch. The aging priest, though beset by the demon drink, was still a good shepherd to his flock. He cupped his battered mouth organ to his alcohol, bitten lips and gently eased back into the pleasant tune of the 'sweet bye and bye'. Ned listened, and joined in, his voice at first calm, steady, then choking a little but still steely determined to show no emotion. Tears coursed down the ruddy cheeks of the old, drink sodden priest as he shuffled the music stick backwards and forwards across his parched lips.

Updike waited. He waited for the time when he thought the condemned man would lose his nerve and snap. That's the moment when he would summon his men and they would drag him screaming and kicking from his cell. None of these things happened, except a distant, familiar chord of the song resonated in his short, cropped skull taking him back to his childhood and unleashing a flood of repressed memories; memories of abject poverty, gnawing hunger, and a drunken violent step father; memories of a pitiful, worn out mother who gathered her little ones about her at night, after scrubbing every dirty shithouse in the neighborhood, and sang her troubles and their cares away in her bone, weary voice. When his mum sang, peace descended like a warm blanket over their ramshackle home and into the sad, little boy. When his mum sang, warmth chased out the numbing cold and his hurt. When his mum sang, joy came to the wounded heart of a troubled child. She went, and the singing stopped. He was split from his siblings and orphaned. There with the other kids, young Updike learnt to do crime. And it kept on, until he reached the age of fifty-four years with nobody to love and everybody to hate. In a wasted lifetime he learnt to hate good. So good that the State paid him for killing the people he hated. Now those lost memories, awakened by the song and the tender scene unfolding in front of him, memories of the one person he loved, tugged and pulled at his barren heart. His upper lip quivered, and unwittingly, he began to mouth the words of the song he had heard the two men sing. They lifted their heads and looked. Updike's gravelly voice was at first tentative, then got more confident and stronger, louder; inviting in the other two, and together their voices harmonized and flowed down the corridor and alerted the inquisitive ears of the gathered audience in the gallows. They looked at each other puzzled by what they heard and impatient at the delay of the gruesome spectacle they had come to witness.

Updike led Ned out of his cell, his hand placed reassuringly on his shoulder. The three men walked easily together. He felt no hate, only compassion. A lifetime of hate was driven from him by the faltering song of an innocent man going to his death like Jesus chasing the devil out of the swine. He knew then he was wrong to treat all condemned prisoners with contempt. The net of justice ensnares both the innocent and guilty. His poor, impoverished mum was innocent of the punishment life gave her.

As the door to the gallows opened, Ned stood quietly at the entrance studying the spacious 'dance floor' as it was commonly known, the area before the beam and trap door, the place where the guilty and sometimes innocent struggled, bargained, prayed cried and begged for their miserable lives. As though vainly hoping for a last-minute miracle, the prisoners would engage the executioner in a life and death struggle as they circled the room grappling, pulling, lunging, stumbling to the floor until finally overcome by the combined strength of executioner's strong men. Finally trussed up like turkey they were held upright on the trap door for the short drop to eternity.

Ned looked across and recognized an old friend. Sarge half lifted his hand as though to wave goodbye. Ned acknowledged his gesture with slight nod of his head. He took the hand of Updike and smiled.

He beckoned as though to dance.

Updike smiled.

He intended to leave his job and thought what have I got to lose, and I like this boy. He pulled his canvas hood over his head and the two waltzed across and around the dark slate floor to the breathless amazement of the gathered audience who came to witness the grizzly event much like the public hangings not so long ago. In this fun-loving fearless boy's mind, he imagined some those dear to him and for whom he had loved and fought were lined up around the dance floor waiting to take his hand in a final loving embrace. He engaged with his sister Kate, his mother, his Dad, Mrs. Jones, Dan, Steve, Joe, and Kev –then suddenly as though in a puff of smoke the room emptied and there stood a grey mare – Music – in all her pure, white, sleek feminine beauty. She had come as she did at Glenrowan to spirit him away- he bent his head to rest on her forehead and stroked her smooth, silky neck looking into her big, dark eyes which seemed to him to understand all things.

'It won't be long,' he said to his mare before he found himself dropping into thin air, plummeting down, down to Earth and like a rubber ball rebounding back and upwards to the sky, and further still, onwards and upwards to another place where wrongs would be righted and loved ones reunited. Updike carefully placed the knot to the correct position on the left, lower jaw, affectionately squeezed his bound hand, and Australia's most wanted bushranger dropped to his death. His knees lifted momentarily, and straightened for the last time. Then all was quiet and still.

The spirit of the wedge tailed eagle fled the body, sped past Kev and Ned's mare waiting outside the jail, knocking Kev's hat from his head. It passed a boy who remembered being saved in a dam. It rapidly climbed upwards to the slipstreams in the blue sky and followed the train track, over the towns, diving and circling once around Glenrowan, and then on to its much loved Strathbogie Ranges where it found a home in an abandoned eagles nest perched high on a craggy cliff.

The authorities were shocked at Updike's familiarity with the prisoner. They wanted to send him to rehab but he said 'I'm handing in my notice.' He told them to stick their job up their arses and that he would rather spend his time with his mum. Before he left, he scribbled on the wall in Ned's cell along with all the other rhymes and graffiti,

'I'll be seeing you in apple blossom time.'

He didn't know why he chose those words but they seemed right. After fifty-four long, hard years and in the twilight of his life, apple blossom time of sorts came to Updike. He had been spending time with his frail, elderly mum with whom he was recently reconciled. He would care for her in her last years.

Back at Glenrowan the schoolteacher was reading the news.

'Kelly hanged,' said the bold headlines.

He put the paper down and said to his wife,

'Ethel...I have sent an innocent man to the gallows. I wish to God I could turn back time. I have felt bad ever since I betrayed that Kelly boy's trust. I don't think I can live with myself.'

'Live,' she said 'I am going down to the Bank this morning to collect part of the reward. We are going to live for the first time in our lives.' and she left.

The schoolteacher walked to his school as he had done many times before, went straight to the front of his classroom and spoke to the children.

'The first lesson of the day, children,' said the schoolteacher, 'is not to sell your mates down the river, not to sell your mates for thirty pieces of silver.'

He picked up his chalk and wrote on the blackboard,

'thirty pieces of silver.'

The children looked at each other perplexed.

'That children is what Judas sold Jesus for. Never be a Judas, children.'

One curious lad asked, 'what happens if you do, Sir?'

'What happens, dear boys and girls,' he said, 'is this.'

He calmly took a revolver from his coat pocket. It was the same revolver a policeman gave him to protect himself from the Kelly's when he stopped the train. The memories returned to the troubled schoolteacher. He placed the barrel to his forehead, and pulled the trigger. He slumped onto his desk, and did not draw another breath. The children ran screaming from the school, and down the main street. Constable Bracken heard the commotion, and ran down to the school with his colt in his hand. He couldn't believe his eyes. He put a sheet over the dead school teacher.

'You didn't see any Irish sympathizers about?' he asked one of the children.

The child said 'no... no one, Sir...he did it to himself.'

'Then who wrote that message on the blackboard?' the police officer asked thinking it was an act of vengeance.

'Our schoolteacher wrote it before he shot himself,' the child replied.

His wife had been to the Bank and filled her bag with fresh notes from the reward. She went straight to the local store and purchased expensive perfumes and powder that she had seen the wealthy Squatters wives buy, and which she had not been able to afford on her husband's modest salary. As she came out the store, she saw Bracken run past and distressed school children in the street. She suspected the worst and quickly walked to the school. Bracken met her at the door.

She said straight away, 'He shot himself, didn't he Constable?'

'Don't go in, Mrs. Kershaw...it's not very nice...I cannot understand why he did this.'

She said 'I do,' and left without explaining.

At night her friend Mabel came to console and be with her and children trying to cope with the terrible tragedy.

'It was such a selfish act. He didn't really love us, Mabel,' said the schoolteacher's wife.

Mabel said, 'well Ethel... he must have thought about you and the kids a little at least. He could have flicked himself before the reward arrived, and then maybe, the Government would have reneged and not paid you anything. You know what them bureaucrats are like, counting their pennies and taking our taxes. They are not too good at giving it back if they can find an excuse.'

Ethel stopped looking into her mirror and brushing her face with the expensive cosmetics she had purchased that day. She thought for a few seconds, returned her new, gold plated make-up brush to its elaborate, shiny, black box, and said,

'Yes... I suppose what you say, Mabel, does put a different complexion on it.'

Music has done a bad, bad thing

Thoughts of rebellion seethed in the fledgling colony. Kelly had been denied a decent burial sought by his supporters. What they did to him after the execution was to them a barbaric and heathen act.

'I'll see you there where I go' was Kelly's sentence on Judge Barrington and the Judge drew his last breath in the same month. The Government, for his efforts in the Kelly trial, wanted to reward his memory with a State funeral. Cobb and Co handled State funerals having the more elaborate carriages and the best horses.

The manager called in his head driver Kev showing him the contract.

'Can I leave this to you, Kev? - you've done a few of these ceremonial funerals before and know what's required. We can use our special funeral hearse for the job. Be careful...the hearse cost us quids, and I want only the best and most reliable horses used. As you know we've got a good reputation for doing these State affairs, and the pay is generous.'

'Who is this cove, Barrington, do you know?'

'He's the one who sent Kelly down,' replied Kev.

'Oh... good, that's one less outlaw we have to worry about. The fellow did over one of our coaches, did you know, Kev?'

'Yeah boss... I was there.'

'He took a horse of ours, didn't he, the grey mare...she was a good mare that one. You trained her didn't you?'

Kev sensed the conversation getting a little close and wanted to leave. The manager kept on,

'I wonder if we can get her back.'

'I think she probably got sold over in N.S.W. boss, but I have another grey mare just like her back home. I've had her for about six months now,' he said to put him off the track. 'She's a nice type, nice lookin mare, well behaved so I might ride her myself for the funeral.'

'Whatever you say Kev...we trust you implicitly in these matters. Remember to get those special state uniforms you have to wear spruced up. The public usually line the streets for these affairs. It's only right too. These Judges give a lot of their time to the community.' Kev had heard enough.

'I reckon they should have given that Kelly boy a State funeral for the guts he showed for his mates,' said Kev in a matter of fact tone as he was won't to do.

'Ah... you country fellas always stick together. Giving an outlaw like Kelly a State funeral...I must remember that one.'

Kev got down to work organizing men, grooming the horses, cleaning the harness, polishing the silver and brass and the timber carvings of ornate carriage to transport the coffin to the Cemetery. That evening after tea, he took his halter and brought Music in from her small paddock. He mixed up a feed of chopped hay, carrots, a little grain with some molasses. Her condition was improving. 'It will be a big day for you tomorrow, my girl,' he said as he brushed and whisked her coat with some straw and blackened her hooves. Her ears pricked, she stopped chewing and appeared to listen as he worked over her. He put a small amount of oil onto a rag and rubbed her coat to get a shine. He trimmed off any long hairs from her hocks and ran his pocket knife through her tail and mane. He remembered she always seemed to enjoy ceremonial occasions in the street with people milling about, and hoped the outing would bring back her usual good appetite. He stopped his work, stood by her side, and looking at her said, 'you'll have to put out of your mind that bugger Barrington...he didn't give Ned much of a go.' Music went back to her tucker. Kev sat down on his stool and watched. He wondered if she understood what had happened. Certainly, the rumors about her at Glenrowan made him think this mare had unusual loyalty and attachment. Kev went back to his house preparing his uniform and polishing his long boots and ceremonial sword. He rose early the following morning, packing his gear into a bag, strapping it to Music and led her to the depot from another horse. The mare looked the best she had for long time. Kev when fitted out in his State uniform looked a picture of elegance mounted on the prettiest mare in the State. He was to ride her as the lead horse in front of the funeral hearse. Kev led the cortege on Music, and two riders were positioned to the rear of the hearse on either side. A drummer walked in front of Kev giving a slow roll of his drums. Luminaries including Judges decked out in their blood, red robes and long wigs and members of the Government walked behind the hearse, and two more uniformed riders took up the rear as the procession made its way slowly to the City cemetery. It was an overcast, dreary day and few people gathered in the streets to see the procession. As it passed the Melbourne Club a loyal and suitably subdued gathering of wealthy Squatters and the Melbourne Club bowed their heads in respect. Nearing the cemetery Kev overheard two spectators,

'What's all this about? who kicked the bucket?'

His mate replied, 'some Supreme Court beak I think.'

'Pity they don't take the opportunity to bury the lot of them...arrogant pricks,' the other replied and they both turned away without so much as an acknowledgement.

At the cemetery, Kev followed the coffin to the grave on his mare where he would stand guard with two other uniformed riders until the sermon was finished. The Anglican Archbishop spoke of the deceased in predictably endearing terms using all the appropriate phrases...pillar of society, a man who spent his life ensuing the orderly conduct of its citizens in a fair and just manner, had the common touch, loved by the citizens of the State, humble servant of the people and so it went on. Kev impolitely yawned as the Archbishop droned on to his silver tails. The Archbishop's humbug drew to a close,

'I invite you, dear friends, to come and deposit your gifts, your flowers into the grave of this humble, obedient servant of God and Her Majesty. Please remember to do this in an orderly manner and whilst this is taking place, our choir from one of our distinguished girl's schools will sing what I am reliably told was one of the deceased's favorite pieces 'Britannia rules the waves'.

The choir master motioned his girls to commence and as their voices lifted above the crowd, the distinguished mourners filed towards the open grave. The Squatters and their families who had profited immensely from the deceased Judges rulings got a little carried away in their enthusiasm and pushed towards the grave containing the coffin and body of the deceased. People were getting squashed. Kev and his two supporting riders had to back their horses onto grave site to prevent the crowd from getting any closer. There in the commotion, the singing and screaming of the crowd, Music tensed her haunches and in full view of the mourners, lifted her tail and pooped balls of steaming manure into the grave and onto the deceased Judge's expensive coffin splattering the ornate gold fittings and expensive timbers. The crowd gasped in horror at what had happened. The photographers with an eye for a good front page photo flashed their cameras. Yells of dismay and anguish came from the mourners. The choir stopped their voices in mid-stream, and as schoolgirls are wont to do, they began to titter and giggle. The choir master, overcome with nervousness, persisted in waving his stick but there was no response and his control was lost in a sea of young faces trying to gag their laughter. The Archbishop went pale, and began to stammer uncontrollably. The funeral broke up in bedlam as orderlies dropped into the grave to clean up the shitty mess. Kev quietly exited not wishing to make matters worse, and took the mare home.

highway to hell

Music seemed to enjoy her outing. When Kev took off her halter in her small paddock at the back of his house, he shook his finger disapprovingly at her. She looked at him for a minute, flung her head back defiantly, and galloped off around her paddock kicking up her heels as she went. Sometimes she could be a contrary mare. The next morning Kev went to get her. He was not ready for what he saw. She was lying still on her side. As he got close, he saw her eyes. They were still and glazed. She was dead. There were no suspicious signs as he looked her over. She had died during the night. He couldn't understand it; she seemed in high spirits after her mischievous antics the day before. Maybe it was her wound from Glenrowan. He knelt beside her for an hour. It hurt to lose the mare so soon but as he grieved, he conceived a plan to give the mare the burial she deserved and that Ned had requested. He sent a coded telegraph to Tom to say he would deliver the mare to Glenrowan and would be leaving by midday.

At work that morning, he had orders to see the manager.

'Sorry about what happened yesterday, but I thought the mare was ready. I'll have to be more careful in future.'

'You ain't telling me anything Kev. I've been expecting a visit from the Minister all morning. If you had not been such a good worker for the firm, you'd be walking Kev, walking right out the door... let me tell you.'

'I know, but I'll make up for it. I'll take that funeral carriage out today and drill the team for an hour or so...get them going real well, and then I'll personally check the other horses.'

Kev harnessed four of their fastest horses, and when nobody was looking put two bags of chaff and grain in the hearse, water containers, ice and left. He traveled quickly to his home, and with the help of his two children, they loaded her into the hearse and made her look comfortable. Kev poured alcohol and scents over Music and iced her up to preserve her for the long trip.

Kenny his son said, 'you sure you want to do this Dad. It doesn't make a lot of sense...you'll lose your job and get jailed for sure.'

'So be it,' said Kev, 'for years I've done what they tell me. Now I'm going to do what I think is right...country right, Boy ...not rules and regulations right...right for the mare and right for Kelly, and to hell with the consequences. I should get about half a day ahead before they get after me. Where I was born, kids, in Casterton, a man's word means a lot...not like here in the big smoke where you do what you're told just to keep a bloody job. I want you kids to remember that.'

'Yeah, yeah...we've heard it all before Dad ...don't say we didn't warn you,' said his teenage daughter, Bella.

'You won't make it to Glenrowan, Dad. The Police will run you down before you are half way there, and they are pretty gun crazy after that Kelly business. I'll get your rifle.'

'I don't need the gun, lad. Just some tea, a few cakes and my kangaroo, stock whip.'

'I'll get it for you Dad. You rest for a while. You're going to need all the energy you have to pull this off. It's a long way, and it will be as hot as hell now it is summer.'

Kev put his arms around his two kids, and playfully wrestled them about.

'I feel good, kids...the best I have felt for a long time.'

The Nation's papers that morning displayed the mare caught in the act. A radical left-wing paper headlined 'a grey mare pays her respects'. The Establishment was not amused and wanted explanations. That day Sarge saw the photograph in the paper. He let out a loud, belly laugh. Four Eyes became inquisitive.

'What's the joke?' he asked.

'Have a gander at this,' he said showing the picture to him. 'It never fails to amaze me what them bloody horses do,' he added shaking his head in disbelief.

Four Eyes studied the photo. He then went to the drawer and took out his magnifying glass.

'I didn't think you need them with your glass bottoms lad,' said Sarge.

'Hell,' exclaimed Four Eyes. 'Do you know whose horse that is?' he asked, his glasses fogging up with excitement of his discovery.

'Look at the horse's brand, Sarge...if I'm not mistaken it's 'E. K.'

It's Ned Kelly's mare. I'm sure of it.'

'Heaven forbid... I think you're right Cyril. If this gets out the Government will be the laughing stock of the Country. All hell will break loose. I'd better telegraph the Police Minister right away.'

When the telegraph reached the Police Minister, he rushed to the offices of Cobb and Co pushing past the receptionist and charging into the Manager's office.

'What sort of game are you playing at here? Do you know whose horse that is featured on the front page of the paper today?'

'Yes...it's one of Kev's.'

'That horse is Ned Kelly's mare ...the damned horse we've been looking for, and there she is... as big as life, crapping into the coffin of one of our most highly respected Supreme Court Judges... the very one who sent him down. The Government will be the laughing stock of the Country. It'll cost me my job.'

The Manager gulped.

'Where's this Kev fellow,' demanded the enraged Minister.

'I'll get him...he should be well back by now. He was upset by what happened yesterday, Minister, and was taking out the funeral hearse to drill the horses for the day.'

No sooner had he said it than an employee came to say that Kev had not returned, but one of the coaches coming back to Melbourne passed him going the other way. He didn't stop and they say he was going like the clappers as only Kev can. He said there was something large in the hearse...looked like a horse but he said that couldn't be right.'

'That's strange,' said the Manager.

'Strange be buggered. I'll wager he was heading for Glenrowan – them Irish have made that burnt out Pub a sacred site.'

'That's right...that's the road he was travelling, Sir,' said the employee nodding his head.

'Cobb and Co are going to pay for this...mark my words... you'll be lucky to get another government contract, and I'll see your license withdrawn if it's the last thing I do,' yelled the Minister.

He took off to the Premier's office. On the way he was told one of his men had visited Kev's house and made inquiries with the neighbors. He was told they saw Kev and his kids carry a dead horse into the hearse about mid-day, and leave quickly. He also heard the news that the rogue horse at the funeral was Kelly's mare had got to the public and the newspapers were going to headline it the next day. The Premier went pale, then red with anger.

'We'll never live this down. The public will see this as a victory for Kelly and we'll never be taken seriously again. I can't afford to lose face with the public. Credibility is everything in this business especially now with the election coming on. We must stop them from having this public exhibition of rebellion, and get that damned horse back at all costs.'

'It's a job for our special mounted unit Sir. You've heard of them I take it. We trained ten of the State's best horsemen and scoured the country for ten of the fastest thoroughbreds to mount them on. They have been in training for six months. We did it in response to the Kelly raids over the last two years. They are one tough, fast, well trained unit led by Steele Sir... he's the one that claimed he disarmed Kelly at Glenrowan. He had the best credentials for the job but is a little impetuous for my liking. They say he was about to shoot Kelly until Sarge stepped in.'

'Sarge, Sarge, that's the man who caught Harry. Telegraph him and see what's cooking up there.'

Sarge telegraphed back.

'Movement in Irish camp - heading to Glenrowan - rumor is there has been purchase of land back of burnt out hotel - will keep you informed.'

The Premier's hand shook as he reads the message.

'The Irish renegades are going to bury Kelly's mare at Glenrowan, right under our noses, for all the fucking world to see...it will ruin us. Get your Posse going and tell them it's a matter of life and death to stop that crazy Cobb and Co driver before he gets to Glenrowan. Put a warrant out for that mare, and one for the driver – habeas corpus, corpus Christi, or whatever the the fuckin lawyers call it. Shoot the bastard on sight if necessary ...he's an enemy of the State and so is the damned mare.... promise your men a year's salary if they stop him. Go now... you haven't a second to lose,' yelled the Premier pushing his Police Minister out the door.

'It's not corpus Christi, Mr. Premier, that's the body of Christ.'

'Whatever, and don't get smart with me or you be walking the beat again rather than toffing it in the expensive office of yours.'

The Police Minister beat a hasty retreat.

The Premier was a demanding man, gritty, pushy and self-made. His pushiness had got him elected to the top Office in the State. He tried to compensate for his lack of presence and education by an aggressive manner, and priding himself with a rude, intemperate language that he would often use when excited. It was, he claimed with certain smugness, the language the common people understood. It was not often that he took a backward step, and if he did, it was only to take two forward. The Premier went to his drinks cabinet and poured a stiff whisky which he tossed down his throat. Beads of perspiration dripped from his irascible face as he rummaged his pockets for a handkerchief to wipe his sweating brow. He was panicky, and for good reason. He knew better than most how fickle the vote of the public was, and that an event such as this, had repercussions well beyond stopping a dead horse from being buried at Glenrowan.

He cursed the name of Kelly.

He was street smart and knew more than others that silly events such as this captured the public's imagination, and where their imagination was, often their votes went too. He didn't have to spell it out...if they didn't stop the hearse, they were finished. He threw his glass against the office wall smashing it into pieces and banged his fists on his desk. His secretary opened the door. She was well endowed.

'Anything the matter, Sir?' she enquired.

'Yeah, some fucker from Cobb and Co is about to break my heart unless I can get the mounted police to stop him before he reaches Glenrowan.'

'Those Kelly problems again...I told you it would not end with his hanging, Mr. Premier...all you did is make him a martyr.'

'Get the fuck out of here before I explode...you stupid woman, Pamela. I want all telegrams delivered immediately to me...do you hear... and not in double Dutch, dots either.... get me an interpreter, so I can understand the bloody things.'

And then he added, 'before I forget, Big Tits, make sure the coppers get that corpus Christi order. I sure as hell don't want to be sued by them bog Irish. Or look up that law passed back in Ireland about two hundred years ago- I am sure our man Barrington, the beak, could make something of that.'

I've got it here Premier. I looked it up when we were thinking of taking the horses off the Kelly sympathizers. It's called a penal law.

'Read it out to me, Big Tits.'

'Pam, if you don't mind.' she said.

'Get on with it... I pay your salary... I'll call you what name I want.'

'Sect 10 Penal Laws - no papist shall be capable of having or keeping for his use, any horse, gelding or mare of five pounds value. any protestant who shall make discovery under oath of such horse shall be authorized with the assistance of a constable, to search for and secure such horse and in the case of resistance to break down any door. and any protestant making such discovery and offering five pounds five shillings to the owner of such horse in the presence of a justice of the peace or chief magistrate shall receive ownership of such horse as though such horse were bought in the market overt.'

'Well, what a beautiful piece of drafting that is... couldn't do better myself... get it delivered to Barrington and tell him I want to use it to get that damned Cobb and Co driver from Casterton arrested and the Kelly's horse impounded.'

'You are forgetting Premier ...he died couple of days ago...you were there for funeral'

'So I was. I am getting a bit rattled with all this, Pam. Get it to his deputy Judge then. Tell him if he wants the top job, he'd better git this done right without the usual shit we have to put up with them know all fuckers. If he tells me it is repealed, tell him to repeal it back again, or go peel his banana for the top job.'

'And is Kev a papist?' asked Pam

'What Kavanagh - he comes from that potato growing country, Casterton...is the Pope a catholic...don't ask me silly questions, Big Tits.'

Desperado

Stonewall Jackson's death

During his last three days, Jackson was often nauseous and in pain; he drifted between periods of lucidity and delirium. On May 10, Dr. McGuire informed Anna Jackson that her husband would die within a few hours. She brought him the news herself. "Very good," he said, "very good. It is all right." Anna sent for their daughter, Julia, so Jackson could kiss the baby good-bye, then she took a seat in a chair beside her husband's bed and waited for the end. It came at about 3:30 in the afternoon. In a clear voice Jackson said, "Let us cross over the river, and rest under the shade of the trees." A few moments later, Stonewall Jackson was dead. In the American civil war T.J. Craughwell

Kev looked straight ahead avoiding the curious stares as the fancy, funeral hearse sped along the dusty, country roads and through the small villages carrying the body of Ned's grey mare. Years of coach driving had taught him how to save his horses and still cover distance. He slowed for the steep inclines, rolled down the gentler hills in a smooth effortless canter, and just now and then a ground covering gallop on the flat all the time trying to keep their breathing steady and relaxed. There was long way to go to reach Glenrowan, and he expected there may be efforts by State to apprehend him before he delivered Music to the Kelly supporters.

That evening he rested on a hill with a small stream below. He took the harness off the four horses and led them to the water two at a time. It was one of those warm summer's evenings, deathly still with no hint of a breeze. With the moonlight reflecting off the silvery stream, he stripped down to his underclothes, grabbed his sponge and washed the dirt clogged sweat and soreness from the tired limbs of his horses. He toweled them dry and felt down the back of their cannon bone for any swelling or inflammation in the tendons and ligaments. He felt a slight swelling in the near foreleg of one of the front horses which he packed with mud like a poultice hoping it would subside by the morning. The horse was not lame but he feared the long stretch of road ahead of them would test any weaknesses to the limit. He let them roll in a sandy patch by the stream before tying them to a rope line strung between two trees. When the horses were done, he fed them grain mixed with a little sunflower oil to bolster their energy reserves for the hard miles ahead. He always enjoyed watching them eat. Their appetite told him they were well. He thought he may have about half a day's break on his pursuers and he would not rest any more than absolutely necessary. He intended to leave before daybreak to make the most of the cool, morning hours and slow down during the heat of the day. He expected to make Glenrowan late that afternoon if he were not overtaken by the Police. He made a small camp fire, boiled up a billy, and made some tea. He climbed back onto the carriage where he sat drinking his tea and eating his rock cake. He watched the sun setting low on the horizon and for the first time in many years he felt free; free of his work; free of the smoke ridden grimy city; and free of the matchbox homes and industrial grime of a big city. He was born a country boy and it was to the country that he wanted to return. He didn't like the smell of sewerage that hung about the streets, the cramped, small cottages or the smog that polluted the air. Out here in the expanse of bush he breathed easily and his mind rested. He knew that his escapade would cost him his job, possibly imprisonment, but he wanted to change. He looked through the etched glass and saw the mare wrapped in ice and serenely still in the half light of the full moon. 'I hope we can make it to Glenrowan, Music,' he said as he tapped on the glass window. He took up the smooth handle of his bull whip beside him and lazily flicked his wrist coiling the leather thong in circles about him and let go one thunderous crack that echoed through the bush gullies and startled the bird life and horses.

He had in his time with stock and horses become expert in the use of short handled bull whip that he now lovingly fingered in his palm. The whip was made of braided kangaroo hide that extended elegantly over the twelve-inch handle, and had a beautiful feel and balance. It was used not for punishment but to guide, direct and encourage the horses when young and headstrong, and the length meant he could reach the front horses of eight horse team sometimes pulling a coach carrying over eighty passengers and their luggage. With his work done for the day and the horses settled, he stretched out on top of the hearse, pulled a blanket over him and slept. As Kev slumbered, little did he know that the specially trained and equipped mounted Police Posse were riding hard through the night to get to him and the mare.

Their commander Steele had a point to prove. Witnesses doubted his evidence of valor at Glenrowan, and he was determined to show them he had the courage and strength to run down this escapee, and put a stop to this Kelly business once and for all. He rode at the front of his men urging them on and not worrying about the dark. They could see an outline of the road in front but it turned black when trees blocked the moon light. A horse tripped in a hole throwing its rider and dislocating his shoulder. Steele ordered that he be left while they galloped on. Another horse stumbled on a exposed tree root and went down. The rider was not hurt but his horse was lame. He too was left. One of the men objected and warned that their horses could not sustain the mad, frenetic pace. Steele pulled his colt revolver, and thrust it to his head.

'Is it a mutiny that you are thinking of, Bronson?'

'No sir...it's just that I think we could go quicker if we look after our horses. Begging your pardon Sir but I reckon we'll run their legs off at this rate...run them to a standstill.'

Putting his colt back in his holster Steele yelled,

'I'm not interested in your opinion, Bronson. You should know better. This misguided fool Kavanagh has the break on us. He expects to be in Glenrowan late tomorrow. We don't have the luxury of taking our time like some Sunday picnic. If he gets Kelly's mare there before we catch him, me, you, and the rest of us will be looking for another job and so will the Government from what I've been told. Kelly and his Gang have made the Police look fools over the last two years because they were too smart and outran us. Hear that Bronson... outran... outrun... outran. In case you don't know Bronson that means go faster. That is why the Minister formed our special mounted horse unit, gave us good thoroughbred horses and put me in charge... so that we could get back some of our pride and chase down these criminals. Restore some dignity and authority to the Government rather than the ridicule we have been copping from the public. And you...you want us to toss in the towel and go slow... not me matey... I don't know about you, but I happen to like my job and what I'm paid, and I'll be buggered if these horses we're riding now, some half-witted Cobb and Co driver, and a dead mare are goin to take it from me.' With his tirade, Steele effectively silenced the officer and any others tempted to support him, and they rode on.

Kev woke well before dawn and in the dimmed light of the camp fire gathered and harnessed the team. It was a ninety-mile dash to his destination with one large town to go through. He was hoping he could pass through unnoticed. The horses moved along briskly in the cool of the morning and refreshed after their short rest. Kev watched the leading horse for signs of soreness and thought that there was something worrying him but he appeared to work out of it. His mind was put at ease by a passing rider who told him the news of his run had filtered from the assembling crowds at Glenrowan to the neighboring towns, and that people were abuzz with interest and excitement. He said the local Police would not interfere because the mare had captured the people's imagination and sympathy, and they did not wish to risk open rebellion. He said it would be left to Steele and his men from the city to carry out the orders of the Minister and a telegram confirmed they were making good time and expected to apprehend him and the mare before the last town. Unfortunately for both Kev and Steele and their horses, the coolness of the morning gave way to a hot, Australian summer day. There was not a cloud in the sky and the sun's rays burnt into his arms and face, reddening his skin, and a wet perspiration soaked his shirt. His horses were slowing, and he could see the sweat glistening off their coats. Kev knew from experience that a horse would drive out the accumulating heat in his body by sweating but that in losing sweat it was losing vital body water and salts, and that could lead to a multitude of serious if not fatal problems. He stopped in the shade of some large, gum trees by a dam and bucketed water over the horses and gave them a drink. They drank greedily draining the bucket. He was only about two miles from the last town and knew that the Police, with no load to pull, would be closing in on him. He left apprehensive about entering the town.

Steele and his men were closing the gap but it was at the expense of their horses. Stopping at the same dam Steele saw the wheel marks of the hearse in the dirt, and noticed the soil was still damp where Kev's horses were washed and watered. They undid their American Army McClelland saddles and washed their tired mounts trying to refresh them. Steele knew the hearse was now within his grasp but the exhaustion and slowing pace of his horses made him irritable. If his horses gave up the ghost Kavanagh might just make it to Glenrowan. He ordered his men to run beside their horses before remounting… he had heard this is what Kelly did. The horses had to be pulled and did not run easily. He ordered his men to remount, and they kicked and spurred their flagging horses on towards the town.

'That hearse can only be minutes in front at the most. I'm sure we'll catch him before Glenrowan if they don't stop him in the town,' said Steele trying to encourage his men.

When Kev saw the town come into view, he thought he could hear a commotion coming from the main street. He passed a few riders coming the other way who waved madly at him but he kept on, paying little attention. As he turned his horses into the main street, he stood and urged them on hoping to push past anyone who wanted to stop them. To his surprise he saw the street lined with cheering, waving people who urged him on and threw flowers covering the roof of the hearse and the road behind him as he passed. The story of the mare and what she did at Glenrowan and the unpopular Judge's funeral excited their passions, much as the Kelly case had done, and they wanted her to be buried at Glenrowan. They resented the unfair treatment Kelly received at the hands of the Police and Judiciary, the way the State had refused to hand his body over and had it butchered by pimply faced medical students. The country folk especially wanted to balance the books and see that the underdog had a fair go. If they would not grant Ned a decent burial, then they would do their best to see that his mare had one. Kev stood upright in his seat, driving the horses on and gratefully acknowledging the support of the crowds who yelled their encouragement. Their generous spontaneity moved him to tears and he hoped he would not let them down. For a split second he thought he saw two familiar faces in the crowd. A rider raced his horse level to the hearse and yelled,

'the Traps are only about two miles behind Kev …you will have to go like the blazes to get to Glenrowan before they overtake you. They armed to the teeth and will shoot on sight. We will do our best to hold them when they get here, but I don't think we will be able to hold them for long.'

Kev shouted his appreciation and fisted the air, and the hearse rattled on down that road to the distant roar of its supporters back in the town. This deadly contest was going to take every bit of experience Kev had learnt in his many years to avoid being caught by the rapidly gaining Posse who now had the town in its sights. Steele thought for a moment when he saw the vast throng of people lining the street that they had already captured the hearse, but as they got closer, the loudening boos and hisses from the angry crowds told him a much different story. His men were jumpy. He told them to be calm as they tried to exit the town. Suddenly in front of them two carts came from nowhere blocking the way ahead. They wheeled their horses around and sped back looking for a side street but there too their retreat was blocked. The people shouted and booed. Then from the roofs of the shops and the street came flour bombs and eggs splattering their dusty, blue uniforms in ugly smears of white and dripping egg yolk. Steele pulled his revolver and fired several shots into the air while ordering his men to dismount and push the carts out of their way. They eventually managed to move the blockage, but the exercise cost them valuable time. They raced on but it was clear that their horses would not sustain the pace any longer without serious injury. A couple of the horses were panting rapidly, and their action dropped to a stumbling, stiff gait telling their riders they couldn't go on.

Steele stopped his men. He decided he would risk his horse, and gallop ahead in the hope that he could overtake the hearse before it reached Glenrowan. If they all went with him they would risk losing too many men, and every man would be needed if there were a confrontation with the sympathizers. His men were to wait and proceed at a walk until their horses sufficiently rested to go on. It didn't worry Steele about his horse. He would catch the hearse, or the exhausted animal could die in the attempt. If he could only get within firing range, he was sure he could stop them. He took a spare ammunition belt and reloaded his colt revolver. He then ripped into the poor animal's hide with his sharp spurs and galloped down the road waving his silver hand piece wildly in the air.

Little did he know that Kev had stopped along the track. His leading horse went lame on the suspect leg, and was unable to go further. Another horse was showing signs of heat exhaustion. He unhitched both and attended to them. The scrub bordered the road, and he led them into the shade. He poured some water into a bucket for them to drink. He was broken hearted, but he would not risk the two horses any more, and the coach was too heavy for the remaining two weakened horses to pull by themselves. He had no hope of making Glenrowan, and would await the coming of the Police, and his inevitable arrest. He sat down on a log and buried his head in his hands. He heard horses approaching.

He could not bear to look. The horses came closer.

A voice said, 'Need a hand, Pop?'

He looked up. There in front of him were his two kids, Bella and Kenny on their horses. He was elated to see them.

Kenny said, 'we thought about what you said Dad... you know about keeping your word and all that. We are family, Dad. We decided to follow you to Glenrowan in case you needed help. We kept just out of sight thinking you would send us home. You sure got one hell of a welcome back there. Did you see us?'

'Stone the crows...I did too. But look, kids, this is too dangerous for you to get into but I have to admit your timing is pretty good. We don't have a second to spare...help me harness up your two horses…they look in good nick. We might still make it to Glenrowan… God willing.'

They hurriedly harnessed the two horses, and scrambled aboard. Just as they were leaving, Bella looked back and saw a speck in the distance rapidly gaining on them. As the figure got closer, they could make out a blue uniform and something glinting from his hand being waved madly about.

'It's a gun,' said Kenny 'I said you should have brought your rifle, Dad.'

'He won't shoot,' said their Dad looking for more speed from his team.

He was wrong. A bullet smashed into the rear plate glass fracturing the pane into a hundred broken pieces.

'Kids…lie flat on the roof behind the metal boxes…I might be able to outrun him. His horse looks pretty tired.'

Steele pulled out his carbine and a fusillade of bullets splintered into the ornate woodwork of the hearse. Kev's two kids were frightened. The rider was now getting close to the coach. They could hear his lunatic abuse. He threw away his rifle and pulled out his colt. He aimed it at Kev and fired. The bullet seared through Kev's left shoulder snapping the ligaments so that it hung helplessly at his side. For a second, he didn't feel anything but then pain like a red-hot poker flushed through his body, and he began to bleed.

The children cried, 'Stop Dad… you're hit… stop before he shoots again.'

'Don't move, kids,' said Kev 'I'll get the mongrel yet given half a chance.'

He slumped and let the reins drop. The horses slowed and Steele drew close. His horse was a mass of thick, sticky foam and blood oozing from its heaving flanks where Steele's spurs had dug and ripped at its flesh. A shallow rasping came from deep within its throat like a death rattle. A murderous grin covered the rider's face when he saw he had winged the driver. He was slumped over and he could just make out the outline of his head as he came alongside the coach and took aim for the second and he hoped final time.

'Stay dead still,' Kev whispered to his children, 'and keep low.'

Suddenly a long, lethal, leather braid, heavy and well oiled, snaked out at Steele, coiling around his neck like an anaconda, yanking him abruptly from his saddle, dragging him along the dirt track as the horses moved slowly forward. Kev's whip choked the slow, cold beat of his mean, authoritarian heart. The hearse stopped and Kev let go the whip he held in his right hand. Steele's horse stood there heaving, on the brink of complete body meltdown and terminal collapse. It was thumping loudly and rapidly. It staggered a few steps, let out a muffled anguished cry and fell awkwardly to the ground. Kev looked at the distressed animal. He was an honest gelding who had kept going where the others had stopped, who had given his best, and he was moved by pity for its plight. He threw down his canvas water bag and towel, and with his good arm struggled off the hearse. He walked to Steele lying face down on the dusty road with the leather braided whip wrapped tightly around his neck. He was a dead. He stepped over Steele's lifeless body to his suffering horse, gasping for air and muscular tremors wracking it's sweat soaked frame. In the gelding's staring eyes, he saw the unmistakable pain of its struggle to survive. He and the children helped the horse to its feet, undid the girth taking off the saddle and bridle. They set about cooling the distressed horse with what water they had left. They rubbed him down with towels and used some of the melting ice from the hearse to cool its overheated body. The horse was steaming but slowly began to show signs of improvement. They led it to the shade of the scrub, and waved wet towels fanning a cool breeze over its exhausted frame. Kev gave a sigh of relief when he saw the gelding begin to taste the water and drink but he was badly wounded. He said to his kids it was time to go before Steele's men arrived. The children help bandage their dad's shoulder.

'It don't look good, Dad...you've lost a lot of blood.'

'I would like to rest in the shade somewhere, kids...I feel crook, real crook,' he said 'but we are not far from Glenrowan now...and I have given my word to Ned which I will keep while there is breath in my body.'

They helped him back onto the hearse, and together with young Kenny driving and Bella holding her wounded Dad, they rolled into Glenrowan, past the ashes of the burnt-out hotel, and down into the open meadow where there were at least two to three thousand welcoming men, women and children gathered by a large grave site that had been recently dug. The ecstatic, cheering crowd looked up and saw the hearse stream down the hill. Kev whispered to his kids,

'get the whip, son, and crack it loud like a real stockman from Casterton...that will make me a proud man.'

The young lad grabbed his dad's whip, stood up on the hearse as it rolled towards the grave site, and let go with volley of loud cracks that echoed around the hills and brought the crowd alive. They couldn't contain themselves and ran wildly to the hearse holding onto the sides and clambering onto the ramps. It was a scene that moved you to tears. The mare had come back home, and with her the spirit of a Ned Kelly. Now they could give them both a decent burial. As the hearse slowed, the crowd parted and Kenny drove a narrow path to the large grave. It came to a halt, and the people closed protectively about them. They saw that Kev was wounded and carried him from the hearse laying him down on soft blankets.

'Billy, go for the doctor will you whilst we attend him. He doesn't look too good,' said Tom. 'You relax Kev...and leave the rest to us...we'll get a doctor to you. God bless you and your courageous children for what you have done for us.'

Several men brought a large timber box held by strong ropes. The mare was slipped into the coffin and carried to the gravesite and their faithful, worn out, alcoholic Priest dressed in his best church gear with big silver crucifix hanging around his neck.

Back along the road, the Police came upon their commander Steele dead on the road.

'There is no bullet wound,' one said.

'There looks like bruising around his neck...maybe his horse fell and he broke his neck...his horse sure looks rooted and probably collapsed under him. They carried him to the side of the road and placed a sheet over him.'

'By the look of the footprints and glass, there has been a bit of a showdown here,' added Bronson now in command. They rode on, now preparing for the worst. At Glenrowan, they met up with about thirty Police who had just arrived from the nearby town to control the gathering crowds.

'There's going to be trouble a plenty,' said Bronson. 'We have a body back along the track.'

The Police prepared their rifles, and rode cautiously into Glenrowan and to the top of the hill overlooking the meadow below where a burial was about to begin. There they saw, crowds massed around a freshly dug hole in the ground. They also saw to their dismay the hearse.

'That Cobb and Co driver from Casterton has beaten us,' said Bronson.

spirit of a horse
Thus the conversation continued for two hours. Young Carson modestly suggested that it would be better if the Spaniards were less cruel in breaking in their horses. "Your horses," said he, "would make excellent buffalo hunters with proper training. I have some horses at camp, that I intend shall see buffalo. But why do you not deal gently with them when they are first caught? You might thus preserve all the spirit they have in the herd. Pardon me, but I think that in taming your horses you break their spirits." "I sometimes think so too," the Spanish gentleman replied. Kit Carson, The Pioneer of the West by John Abbott.

Branson tied a white handkerchief on his rifle, and walked his horse down to speak to them. Tom made his way through the crowd. Bronson said,

'I have a warrant for the return of the hearse and to take possession of Kelly's grey mare. I also want a Mr. Kevin Kavanagh for questioning about larceny of the hearse and possible murder.'

Tom replied, 'I'll not be releasing the mare or Kavanagh to you, Officer. The mare is ours. You might not understand this but we see this mare as one of us the same as Kev. Steele has attacked and wounded Kavanagh who was doing no more than delivering the mare to us, and he defended himself with his whip. I have sent for the doctor. His condition is not good, but you will only take him over our dead bodies.'

'You leave me little choice. I had hoped to avoid a confrontation but I have my orders. I will allow you ten minutes to hand him over and the mare. After that I take no responsibility.'

'For God's sake man, leave us in peace. There are women and children here. We do not carry guns and have to come to a peaceful funeral hoping not to be disturbed. You can take the hearse...that is all.'

'You have heard the last of what I have to say. I remind you ten minutes is all that I will allow,' and he swung his horse around and trotted back up the hill.

Back in the city, the Police Minister and his Premier heard the news of the public's reaction to the Police. Sarge had sent a telegraph warning of the worsening mood, the gathering of many of the sympathizers at Glenrowan, and the possibility of a civil uprising. 'It's got out of hand,' the Premier said, 'now that Kavanagh has beaten us to Glenrowan, it is probably better to let the show go ahead than risk open rebellion. I will telegraph Sarge, who has some influence up there, to ride to Glenrowan and order our men to withdraw. I hope it is not too late. You can also say that the Government will investigate, with an independent inquiry, the grievances and complaints of the selectors and Kelly sympathizers including police harassment and land grants.'

The telegram was sent.

Sarge was pacing his office when the telegram arrived.

'Some common sense at last,' he said to his clerk flourishing the telegram in front of him. 'I'm going to leave immediately. There is not a minute to lose before this whole affair explodes in our faces.'

'I'll come too,' said his clerk. 'I missed out on the siege sitting in the office here doing bookwork and I don't want to miss out on this.'

The two left the town in a hurry. They had about ten miles to ride to Glenrowan.

Sarge soon left his floundering clerk far behind. The big, cold blooded mare had a stubborn, contented look on her face refusing to break into a canter. She rightly thought the trot was more suited to her bulk and the futile attempts of the red-faced clerk to get her to canter was no more trouble to her thick, leathery hide than that of a bot fly.

'That's a relief,' said Sarge as he saw the two fade into the distance behind him. 'It would be bloody embarrassin to be seen with Cyril and his big clomper.'

The old fella fairly flew along the road to Glenrowan. Sarge rode on, past the hotel ruins, and up to the hill. On top of the hill, Sarge saw the Police descending the hill with their carbines leveled at the crowd. The women and children had separated leaving the men tightly surrounding Kev and his mare. He spurred his horse and raced between the two groups yelling,

'stop, stop...on the orders of the Premier,' and waving the telegram above his head. 'The Premier has ordered that you withdraw... there are to be no arrests, and to allow the funeral to proceed.'

Tom came out from his men to read the telegram with Bronson. Both looked relieved. Bronson knew his men had little heart for the fight. He had instructed them to fire over their heads in the hope that it may disperse the crowd. After that he wasn't sure what was going to happen. A distant echo of a horse approaching interrupted their conversation. The crowd turned as one and saw a large, ponderous, horse with feathery hocks descending on them like a charging elephant. As it neared, it broke into a lumbering canter much to the excitement of its bespectacled rider.

'Sarge...I told you I could canter,' yelled Cyril excitedly barely able to restrain himself. The huge, stubborn animal came to a jarring halt, recognizing its mate in Sarge's horse, and flinging its rider out of the saddle and spread-eagled onto its neck. There, for what seemed an eternity, he slowly rotated, still holding on, but now looking at the sky with his spindly legs awkwardly clamped around the big horse's withers. Sarge felt an acute embarrassment at the spectacle unfolding in front of him and watched with amusement by both the troopers and mourners alike. Despite the solemnity of the occasion, the spectators began to convulse with laughter.

'Let go, you stupid boy, let go,' demanded Sarge.

The clerk slowly released his leg grip and slipped to the ground.

He saw Sarge coming for him.

He quickly pulled himself up, dusted his coat, snapped his feet to attention and saluted. The unintentional comedy visibly eased the tension between the two groups. Tom invited Sarge, Bronson and his men to join them.

'I hope you can see your way clear to give a little time for this mare...no matter what side you're on. We would be honored to have you join us...let the mare bring us together in a way that our politicians have failed to do. We used to get on. Then he looked directly at Sarge and Bronson and said,

'Can we have fairness and justice in the administration of the States laws?'

Bronson looked at Sarge.

Sarge nodded, and replied 'I cannot see why not, Tom. I have the assurance of the Premier there will be an inquiry into the Courts and Police. We need your cooperation to make things better.'

There were no political speeches, no sermons. Only a slip of a girl dressed in black with a lace shawl covering her head, Grace Kelly, came forward and sang her song. A song taught to her by a Ole Southern General, Virgil, and one which she had and kept locked in her heart until the time had come. Now she knew it had. The child was blessed with a exquisite voice. In a reedy, delicate voice she sang 'Danny boy', a poignant and moving song of sad memories, of lost and gone away love, of the grave, death and a loved one's return. Its tender, bitter sweet melodies drifted and warbled out across the meadow to the Strathbogie Ranges, and into the hearts of the people gathered there so that their tears flowed freely for the loss of an uncommon mare and the young man who rode her and the insanity of violence by one to another. The voices of the Police along with the sympathizers could be heard on the higher notes of that revered and holy song,

'but come ye back when summers in the meadow....'

Kev woke and looked up from his bed. He saw legions of angels descending from heaven, and roosting in the spreading branches of the nearby gums. One was beckoning him to come. He saw a wedge tailed eagle spiraling high above in the sky.

'Look,' he said to Bella, 'they've come for me and the mare,' pointing with his one good arm to the nearby gums.

'He's delirious,' his boy said.

Grace looked out at the large, spreading gums. She saw what Kev saw. What the Ole Southern General said was true. The angels did desert their posts in the heavens and descend to earth to hear her song. She waved to them in the trees, and they smiled, flapped their snow-white wings, and waved back. Enthused by her heavenly audience, the child drew deeply into her lungs, and her voice, so sweet and tender, rose clear and strong above the crowd to the highest branches of the surrounding gums so that the angels and those rooted to the earth wept openly and unashamedly in that little valley behind the blackened remains of the now infamous Glenrowan pub.

Kev's two kids held him as he lapsed back into unconsciousness. His mind was dreaming, taking him far away to a strange land. He was riding in a weird almost fairytale landscape on Music, and the road led up into the sky. The mare was singing, and she floated, her hooves not touching the ground. He could see that her coat was changing color from gray to chestnut, to bay, to black, to dun, to piebald, to skewbald and finally to appaloosa colorings, to all the wonderful colors of the horses that inhabited the earth as she shimmied along her ascending path. He then saw a hotel, up ahead, lit up with the brightest lamps he had ever seen. The sign out the front said 'the half way pub' and he could hear much celebration going on inside. As he got near, he saw a bushman come flying out backwards through the swinging doors landing heavily on his rump. He stood up and began to swear and shake his fist at those inside, but on hearing the horse approach, stopped, shielded his eyes with his hand and studied them intently.

A look of fond recognition and joy beamed over his face as he rushed to and hugged them

'My mare...Kev...I've been waiting for you two a long time, drinking in this half way pub...seeing you two I feel as if I have come home. Have you got room for me?

'There's room for two,' said Kev and hoisted Ned up behind him.

'Had enough back there?' asked Ned.

'I wouldn't have minded a bit more,' said Kev.

'Yeah... same with me,' said Ned, 'you me and the boys -we were not much more than children Kev and they took us away.'

'Do you think we will make it to Paradise, Ned?' asked Kev.

'You are about to find out mate...what I do know is that we wouldn't have a chance if we were not mounted on this mare. But before we go I have some friends behind the pub I would like you to meet'. Kev dismounted and they walked to the rear of the noisy hotel. There much to his amazement was six persons mounted and ready. Joe, Dan, Steve and Tennessee. The remaining two were young girls-one Chinese and dressed and painted like Indian brave-Gong and the other with black hair combed in a bouffant style, and her nose in a book-Val.

'I have heard about you lot but not met you,' and Kev went to each shaking their hand and giving Val and Gong a hug.

'My Gang has grown,' said Ned 'Roy is here but he has to wait for another year before he can enter and I think that is fair enough- hasn't stopped him trying to make a dollar in the pub though. Now we have a long and difficult ride ahead of us. I have heard there is some debate as to whether we can enter Paradise. So, we are going in together or none at all. That's the way it is. I am going to ride double with Kev on Music – he can steer and I am going to need my hands free,' he said as he holstered a silver colt 44.

The Gang took off at an easy canter with Music leading the way. Val put her book in her saddle bag and concentrated on her riding. The landscape was amazing. In the beginning they were riding through country like the Wombat Ranges-scrub, creeks, rivers with cockatoos in the gums and kangaroos grazing in the clearings. They rode silently through camps Aboriginal camps with their humpy's, American Indian camps with their tepees and finally a Chinese mining camp. The inhabitants were going about their daily activities. as they silently passed but the people did not look or the dogs bark. It was as though they were invisible. Ned told them not to talk or wave. They were to continue on. They eventually came to a fork in the road. One sign said 'highway to 'hell', purgatory was where they had come from and behind them and the third said 'Paradise but present identification'.

'Which way?' said Kev.

'Let the mare choose...she knows best,' said Ned.

She put her nose to the ground and sniffed as she ran.

She took the road leading them to hell. The two riders stiffened in the saddle. The mare sniffed the ground again, did a roll back that nearly unseated her two passengers, and then veered off cutting over to the road to Paradise.

She gave deep laugh much like the hew-haw of a donkey.

Kev gave a sigh of relief.

Ned laughed.

'She was always the joker,' he said as he gave her a friendly whack on the rump. 'I think she picked up her mum's trail going to hell for doin in the Old Man.'

Listen Gang...they want identification. and I'm not sure that our names are on the good book. I've got my colt revolver with me. We'll crash them big gates and give St Peter a bit of a hurry up. It seems a pity to waste all the experience we gained down there on Earth, don't you reckon?'

'We are with you, Ned, ride on.'

The mare's stride lengthened and she sped up the hill towards the big, pearly gates. The road was lined with beds of brightly colored roses of every conceivable color, even blue, sun flowers and yellow corn ripening on the husk. The others braced, rose in their stirrups and began to whoop and yell.

Ned spun the chamber of his silver colt checking that it was loaded.

They could make out an elderly man standing in the middle of the road with one hand holding a large book, a halo over his head, and holding up his other hand to show he wanted them to stop.

'Duck your head a bit, Kev,' said Ned as he took aim and fired off three shots.

One split the halo over St Peter's head, and the other two burst the padlocks on the large gates so that they slowly swung open revealing a bright, incandescent light. St Peter dropped his book, gathered up his white robes, and bolted for cover. Ned bent over as they passed, scooped up his book and began scribbling in the names.

'Gun her for the gates Kevy boy...by the time we get through I will have scribbled our names in and nobody will know any different.'

'I think we are supposed to knock on the big door - you sure are a larrikin Ned. - that fat turd Barrington was right about you.'

'No knockin Kev - this is a break and enter – and them big Gates are slowly closing.'

The gallant, little mare flattened her ears, and sped towards the narrowing opening.

Ned whooped.

'Kev gave a loud yeee – haaa and said

'This mare sure has some spirit, Ned.'

'You did a great job breaking her in, Kev,' Ned yelled.

'Give me half a chance, and you and your Gang won't catch me a second time,' said Kev.

Ned wrapped his arms around Kev, Kev clamped onto the mare's neck, and the rest of the Gang held hands as they galloped at breakneck speed to the Pearly Gates of Paradise shielding their eyes from the brilliant, eternal light. As you might expect, Val fell from her horse. Gong skidded Panda to a stop, spun around and accelerated to her. She pulled her on behind and together they went hell for leather to the small opening just entering before it closed shut to the welcoming shouts and arms of their dear friends.

In the Glenrowan valley where the people had congregated, Kev stirred, half raised himself and opened his eyes.

'Yeee - haaa,' he said in faltering voice, and fell back dead still. Those were his last words.

His children held him tight as he galloped headlong into another world with his Gang. They buried him with the Glenrowan mare. And in the mare was the spirit of Ned Kelly.

Bibliography

I am indebted to all the following books, novels and newspaper articles which have in informed, enlightened, amused and entertained me in the writing of this story.

A Short Life - Ian Jones

The Kelly Gang unmasked - Ian Macfarlane

Glenrowan - Ian Shaw

Ned Kelly - Keith McMenomy

Ned Kelly - Peter Fitzsimmons

Ned and the Others - D Balcarek and G Dean

Ned Kelly - Ian Jones

The trial of Ned Kelly - John H Phillips

Custerology - Michael A. Elliott

Life amongst the Apaches - J C Cremony

Ride the Wind - Lucia St Clair Robson

The Story of the Pony Express - Glenn Danford

Derek Deane - Ballet talking about English ballerinas - Australian newspaper

'Co. Aytch' - Maury Grays, First Tennessee Regiment

Jack Hinson's one-man war - Tom C. McKenney

Texas Cowboys - Memories of the Early Days - James Lanning and Judy Lanning

Irish Brigade in the American Civil War Thomas J. Craughwell

Wild ride – Sam Everingham

Six Years with the Texas Rangers - James B. Gillet

Ned Kelly-Extracts from the Argus - William Kerr

American Indians - Frederick Starr

Why the Irish Hate the English - Jonathan Madden

'500 Nations' - Alvin M Josephy Jnr

'Fools Crow' - T Mails

Australia, its history and present condition - William Pridden

The American West – Dee Brown

Famine to Freedom - The Irish in the American Civil War J.J. Collins

Genghis Khan – Michael Hoang

The Age Saturday October 10th 2009

Nine Years among the Indians - Herman Lehmann

With Lee in Virginia-A Story of the American Civil War - G. A. Henty

Comanches - Wallace and Hoebel University of Oklahoma Press

Argus Newspaper 26th May 1859

The 'Sojourners' by Eric Rolls U.Q.P.

'Our Antipodes' - Lieutenant Colonel Mundy

'An interview with Harry Power' - by James Stanley the Argus and the Age

The American West – Dee Brown pg 193-
Life among the Apaches - J. C. Cremony
William Cody – Buffalo Bill 1859
My life as an Indian – J.W. Schultz
Sir Henry Irving 'The American West' - Dee Brown
Major Lemly on Crazy Horse's death
The Comanches-Lords of the South Plains - by E Wallace and E Hoebe
'Lame deer – Seeker of visions' - by John Fire and Richard Erdoes,
Down all the days - Christy Brown
The Making of Ireland - James Lydon
War Years with JEB Stuart - Lieutenant Colonel Blackford
The Texas Rangers - WP Webb
The West - John Lewis
The Native American Warrior - Chris Mc Nab
The Custer Companion - Thom Hatch
Warrior and Pioneers - TJ Stiles
Long Death - R.K. Andrist
Captured by the Indians - Frederick Drimmer
Son of the Morning Star - Evan Connell
Crazy Horse and Custer - S.E. Ambrose
Sharpshooting in the Civil War - Major John Plaster
Kublai Khan - John Man
Comanches - T R Fehrenbach
Marching to Valhalla - Michael Blake
I rode with JEB Stuart - Major Henry B McClellan
Killing Custer - James Welch
North American Indians - Lewis Spence
Civil War Book - Berry Benson
Battles and Leaders of the Civil War - Ned Bradford
The Life of Johnny Reb - Bell Irvin Wiley
When the sky fell down - Keith Willey
Captain Rock - James S Donnelly
Mosby's Rangers - J D Wert
History of Australian Gold Rushes - Nancy Keesing
The Gold Rush - David Hill
Life among the Indians - George Catlin
The Hempen Collar - executions in S.A. 1838-1964 D Towler T Porter
Confederates in the Attic - Tony Horwitz
I fought with Custer - F and R Hunt
My Life as an Indian - J.W. Schultz

with Custer on the little Bighorn - William O Taylor
The Great Wall - Julia Lovell
The Penguin book of the Horse - Candida Baker
True Grit - Charles Portis
History of the Indians of the United States - Angie Debo
Irish Penal Laws - Queen Elizabeth 1 of England
Indian child life - CA Eastman
The American Indian in early US history E Eggleston
Traditions of the North American Indian vol 1,2,3 - W.J. Jones
The Siouan Indians - W J McGee
The soul of the Indian- Charles Eastman
Old Indian days - Charles Eastman
Native American tribes - Charles River Editors
Indian frontier policy - John Miller
Across the plains in 1844 - Catherine Sager
The Battle of Massard Prairie - Dale Cox
Irish landed gentry when Cromwell came to Ireland
Ned Kelly extracts from the Benalla Standard
The authentic life of Billy the Kid - Pat Garrett
A Collection of plain horse tales - Robert Wolfe
Genghis Khan - Jacob Abbott
Life of the Hon. William Cody
Confessions of a horse dealer - Frederick Taylor
Last of the great scouts - Helen Wetmore
The scouts of Stonewall - J Altsheler
The Horse in history - Basil Tozer
The annals of the civil war - Charles River editors
The camp girls behind the lines - Margaret Vandercook
The harness horse - Walter Gilbey
Little union scout - Joel Harris
My first campaign - J.W. Grant
The pony rider boys with the Texas rangers - Frank Patchin
Reminiscences of a Rebel- Waylaid Dunaway
The war trail - Mayne Reid
Three years on the plains - Edmund Tuttle
Thoroughbreds - William Fraser
Personal memoirs of U.S. Grant
On horsemanship - H.G. Dakyns
The life of Kit Carson- Edward Ellis
The life of General Robert E Lee - John Cooke

The horse and war - Sidney Galtrey

Horse breeding recollections- G Lehndorff

Horse and man - CS March Phillips

Historic papers on the causes of the civil war - E Potts

From Bull run to Appomattox - L Hopkins

French and Indian cruelty - Peter Williamson

Essays on horse subjects - F Grenside

Civil war experiences - Henry Codington Meyer

Buying a horse - William Dean

Bullets and billets - B Bainrnsfather

The Broncho rider boys - Frank Fowler

The Arab the horse of the future - J Boucaut

Waiting for daylight - Henry Major Tomlinson

What horse for the cavalry - Spencer Borden

With Lee in Virginia - G A Henty

Army life in the black regiment - T Higginson

Ned Kelly - extracts from the Argus

Six years with the Texas Rangers - J Gillett

Ride the wind - Lucia St Clair Robson

The story of the Pony Express - G Bradley

A fate worse than death - G and S Michno

The story of Cole Younger by himself

Boot and saddles - Elizabeth Custer

Causes of the Irish famine - John Hughes

The story of Ireland - Emily lawless

Memoirs of General W T Sherman

In the time of famine - Michael Grant

Famine to freedom - the Irish J. J. Collins

The confederate girl's diary - Sarah Dawson

The Comanche empire - P Hamalainen

Old plantation days - N Saussure

Personal recollections of cavalryman with Custer - James Harvey Kidd

The graves are walking - John Kelly

Classic slave narratives - F Douglass Harriot Jacobs

Prairie traveller - R B Marcy

The Iroquois book of rites - Horatio Hale

The story of the outlaw - Emerson Hough

Gun - Logan Thompson

The life and art of the North American Indian - J A Warner

Native Americans a portrait - C Bird, G Caitlin and K Bodmer - - R J Moore

Warriors - N Bancroft-Hunt

Blackskin and Buffalo - Colin F Taylor

The Trailblazers - Bil Gilbert

North American art - David Penney

Warrior artists - Herman Viola

Charles Russell - Peter Hassrick

Native American traditions - Arthur Versluis

An album of Chinese Art - national gallery of Victoria

China - the land of the heavenly dragon - professor EL Shaughnessy

The noble horse - M and H Dossenbach

The Ned Kelly Paintings - Museum of Modern Art

The Celts - John Davies

Castlemaine from camp to City 1835-1900 G Hocking

Gettysburg - Champ Clark

The story of the West - Robin May

The Civil War - Stephen Sears